MW01221771

SICK and HURT

Medical Events

in

O'Brian's Aubrey Novels

by
Eric Shulenberger PhD JD

Publication Information
ISBN 13:   978-1533484048
ISBN 10:   153348404X

Shulenberger Publishing
3912 NE 127th St., Seattle WA 98125
ericshul@hotmail.com

Library of Congress Control Number 2016910219
Editor = Eric Shulenberger

Thanks

Special thanks are due my wife, Susan Wessman, who helped enormously throughout the longish process of producing this book. Fortunately for me, she has fallen in love with O'Brian's delicious prose, which made the final third of this book-writing process into a much more interesting exercise than it would otherwise have been.

And (of course) thanks to Patrick O'Brian for his years of work providing us lesser mortals with education, amusement, shining examples of 'how to write', and in general a rousing good time. The title is from the Royal Navy's "Sick and Hurt Board" – the official supplier of medical support and materials to the Navy

Note on Sources

This work uses as reference points the chapters and page numbers in the individual novels. The specific text I used was the twenty-volume (paperback) boxed set of "Aubrey-Maturin" novels published by W.W. Norton & Company, New York about 2005. In that set, the ISBN of book #1 (Master and Commander) is [0-393-30705-0]. The novels have been reprinted many times, my copy (in the boxed set) of Book 1 is printing #32 (probably that refers to the version published by Norton: there were other earlier printings by other printers that may not be in the same format). Regardless of printing and binding, O'Brian's chapter-breaks should remain in their proper places, letting a reader of this work easily find items of interest.

Contents

SICK & HURT:
MEDICAL EVENTS
in O'BRIAN'S AUBREY NOVELS

Preamble and introduction

I am an enormous fan of Patrick O'Brian's "Jack Aubrey" series. Some years ago, for Christmas, my in-laws gave me a boxed set of all twenty novels, in paperback. I have read the entire series straight through at least five times, probably more... to the point where the covers are beginning to come off. Jack Aubrey's name supposedly was chosen to give initials matching "Jane Austen" – a writer he apparently idolized (and whom he has far surpassed, in my view). I love these books, the characters in them, the age in which they are set, the details of social and political activities and intriguing. Not even to mention the phenomenal wealth of fanatically-accurate detail of the rigging and sailing of square-rigged men-o-war (a favorite hobby of mine). I have bought as gifts I do not know how many copies of Master and Commander (book #1 in the series)... none of the recipients seems to have escaped unscathed – they are all converts (or addicts?). Read these novels for their language and their stories, and you will be drawn inexorably into O'Brian's naval and political world of about 1800, a world now utterly lost, but accurately resurrectable (with a great deal of work) in bits, as done for us all by O'Brian.

Not even my wife could escape O'Brian's clutches – Susan was without the vaguest interest in things naval (much less internal details of medicine and naval intelligence service in that era), but my reading aloud various sterling passages intrigued her – she is now on the fourth or fifth novel, and feels the author's skill with words and stories far surpasses that of both Ms Austen and Charles Dickens himself, both of whom my wife (like O'Brian) though unsurpassable. Without even realizing it, she is becoming fluent in the language and customs, the naval duties and social milieu of that era. Even hardware - the other day she correctly used, perfectly casually, the term 'great guns' – much to her surprise but not to mine – I could see it coming.

Like many others, I have proselytized about the depth and reality of the stories, and the exquisite elegance of the writing. After many readings, I have decided that the popular nickname for the twenty novels (or, more accurately, one long novel in twenty volumes) is wrong – if one studies the characters, the depth in the story comes not from Jack Aubrey, but from his sidekick, surgeon Stephen Maturin. In short, this is really not the "Jack Aubrey" series, rather it is the Stephen Maturin series – with the more flashy "shoot-em-up-BANG!" Jack Aubrey being much more Stephen's sidekick than the converse.

Mr O'Brian is nothing short of incredibly gifted as both a story-teller and wordsmith... as a writer about the realities of 1800s naval life and doings, he is light-years beyond his only competitor, CS Forester and his Hornblower books. By comparison, Forester seems stilted, cold, juiceless and almost devoid of descriptive capability. Plus Forester's books have nothing like O'Brian's alternative hero, Stephen Maturin. O'Brian's authorial skill is incredible - the "Literature 101" adage goes that there are only six core themes in all of literature: (1) man against himself; (2) man against man; (3) man against woman; (4) man against nature; (5) man against fate; (6) man against the gods. It takes a fine writer to tackle perhaps two of these in a single volume... O'Brian commonly deals with all six in a single paragraph of exquisitely crafted prose carrying five levels of meaning. The man is the Rembrandt of English-language writing.

Jack is simple and brutally direct, a superb fighting captain and a nearly complete social stumblebum whenever ashore. Jack's inner turmoils are like the rest of his activities, direct and straightforward. Stephen's is the complicated mind we get to explore, in great depth and on a wide range of important topics... all presented totally within the social and knowledge base of the day.

Stephen Maturin, MD, FRS, is the complex character, with several well-developed personae: he is simultaneously a renowned medical doctor (he is ship's surgeon for Jack's commands through Jack's career), an extremely effective agent for Royal Navy Intelligence, and a world-class natural historian. In his persona as a medical doctor of the very early 1800s, he is set in an extraordinarily violent world, and knows only too well just how little mankind knows about our own animal's workings - how little doctors can actually do. For medicine in the Royal Navy of the times, the bone-saw was the major curative principle. Plus, of course, large quantities of rhubarb to cure persistent constipation.

Although both Aubrey and Maturin are Fellows of the Royal Society (a signal scientific honor both then and today), in fact, on things intellectual, Jack can compete with Stephen in only the most limited manner. Jack is, overall, rather well educated for the day and his station in life, but cannot hold a candle to Maturin's erudition, which extends across many fields. Jack is entirely self-taught in mathematics (at which Maturin is utterly hopeless), and constructs his own telescopes: he presents, at Royal Society meetings, his occasional papers on a new technique for calculating a ship's position by using measurements of the moon's altitude. Stephen is a more frequent presenter, and mumbles his way through his own contributions in natural history, most especially in 'comparative osteology' (the comparison of skeleton feathers of various species).

So – Why this book?

At some point in my fourth (or so) reading of the series, I found myself increasingly fascinated by the variety and frequency of often-mysterious medical treatments and procedures in which Stephen was directly involved. I began making lists of "what happened to whom and why, and on what page?" That led me to gentle digging about in the internet, to find out what various conditions, procedures, medicines, and diseases from back then are called today – not necessarily an easy quest. I have a strong background in mammalian physiology, which helped.

SO – for the genuine fan (like me) of the "Aubrey" series, I present here a list (with explanations embedded) of all the medical procedures and events and ruminations of Dr Maturin (the real 'main character') over the course of the twenty novels. The frequency of occurrence of blood-and-guts events starts high, and gradually decreases as the novels progress. By the later volumes, I think O'Brian had had his fun with inventing nostrums and having his characters embedded in gore – the last few novels have many chapters in which no medical events occur (this is so noted in this present text).

This book – how to read it. I treat each book as a self-contained unit, as did O'Brian. Most of the novels have 10 or 11 chapters: I treat each chapter also as a self-contained subunit. I provide a very personalized (to me) précis of the chapter, to remind the reader (me, mostly) where (s)he/we/I are/am in the novels. Then after the précis for a chapter, I list (by page number) all the medical events mentioned in the chapter. I then iterate through the chapters – précis, explanatory list: précis, explanatory list. Through all 20 novels. (I chose not to deal with the intriguing incompletenesses of the ~90 pages we have of Book 21.)

The novels have generated their own firestorm of ancillary materials, on things medical, things sailing, things cooking, and other topics. This book is another such specialty volume for those of us who have sailed over the far edge of our own little world due to our obsession with and immersion in O'Brian's, Aubrey's, and Maturin's universe.

SICK and HURT

✶✶✶✶✶

Medical Events
in O'Brian's Aubrey Novels

by

ERIC SHULENBERGER, PhD JD

Book 1 - Master and Commander

Book 1 Chapter 1 - p7-33: (overview) Book opens in the music room of the Governor's House at Port Mahon, the important British naval base on the island of Minorca, eastern Mediterranean. Jack Aubrey, Lieutenant, RN, meets Stephen Maturin, MD - an acrimonious meeting. Jack is without a ship, Stephen without a patient for financial support. Jack is appointed captain of HMS Sophie, his first command, an elderly, small, out-of-date sloop. Mr. Baldick (current Lieutenant of Sophie) interviewed by Jack in hospital ashore. Baldick is self-admitted, for "low fever", but really came to hospital to escape from Sophie's surgeon whom he despises. Said surgeon has apparently left the ship now: Baldick wonders where Jack will find a replacement - surgeons are scarce in the Mediterranean. Jack and Stephen become friends over dinner. This opens the way for Jack to invite Stephen to become a Sophie.

24 - First "medical note" of the series. David Richards, civilian, put forth by Jack's financial agent as a candidate for purser of HMS Sophie - has severe acne. (Mention only - pre Stephen)

25 - Sophie's Lt Baldick is a confirmed alcoholic who does extensive self-treatment with various nostrums. Treatment proposed for him by Sophie's surgeon is mainly "water cure" and "low diet". (NOTE: "Water cure" is a broad generic term: it included extensive bathing [in salt or fresh water], and drinking large quantities of water, often sulfurous. Here, drinking plain water is the most likely form. "Low diet" probably means low-fiber hence low volume of feces.) Nostrums he swears by include Ward's Pill and Ward's Drop. These "medicines" reappear throughout the 20 novels, and seem to be O'Brian's inventions perfectly in line with the medical realities of the day. Baldick is convinced the Ward's nostrums saved him from the yellow jack, scurvy, sciatica, rheumatism and the bloody flux (severe dysentery).

27 - Baldick, in discussing members of Sophie's crew with Jack, mentions in passing that Mr Day (later identified as HMS Sophie's

Master Gunner) is "...a good man, too, when he's well, but he has a silly way of dosing himself." Presumably Day (as well as Mr Baldick: pot calling the kettle black!) takes various nostrums for real or imagined problems, and occasionally renders himself unfit for duty thereby.

30 - Aboard Sophie, in Port Mahon. Sophie's gunner (unnamed here - later identified as Mr George Day, Master Gunner) has an unspecified illness that keeps him away from Jack's initial inspection of the ship. Presumably he has overdosed himself with some nostrum, per Baldick's characterization (p27). Recovers p129; diagnosis p138.

Book 1 Chapter 2 - p34-82: (overview) Stephen and Jack further develop their friendship over dinner ashore, exchange background information. HMS Sophie goes to sea for shakedown of crew and to test two 12-pounders as bow chasers - too heavy and powerful for Sophie. Returns to Port Mahon. Jack ordered to convoy twelve merchant vessels to Cagliari (port at south end of Sardinia, in the Italian Mediterranean). Sophie and convoy set sail.

37 - Stephen's unnamed patient, whose care in Minorca provided Stephen's income, had died at sea, of "...the last stages of phthisis" (i.e., pulmonary tuberculosis), about a week before Stephen and Jack met. This death left Stephen both unemployed and stranded, and is the immediate reason for Stephen's readily agreeing to go to sea as ship's surgeon with Jack. Stephen informs Jack that he is a physician (a rare animal, a university-trained medical doctor), not a mere surgeon, most of whom are literally butchers or barbers, untrained in medicine but with a license to practice medicine aboard His Majesty's ships. Jack is suitably impressed.

47 - New crewman taken aboard, a Negro named Alfred King, whose tongue has been cut out by the Moors.

69 - Crewmen know about and comment upon First Officer Williams' pederastic (homoerotic) tastes, observe that Williams is clearly enamored of Jack. Jack is utterly oblivious, cannot possibly be told, and would not believe it if told.

81 - Stephen recruited by Jack, comes aboard as Sophie's Surgeon.

73 - Jack studies the Sophie's recent log, finds entry "Richard Sutton Lt, discharged dead" - he was killed in action with a French privateer (no injury details).

Book 1 Chapter 3 - p83-119: (overview) Sophie and convoy proceeding under good weather; details of several characters revealed.

89 - Stephen, unused to the very low ceiling of his quarters, is startled by the rush of feet as the men go to their duty stations, stands up and strikes his head, almost cold-cocking himself - but does no real damage.

92 - Formal muster of all hands, 92 souls on board Sophie. Isaac Wilson fails to answer, cause unspecified, but it is likely (see p116) he's been scragged (killed by his shipmates) for committing sodomy with the ship's milk-goat.

105-106 - Stephen gets a tour of crew's berthing and sanitation arrangements, is appalled.

116 - Still at sea, Jack begins work on a pile of unfinished business left behind by Capt. Allen, his predecessor: item #1 is a request from Allen to Admiral Keith, that the Admiral "... order a Court Martial to be held on Isaac Wilson (seaman) .... for having committed the unnatural Crime of Sodomy on a Goat...." Jack and Stephen discuss the topic, then both decline goat's milk for their tea.

Book 1 Chapter 4 - p120-151: (overview) Sophie and her convoy have a running fight with a small fleet of Algerine (= Algerian) galleys (fast, maneuverable oar-powered craft, each with one heavy cannon) - aka privateers or pirates. Algerines take the convoy's cat (a small merchantman); Sophie in pursuit. Cat retaken. Convoy arrives in Cagliari without further problems. Jack reports to Admiral Keith, whose new much-younger wife Queenie was Jack's childhood protector and teacher... and occasional innocent childhood bedmate, a situation known by, and not pleasing to, the Admiral. Admiral gives Sophie a solo cruise down to Cape Nao (also spelt NAU) - a prominent eastward-pointing projection on the Spanish Mediterranean coast. Sophie seems to have left on the Cape Nao cruise immediately.

127 - All hands including lookouts are distracted by gunnery practice: only Stephen (who is the ultimate land-lubber) notices that strange new ships seem to have joined the convoy. Stephen asks what is going on. Pirates are attacking the last ship in the convoy, a Norwegian cat. Pandemonium ensues: the professional crew haven't been sufficiently on guard and alert.

129 - Master-Gunner Day somewhat recovered from unnamed ailment (p30), appears on deck in time for action - apparently cured by treatment prescribed by Stephen. Of Stephen's prescription, Mr Day says "It worked, sir, like a maiden's dream." His ailment is eventually specified (p138) as severe constipation, self-induced by overuse of "Peruvian bark." (Aka "Jesuit's bark" - inner bark of the Cinchona tree, from which the word QUININE - an effective anti-malarial even today.) Patient not helped at all by applying the seaman's medical philosophy, "If it works for X then it must work for Y, and more is ALWAYS better!" Not specified here, but rhubarb is part of Stephen's pharmacopeia - a powerful and often-used laxative. Large casks of rhubarb are carried in the medical-supplies inventory.

130 - Before battle Stephen consults Northcote's "Marine Practice" about amputations, because he has no experience whatever with war-related injuries. NOTE - This is a real book, widely studied and followed for decades in the Royal Navy - the Navy's medical bible. Full title -

> *"The Marine Practice of Physic and Surgery: including that in the Hot Countries, Particularly Useful to All who Visit the East and West Indies, Or the Coast of Africa, to which is Added Pharmacopoeia Marina..."* - by William Northcote, first published 1770, 491pp. A copy was issued as part of the standard ship's medicine chest, along with medicines and surgical implements.

132 - Sophie hit by 18-pound (18#) shot from Algerine galley (Sophie carries only four-pounders, mere popguns by comparison). William Musgrave, sailor, hit by splinter, carried below bleeding. Stephen ligatures (sews; repairs using thread or gut) his "spouting femoral artery". This is Stephen's first encounter with the most common and vicious battle injury, namely splinter wounds: he finds it difficult to believe that a flying chunk of wood could cause such damage. His surprise fades quickly.

133 - Gunner hit on skull by heavy lump of wood blasted from main topmast cap (cap − the heavy wooden fitting that joins two masts together vertically) by Algerine cannon fire. Injury diagnosed on p138.

133 - Sponger of #4 gun failed to clear sparks from barrel, new charge explodes upon insertion, drives rammer's wooden handle through his upper arm, burns his face badly. Treated on p138. A rammer was used to drive the new powder charge down the barrel: a long wooden rod, like a lawn-rake handle, perhaps larger in diameter, with a bore-sized wooden disc at the powder end.

134 - Jack's ear nicked by an Algerine musket ball - bleeds freely, minor injury.

135 - Pring, captain of a bow gun, announced as dead during battle, no cause given.

136 - John Lakey, seaman, hit "In the ballocks" (testicles) by an Algerine musketoon ball. No further details provided, but we find out what happened at p201 in Post Captain (Book 2). ("Musketoon" = short-barreled musket; a carbine, a thoroughly inaccurate and clumsy single-shot weapon usually best deployed as a club.)

137 - Stephen asks "Has the battle begun again?" and is told "Oh, no. That was only a shot across the cat's bows." Stephen comments "It is nearly impossible to sew one's flaps neatly with the jarring of the guns." "Flaps" indicates an amputation (as yet unreported) - flaps presumably means the still-attached muscle and skin that have

13

been preserved to be folded over the cut end of the bone, then sewn down as a cushion or padding.

138 - Sponger's wound discussed - rammer handle had been driven through the head of the biceps, but missed the ulnar nerve. A good recovery seems likely if no infection occurs. Gunner Day's earlier health problem identified as "…the grossest self-induced costiveness it has ever been my privilege to see…" (costiveness = constipation). Gunner Day's head injury is a depressed skull fracture - he is unconscious. Stephen will have to trephine Day's skull - i.e., cut a hole using a circular saw, to relieve pressure on the brain due to the brain swelling. Details of the procedure are not given until p284 of Post Captain (Book 2).

139 - Aboard re-captured cat (member of Sophie's convoy), discussion of the enemy dead. Considerable slaughter (at least three dead Algerines) has occurred aboard the cat: no details on the action. Sophie's Negro seaman Alfred King, a member of the boarding party, is covered with blood, holding a battle-axe. He may have gone berserker and is being restrained by his mates. His tongue was cut out by "Moors" which here is synonymous with Algerines: perhaps he has had his revenge? Nobody will tell Jack what happened. He does not press the question.

142 - Sophie's warrant officers tell Jack they wish Stephen to share in their portion of any prize monies, "…as an acknowledgement of his conduct considered very handsome by all hands." The crew are being appropriately noble and appreciative here - they know the Doctor is a volunteer and therefore not entitled to share in prizes.

147 - Back aboard Sophie, in port. Jack and Stephen discuss very obliquely the likelihood of Queenie getting pregnant by the Admiral, who is sixty. In Italian, "Very possible!" says Stephen, to Jack's astonishment.

Book 1 Chapter 5 - p152-179: (overview) Sophie continues towards Cape Nao, and takes L'Amiable Louise, a French polacre (a small three-masted cargo vessel). Sophie meets Norwegian ship Clomer, a near-identical copy of Sophie. Amazement all around. Sophie returns to Port Mahon (no details of that passage).

152 - At sea. From Sophie's log: "Departed this life Henry Gouges, loblolly-boy." Gouges was Stephen's assistant, aka loblolly-boy, a ship's surgeon's aide, usually someone picked from the crew because of a particular talent, and trained aboard ship. No cause of death given until p153.

153 - Gouge's death apparently due to massive stroke or heart attack, or burst aneurysm: this is his 50th birthday, he was sitting at table with messmates. From convivial chattering to stone dead in a second.

155 - Sophie encounters a felucca (quite a small craft, single-mast, low-freeboard, for coastal work) in distress. Upon approaching her, they can see bodies on deck, and get no answer to their hail. With a telescope Stephen examines her from afar, declares that one visible body "...died of plague." When asked if he is certain, Stephen replies 'yes' and demands to go across to see if he can provide assistance "...there may be some survivors". Sophie sheers off, departs instantly, nobody is allowed to touch the felucca. Stephen is furious, but Jack is adamant. They sail away. Jack's reaction is actually much the more rational.

161 - Sophie pursues another polacre: Stephen upbraids Jack for walking about in the rain inadequately clothed. "Think of the night air, the falling damps, the fluxion of the humors..." Jack is ordered to wear wool.

167 - Sophie takes Citoyen Durand, a massively-overloaded French gunpowder ship – one of the most dangerous objects in the world at the time. Master's wife is giving birth. Stephen goes to her aid. Sophie's entire crew unnerved by the mother's screams.

169 - Stephen, still aboard C. Durand: "A perfectly straightforward delivery; just a little long..."

Book 1 Chapter 6 - p180-199: (overview) Un-chronicled return of Sophie to Port Mahon. Sophie then sent to continue her cruise near Minorca.

189-190 - Ashore, after Molly Harte's large party or rout, at which Jack (drunk) has made an utter ass of himself, very publicly. Jessop, cook's mate, broke a leg falling down Pigtail Stairs at the waterfront - presumably dead drunk. Several Sophie crewmen are unconscious from alcohol - a common occurrence, not at all remarkable. Sophie returns to her cruising ground (presumably still the region assigned by Admiral Harte).

193 - Flogging of several men, Stephen's first view of the process. Stephen treats with an ointment some men's flayed backs.

195-196 - Stephen talks to seaman Cheslin (a hare-lip), whose medical problem is unspecified but probably psychological. Cheslin is a "sin-eater" and is being absolutely ostracized by the entire crew. "He is dying from inanition" says Stephen (p197). Inanition is a lack of will to live.

Book 1 Chapter 7 - p200-243: (overview) Action against five ships led by privateer Gloire. At dawn, Sophie finds Gloire et al. very close, engages at once. Gloire retires. Sophies plan a landing party to attack battery of fortress Almoraira.

212 - Christian Pram, seaman at the wheel, has forearm "...ploughed open from wrist to elbow", presumably by a splinter.

214 - Gunner Day on duty again, apparently recovered from trepanning. NOTE: the results of Day's operation are disclosed piecemeal over several books. Day was trepanned on deck, with the whole crew watching, a thoroughly famous event known in detail across the entire Navy. The hole in his skull is covered with a screwed-down dome made from a silver three-shilling piece (this may be anachronistic – the 3-shilling coin was issued from 1811-1816, later than this

story's time frame). Day recovers fully. Stephen's fleet-wide reputation as a medical miracle-worker begins here.

215 - Butcher's bill (list of killed and wounded) for the Gloire action declared trivial - no deaths. Stephen lists sickbay denizens - Pram's forearm is "moderately scored". Some splinters that must be removed - mere bandaging. Plus one gleet (= pus discharge, probably from the penis and due to gonorrhea) and one inguinal hernia (lower abdomen - aka 'burstin belly').

225 - Killed in the attack ashore: John Hayter (Marine). Wounded, James Nightingale and Thomas Thompson (seamen) - wounds not specified. Jack et al, detonate fortress's powder magazine. The unexpectedly violent explosion badly burns his face and neck, singes off all hair on left side. French volunteer LaHire also "somewhat bruised and singed" helping fire (i.e., explode) the magazine.

229 - At sea. Loblolly boy (Cheslin - hare-lipped sin-eater) found to be "...grinding creta alba into their [the crew's] gruel..." Creta alba is plain white chalk - chalk was mixed with various medicinal substances to make up pills (aka boluses). It has no medical effects, and is often variously colored to convince superstitious mariners that they are getting some special or potent medicine. Cheslin does not know this, and has been putting chalk in the crew's food, in retaliation for being ostracized. Stephen decides to keep his medicals locked up.

231 - Sword-fight. Dillon, First Officer of Sophie and extraordinarily touchy about "matters of honor", reports having dueled ashore with a soldier, whom he killed "in two passes".

Book 1 Chapter 8 - p244-276: (overview) At sea, arriving on Spanish Mediterranean coast. Sophie disguised as merchantman: encounters the much larger and more powerful Cacafuego (32: the name translates "Shit-fire"), a Spanish xebec-frigate 4x Sophie's tonnage and with well over twice her crew, not to mention a surfeit of firepower. The two ships run close alongside to speak one another, Cacafuego is prepared to board Sophie but does not because Stephen declares Sophie a plague ship and is believed.

First Officer Dillon is convinced Jack is a coward for not attacking Cacafuego despite the impossibly long odds, fulminates silently but Jack intuits his feelings. Sophie returns to Port Mahon. Admiral Keith criticizes Jack for various faults, then gives him yet another cruise because Jack is lucky (and the Admiral himself profits thereby, getting a hefty percentage of Jack's share of any prizes). Jack tells Stephen that before their next cruise (per p263) Sophie will run "...an errand to Sir Sidney Smith's squadron at Alexandria..." in Egypt.

255 - Stephen -wearing his custom-made lead-soled boots- falls overboard during swim-call, sinks (he cannot swim in any case), is rescued by several crew including Jack. Jack is famous for having saved perhaps 20 men from drowning. Jack thinks nothing of it.

261 - Sophie escapes without battle due to Stephen's Spanish-language subterfuge, pretending Sophie is a plague ship. Cacafuego wants nothing to do with Sophie, refuses any contact, departs.

269 - Still ashore, Jack is recovering slowly from his burns: at present, "...his left-hand aspect was not unlike that of the great West African mandrill." The mandrill is justly famous for its brilliantly polychromed face and hind end.

Book 1 Chapter 9 - p277-300: (overview) Jack is internally angry at Dillon. In Sicilian Channel, Sophie encounters French frigate Dedaigneuse (44): the sighting interrupts poetry recitations by some officers. Sophie runs, is closely pursued. Man goes overboard during chase, Jack turns and stops to pick him up. Poetry resumed, but is again interrupted - this time by a twelve-pound ball from their pursuer. At nightfall, Sophie launches a decoy raft, successfully confuses Dedaigneuse. Sophie escapes, sails to Port Mahon, Minorca on 1/4 allowance of water. Jack goes ashore expecting a tryst with his lover Molly Harte (his Admiral's wife), finds she has been cut out by a Marine officer. Returns in foul mood, Sophie sails immediately, cruising near Cape Salou, Spain, then off Barcelona. Jack's father, the General (age 64) marries his kitchen-maid (age 20), who was one of Jack's "hay-loft" conquests when he was younger.

18

284 - Henry Ellis overboard while Sophie is being chased by Dedaigneuse: Jack stops for him. Frigate much closer due to this stop. Ellis brought aboard drowned, dead.

285 - Ellis has no pulse. Stephen hangs him up by the heels, uses a bellows to pump cigar smoke into his lungs. Ellis revives. Crew is pleased, but not astounded - Stephen can repair ANY injury!

293 - In Port Mahon, Stephen returns aboard with "...a leg wrapped in sailcloth, quite a fresh leg, a present from Mr Florey." This is a human leg, for anatomical dissection, a particular passion of his.

294 - Sophie's crew ashore on liberty, with prize money, which enables especially bad behavior. Four crewmen in jail for rape; four lost somewhere in the red-light district; one with broken collarbone and wrist.

300 - Crewman Simmons reports in sick, fails to report for duty on Captain's barge. "His birthday, sir." Presumably Simmons is seriously drunk, but not so stated.

Book 1 Chapter 10 - p301-333: (overview) Sophie adopts minimalist disguise to fool potential enemy/prey. Sophie meets disguised merchantman Pola (a tartan, a two-masted species of small coastal freighter), sends seamen Codpiece (sic!) and Baptist aboard to check documents. Pola taken as lawful prize. Gunfire in distance, Sophie sails to investigate it, encounters small Spanish privateer Felipe V (7) enroute to same gunfire: Sophie takes Felipe in 12 minutes. Several gunboats (more than 11) come out from Barcelona to meet and engage Sophie. No definitive result. Sophie re-encounters Cacafuego (32). Closing to yardarms distance, heavy battle. Sophie outmanned 2: or 3:1: a surprise boarding is Jack's only option despite Cacafuego having a much larger crew. Cacafuego engagement ends: Sophie victorious: this becomes the stuff of legends, David vs Goliath, Jack gains fame. Stephen philosophizes on moral law and honor.

305 - Crewman Tom Simmons dies after four days in an alcoholic coma: Stephen is dispirited. Popular with his messmates, Simmons had been given a full quart of straight rum as a birthday present, which he apparently drank at one sitting. Stephen finds out the quantity only after Simmons has been sewn into his shroud with roundshot at his feet, for burial at sea. Stephen begins a crusade to get rid of the crew's daily rum ration. The crusade, needless to say, fails.

311 - In a storm, Ellis, the recently-resuscitated man-overboard, is busy being violently seasick.

315 - Ellis instantly restored to health, seasickness evaporated, by the prospect of action.

319 - Stephen and Jack have a philosophical discussion of parallel sets of contradictory rules of human behavior in society. Stephen bleeds and "physicks" Jack with some sort of bolus. In passing, Sophie does not issue soap to the crew. Nor is there fresh water for bathing or laundry.

325 - Sophie re-encounters Cacafuego - the flotilla of gunboats may have been a ruse to get Sophie close to Cacafuego.

330 - A violent close-quarters battle ensues. Jack orders Sophies to board Cacafuego, Stephen declines to go but volunteers to steer Sophie to hold her alongside Cacafuego during boarding. This is perhaps the only time in the entire series when Stephen displays any capacity whatever for dealing with ships or their equipment, tactics and operation… certainly it is his only active participation in maneuvering any vessel larger than his personal two-man rowboat, which he can handle only marginally.

332 - During hand-to-hand combat of boarding, Jack receives a deep flesh wound in the ribs, from a pikeman. Bonden (Jack's coxswain) fires a pistol, which kills the pikeman... and also blows off "the lower part of Jack's ear."

333 - Dillon (Jack's First Officer) found dead aboard Cacafuego, wounded in the heart during the boarding action.

20

Book 1 Chapter 11 - p334-377: (overview) Cacafuego to Port Mahon, enthusiastic congratulations from all vessels, personnel and civilians. Admiral Harte, only too well aware of the Jack/Molly affair, contrives to NOT have Sophie's victory Gazetted (i.e., written up for public and professional consumption in the Navy's official informational publication, the Gazette), and also to keep Jack from being made Post for the action. He also does not confirm (promote) Jack's Lieutenant, Thomas Pullings. Jack ordered to Malta for refitting and repairs, returns to Port Mahon, still owed 37 days of cruising. Admiral Harte comes aboard, does not promote Jack, cancels Sophie's cruise. Sophie to convoy a slow civilian, presumably carrying the delayed copy of Jack's report of the Cacafuego action. Admiral Harte be damned, other naval vessels formally cheer Sophie on her way to sea. Sophie, leading the very slow packet, has time to poke about inshore, sets fire to a whole shipload of olive oil at night. This attracts the French ship of the line Desaix (74). Sophie tries everything but cannot avoid capture by the larger, faster and more powerful Desaix and her fellows. Jack is taken aboard Desaix, has full freedom of movement. Captain Christy-Palliere is a gracious host, speaks English, has a superb chef aboard and has relatives and mutual acquaintances with Jack in England.

334 - Jack's official letter mentions "Mr Ellis" (supernumerary) as killed in the Cacafuego action (no details). Ellis is a very young man (today's term would be "boy") taken aboard at his parents' insistence, abetted by their friend, Jack's Admiral Harte. They had hoping to launch the boy on a naval career. Also listed as wounded were Mr Watt (boatswain) and five seamen (no specific injuries reported). Official letter lists 3 killed, 8 wounded.

338 - Jack gets a secret invitation (presumably for a rendezvous) from Molly Harte: his recent shoulder-wound (saber-cut) opens due to unnamed (probably amorous) exertions, and Stephen treats it again.

343 - Stephen and Florey are dissecting a porpoise, and on an adjacent table is a young female human corpse, cause of death unknown, but perhaps battering and/or drowning. She is partly dissected (the body cavity has been opened by Foley) and covered with a sheet.

Sanitation of the times: they are eating as they work, and use a knife straight from the human dissection to carve their cold roast beef. "Perhaps we ought to wash it,' said Mr Florey. "Oh, a wipe will do," said Stephen, using a corner of the sheet.

348 - Having been feted ashore after the Cacafuego action, Jack consults with Stephen, is diagnosed with a (mild? and unspecified) venereal disease (VD): "Some lady of your acquaintance has been too liberal with her favors, too universally kind." The only possible Lady seems to be Molly Harte, widely acknowledged to be readily available to successful officers both Army and Navy. Somehow, this is Jack's first such encounter with VD. Because it seems amenable to treatment, this is likely a first-stage case of syphilis, treatable at that time with compounds of mercury. Additions to "treatment" include drinking only barley-water, eating only thin gruel (no beef, mutton, wine, spirits). Mortification of the soul and/or flesh is a common treatment indeed.

349 - Stephen's thoughts on venereal diseases and medical dosages. Stephen considers how to deal with the persistent problem of sailors absolutely believing that when it comes to medicine, more is inherently better… and finding ways to overdose themselves in the face of all contrary advice. Stephen carefully locks away the remaining medicines. He then mixes 50% too much VD medicine for Jack, reserves the excess for midshipman Babbington, whose sole interest ashore is pursuing women (in which he has great, and mystifying, success), and whom Stephen therefore expects to have to treat for the same problem momentarily.

364 - Sophie, at sea. "Young Mr Ricketts [a 'young gentleman' aka midshipman] has swallowed a musket ball and they can't get it out. Choking to death, sir, if you please." Stephen leaves his wine to successfully administer a strong emetic, returns in under five minutes. No explanation of why Ricketts had the ball in his mouth. A standard musket ball was a lead sphere about 7/10 inch in diameter.

370 - Sophie trying to avoid being captured by Desaix et al. in a calm, by rowing. Stephen abrades the skin from his palms helping man the sweeps (large, multi-man oars used in a flat calm or emer-

22

gency by ships up to Sophie's size). Stephen's hands are "neatly mittened" shortly after he finishes his stint as a volunteer galley-slave.

Book 1 Chapter 12 - p378-412: (overview) Sophie has been taken, Jack and Stephen are 'guests' aboard Desaix: they are part of a large French fleet at anchor. English ships arrive, a battle ensues (with the French fleet hunkered down in defense, at anchor close to shore) which they watch from Desaix. On the French Admiral's orders, Desaix is run aground. They go ashore as prisoners (but give their parole, hence have freedom of movement). From a high hillside, they watch French and English fleets maneuver towards an eventual offshore battle. The fleets are close enough to shore at the moment that the Spanish shore batteries join in the action, on the French side. British and French fleets sail out of sight even to Jack and Stephen. In the dark, beyond the horizon, two ships blow up - no idea whose. In the event, the English won the fleet action. Jack and Stephen given quarters ashore, above Algiceras: soon sent to Gibraltar to be exchanged for French prisoners. Returned to London for the requisite court-martial due to loss of HMS Sophie. Jack and all of Sophie's officers are acquitted with honor.

379 - Stephen visits the Desaix's sick-bay with his French counterpart, Dr Ramis. French sickbay is "sparsely populated" (Desaix's crew numbers 600-700). "...a dozen of the usual diseases" [unspecified]; "a fair amount of pox" [possibly smallpox, more likely other diseases less contagious and less fatal – measles or even syphilis, etc.]; four invalids from Sophie (maladies unspecified); all the ships' wounded [wounds and numbers unspecified], and three men "...bitten by Mr Dalziel's little bitch" and confined for fear of rabies.

380 - In a discussion of possible interactions between mind and the physical body, Stephen and Dr Ramis do an experiment to see if mental processes (here, intentional imagining of distressing situations) can affect the physical body. They find indeed such effects are readily produced - their pulse rates rise as they imagine various unsettling scenarios.

384 - Jack is standing exposed on the Desaix's deck watching the battle develop when "…a cannonball at head height reaped a file of marines on Desaix's poop…" Presumably multiple decapitations, number unspecified. A not unusual occurrence.

388 - Stephen has volunteered to help the French surgeons with their surgery aboard Desaix, which is intentionally aground and has heavy casualties (p-389, "about a hundred killed and a hundred wounded"). Other French ships sustained similar casualties. Jack's friend English Captain Ferris of the Hannibal, just now taken by the French, is also aboard Desaix as a prisoner (Hannibal's casualties are 75 killed plus 52 wounded): he and Jack are talking on the Desaix's deck when Stephen joins them after operating for some time: he is literally soaked with blood, all garments, head to foot. Jack attempts to introduce the men to one another: "May I name Dr Maturin? Captain Ferris. My God, Stephen!" Jack thinks that Stephen "…might have come straight out of a busy slaughterhouse."

390 - Captain Ferris, badly distraught at having struck to the French, asks Stephen to prescribe for him a sedative or soporific, "…something in the poppy or mandragora line."

399 - Jack and Stephen, from a high hillside, watch the French fleet weighing, forming up and setting off in line-of-battle order for an offshore fleet confrontation with the English. Stephen arrives somewhat late, missing part of the French fleet's "getting underway" maneuvers, apparently because some "damned fellow in Ward B…" has attempted to cut his own throat. Treatment and outcome not specified.

411 - Returned to London in a prisoner-exchange, Jack undergoes the formal court martial required for every English captain who loses a ship (regardless of the circumstances). In theory, the court sits in judgment on the entire body of ship's officers, including the surgeon. Stephen is called to testify. Jack is so distraught and preoccupied that when he is returning to the courtroom to hear the verdict, he "…struck the lintel of the door with a force that left a patch of yellow hair and scalp on the wood."

Book 2 - Post Captain

Book 2 Chapter 1 - p9-32: (overview)   Aboard HMS Charwell, returning from captivity, Jack is a passenger, watching as she overtakes an unidentified ship in the Channel, expecting a battle. That vessel sends its cutter to Charwell to announce that peace has broken out and to offer fresh newspapers for sale. Given peace, Jack's naval career is at best on hold, at worst quite over. Jack explains this to Stephen. Foxhunting whilst looking for a suitable rental. Diana Villiers appears, riding extraordinarily well, a beauty, widowed young whilst in India. Mrs. Williams and her daughters Sophia (Jack's eventual wife), Frances, and Cecelia (all cousins of Diana) are introduced, as is their home, Mapes Court. Jack and Stephen rent nearby Melbery estate for a year. Retired Admiral Haddock, the Williams' family friend, extols to them Jack and his Cacafuego action. (Possible confusion – Jack's eventual lady is named SophiA, but nicknamed throughout the books "SophiE – which nickname mirrors the Royal Navy's small man-o-war named "Sophie" which is one of Jack's commands.)

21 - Riding to fox, Jack is thrown, then dragged by his horse. No serious injury, but his "...raw bones and bloody head..." are mentioned.

Book 2 Chapter 2 - p33-55: (overview) [NOTE - Nothing health/medical occurs in Chapter 2.] Jack, Stephen, and the Williams entertained by retired Adm. Haddock, then living at Mapes. Jack entranced by both Sophie and Diana. Introductions, inspections, etc. flow. Jack rents nearby Melbery Lodge, hosts a formal ball. "Acquaintances ripened but did not mature." Foxhunting. Signal flags as decoration in Jack's ballroom read "Engage the enemy more closely". Emotional and intellectual interactions at the ball, especially between Stephen and Diana (Stephen's eventual wife, years hence). Diana expert at driving a four-in-hand coach.

Book 2 Chapter 3 - p56-88: (overview) Stephen's diaries; self-examination of motives and behavior. International politics. Stephen's role as expert unpaid secret agent for England (read, anti-Buonaparte, anti-colonialism). Jack's prize agent has absconded with all of Jack's prize monies. Even worse, Jack has also lost appeals on two prizes and must repay those funds - but that is the money his agent stole. He is facing arrest and prison for debt. To avoid this he must have a command and get to sea, beyond the reach of the law, and where there is some possibility of prize money. Jack at the Admiralty, London. He has never been rewarded for taking Cacafuego, appeals for any command whatever. He makes a cock of his interview with the Admiral.

62 - Stephen's medical merits mentioned, including his book "Tar water reconsidered" (an O'Brian invention), his remarks on suprapubic cystotomy (an operation to remove kidney or bladder stones).

63 - Riding home with Jack through rain in a dangerous forest. Jack check's Stephen's pistol holsters, finds a bottled dormouse and a teratoma (a benign internal human tumor, often containing random bits of mis-placed anatomy e.g., teeth, hair). No pistols. Jack is disgusted on both accounts - his own squeamishness and Stephen's lack of arms for self-defense.

Book 2 Chapter 4 - p89-114: (overview) Stephen and Killick see sheriff's officers ('tipstaffs'; 'bums') lurking about in hopes of arresting Jack. Stephen orders Killick to pack Jack's sea-chest at once, heads out to find Jack and warn him. Stephen and Jack head for Dover to find a ship they can get aboard: they go to France. At Toulon, they visit Capt. Christy-Palliere aboard his ship: enthusiastic reception. Jack and Christy-Palliere commiserate - the two navies are amazingly similar, their professional problems identical. Seven French ships of the line in port. Busy preparations for war with England, but war not yet declared. Christy-Palliere intimates strongly that Jack and Stephen ought perhaps to leave the country ASAP - preferably ending up in Spain. Jack doesn't understand but Stephen does - war is about to break out and if they do not leave they will spend the duration in a nasty French prison.

Sophie reported to be engaged to another man. Jack angry with himself about his inability to move on Sophie. Stephen feels he has badly mishandled his relationship with Diana. Stephen and Jack are both back to 'courting' Diana - things are very uncomfortable. Jack gets a letter direct from Sophie saying she is NOT engaged elsewhere: Jack tells this to Stephen, they relax.

92 - Mention in passing by Christy-Palliere of "...our cholera outburst and the new Egyptian pox." Pox is never identified to species ('pox' was a generic term covering a wide variety of sicknesses).

99 - Stephen and French colleague Dr Ramis discuss "...the whole range of disorders that have their origin in the mind..." (false pregnancies, hysterias, impotence, etc.) and consider why such disorders are rare aboard ship. Discussion of 'quality of mind' in sailors vs that in landsmen.

102 - Stephen and Jack act on Palliere's accurate warning, and are escaping from France to Stephen's quite large estates in Catalonia. Jack is disguised as a dancing bear and the pair have been walking cross-country for some weeks: he is covered with "small rasping wounds" where the costume abrades his skin.

111 - Jack (always in bear suit) and Stephen continue their trek towards Catalonia: Stephen carries a pack with all their possessions in it (about 50 pounds). Jack notes how Stephen has bloody welts from the pack.

114 - They reach Stephen's property in Catalonia (Eastern Spain), whence they eventually arrive at Gibraltar and take passage to England aboard the heavily-armed East-Indiaman Lord Nelson, Capt. Spottiswood.

Book 2 Chapter 5 - p115-148: (overview) Going to England from Gibraltar. Jack's former masters-mate Pullings is First Officer on Lord Nelson. Battle with French privateer Bellone.

121 - Aboard Lord Nelson in the Mediterranean, enroute home, Jack discusses with two female passengers his (unspecified) illness whilst in Catalonia. Treatment consisted of application of leeches

twice per day ('Mother Nature's blood-letters'); "pap" as food; warm goat's milk; plus bleeding and "doses" from Stephen.

122 - Stephen announces that Lord Nelson's Lascars (crewmen from SE Asia or India) are ill with Spanish influenza, not some exotic disease that they brought with them from afar. In an attempt to prevent the disease spreading aboard ship. Stephen declares "But I shall dose them; oh, I shall dose them!" No particulars are ever given. This disease renders Lord Nelson seriously short-handed for the coming battle. He also provides the two women passengers with some sort of unexplained preventive medicine ("prophylactic bottles"), of which he reserves a larger dose for Major Hill.

123 - Lord Nelson encounters privateer Bellone (26), Capt Dumanoir, out of Bordeaux. Lord Nelson is legitimate prey for a French privateer: Bellone gives chase. Lord Nelson is a large East-Indiaman with considerable armament aboard (12 and 18-pounders) for self-protection. Lord Nelson flees, but is also preparing for battle. Jack assumes command of some of the long guns.

127 - During the battle, gun-crewman Lascar Kalim is not at his station, reported "...nearly dead-can't speak" presumably due to Spanish influenza.

131 - Jack is firing Lord Nelson's port-side guns when #7 explodes, dazing Jack and killing three of its servers including the gun-captain, whose head was blown to pieces: his jawbone gouges a wound in Jack's forearm. Shrapnel from #7 wounds an unspecified number of men. At p135 the captain of #7 is identified as "Haynes", known to Jack from time aboard HMS Resolution years ago.

133 - Battle still raging aboard Lord Nelson, which the Bellones are attempting to take by boarding. Jack carries "...a boy down into the cockpit" (aka Stephen's below-decks improvised operating theater). Both of the boy's arms are slashed -probably by a boarder's cutlass. Stephen shows Jack where to press to stop the boy's bleeding.

135 - Bellone has taken Lord Nelson. Jack awakens in the Bellone's cockpit amidst Stephen's other patients. Jack fell headfirst down the fore-hatch near the end of the Bellone engagement. He has been unconscious for some days. Stephen says of Jack's condition,

"...Coma was all I feared these last few days." Stephen then prescribes an "Almoravian draught" for Jack. This treatment is nowhere described and seems to not to appear in any other author's writings. Probably another of O'Brian's invented nostrums. Presumably it is a liquid prepared in advance and likely containing a good deal of alcohol and/or opium- Stephen tells Jack "....they did not find half my Almoravian draught."

136 - Stephen informs Jack that Lord Nelson was taken and had thirty-six killed and wounded (no further breakdown). Stephen removed a ball (musket, pistol) from the shoulder of Bellone's captain, M. Dumanoir, after the battle. More of Lord Nelson's Lascars are down with the Spanish influenza.

137 - Pullings' "Bellone" wounds include grape-shot in the thigh, two broken ribs, and a sword-cut on the shoulder. Major Hill still has the Spanish influenza but can take the air on deck, supported (as was Pullings) by the two Misses Lamb, passengers, who during the battle dressed in men's clothing and carried powder and shot. They are being respectfully treated and are acting as nurses for Lord Nelson's sickbay.

148 - After several minor battles with privateers, which Jack and Stephen watch from within, the captured Lord Nelson is herself taken by a squadron of four English ships of the line.

Book 2 Chapter 6 - p149-196: (overview) Jack goes to the Admiralty to see about a ship - ANY ship: they are in short supply, no promises. Jack continues to fear arrest for debt, takes various evasive actions. Jack philosophizes about rank and promotion in the Navy. Stephen is a terrible roommate, dirty in person and habits (but typical of the era). Stephen muses on Jack's dual/contradictory characters - the gentle sentimental soft-hearted musician, vs the ferocious warrior. Both men attend Queenie's rout (she is both Adm. Keith's wife and Jack's childhood mentor), where Jack encounters Canning (exceedingly wealthy Jewish merchant who is monopolizing Diana). Canning offers Jack captaincy of his new-built privateer frigate. Jack is also offered HMS Polychrest ("The Carpenter's Mistake") by the Admiralty and accepts – refusing an assignment is a serious black mark in an officer's record. Enroute home from the rout Jack meets and captures a footpad, takes him back to the inn. Stephen upsets Jack mightily by saying he cannot go with him on Polychrest - inter alia, Stephen has been offered the position of Physician of the Fleet, aboard the flagship - a considerable honor, which he declines. Shortly, Stephen apologizes, agrees to go with Jack, if given a few days to conduct personal business first.

156 - At their shared quarters ashore, Stephen is revealed to be exceedingly slovenly in personal cleanliness and habits: he upbraids Jack for his "...peevish attention to cleanliness..." and claims Jack's behavior is "...not far removed from cacothymia." - a mental disorder due to a malfunctioning thymus gland. Jack is unimpressed.

167 - Jack and Stephen have returned to England and are at Lady Keith's (Queenie's) gala. Sophie is absent, her mother present: in talking to his future mother-in-law Jack mentions "...a most devilish fever I caught in the mountains..." - presumably during the bear-suit escape from France to Catalonia. He credits his survival to Stephen's medical skills. Stephen's ownership of a castle in Spain and "...a thumping great estate..." are revealed: the Williams are astonished.

179 - Jack is walking home alone in the dark after Queenie's rout and is approached by a footpad (aka robber, on foot). Jack instantly hits the man hard on the right ear, ripping the ear and knocking him out. Worried about leaving an unconscious man on the ground when it is likely to drop to freezing, Jack takes him prisoner and physically carries him to his and Stephen's room at the inn.

180 - Stephen arrives at the inn: the footpad is bound in a chair. Stephen comments on a body-louse he sees crawling on Jack's neck, courtesy the footpad. All Jack's clothing will need to be boiled as a result. The footpad is a literary man (translator, writer of pamphlets etc for hire), is quite ashamed of himself, apologizes profusely.

192 - The footpad's badly-injured ear has been treated by Stephen, with "...an ointment from the oriental apothecary..." As part of his treatment, Mr Scriven (here we get his name) has been "shaved all over" and "parboiled", and his cloak has been baked, all to eliminate lice.

Book 2 Chapter 7- p197-244: (overview) HMS Polychrest adventure begins. She is the mobile part of an abandoned secret weapon project (presumably a huge ship-launched rocket) which killed its inventor first shot. She is pointed at both ends (to absorb recoil), everything about her is weird. Seriously shorthanded, Jack has former footpad Scriven write and print advertizing handbills, gets good seamen. First Officer Parker is poor quality, intensely mistrusted and disliked by Jack. Bailiffs try to arrest Jack for debt: he escapes via window, they pursue, encounter Polychrest crewmen, are pressed by Jack. Problems fitting out at Portsmouth for sea trials. Stephen ruminates on many topics. Jack's protégé Pullings is promoted Lieutenant, assigned to Polychrest. To sea: ship can barely tack, makes 4x normal leeway - a design disaster. Week-long bad storm solidifies crew somewhat. Polychrest assigned to escort a small merchant convoy, can barely manage.

201 - We find out what happened to John Lakey, foretopman, who was shot "...in the ballocks" in Master and Commander (p136) during Sophie's encounter with the Algerine privateers. Lakey has been assigned to Polychrest by the Admiralty. Says Pullings to Stephen, "...and John Lakey, maintop. Do you remember him? You sewed him up very near the first time you ever sailed with us and we had a brush with an Algerine. He swears you saved his -- his privates, sir, and is most uncommon grateful: would feel proper old-fashioned without 'em, he says."

203 - Stephen points out two bailiffs following Jack - they cannot arrest for debt on a Sunday.

212-215 - Pullings' family has Stephen and Jack to dinner at their London inn. One dish is a deep meat pie replete with truffles, which amaze Stephen: he ruminates on truffles and other fungi - safe if not overindulged in, and even if overdone "...only a few cases of convulsions, a certain rigidity of the neck over in two or three days - nonsense to complain." Bailiffs (aka tipstaffs - King's officers who arrest people for debt among their other duties) rush in at dinner's end to arrest Jack for debt resulting from his legal reverses concerning the "neutrality" of some of his earlier prizes. Jack's coxswain Bonden disarms a bailiff, then knocks him out with a stretcher (wooden bar from a ship's boat). Jack immediately presses two of the bailiffs.

225 - Youngster Parslow has tried to shave (unneeded!) and cut himself from ear to chin. His explanation: he was "Shaving, sir, and a huge great wave came." Parslow is sent to Stephen for treatment (not specified, probably styptic and sticking plasters).

230 - In a severe storm lasting several days, First Officer Parker was "shot down the main hatchway", injuring his shoulder, and is now confined to his cot. Jack intensely dislikes Parker, who is neither intelligent nor a good seaman, and tries to get Stephen to declare the man unfit for duty - which Stephen declines to do for lack of a medical reason.

231 - End of the several-day-long storm. Polychrest has "17 men in the sick-bay" (out of a complement of about 90): two hernias; five who fell and broke unspecified bones: the rest are "the usual wounds from falling spars or blocks, or ropes crossing a hand or a leg." One new recruit has gone "raving, staring, barking mad", and yet another landsman (raw recruit, an out-of-work glover, pressed) was lost overboard. The lunatic is probably already sedated with laudanum, for on p235 Stephen talks of giving the man "more". (Laudanum = an alcoholic solution of opium used here as a sedative - used with rum it is the closest thing to an anesthetic available at the time.)

232 - "Child midshipman" Parslow is made drunk by 'friends', is overtly insubordinate to Jack in view of all, is whipped for it. Stephen suggests pouring all the rum over the side, Jack declines for fear of instant mutiny.

235 - Stephen listens to the lunatic "barking" in time with the chain-pumps, and thinks "I must give that man some more of my laudanum." Jack inquires about First Officer Parker's shoulder: no details are given of the injury, but treatment seems to be rest and "Dr Ramis' thin-water gruel and the low diet". Parker can return to duty next day, and Jack is disappointed.

239 - Newly-pressed landsman with rotten teeth being punished for trivial infractions by having his jaws tied closed around an iron marlinspike (crushing two molars) and being whipped around the

32

deck, all at the direct orders of Mr Parker, Jack's intensely-disliked and deeply stupid First Officer. Stephen stops the punishment and verbally assaults Parker for stupidity and cruelty. Parker reports that to Jack: Stephen and Jack have a furious encounter over the incident. Stephen and Parker forced into mutual apologies by Jack.

Book 2 Chapter 8 - p245-290: (overview) Stephen visits Mapes. Stephen tries to get Sophie to at least write Jack a letter: she refuses... that would be altogether too forward. Sophie and Diana's catfight. Stephen tells Sophie of his attraction to Diana Stephen visits Diana also: he returns to Polychrest in Plymouth. Civilian dentistry exists. Killick reappears, bearing large amounts of food from Mapes. Polychrest gets orders to clandestinely pick up a person on the coast of France - likely a returning spy or a defector, but not specified. Bailiffs are still looking for Jack: he must stay afloat to avoid arrest. Jack hosts a successful dinner for Canning, aboard ship. Pickup fails, fatally. By attending to his duty, Jack misses a small, very rich prize: Admiral is upset over the prize, not over mission failure. Stephen discovers tides.

245 - Polychrest's shakedown cruise completed, Jack and Stephen are once more ashore in England. Jack goes to visit his amour, Sophie Williams, at her home. Sophie has taken younger-sister Frankie to town "...to have her teeth filed [sic], poor pet." Unclear whether this is a typo for 'filled'. The idea of "filing" teeth seems out of place in upper-middle-crust early nineteenth century England - as does the idea (ca 1805) of "fillings" (modern sense). At any rate, it is some form of active professional dental care.

247 - Stephen visits with Sophie, declares her underweight (8 stone 5 pounds --- 117 pounds), prescribes a daily pint of porter with dinner, until further notice. By contrast, Jack is "...digging his grave with his teeth..." Throughout the series, Stephen will nag Jack about his weight and huge appetite.

256 - Aboard Polychrest in port, Stephen watches Jack change from work clothes into dress uniform, notes the wide variety of scars Jack has accumulated, from bullets, splinters, cutlasses, pike and

boarding axe. The pike gouge along his ribs is still "red about the edges".

257 - Aboard Polychrest in port: Stephen has helped at a (naval?) hospital where he reduced (i.e., set) a broken femur (perhaps sutured the tissues if it were a compound fracture) and "...the leg may be saved." Stephen has also fobbed off on the shore hospital his barking lunatic, who has been calmed by a Stephen slime-draught. The "slime draught" seems to be O'Brian's invention (like the marthambles and Stephen's "Almoravian draught"). The basic concept is a medicine so horribly nasty in texture, taste/smell, and color as to make any person who must take it KNOW, beyond a shadow of a doubt, that s/he has been "physicked" - that is, adequately treated for the ailment du jour. Most likely the slime draught had no overt medicinal activity or benefits beyond the psychological.

261 - Jack sends Midshipman Babbington ashore in command of a boat-party. Babbington can seldom stay away from the ladies, and is remarkably successful with them, at all ports of call (despite being 5'6" and missing many teeth!). Jack has Babbington empty his pockets before leaving, and confiscates all his cash, saying to Stephen "It is the only way of keeping him even passably chaste." Jack's steward arrives with extensive foodstuffs from Sophie, plus a roebuck run down by Killick's horse-cart, injured, and therefore of necessity killed for the kitchen, not to be wasted.

270 - Polychrest, moored. Jack invites civilian ship-owner and privateer-sponsor Canning aboard for a fine Navy dinner, during which Canning (who has significant seagoing experience) stands up, smashes his skull into a low overhead beam, and cold-cocks himself momentarily. His self-criticism and comments upon recovering moments later endear him to the entire officer's corps of Polychrest.

280 - Polychrest at sea, holding just off the coast of France. Jack is supposed to pick up one or more men who are leaving France clandestinely. As they row out towards Polychrest, they are pursued by a boat full of marksmen. The man whom Polychrest is supposed to pick up, Jean Anquetil, has his aorta nicked by a bullet and bleeds to death on the Polychrest's deck with Stephen helpless to do anything.

282 - Polychrest, at sea. Jack reluctantly imposes a rare punishment of lashing on about a half dozen crewmen. The mess from their flogging (presumably blood on the deck) is cleaned up by swabbers. Some of the flogged men report to Stephen to be anointed or patched.

284 - We finally, a book after the fact, get details of the trepanning of Gunner Day (wounded aboard Sophie in Master and Commander, at p133, 138) as part of the bragging by a Polychrest seaman who has sailed with Stephen and regards the Doctor as a miracle-worker.

285 - Stephen is ashore with a boat's crew, but has been allowed (against all better judgment) to wander off alone to collect specimens. He has doffed his valuable lead-soled boots but forgotten or ignored the existence of pronounced tides (this being the Atlantic instead of the Mediterranean). He finds where he left the boots, which are now far beneath the surface because the tide has risen. He decides to dive to retrieve them - but he is not actually a swimmer. His going subsurface provokes the boat's crew to rescue him, in the course of which they get a boathook around one ankle, hit him in the nape of the neck with an oar, and drive his face into the sand. He emerges without significant injury and under intense and vociferous criticism from the sailors. Each sailor has helpful health advice to give him: food, drink, warmth, clothing...a wide variety of suggestions.

288 - Polychrest at sea for convoy duty. Purser Jones asks Stephen for an anaphrodisiac (i.e. a sex-drive depressant) because his wife is not interested and he doesn't wish to impose his needs on her. Stephen tells him that no such medicine exists.

Book 2 Chapter 9 - p291-322: (overview) Polychrest drops off convoy, returns home: she is a disgraceful sailing machine, an impediment to the merchantmen. Midnight collision with merchantman, Polychrest's fault. Jack reconfigures sails and ballast per his own ideas: sailing qualities markedly improve. Jack rescues yet another man-overboard. Stephen decides he will learn to swim - progenitor of many problems in later novels. To everyone's surprise, Stephen is revealed as an extraordinarily dangerous, highly skilled swordsman and marksman. Polychrest leaves the convoy which she has successfully escorted. The ship has 87

35

men and boys and is 33 short of full complement.. Enroute home, Polychrest encounters Bellone (34), a French privateer frigate and superb sailer, accompanying several ships. Jack attacks Bellone, catching her off-guard. Polychrest's still-poor handling qualities plus poorly worked-up shorthanded crew deprive Jack of his victory and possible prizes. Jack pursues Bellone, ultimately driving her ashore and destroying her. From the Admiral he of course gets no credit for the action.

297 - Stephen has only one patient in sick-bay, a young topman who has a VD (unspecified - "Which she told me she was a virgin."): Stephen forbids him grog or other ardent spirits "...until you are cured."

298 - Seaman Bolton (drunk) falls from a yard, avoids death by landing on a backstay, which bounces him overboard. He cannot swim. Jack is a powerful swimmer and has rescued above twenty men over the years. He dives in and first calms, then rescues Bolton, whose only injury is a mild contusion across his chest from impacting the backstay.

307 - Midnight encounter with a small flotilla of ships, maneuvering together, nationality unknown. Then their escort is identified - Bellone (34), French privateer frigate. Jack engages Bellone at pistol-shot range.

313 - Macdonald, the new commander of Polychrest's Marines, is shot in the arm.

314 - There are Polychrest bodies on the Polychrest's forecastle, never identified.

316 - At sea, the two vessels have exchanged considerable fire and done extensive damage to one another. Here, the Polychrest's "...wounded [are] carried below" but names, wounds and body count of wounded are not specified.

317- A Bellone cannonball kills a Polychrest seaman near the wheel: the mutilated body lands on child-midshipman Parslow, who is uninjured.

319 - Overheated gun bursts, killing the gunner, wounding three. Wounded taken below to Stephen, wounds not specified.

Book 2 Chapter 10 - p323- 360: (overview) Stephen visits Diana - tension and artificial smiles. Stephen andJack advise one another on relationships, do not see their parallelity: both are artificially and socially constrained from acting as they would like. Stephen, secret agent, has disappeared for a while, "to Ireland on tedious family business." Jack's long-time friend Dundas tells Stephen to warn Jack that he is spending too much time ashore, wenching - it is known even at high levels, and not appreciated. Stephen much puzzled at how to tell this to Jack. Marine commander Macdonald replaced by Smithers, an insufferable braggart. Jack buys for naturalist Stephen a perfect narwhal tooth, as a gift. Stephen tries to give Jack Dundas's messages, and as a result they have an almighty row specifically over Diana, during which Jack calls Stephen a bald-faced liar and a bastard, while Stephen calls Jack a coward and a liar. Neither will retract. Stephen challenges Jack to a duel. Neither will apologize. Seconds are chosen, as is a meeting ground. Polychrest gets orders to sea before any meeting can occur. After the challenge, Jack goes to Diana's home in Dover, is told she is not at home but he can tell she is. He uses a construction pulley to hoist himself to her floor level, and discovers that Canning is with her, in her bedroom... thus dashing all his hopes and making nonsense of the deepest grounds for the duel, which is —eventually- tactfully forgotten/forgiven by both parties.

325 - Ashore in England. Stephen is off, ostensibly to do some dismal "law-business". He is leaving his Polychrest practice in the hands of "...a good-natured foolish young man with scrofulous ears..." who has been assigned to be his assistant.

334 - First Officer Parker is behaving irrationally and violently in giving orders to the crew - Stephen arrives on board, observes, wonders if Parker is genuinely mad.

335 - Stephen's assistant Mr Thompson had earlier attempted a "Cheseldon's Lithotomy" which now has the unfortunately too-common odor of gangrene - rotting flesh - caused by an infection curable only by amputation, hence fatal if it occurs in the body (as here). Cheseldon was a pioneering surgeon (he attended Isaac Newton on

37

his death bed). This procedure (named from the Greek words for stone and cutting) is Cheseldon's innovative, quick, straightforward operation to remove kidney or bladder stones - which were a common ailment of the day. Actual 'cutting time' for Cheseldon himself reported to be under a minute, seldom as much as two. In his hands, the operation had the amazing survival rate of over 50%. Another patient has 'gummata" or soft swellings, over an old depressed skull fracture, is terrified that Mr Thompson may touch them. Thomson seems ham-handed and insensitive.

338 - Aboard Polychrest, Jack dislikes what he sees of himself in the mirror, asks Stephen for a "treble-shotted slime-draught to get me to sleep."

341 - Both Stephen and Jack are courting Diana, each is aware of the other's machinations. Both men are at a high-pitch of what Stephen would call "sexuality-driven tension". Angry words result in a challenge and acceptance. Neither man will back down.

346 - In the sick-bay, a number of patients mentioned in passing... "Stephen's patient" (not identified); several men in a corner, chatting and drinking grog; two Highlanders soothing a flogged Irish comrade.

347 - Stephen goes to the hospital at Dover to see his patients. The barking-madman is rolled into a ball. Marine Macdonald's arm-stump is "healing well", with nicely-done flaps on which the hair retains its original growth orientation. Stephen's amputation of the arm (wounded by a shot from a Bellone musket - p313) is not chronicled. Stephen borrows Macdonald's pistols for the duel.

354 - Jack gets orders to look into Chaulieu (on the French coast) for French corvette Fanciulla and associated gunboats; utmost dispatch. An extremely dangerous undertaking. Stephen and Jack both return to the ship (separately) for immediate departure - no time for the duel.

Book 2 Chapter 11 - p361-384: (overview) Stephen, monumentally uncomfortable, warns Jack of a likely mutiny that night. Jack wants to apologize, but cannot bring himself to do so. Resigns himself to being punctured at Stephen's discretion in their postponed duel. Jack takes strong action to prevent mutiny, re-

38

enlists the crew to their orders, promises no mention in the record of the mutinous proceedings. Men say out loud that the cause of the problem is Parker. With Chaulieu and Fanciulla as their goals, the men rally to Jack. Sailing in to Chaulieu in the dark and fog, they go firmly aground. Their target Fanciulla is moored under the fortress's guns: Fanciulla and fortress both mount fire at Polychrest, which is taking a serious battering. Jack takes volunteers in the small-craft to cut out Fanciulla: they board successfully. Jack and Bonden collar the captain, and Fanciulla strikes. They make good their escape in Fanciulla: Polychrest is shot-riddled and coming apart. Jack manages to tow her free but she sinks in shallow water.

361 - Aboard Polychrest, Stephen is checking an unidentified patient for an unspecified problem, and believes he had "... almost certainly pulled him though."

375 - Boarding the moored Fanciulla, Babbington goes down (apparently to a musket shot at close range) whilst Jack is 'half decapitating' a defender. Jack is stabbed in the shoulder.

378 - Aboard the taken Fanciulla, while bringing her out of the harbor, bombardment from the shore becomes intense and a shell from a heavy land-based mortar kills four of Polychrest's boarding party who are working at the corvette's capstan-bars.

379 - The battle still raging, Jack is hit on the head by shrapnel as he dives from the corvette into the harbor to carry a cable to the Fanciulla, where he is hauled aboard. (Injury detail, p441.) He then swims the cable to Polychrest, which is aground and very badly damaged.

381 - Aboard Polychrest again, Polychrest still aground. Jack's cable serves, the crew re-floats Polychrest but she is "opening like a rose" - literally coming apart due to shoddy construction plus extensive battle-damage. In trying to work her out of the harbor, Jack calls for Mr Rolfe (gunner?), but Rolfe is dead.

382 - Babbington has been wounded in one arm ("...one sleeve hanging empty") but carries on: he reports to Jack about the towline despite the injury.

384 - At the end of the Polychrest battle, with Polychrest having sunk, Stephen takes an exhausted Jack into the Fanciulla's sick-bay. It is here, apparently, that the looming duel between Stephen and Jack is simply forgotten. NO explicit resolution of the already-arranged duel is ever given (but see p475 for the likely resolution).

Book 2 Chapter 12 - p385-431: (overview)   Jack writes to relatives of the casualties. Jack's and Stephen's relationship seem to be on an even keel again. Prize money yes, but not enough to clear his debts. Jack summoned to the Admiralty. Fearing the worst, Jack is pleasantly surprised when greeted by and congratulated by the First Lord, Melville, who personally gives Jack his critical promotion to Post Captain. Jack is offered the frigate Blackwater, now a-building and to be launched in six months. But Jack needs something instantly (the debt problem). Appointed acting captain to HMS Lively (34), a well-known crack frigate. Jack's thoughts on limits and uses of authority by acting captains. Jack's reputation precedes him to Lively - rake, protégé of Lord Melville, fine seaman, fighter. Lively's crew is superb, show off for Jack by making sail from their moorings, with a single command "Make sail". Jack is flabbergasted. Later, Jack decides to properly train Lively's gun-crews by bombarding to destruction every French coastal defense battery he can find. This is a legitimate expenditure of His Majesty's powder and shot, and will satisfy the bean-counters at the Admiralty.

385 - Back in England, aboard Fanciulla at The Downs. Jack's letter to Babbington's parents says that amputation of the injured [left] arm is quite likely, but the parents are not to worry - Dr Stephen is "...the best hand in the Fleet with a saw, if it comes to that..." This demonstrates Jack's tact at its finest.

387 - Stephen is off for some days of personal business, leaves prescriptions for Jack: physic, bolus, a quart of porter at breakfast and again at mid-day, a glass of cold negus (basically, mulled wine) before retiring, no beef or mutton --- fish, rabbits, chicken are okay. And NO SEX. Jack's treatment is left explicitly in his steward's (Killick's) hands. Under Stephen's directives, Killick terrorizes his

captain as to dosages and schedules and restrictions. Killick thoroughly enjoys the authority. Jack does not, but cannot fight - Killick is in charge.

390-391 - Highly favorable response in the press to Jack's report of the action (17 dead, 23 wounded: last muster before the Fanciulla action was 97 souls aboard).

392 - Because the Admiral asks, we find out what injuries Jack got when he was swimming the cable from ship to ship (p379) - "tearing off a hands-breadth of scalp", plus an un-noticed (at the time) sword cut that caused Jack severe bleeding. Jack is still bandaged from the head wound.

393 - Lord Melville gives Jack his Post-Captaincy. Offers HMS Blackwater, frigate, now a-building. Jack needs a ship NOW to avoid arrest.

401 - Jack posted as temporary (acting) captain to HMS Lively, 34, a well-reputed crack frigate whose Capt. Hammond is off to Parliament. Jack invites Stephen to join him. When they report aboard together, Stephen makes several major faux pas before the entire crew- his dress and comments on the ship (not to mention his 60,000 bees) are well meant but misunderstood. He is known by reputation, however, and the behavior is accommodated.

410 - Lively's surgeon Mr Floris tells crew Stephen is a great man, enormously respected. Floris claims, "I have read his book until it is dog-eared - a most luminous exposition...." We are told neither title nor topic of this book - perhaps it is "Tar-water reconsidered"? Floris wants Stephen's thoughts about a patient, Mr Wallace.

411 - In the wardroom, multiple topics of discussion, including the health of Cassandra, the last survivor of the ship's pet gibbons.

418 - Jack finds that Lively's Capt Hammond, like Jack himself, disliked punishing men via the cat - a few hours at the pumps was the Lively's usual punishment when needed. Jack thinks it a fine idea. Stephen is called on by Jack to decide which of two claimants for a shrunken ape's-head is the true owner. One claims "his ape" was male - the other claimant says HIS ape was female. Stephen pronounces the head male, confiscates it temporarily for study.

422 - Stephen's experiments on bees' abilities to navigate and communicate go awry - the bees get into the gun-room's cocoa. Killick terrified of bees.

424 - Cassandra, the last of several gibbons brought aboard, is now a confirmed alcoholic (so diagnosed by Stephen) due to "gifts" from seamen. An earlier pet, a monk seal, had died of alcohol abuse made possible only by her 'friends' amongst the crew. Stephen's eagerness to dissect the ape when it dies upsets the wardroom during Jack's formal dinner. One midshipman is aged all of five, and is sucking his thumb - son of the Lively's 2nd Lt.

430 - Stephen will be going ashore to pick up "...some stores, and salve against bee-stings." He will also visit Polychrest's wounded in the hospital.

> **Book 2 Chapter 13 - p432-444: (overview)** Ashore, Stephen visits Diana's vacated quarters, ponders events. Helps surgeon Mr Floris with surgery: the patient survives. Stephen's bees get into the crew's cocoa. Crew needs live-firing practice with great guns but there is almost no allowance for ammunition for practice. Jack takes Lively close inshore to bombard coastal fortresses (this being legitimate combat under his orders) thus circumventing the restrictions. Crew enthusiastic, improves quickly.... "...short of shooting at their fellow man, there is nothing the crew like better than smashing an enemy's glass and stone at half a mile." Jack's jackass father elected to Parliament. Returning to England, Lively gets orders to immediately escort a north-bound convoy. Jack is offered a chance to visit with Sophie at Adm. Haddock's home, declines for want of self-confidence.

432 - Ashore. Midshipman Babbington's arm has been saved, and one "shocking belly-wound had astonished him [Stephen] by living." (Patient and wound not specified.) Stephen, visiting the now uninhabited former home of his beloved Diana, opens the house gate with a wire and the kitchen door with a Morton's retractor (a surgical instrument). Why he would have it with him, unless with malice aforethought, seems strange.

434 - Stephen is the acknowledged master of the "suprapubic cystotomy", an operation to remove kidney or bladder stones, and accepts an invitation to aid Dr Floris with that operation on Floris' patient, Mr Wallace, the operation to be done in the ship's sick-bay.

436 - Anesthesia for Mr Wallace's cystotomy - laudanum and rum. Wallace is strapped and chained to the operating table by his mates, who give him a bullet to bite on.

439 - With respect to Mr Wallace's suprapubic cystotomy, "...and the patient survived."

Book 2 Chapter 14 - p445-496: (overview) Lively is ordered to Plymouth to take charge of a convoy. Ashore, Stephen finds that Sophie is staying nearby at Adm. Haddock's home, tells Jack. Jack refuses to go visit or to write, feeling he has nothing whatever to offer her. Diana has become mistress to Canning. Stephen tries to get Sophie and sister to ask for passage to the Downs aboard Lively enroute to the convoy. Sophie refuses - utterly improper, entirely too forward! Inspired by music, Stephen philosophizes about the human condition. Back aboard ship, he is startled to look out the stern-window and see Sophie glide past - she has decided to come aboard per his suggestion, arrives with sister Cecelia and escorted by Adm. Haddock. Jack's father, retired general now in Parliament is making an ass of himself in his speeches - and it reflects badly on Jack, who can do nothing about it. Spain is coming into the war on the side of France - and is shipping some 5 million pieces of eight in several ships from Montevideo to Cadiz. The money's safe arrival will be the signal for Spain to declare war. Stephen, through his contacts, makes certain that Lively will be in the center of any action. At p475 we get the closest thing to an apology from Jack to Stephen for having called Stephen a liar and caused the aborted duel...Jack's orders require him to consult on political matters with Stephen: Stephen points out that in his business (intelligence) he is unable to be forthcoming and must indeed often lie. The implication is that "required lying" was the basis upon which Jack's challenge was issued, hence the challenge was unwarranted had Jack only understood Stephen's job and its obligations...which Stephen could not disclose... a perfect Catch-22. Jack claims not to have been in his right mind when he gave Stephen the lie....in context of the era, this is a formal apology. Stephen, equally indirectly, accepts. Stephen has been given a temporary commission as a naval officer for this cruise. Very odd indeed. This time it is Jack who understands - Stephen's boss, foreseeing possible large prizes and having never been able to properly reward his best agent (Stephen is an unpaid volunteer!), has thereby assured Stephen of indirect reward for his services, since as a commissioned officer aboard ship he will share in any prizes - e.g., the Spanish 5 millions. At sea, Stephen negotiates with the Spanish commodore as to possible surrender of his fleet. The fleets face one another point-blank whilst negotiations proceed. They fail, battle ensues. Lively pursues the actual treasure ship, Fama. Lively catches and takes Fama - the implication is of great wealth from prize monies, plus perhaps Spain will not declare against England after all. The captured Spanish officers dine aboard Lively, and all toast Jack's "Sophie".

446- Details about Jack's head-wound (p379, 371) are revealed by Stephen to Sophie: "... a mere scalp wound. Not above a dozen stitches".

477 - Samantha the Gibbon has died, presumably of alcoholism, and another child midshipman, Randall, wept for her.

480 - At sea in Lively. Stephen becomes violently seasick for the first time ever - during a severe but short-lived storm. Stephen reports that he has been bitten by a tame female horseshoe bat, and now thinks he may be experiencing the onset of rabies. The implication is that Stephen is embarrassed by seasickness and uses the putative bite as an explanation/excuse for the seasickness. Jack sends Killick to Stephen with a basin - a vomit-catcher. The storm renders Jack senior captain on the scene - he is now in charge.

481 - Post storm, Stephen and Mr Floris spend the morning dosing one another for various diseases and conditions, including orchitis (inflammation of the testicles, usually due to mumps), scurvy (simple vitamin-C deficiency), and the ""fell Ludolphus' palsy" [aka rabies], thus demonstrating that imagination and superstition about things medical are NOT the exclusive purview of the ignorant and uneducated seamen.

491 - Stephen investigates laughter coming from the sick-bay - a unique and unsettling experience. Two of Floris' assistants and three patients are sitting about, chatting and drinking. Stephen's arrival unsettles them, but they explain that the entire butcher's bill for the latest combat is two splinter-wounds, one musket ball and one broken femur. Plus, of course two men cut in half by the ship's figurehead when it was shattered by cannon fire.

Book 3 - H.M.S. Surprise

Book 3 Chapter 1 - p5-27: (overview) At the Admiralty - debate about whether Jack's capture of Spanish treasure ship Fama should be treated as a prize, or the 5 million pieces of eight confiscated by the English Crown. Debate mismanaged, decision is to confiscate, then to make a nominal ex-gratia payment in lieu of prize monies. New incompetent First Lord of the Admiralty clumsily imperils Stephen's cover as intelligence agent. Stephen's inamorata Diana is in India as Canning's mistress (and him a Jew!). Stephen has intelligence reports on both of them. Aubrey is away serving as acting captain of frigate HMS Lively (34), whose Captain Hamond is sitting Parliament. Stephen tries to explain to Sophia the complex and fluid international scene, largely fails. Sir Joseph, head of naval intelligence (also Stephen's boss, scientific colleague, and friend), explains the prize-money decision to Stephen, for relay to Jack. The ex-gratia payment is unlikely to clear Jack of debt - he will still have to dodge the bailiffs.

13 - Stephen visiting Jack's fiancée Sophie at her residence "Mapes", tells her she is getting too fat ... whereas six months ago, she was too thin.

Book 3 Chapter 2 - p28-55: (overview) English fleet at sea, blockading the French in Toulon. Lively pokes inshore daily to inventory French men-o-war in harbor. Blockading is boring, wearing work. Lively et al are long overdue for provisions. Cutter Weasel arrives with mail and orders for Lively to generally go raise hell with enemy "shipping, installations and communications" (i.e., independent cruising, Jack's perfect assignment). Jack immediately sets sail for Calvette (an imaginary destination). Lively will pick up Stephen at Minorca - as a renowned naturalist Stephen "has a pass" to travel even in enemy country, which Minorca is at present. However, unknown to Jack, Stephen is ashore on an intelligence assignment, not for science. One of Lively's midshipman finds a newspaper announcement of Jack's betrothal to Sophia, proposes a toast. Jack takes parties ashore to destroy various enemy facilities. Jack attempts to pick up Stephen in the dark, is given a partly garbled message purporting to be from Stephen in prison, where he is being tortured by French intelligence.

29 - Lively et al. have been on short rations for some time: two "thin midshipmen" rhapsodize over the idea of bacon, sausages, etc.

32- Like his midshipmen, Jack is daydreaming of food - specifically of a meal when he and Stephen were prisoners aboard Christy-Palliere's ship (a French 74) just before the current hostilities began. Officers were responsible for their own food supplies aboard ship: a "murrain" had decimated the Lively's officers' sheep, and measles was rampant in the pig-sty. "Murrain" is generic and covered what are today several separate diseases... e.g., hoof-and-mouth; anthrax. Pigs are anatomically and physiologically very similar to humans, and share with us some diseases, including measles. Jack has "...a small shoulder of not altogether healthy mutton..." available for dinner.

33 - For a month the young gentlemen (aka midshipmen) have been catching rats in the hold, skinning and either selling or eating them (now 5p each, and rising). This was a timeless tradition in most navies of the day, and one in which Jack had participated when he was temporarily de-rated and put before the mast.

38 - At Jack's dinner, a discussion of the relative taste (when eaten) and other merits of two varieties of weevil found in ship's biscuit.

39 - Still at Jack's table, a discussion of laurel (aka bay leaves) - usable as a seasoning, but more than a taste "...a deadly poison". (Not true.)

46 - Jack remembers the gruesomeness of the combat when Lively boarded a French gunboat - Lively's Chinese crewmen were utterly cold-blooded, used only knives and garrotes, decapitating all the dead, cutting into bodies looking for hidden valuables. No prisoners. Jack is nauseated by the sight and attitude, but the Chinese are prime seamen. Jack's arm has been cut and bandaged: the bandage is still oozing blood. No details.

51 - Discussion about the captured gunboat - the Chinese seamen involved were taken by Lively from an armed junk - probably a pirate - and are not to be trusted. They are suspected of having eaten the

evidence of some of their crimes (i.e., cannibalism). Jack agrees it best not to use Chinese as part of the prize crew.

55 - At Minorca, a message (supposedly from Stephen) reaches Jack: Stephen has been captured and is being tortured by the French intelligence service.

Book 3 Chapter 3 - p56-73: (overview) [NOTE: nothing "medical" or "health" occurs in Chapter 3.] We know that Stephen has been tortured, we suspect it may have involved his hands [this because of the illegibility of his note to Jack], and back or legs [he cannot negotiate stairs]. Details slowly emerge farther along in the story.] Stephen's written message is hard to decipher, but courier Maragall explains the situation, and is eager to help. Stephen is being held at a known site in Port Mahon, which city Jack knows very well. Jack instantly plans and mounts a rescue effort: he cannot allow any of his officers to come along, which disappoints them. Maragall insists that as a smokescreen, ALL prisoners (there are several) must be freed, not just Stephen. Jack agrees. Rescue party rows ashore, finds the building. Maragall fires a warehouse as a distraction. Raiding party takes the prison in a sharp, furious battle, frees prisoners (including one man, perhaps Stephen himself, being broken on a wheel, a la the Inquisition), kills several of the guards but the man in charge, Dutourd, escapes. ["Dutourd" is an obvious play on words, translating "Of/from a turd": he is a high-level (and recurring) bad-guy in the series of novels.] The Surprises carry Stephen to the ship, after stripping the facility of all interrogation-related records and paperwork, then firing the municipal records-office to confuse the enemy further. Blaine announces his imminent retirement, identifies his successor. Stephen gives Blain papers taken from the prison, which papers ("authentic even to the bloodstains") identify in detail the French Intelligence Service's network of secret agents and contacts. Sir Joseph is beside himself with glee.

Book 3 Chapter 4 - p74-97: (overview) Back in Portsmouth, ashore at the Crown Inn. Stephen mending rapidly under intensive amateur but well-meaning care, which irritates him mightily. Jack is arrested for £700 of debt, hauled off to a 'sponging house', i.e., a short-term debtors' prison, this one located in Vulture's Lane (of course). Jack is still waiting for the Crown's ex-gratia payment. Sir Joseph, to thank Jack for Stephen's rescue, volunteers to personally guarantee the £700, thus releasing Jack. At the hot springs in Bath, Sir Joseph and his replacement Mr Waring discuss Stephen's ancestry and politics. Later, Sophie is visiting Stephen in his room at the inn when Sir Joseph et al. arrive, are astounded and impressed to find such a beautiful young woman attending the wizened gnome-ish Dr Maturin - he eventually introduces Sophie as Jack's fiancée. Sir Joseph offers a semi-tropical cruise (warmth for Stephen's recovery), a frigate preparing to take HRH's official Envoy Mr Stanhope to the Sultan of Kampong (fictional - but set in the East Indies) - a very long ocean voyage indeed. Would Jack be interested in the command? Jack is available, having been released from the sponging house. Bonden (Jack's longtime personal coxswain) proves illiterate: Stephen will teach him at sea. Stephen writes to Jack "We have a ship, HMS Surprise, for the East Indies..." to be met by all at Portsmouth immediately. Surprise (28), a smallish, old, nearly obsolete frigate, was Jack's first major ship as a midshipman long ago. Enroute to the ship, Stephen arranges a clandestine, midnight half-hour meeting for Jack and Sophie, who has never been out at night before. Sophie and Jack agree to wait for one another for marriage, but that theirs is NOT an "official" engagement. Discussion of Jack's ability to respond instantly to physical danger, and to be wise at sea, yet be a complete ninny ashore. Discussion of French inhumanity in interrogation contrasted with the otherwise high moral character of French behavior generally.

74 - Stephen being cared for by civilians and Jack. Overly-warm coach and greatcoat. Endless possets (hot milk curdled with alcohol, usually strongly spiced - a cold remedy); caudels (like a posset thickened with eggs or bread). Jack provides a bottle of "Dr Mead's Instant Invigorator". "It contains iron!" - so Jack tells him, as he adds the elixir to a posset. Another of O'Brian's invented medical nostrums. At least, the need for iron in the diet has been discovered.

76 - Stephen is visited by his boss, Sir Joseph Blain of Naval Intelligence, who is shocked at Stephen's appearance (no details given). Stephen protests that what bothers Blaine is superficial damage, "There is no essential lesion." Stephen, we find in passing, cannot yet negotiate stairs. Stephen's landlady is doctoring him with the patent

49

medicines 'Godfrey's Cordial' and 'Ward's Drop'. Sir Joseph decides against recommending that Stephen take the waters at Bath.

78 - Stephen tries to use his hands, falls back muttering "No grip...." His hands were severely damaged by the French torture. Stephen volunteers that he will go to Bath for the waters - Sir Joseph waxes enthusiastic, happy he didn't need to make the recommendation himself.

79 - Even Jack's Coxswain Bonden is dosing Stephen - with raw eggs beaten up in brandy – in terms of medicinal effect, this is probably the best option available.

86 - At Bath, Stephen is soaking in hot water and sunshine, aided by Bonden. Sir Joseph is also present: "...He is doing far better today." Stephen walked nearly a mile yesterday. Clearly his torture involved more than his hands, at which Sir Joseph cannot even look.

88 - Before leaving Stephen, Sophia feeds him yet another unnamed "glaucus [pale bluish gray] liquid" plus pills. He takes them graciously. He is recovering well, plans for the evening include working with a friend: they will dissect "…an aged male pauper".

91 - At Mapes, Stephen listens to the calls of an itinerant corn-cutter (callus remover), ruminates on the development of corns.

95 - Stephen comments to Sophia that a heavy coat is actually harmful to the wearer, if he has a certain "depth of skin" - a depth created by prolonged exposure and aiding in heat retention.

Book 3 Chapter 5 - p98-132: (overview)   Weeks into her long voyage, Surprise is becalmed at 30W, carrying HRH's Envoy His Excellency Mr Stanhope to his duties: diplomatic party clueless about naval customs and manners. Stephen learning to swim – can now weakly paddle the length of Surprise. Stephen is experimenting on rats: the midshipmen have eaten the experiment. Doldrums break. All-hands formal inspection. Unknown ship sighted, turns out to be St Paul's Rocks. Stephen goes ashore on St Paul's Rock to investigate the flora and fauna: the Rocks are feet-deep in bird guano. Struck by an intense squall, Stephen's companion Nicolls and their rowboat are lost: the same squall partially dismasts Surprise, drives her leagues away. Stephen is marooned alone, watches Surprise disappear over the horizon.

98 - Stephen is sleeping on deck with his head in a cloth bag, to protect against "moon pall" - a fictional condition or entity invented by a "Dr Tufts" in London about 1700.

103 - Acne! Boys whose voices have not yet broken - especially the very young (5-10 years) are 'squeakers'. The 'squeaker' Jack invites to breakfast (Mr Callow) "...had burst out into an eruption of adolescent spots, enough to put a man off his appetite." Callow inhales 27 slices of bacon, with Jack's urging.

104 - "His Excellency is much better today" - chronic seasickness.

105 - Stanhope's gout (first mention of it) has "...flown to his stomach" and is now aggravated (e.g., by the ship's motion; diet; etc.). Perhaps he also has an ulcer? Midshipmen's mess is down to catching and eating rats.

110 - Seamen Kelynach (who fell overboard from a yard yesterday, but was not injured) and Garland both are listless, dull. Jack knows, but we are not informed, what the condition is.

112 - Several more listless dispirited men amongst the crew.

113 - The listless dull crewmen are exhibiting preliminary signs of scurvy, despite the voyage being young. Worries that the symptoms might indicate other more virulent things. Stephen has a "...raw-boned Scotch assistant" as yet unnamed. Sickbay roster today includes one broken arm, one hernia with pox, four 'plain poxes'.

114 - Ship's cat and parrot prostrated by the heat.

117 - Stephen reading the 'scurvy' chapter of Blane's Diseases of Seamen: This is a real book, and was a standard Royal Navy medical treatise: _Gilbert Blane MD (Physician to the Fleet): 1785; "Observations on the diseases incident to seamen" - 546 pp, London_.

118 - Stephen confirms Jack's impression - it is scurvy. Scurvy's early-onset symptoms include weakness, muscle pains, tender gums, petechiae (bruise-like splotches of color under the skin, due to burst capillaries). It is affecting only men received off another ship (Racoon) which had been at sea for months without greenstuff (= green plants, at least somewhat edible and containing usable vitamin C) be-

fore the men were sent (without recuperative shore leave) to Surprise. Stephen worries that Surprise's supply of lime juice may be useless.

119 - Stephen disabuses Jack as to what physicians can actually do in the way of effective treatments. Differentiates between 'surgery' and 'medicine'. "I can purge you, bleed you, worm you, set your leg or take it off, and that is very nearly all." Not an inaccurate assessment of the state of the physician's art. Regardless, the men have infinite faith in Stephen's abilities.

121 - Surprise's purser, Mr Bowes (an honest man hence a rarity amongst pursers), bought his position and went to sea despite having a club-foot: has participated well in several cutting-out expeditions.

125 - Nicolls volunteers to row Stephen to St Paul's Rocks to do his research. Stephen speculates on what is wrong with Nicolls, who looks distinctly unhealthy - not scurvy - perhaps syphilis or worms?

128 - Atop the Rocks, Stephen considers Nicolls, who is miserable, seriously depressed - had told Stephen of a powerful long-standing disagreement with his wife, which all his efforts have failed to fix - he gets no mail, ever, is intensely lonely.

Book 3 Chapter 6 - p133-189: (overview) Stephen marooned for a week, alone, drinking from rainwater puddles heavily infused with guano and strongly heated by the sun. Surprise lost four men overboard to the squall, almost lost the ship. Stephen rescued by Surprise's crew, arrives at the ship naked, is suavely greeted by Mr Stanhope. Scurvy strikes hard, Surprise detours to Cape St Roque, Brazil, to get anti-scurvy greenstuff. Babbington given conditional promotion to Acting 3rd Lt, confesses to having eaten of Stephen's missing experimental rats. Stephen's new acquisition, a Brazilian sloth, becomes ship's mascot, is perturbed by cannon-fire, becomes an alcoholic due to Jack's gifts -biscuit soaked in grog. Arrival at Rio de Janeiro. Mail call. Jack gets £9,755 13s 4d ex gratia for Fama. Jack unloads and re-stows the ship's stores, adjusting ballast to get best ship's trim. Stephen gets a week for natural history. Surprise resumes southward course to round the Cape. Albatrosses at last. Bonden is very bright and a good learner -can now read and write thanks to Stephen. Worrying about icebergs. Huge Southern swell imperils ship. Northwards into the Indian Ocean, towards Bombay, weather moderating. Stephen and Bonden ruminating in the fighting top. The crew are surprisingly talented at composing and reciting poetry: also, musical ability high and wide-spread onboard (a not uncommon thing in the Navy of the time).

137 - Mention of "Stephen's scrofulous shrunken belly" - 'scrofulous' usually refers to having tuberculosis bacteria in the lymph glands of the neck - alternative meaning is morally contaminated - corrupt. Neither seems to make sense here. Stephen claims that baking for a week on the island has greatly aided his recovery from the French interrogation.

138 - Asked by Jack what he had had to drink on the Rock, Stephen replies "Boiled shit," then elaborates to include seabird blood mixed with seawater and juice from kelp (seaweeds).

139 - Scurvy now affecting all Racoons, many Surprises, and four landsmen. Squall thoroughly tumbled and wetted the contents of Stephen's medical chest.

140 - Stephen demands that for medical reasons Surprise head for the nearest land and source of greenstuff, to cure the scurvy. Due to scurvy, many old wounds - long healed - are re-opening, including amputations. Men's gums are beginning to bleed and soften; teeth will fall out shortly.

141 - Stephen's experimental rats have vanished. Jack initially refuses to consider detouring to get greenstuff. Jack is shown (and can ignore) the re-opening wounds, but yields when presented with a box full of men's teeth that have fallen out due to scurvy.

143 - Babbington confesses to having eaten some of Stephen's missing rats.

144 - Due to Babbington's confession, Stephen prepares unexplained 'boluses' for the six rat-eaters, aka midshipmen.

146 - Hove to on the Brazilian coastline, Stephen ashore for greenstuff. Lots of minor ship repair, but all midshipmen are unavailable, largely confined to the head for reasons Jack does not understand - Stephen's revenge was a very strong laxative in the midshipmen's boluses.

148 - Stephen returns to Surprise with large supplies of fruit, meat, greenstuff - plus a sloth which becomes a mascot.... it is perfectly adapted for a life at sea - uncomplaining, requires no fresh air or light, thrives in a damp, confined atmosphere, can sleep in any circumstance, is tenacious of life, puts up with any hardship, and accepts biscuit gratefully. For quarters, any bit of horizontal rope will do. Stephen wins a bet about his ability to read a book by bioluminescence in the ship's bow wave.

150 - With vitamin C from greenstuff, recovery from scurvy is very quick - sickbay empty within a week.

159 - Word about Sophie's mother's health - it is "breaking down". Mother still against the idea of Sophie + Jack, encouraging new suitor Mr Hincksey, the new parson of Swiving Rectory (swiving = old English word meaning 'fucking'---undoubtedly the author's joke or personal opinion).

161 - Mr Stanhope, the envoy for whom the trip is undertaken, has been monstrously and continually seasick - time ashore helps but does not cure or rejuvenate him. Surprise sails, Stanhope immediately seasick again.

166 - Cask #113, of 3-year-old pork, has filled the sickbay with dysentery cases. Also in sickbay are two pneumonias.

173 - Stanhope still dry-seasick continuously. Sickbay houses "...the usual accidents, bangs and bruises of a furious storm." one man bashed bodily into an anchor fluke, a second pitched headfirst down the fore-hatch, a third impaled himself on his own marlinspike. Seaman Woods is dying of pneumonia, Jack attends: "an easy death".

176 - In a furious, near-fatal high-latitude storm, one of Stanhope's party has '...managed to blow himself up with a spirit-stove..." (small alcohol-burning portable stove, just barely usable under these conditions) and is "miserably burnt". Fires in such conditions are both exceedingly foolish and against all regulations. He has also managed to fall heavily on a great gun...and is being patched up.

178 - Ship nearly pooped, almost broaches to but recovers - during recovery "some" hands were injured - no specifics.

184 - In the Indian Ocean, weather having moderated and warmed to 'hot and muggy', Mr Stanhope is clearly failing due to prolonged seasickness.

Book 3 Chapter 7 - p190-238: (overview)   Landfall, Malabar Hill in Bombay. Scents from the land. At Bombay, Surprise goes immediately into the Navy Yard for extensive overhaul and refitting. Mr Stanhope's presence convinces the Port Admiral to be unusually helpful. Stephen feels he himself must spend significant time ashore – to which a ship-preoccupied Jack agrees. Stephen knows Diana is living with Canning in Bombay, wants to see her and also to explore this entirely new world. Stephen's re actions to and thoughts about, and explorations of, many aspects of Bombay society. Stephen adopts/is adopted by a native girl of perhaps 9 years, who becomes his mentor and guide. She is offered for sale to him, he declines. He buys silver bracelets for her, thugs murder her while stealing them. Stephen declares himself to be of her caste, pays for her funeral pyre. Long discussions/ thoughts about marriage, gender-relationships, 'what-to-do?' re Stephen/Diana and Jack/Sophie. Extensive descriptions of Stephen's doings ashore, including society's behavior on various subjects. Diana is miserable with her keeper, Canning: Stephen renews his offer of marriage as an escape route but Diana declines.

190 - Fresh fruit and huge meals.

191 - Stephen's patients are moved to the naval hospital, Mr Stanhope is ashore and recovering (still looming is the sea-trip from Bombay to his duty station at Kampong).

194 - Stephen's 'adoptee', the girl Dil, is very protective of him, beats "with a brickbat" a boy who tried to intrude on their relationship.

195 - Stephen's thoughts about death, occasioned by watching vultures scavenge the human dead exposed on sacred ground - leftover bones not to be carried away

200 - Babbington is successfully working the local women, as usual; this time a 'preacher's daughter'. Stephen reminds Babbington of the gruesome potential consequences of various VDs, declares

"Any woman is a source of great potential danger to a sailorman." Babbington agrees, then asks for (and presumably gets) a loan of pocket money to continue his pursuit.

218 - Emotional reunion -aided by a large scorpion - of Diana and Stephen, in her quarters in Canning's house.

221 - Stephen asks Diana how many teeth she has, she says "All of them!"

222 - Diana notices Stephen's mangled hands, he explains that he has recovered, the hands were caught in a machine.

225 - Stanhope confides in Stephen that he is being treated by a Dr Clowe - slime-baths (!) and bleeding, and worries they may be leaving Bombay three weeks earlier than he'd thought. Stanhope says that Clowe's treatment "...has not prevailed upon the liver complaint..." and the doctors are afraid the complaint may "...fly to the stomach and attach itself there...."

226 - During Diana's picnic to examine famous cave sculptures - probably erotic but not clearly so described. (Parallel to events in Passage to India). Mr White (chaplain) has been bitten on the left buttock by an unidentified creature, when White sat upon it. Members of the party are variously impressed with, or outraged by, the sculptures.

233 - Stephen heads for his own home late at night, encounters a band of Moplahs (thugs, robbers) with a victim. The attackers flee, Stephen finds the victim dead, then at home finds Bonden asleep on a table, with "bandaged arms" (no cause or specific injury given).

234 - Bonden informs Stephen that the ship is ready to sail and Jack wishes to do so - Jack is in a fury over his crew's inability to find the doctor. Bonden's arms were burnt by boiling tar, a work mishap aboard Surprise.

235 - Bonden gives Stephen Jack's written peremptory order to return to the ship at once. Enroute, Stephen encounters his guide-girl Dil, who has been murdered for the bangles Stephen gave her, a genuinely fatal gift. At the body, people are trying unsuccessfully to collect funds from the crowd for her funeral. Stephen declares himself to be of Dil's caste, pays for her cremation.

Book 3 Chapter 8 - p239-273: (overview)   Aboard Surprise, at single anchor in the Bombay channel. Jack's new officer Stourton reports aboard. He has a reputation as a "hard horse" i.e. being a strict and mostly petty disciplinarian. Jack explains his own -very different- philosophy of discipline. Stephen finally arrives. Surprise sails, headed "...south around Ceylon and [then] bear away for Kampong." French Admiral Linois (who once captured Jack) and his squadron rumored to be nearby. Jack and Stephen discuss marriage. Jack was a midshipman years ago in Surprise, shows Stephen his initials JA which he carved into the foremast cap back then. Unknown sail spotted: could be Linois's squadron. Jack cracks on to position Surprise for a 'fight or flight' decision. Stranger is Indiaman named Seringapatam, Captain Theobad, who is well known to both Jack and Killick. Jack compares being filthy rich vs flying one's admiral's flag, the flag wins hands down. Discussion of the burdens of sex (particularly on the male - e.g., the peacock's tail). Stephen wonders if castrated males (whatever species) may not have the best of all worlds. Stanhope and party rehearse for his investiture ceremony in Kampong. Stanhope taken seriously ill (a 'calenture' - resembling stroke), eventually dies before reaching Kampong. The entire trip is written off by Jack: "We came on a fool's errand."

244 - Jack mentions in a letter to Sophie that Stephen is depressed and looking gray. Jack wishes for some medical contingency to snap Stephen's bad mood, but the sickbay has only Babbington (the silent implication is that he has yet another dose of VD, probably from the 'preacher's daughter'), and "...a couple of men with the sun-stroke."

249 - Stephen goes to the foretop with Jack, they inadvertently interrupt a dice-game; gambling aboard ship is a serious crime. Jack understands what is happening, plays blind and ignorant... the dice are quickly hidden in seaman Faster Doudle's mouth. Then Stephen asks Faster how his bowels are doing, and says "...show me your tongue". Jack interrupts, saves Doudle from exposure and mandatory punishment.

258 - Capt Theobald of intercepted Indiaman comes aboard; has "...contrived to blow off his leg", hence is out of the Navy and cap-

taining the Indiaman. Tells Jack that Linois is thousands of miles away.

262 - Stanhope has only a week of seasickness, then recovers, probably due to the looming end of this interminable voyage to his post. Mr Smyth, the "nigger" translator assigned to Stanhope, is "suffering from his liver". .. and his very presence is deeply offensive to Atkins, Stanhope's chief of staff. So incensed is he (although Smyth has done nothing to provoke him) that he goes into a rant about niggers and caste and dueling. Atkin's outrage brings blood to his ears and nose: Stephen tries to calm him, saying that "In these latitudes, indulgence in passion may bring on a calenture..." (Modern definitions of calenture differ: the condition involves a fever, variously described as 'mild' or 'violent', with or without mention of accompanying 'dementia'. It is also said to resemble sunstroke. Here it probably means today's "stroke".)

263 - "Yet it was Mister Stanhope that suffered from the calenture."

264 - Stanhope has a weak pulse, high fever, dry skin. Stephen prescribes bark, his favorite slime-draught, and a blue placebo. No strength, no appetite. Turns yellow. Thorough perusal of all medical references leaves Stephen and loblolly boy M'Alister "at sea". Stephen forbids Atkins from entering Stanhope's presence, spends much time nursing Stanhope, to no avail. Stephen reflects that this close personal care is what he is best suited for (vs pursuing Diana).

265 - Stanhope delirious, Stephen helpless. Sponging. "...petty crisis at four with a laudable exudation." (Laudable meaning 'good', healthy: exudation most likely meaning simply 'sweating'.) Stephen feels as if Stanhope is recovering, has passed some important crisis.

266 - Stanhope seems to be regaining weight and spirit.

267 - Stanhope seriously stricken in some way. Crew rumors have him dead, or just struck down by the 'strong fives' (another O'Brian-invented medical problem), apoplexy, choking on his food, internal bleeding. Stephen demands that they head for the nearest land.

271 - Surprise at anchor, Stephen et al. ashore with Stanhope. Stephen prepared to operate (for what we are never clearly told), warns Stanhope that the operation is the only hope, not doing so is guaranteed fatal: Stanhope elects for surgery. Stanhope dies at three AM: whether ever operated on or not is unclear but probably not. Buried that morning.

273 - Surprise "homeward bound" before the paint is dry on Stanhope's grave-marker. Ship is required to touch at Calcutta enroute.

Book 3 Chapter 9 - p274-330:(overview) A chapter full of complex naval maneuvering and discussions thereof. At Lat 89E, Surprise encounters but does not join a 40-ship commercial convoy -the China Fleet-, mostly Indiamen for Calcutta. "The wealth of the orient" on display (apparently £6M cash in one ship alone). Leading Indiaman ('Lushington', Capt. Muffit) invites all ships' officers + pretty repeat pretty female passengers" to a formal dinner. Muffit and Jack hit it off very well. Surprise returns to solo sailing. Jack experiments with "unorthodox" masts and sails. They sight the French squadron under Linois, which has clearly seen and is already pursuing Surprise. Jack must defend the China Fleet at all costs. Surprise runs, Linois pursues. Surprise is faster than the French. Jack clandestinely slows Surprise during pursuit, and maneuvers to identify his opponents, studying how they sail. French vessels and capabilities identified: ships are 4:1. French crews and ships seem weary from long deployment - now cautious. Jack misleads Linois, pulls off a daring maneuver while traveling faster than he ever has before, then rejoins the China Fleet. Jack convenes a council of war of the Fleet's captains, aided by Capt Muffit. Most Indiamen are armed, some heavily, but none have much experience firing, or enough hands to properly man, their great guns. Jack sends Surprises aboard all major vessels to handle gunnery, dressed in Royal Navy uniforms lent by Surprise's officers. The Fleet's ships are well sailed, can perform the needed "naval fleet" coordinated maneuvers, including forming a traditional 'line of battle'. The Fleet's aggressive show of force fools the cautious Linois, who hesitates, unsure of what he faces. Complex battle ensues between the French Squadron and China Fleet, involving fine sailing and great initiative by the Indiamen. Linois retires, defeated. Indiamen unanimously incredulous that they have pulled off this miracle - the Fleet is intact! Muffit comes aboard Surprise after the battle, is appalled at the damage. Jack bemoans the lack of a good navy yard to repair and refit the very-badly-damaged Surprise - Muffit guarantees him the unlimited support of the Company's extensive Calcutta shipyard facilities....no charge. Offered a tow, Jack almost indignantly refuses - Surprise is still the convoy's escort!

297 - Mr Callow carried below, hit on the head by a falling block.

298 - Jack to sickbay to check on casualties: three splinter wounds, one concussion. Jack instantly asks if Stephen will open Callow's skull (trephination having become almost a routine for Stephen and always being intensely interesting to the crew). No need for such measures. Jenkins, a splinter recipient, missed death by a twentieth of an inch - the distance by which the splinter missed the inominate. (The inominate is a large, high-pressure blood vessel; it arises from the aorta deep in the chest, quite close to the heart.) Jenkins must have received what amounts to a spear-thrust by the splinter. He is talkative, is holding the splinter that wounded him- it is two feet long. The other two casualties - a forearm laid open, and a bad scalp wound. Mr White is rolled up in a ball on the floor, having passed out when asked to help in surgery by holding the patient's scalp. as it was sutured back into place.

323 - French Marengo fires a point-blank broadside into Surprise. Harrowby at the wheel is cut in two. Unattributed screaming from somewhere forward.

324 - During the action, a loose 36# shot rolls into Jack's ankle, knocking him down and injuring the ankle and foot.

325 - Bonden's left arm is "sprung" - apparently unusable. He stays on deck and active...tells Jack that Carlow has been killed. Harrowby's body thrown overboard.

329 - Jack becomes aware of his painfully-damaged ankle.

Book 3 Chapter 10 - p311-348:(overview) Calcutta: the Company honors Jack and Surprise with thank-you banquets and parties. Crew permanently drunk. Jack meets Canning again; he and

Jack become good friends quickly. Canning, for the Company, wants to reward Jack - by having him carry "freight" (meaning private or governmental treasure of some sort) - in this case, a significant parcel of emeralds - for which service Jack gets a percentage of the value. It is apparently a considerable sum, for Jack writes Sophie that it will "...clear me of debt and set us up in a neat cottage..." Jack asks his long-term friend Captain Heneage Dundas to give Sophie a lift to Madeira, where he can meet her. Stephen, not overly bright despite all his philosophical meditations and agonizing over relationships, goes to visit Diana who is still Canning's mistress. Canning finds them together, kissing: the result is Stephen receiving a blow and challenging Canning to a duel. In the event, Stephen, a superb pistol marksman, misses his aim due to his torture-damaged hands and accidentally kills Canning - a bullet to the jugular. Stephen is himself seriously wounded by Canniing's shot. Jack, wallowing in self doubts, refuses to take Diana home as a passenger on Surprise. Diana books passage home on Lushington. Stephen operates on himself to remove the ball, suffers delirium and raving fevers enroute home, nursed by Jack. Stephen recovers: in the Indian Ocean they stop on a poorly charted island to get its position correctly, Stephen finds an undescribed giant tortoise, names it *Testudo aubreii*. Landfall at St Helens: no orders for Surprise. At Madeira, Surprise is saluted by the Indiamen in harbor. Jack sees Lushington's passenger list: it has both Diana and the American Mr Johnstone, who was pursuing her in India, behind Canning's back. Sophie has not arrived at Madeira. Back to sea, late at night Surprise spots a mysterious sail, closes on it stealthily, is within pistol shot when seen by Euryalus. Companion vessel to Euryalus is Ethlion, which signals "Captain Surprise, I have two women for you. One young. Please come to breakfast." Sophie has arrived. They will be married at once when they get home. Stephen is arranging an operating theater in the great cabin. He intends to operate on himself to remove the ball, rather than trust himself to on-shore naval facilities and doctors. Doing this is also very clearly some sort of personally-imposed penance for having killed Canning, and even more for having allowed himself to be drawn into the duel in the first place. Stephen has designed a special extractor for removing the ball, which seems to be lodged under the ribs near the heart and therefore requires some opening of the chest. Jack volunteers to help, is almost ill: the operation is a success. Jack exclaims after-

61

wards to Bonden that he could see Stephen's heart pumping away. Bonden is not impressed: "Ah, sir, there's surgery for you. It would not surprise any old Sophie, however....you remember the gunner, sir? Never let it put you off your dinner."

331 - Stephen is busy with the wounded - the sickbay is full, there are many operations that need doing, including fixing Bowes's head.

332 - Bowes dies, is buried. Jack is soaking his injured ankle in a bucket of warm sesame oil.

347 - Stephen and Canning duel. Stephen is shot in the chest. Reeling from the impact, Stephen misses his aim and accidentally kills Canning with a bullet to the aorta. From the position of Stephen's wound, it is clear that Canning had intended to kill him. This seems to astonish Stephen, for whom duels were generally intended only to inflict an "honor-satisfying" wound. Deadly-earnest dueling with overt intent to kill the opponent was not the rule.

349 - The ball in Stephen's chest is "badly lodged".

351 - With a bit of help from Jack, Stephen operates on himself, successfully removing the ball from his chest.

356 - Diana comes to Surprise to visit Stephen, who is mending well, has eaten an egg already today. Still feverish.

358 - At sea enroute home, Surprise. Jack acts as nurse for Stephen, who is occasionally raving from his post-operation fevers. Stephen talks extensively, discloses hours of secrets about himself, his feelings, his secret work. Jack cannot turn over the night-nursing to anyone else lest Stephen's secrets become public.

360 - Stephen's fever breaks, is held down with copious tea and bark, administered by M'Alister, loblolly-boy.

363 - Ashore on a poorly-charted island, Stephen discovers a new species of giant tortoise, names it _Testudo aubreii_. This success, plus the tropic sun, mends Stephen quickly.

364 - Stephen back to work as ship's surgeon, but little to do - M'Alister has long since dealt with "...the usual sailors' diseases the men had brought with them from Calcutta."

Book 4 - The Mauritius Command

Book 4 Chapter 1 - p15-51: (overview)   Jack re-introduced and summed up. Jack is at home (Ashgrove Cottage) between commands, maintaining his wife (Sophie), fraternal-twin children, mother in law (Mrs Williams) and several others on his "inactive" half-pay of nine shillings a day. Williams has lost to a con-artist the family home (Mapes Court) and all her investments, including Sophie's dowry. Stephen arrives with a bag of wild mushrooms - Mrs Williams throws them out immediately. The cook resigns: cannot take Mrs Williams' abuse. Jack is grinding lenses for his telescopes, aided by Ms Herschel, the famous astronomer's sister: they work closely together and Sophie may be perturbed. An Army General is now First Lord of the Admiralty - the Earth shudders. Discussions of sexuality, motherhood, cabbages and silver mines, sons vs daughters. Of marriage, Jack had "...thought there was more friendship and confidence and unreserve in it than the case allows." Stephen has developed a secret-mission command for Jack but does not want to seem responsible for his good fortune in getting it. Word of Jack's "secret" assignment reaches Ashgrove Cottage in the form of a letter from a naval wife requesting transportation --- this arrives well before the official "secret" orders for Jack. Stephen must explain things to Jack. Four new French frigates are at Mauritius and stymieing British trade. Jack is to be made Commodore (a post, not a rank) and given a squadron, to deal forcefully with the situation. Functionally, Commodore is just short of flag rank. Jack is ecstatic, fearful the command may not happen. Stephen is infinitely critical of English (especially Royal Navy) "security".

20 - Stephen tells Jack that he's "taken the waters" at Caldas de Bohi recently, feels fine. ("Taking the waters" of a spa usually involves drinking lots of water from the spa, and long soaks in various temperatures of water, often sulfur-laden volcanic spring water.)

22 - Discussing Jack's barren heifer which refuses the bull, Stephen philosophizes about the perils and rewards of motherhood in general... but particularly when one's offspring are destined to become veal.

29 - Veiled discussion of Sophie's being insufficiently interested in sex to keep Jack satisfied.

30 - Stephen asked for his 'medical' opinion of the twins, waxes diplomatic. Ordinary children, apparently healthy, but pediatrics is not his bag.

31 - Jack claims to Stephen in private that there is no likelihood whatever of there being any more children - probably a doubly-veiled reference to Jack/Sophie sexual dysfunction. Stephen was not present for the twins' birth but has been told it was long and difficult, perhaps rendering her (understandably) cooler than she might otherwise have been.

36 - Reference to Stephen having been called in to treat the Duke of Clarence (son of the English King: also an Admiral by training) - his doing so is well known in the fleet, at all levels.

38 - Stephen stops a twin from playing with the case clock's (grandfather clock's) pendulum, which is filled with poisonous mercury - Stephen has to explain that to the ladies.

44 - Informal word of Jack's position and mission arrive at Ashgrove Cottage well before official orders (via Lady Clonfert, seeking a free ride to her husband's duty station) – there actually seems to be no such thing as "Naval secrecy". Jack will likely have the frigate Boadicea. He wonders, but wisely refrains from asking - might Stephen have somehow arranged the illness of Boadicea's Captain Loveless\ (Stephen's patient), which so fortuitously made both ship and position available?

49 - Jack and Stephen try to leave amidst domestic uproar, but decide to spend one last night at Ashgrove, inasmuch as the tide is not favorable to leaving before tomorrow. Jack's eventual legitimate son is conceived that night.

Book 4 Chapter 2 - p52-80: (overview) At sea aboard HMS Boadicea, just off the Dry Salvages. By subterfuge, Jack has avoided carrying Lady Clonfert as a passenger. Boadicea has taken a small, nearly antique French frigate named Hebe, and her prize, an English "Guineaman" named Intrepid Fox, a rich prize. Hebe was originally HMS Hyaena, now restored to the Royal Navy and returned to her proper name. Jack dawdles purposely before actually boarding his captured civilian Intrepid Fox, perturbing Stephen, who does not know the law - any captured English civilian vessel retaken within 24 hours is considered NOT to have been captured at all. In any case, one cannot make a fellow countryman a prize. But a captured English vessel retaken beyond 24 hours is considered "salvage", and under world-wide maritime law and custom, significant prize like rewards accrue to the salvors (here Boadicea). Jack expects to get personally 1/8 the value of ship and cargo. As salvage instead of prize, the Admiral does not share. (NOTE - the laws of maritime salvage are byzantine.) Intrepid Fox is dispatched to Gibraltar immediately. For the only time in the novels, Jack has an oversupply of seamen and is happy to see many hands depart. Boadicea heads for the Cape. Extensive intensive training with the great guns. Mr Farquhar and Stephen closet themselves and make plans for their own activities on La Reunion. Long exposition by Jack on the differences between being captain of a single vessel, vs commodore or admiral in charge of several ships - one is no longer DOING personally, but rather sending OTHERS in to do the work... depending on the initiative etc of others, not one's self.

53 - Two Boadiceans (Arklow, Bates) mentioned as slightly wounded in taking the Hebe et al.

55 - Stephen is patching up the French "...commanding officer..." (no wound specified).

57 - Stephen's patient has "...lost a great deal of blood..." but seems otherwise well enough. Confusion in the text as to events and positions - here, Stephen says to Jack, about his patient, "He has the late captain's cook with him, a famous artist...." Apparently the French Captain was killed and the patient is some lower officer who took over, hence was earlier referred to as "the commander".

58 - Jack is oversupplied with hands, gets rid of "...eight sodomites, three notorious thieves, four men whose wits were quite astray, and a parcel of inveterate skulkers and sea-lawyers..." plus one ob-

noxious midshipman and Mr Akers, the 1st Lt., whom Jack distrusts as "no seaman" and otherwise despises (but Akers is in chronic pain from an amputated leg, making him "savagely ill-tempered").

65 - Passenger Mr Farquhar recovers from prolonged sea-sickness, now working with Stephen on plans to subvert the government of Mauritius, preferably without bloodshed if possible.

67 - Boadicea becalmed in the doldrums, floating in a sea of her own filth and trash.

68 - Seaman's diet outlined - dinner (noon meal) consists of cheese and duff on Monday; 2 pounds salt beef on Tuesday; dried peas and duff on Wednesday; one pound salt pork on Thursday; dried peas and cheese on Friday; 2 pounds dried beef on Saturday; one pound salt pork and a treat (e.g., pudding) on Sunday. Plus one pound of biscuit per day, and two pints of grog. A scurvy-producing diet.

Book 4 Chapter 3 - p81-120: (overview)   Near the Cape, at False Bay. Jack is likely to get the post of Commodore, orders, and a selection of available vessels, but nothing is guaranteed. Admiral of the local fleet is Bertie, who Jack knows well, he has aged immensely, Jack wonders about himself. Bertie briefs Jack on the situation - the four powerful new French frigates based in Mauritius are raising hell with English trade over the entire Indian Ocean, must be stopped - but few ships are available for Jack's ad-hoc squadron. Discusses available ships and their captains... some not good. Stephen encounters Bonden, Jack's coxswain, who has been flogged aboard another vessel and asks if he might get Jack to take him and Killick back aboard any ship of Jack's. Bonden expects Corbett, his current captain and one of Jack's squadron, will be scragged shortly. Jack's orders are clear and precise for a change--seek out and destroy the French cruisers, try to take several islands from the French - particularly Mauritius, which is the main French naval base in the Indian Ocean. Jack is given a very free hand. The crew have known for 4,000 miles what is afoot, have prepared the Broad Pennant - it is flown immediately upon Jack's return to Boadicea. The whole squadron knows - salutes begin immediately. Jack's "all captains" meeting goes reasonably well. Lord Clonfert is a pompous showoff, and braggart and, from Jack's personal experience with him, the man is also a coward - he intentionally hung back in a cutting-out expedition, forcing Jack's group to do the dirty work alone, and Clonfert has been embarrassed by the memory ever since - Jack's presence and success are needles in Clonfert's psyche. Other captains are fair to very good, per Adm Bertie's evaluation. Corbett and Clonfert are NEVER to be assigned to work together. Jack reclaims Bonden and Killick for himself. Detailed analyses of each captain and vessel in the squadron. Clonfert claims to Jack that Jack's narwhal tusk is actually a unicorn's horn and that he had himself cut such horns from several animals' foreheads. Later, further extensive discussions on the various captains and their abilities. Jack finally gets his orders and flies his broad pennant. Jack retrieves Bonden and Killick from Corbett's grasp. "Like old times - only better!" says Bonden.

89 - Stephen, ashore, returns to his inn with a batch of orchids, which he sets on his table. Two officers (one from a Russian ship; the other is HMS Otter's surgeon, Mr McAdam) are having a drinking contest, have predicted which way they will fall (forward vs backward) when they pass out. Stephen acts as judge. The Russian drunk talks to Stephen's orchids, weeping. The other is a naval surgeon: discussion with Stephen about mind vs body in matters of health... false pregnancies, remissions of various conditions, proven effectiveness of placebos. The Russian passes out, falls sideways.

93 - Stephen encounters Jack's long-term coxswain Bonden, now crew on another vessel. Together they return the drunk surgeon to his ship. Stephen notices Bonden is stiff, asks if he has "...rheumatism from the falling damps..." Bonden has been flogged fifty lashes. Stephen is astounded... Bonden is the steadiest man he knows. Bonden's captain -Corbett- is a flogging tyrant: his crew desert whenever possible.

96 - Aboard Boadicea, Stephen has an alcoholic patient in a coma, who suddenly begins to gush blood at the ears. Stephen and Jack both seriously hung over.

98 - Stephen tells Jack of Bonden's mistreatment. Jack apoplectic.

114 - Killick gives Jack two "massive pieces of coral" for the twins to use in teething. (At the time, the term "coral" meant a string of beads, made from coral and given to a teething baby as a sort of pacifier and teething aid.) Killick waxes almost poetical in reminiscing with Jack about the Aubrey homestead.

Book 4 Chapter 4 - p121-160: (overview) Squadron is at sea (6 miscellaneous men-of-war - Sirius, Nereide, Raisonable, Boadicea, Otter, Wasp) off La Reunion Island, near Madagascar, Indian Ocean. Mauritius is ~100 miles NE of La Reunion. Mauritius is a lozenge-shaped island about 25x40 miles, long axis nearly NS. Extensive gunnery practice - Jack demands speed and accuracy. The smaller, outlying island La Reunion must be taken before one can go after Mauritius. Stephen goes ashore clandestinely on La Reunion to reconnoiter and make contacts with guerrilla forces, returns safely with detailed information. The French do not know about Jack's Squadron. The population is disaffected with their French overlords. Several of the French vessels are temporarily out of commission. Stephen complains that he never gets time to do his natural history investigations - the Navy continually tantalizes him with unexplored places, and bypasses them. Squadron sails to Rodriguez ~500 miles E of Mauritius, held by English, garrisoned by several hundred soldiers led by Col. Keating. Keating and Jack hatch a plan to take La Reunion, then Mauritius, on their own initiative. Stephen insists that the troops on La Reunion be treated with utmost respect - it may be possible to arrange a nearly-bloodless transfer of power after an initial assault. Nereide embarks 368 soldiers, puts them ashore through bad surf on La Reunion. French man of war Caroline, in the harbor, inflicts considerable damage on the oncoming HMS Raisonable (Jack's flagship), then strikes her colors. Soldiers take the town and fortifications: the soldiers' behavior is exemplary. Raisonable is so old she sprang a butt from her guns' recoil, has to be laid on her side in the mud for repair. Enemy troops seen, from sea, marching towards the town to retake it. Keating says the French army's efforts will not work due to rugged terrain. Burned the governmental archives to confuse the enemy. Clonfert and Corbett both get traditional victors' promotions from Jack (to be confirmed later by the

Admiralty). Clonfert depressed over having mistakenly burnt a warehouse full of silk, valued at £500,000.

127 - Dinner on Boadicea just before Stephen goes ashore on La Reunion - dress uniforms are required, seem likely to give their wearers heat-stroke.

139 - Stephen finally gets several hours to botanize, but as he sets out he is waylaid and begged to come help Dr McAdam (another ship's surgeon) with a difficult, urgent case.

140 - McAdam's patient is Captain Lord Clonfert, who is "in crisis" with the "strong gripes", doubled up with pain. Looks like some form of dysentery, or colonic spasm. A peek into the medical philosophy and medical chest. Stephen pooh-poohs McAdam's thinking, will have nothing to do with "iliac passion' (a mechanical blockage of the intestine that prevents it from moving contents along in normal fashion) or Lucatellus' balsam (olive oil, wax, and turpentine mixture). Stephen recommends a strong dose of *Helleborus niger* (a plant with pronounced toxic and purgative effects, often used anciently for insanity of various sorts) plus "thebaic tincture" (likely named after Thebes Egypt, probably a solution of opium, resembling laudanum) and "antimonial wine" (tartar emetic mixed with sherry), plus "…naturally, of course…" a little Armenian bole (a red clay used in treating diarrhea and dysentery - this seems antithetical to Stephen's other idea, that there is a blockage (but not a tormina) which enemas might help). Discussion of 'tormina' (twisted bowel - common and fatal in horses). The above medications seem mostly to be related to emptying the gut - enemas also used here. Stephen's aside about "…delighted to attend the opening of the body, in the event of a contrary result…" is overheard by the crew, who do not appreciate it.

141 - Long consultation between Stephen and McAdam ashore: they decide Clonfert's problem is actually mental, with physical manifestations. They consider homosexuality as a possible cause but reject it - he is a well-known and highly successful ladies' man. Conclusion: some strange mental twist concerning honor and courage is causing the physical symptoms. The present crisis perhaps brought on

by Aubrey's private criticism of some of Clonfert's behavior, abilities and habits... plus jealousy. Clonfert feels he, not Jack, should have been given this task. Surgeon McAdam drinks himself into a stupor thereafter... his normal behavior.

151 - French man of war Caroline strikes her colors after being horribly battered.

153 - During the taking of the town and fortifications, French man-of-war Caroline had put up major resistance, was shelled by most of the Squadron, received massive damage. Over half her men (say, 200-250 souls), and her captain, are wounded: all are sent ashore to hospital after the battle.

159 - Jack tells Stephen that he, Jack, is playing a psychological game with his crews by putting some of them under Lord Clonfert..."His men will follow him anywhere...." and "...your foremast jack does dearly love a Lord." Then "I must take advantage of that just as I should take advantage of a tide or a shift in the wind."

Book 4 Chapter 5 - p161-197: (overview) Squadron returns to the Cape. Admiral Bertie is pleased with the results so far. Jack likely to get an entire issue of the Gazette dedicated to himself (actual title of this very real periodical is "The Naval Chronicle"). Admiral hugely impressed by Stephen's credentials. Stephen, Mr Farquhar prepare handbills to convince LaReunion-ites not to resist an invasion. Discussion of the differences between legal systems - English Common Law vs France's new Napoleonic Code. Stephen obtains and sketches an aardvark. French resume depredations on shipping with a vengeance: Squadron strengthened, sent to sea again, trying to intercept French with their prizes before they get to Mauritius. Jack's flagship now Boadicea. Enroute La Reunion, Stephen's sea-chest full of gold (for subversion) spills, impresses Jack who helps clean up. Stephen not impressed by bought intelligence or loyalty. Lying off Port Louis on Mauritius they survey the town and its military preparedness. Bonden and Stephen take a vest packed full of gold, head ashore to subvert the enemy if possible. They return with intelligence and fresh coffee. Jack visits his captains: Clonfert is a fop, although not gay: his quarters onboard look "...as though a brothel had moved

into a monastery, and as though it had not yet settled down."
While the fleet is reconnoitering La Reunion, Stephen goes
ashore and does natural history investigations to his heart's content, aided even by the soldiers, who drain a swamp for him, from
which he recovers bones to make a nearly complete skeleton of
the recently extinct dodo. Huge hurricane scatters and largely
dismasts the Squadron, lightning strikes and melts Boadicea's
best-bower anchor. Boadicea becomes last-resort refuge for thousands of birds blown offshore by the storm.

168 - Stephen ruminates again on mind/body interaction, considering Clonfert's intestinal problems anew. Wonders what, if anything,
might relieve Clonfert's mind.

171 - Stephen considers Jack, feels his youth is going fast due to
heavy responsibilities. Jack's overall joie de vivre is cooling, in every
aspect of life.

179 - Coffee today has an odd tang to it due to rat-droppings…
rats have eaten most of the beans and replaced them with the species'
calling cards.

186 - Aboard Squadron ship Magicienne, the yeoman of the
sheets has stabbed the ship's corporal in the belly with a marlinspike… a pointed two-foot metal or oak rod about 2" in diameter at
the butt end. No further mention.

188 - Stephen visits Clonfert aboard his ship: is thanked for
treatment of Clonfert's intestinal seizure. Stephen tells him that there
is nothing discreditable in the malady, pleases the Lord by saying
he'd never seen such pain before.

189 - Stephen visits with McAdam, surgeon of HMS Nereide,
consults about a seaman with "inoperable gummata" that are "pressing on his brain" - gummata are soft-tissue growths in connective tissue (including that in the brain), and typical of the terminal stages of
syphilis.

190 - Stephen and McAdam discuss problems of idiocy (whether,
e.g., to chain the afflicted and beat them, as done in Beldam Pris-
on/Hospital). Psychiatric problems also discussed - says McAdam, "I

have not had a decent melancholia from the lower deck this commission. Manias, yes: but they are two a penny. No, it is aft [NOTE - i.e., among the officers] that you must look for your fine flower of derangement." (Melancholia = persistent depression with illogical fears. Mania = mental illness marked by periods of excitement, euphoria, delusions.) Discussion of Capt Lord Clonfert's overall condition - he has terrible sweating fits, of the right side of the chest - so strong that his coats are asymmetrically colored from scrubbing that side alone. Fits seem to be connected with Clonfert's interacting with, or even thinking about, Jack. The doctors arrive at no consensus as to condition, causes, or treatments.

191 - Stephen goes ashore with Clonfert to further reconnoiter, has his opinion of Clonfert as a very intelligent sensitive and high-function individual reinforced. Stephen feels Clonfert and his problems are a direct product of the Irish social system of the day.

192 - Christmas dinner involves a barrel of "...providentially salted penguins from off the Cape serving as geese or turkeys..."

193 - Midshipmen serve the officers the wrong species of turtle at dinner - the shell turns to glue and all who ate the meat piss emerald green.

194 - Ship's motions in a hurricane have wound one crewman into his hammock "...like a cocoon." The seaman is the sick-bay's only patient (some sort of pox).

195 - Casualties of the violent storm arrive in sick-bay. A seaman with ribs cracked by the wheel; a light-weight reefer thrown into the hances by wind and now unconscious; Mr Peter who fell headlong down two decks through the hatches; miscellaneous broken ribs and limbs. Lightning leaves one man dead plus three dazed. An unspecified number of broken clavicles.

196 - Stephen, going forward to view the lightning-damaged anchor, is flung down and dazed by another lightning strike, a triple stroke, which also set off one of the forward great guns. Stephen stumbles back to sickbay to await the wounded, but there are none.

72

Book 4 Chapter 6 - p198-233: (overview) [NOTE: very little of medical/health import occurs in this chapter, which is almost entirely taken up with planning and executing an invasion of island La Reunion, as a necessary precursor to invading Mauritius itself.] Squadron returns to Cape. No banquets this time. Small, corrupt navy yard makes repair and refit difficult. Stephen is ashore, botanizing. Mail arrives, utterly soaked and nearly unreadable: what can be made out engenders only confusion. Jack defends crew members against prize agent's sharp tactics. Col Keating's garrison on Rodriguez reinforced, now adequate to storming La Reunion. HMS Magicienne and Iphigenia sent to blockade Port-Louis on Mauritius, to bottle up the French ships and keep them away from La Reunion. Discussion over dinner of hanging as a punishment; of punishments vs crime generally... political discussions, however, are eschewed. Mr Farquhar is identified as the pre-appointed new (English) Governor for La Reunion and then Mauritius, given success. Extensive descriptions of ships' movements, military plans. Soldiers fill the transports: their discipline impresses the Navy. The mini-fleet of troop-transporting ships sails for La Reunion: a pair of landings is planned to pincer the main port, St Denis. A falling barometer is worrisome - surf is an enemy of landing soldiers. The landing and land battle going well, Stephen goes ashore to aid in getting the populace over onto the English side. Just as Col Keating et al. have finished laying the perfect battle-plan, Stephen brings to them a pair of civilian dignitaries and a French officer, who wish to see a peaceful surrender and changeover. Col Keating is deeply annoyed with Stephen for this - his chance for a traditional glorious battle just evaporated: "...Your friend has done us out of our battle, as neat a battle as you could wish to see.... then, quite out of order, a capitulation is proposed, t*o avert the effusion of human blood*, forsooth..." Farquhar can now assume duty as Governor of La Reunion - and thereby finally be reinstated to the payroll. He will presumably be Governor of Mauritius as well (implied on p233) should the English take it.

200 - Mr Collins, 18, now Boadicea's senior master's mate, is informed that two weeks is insufficient time within which his ladylove could have determined for sure that his attentions had rendered all her girdles too small. He need NOT marry her on such notice. After all,

she might be suffering from indigestion (if indeed from anything at all).

201 - Surgeon McAdam is also ashore: he and Stephen ponder Lord Clonfert's present elevated mood and extreme -almost frenetic- activity in the Squadron's cause. Stephen asks whether the man's '...humours might have been restored to equilibrio...' through use of two stimulants - coffee and tobacco. Stephen rhapsodizes over tobacco as a panacea. McAdam's more rationally says Clonfert is jealous of Jack and (p202) "He will outdo the Commodore though he burst."

206 - Capt Lambert, HMS Iphigenia, worried about the state of the ship's lime juice. (NOTE - the Royal Navy's bizarrely corrupt supply system seemed incapable of supplying unadulterated (or even REAL) citrus juices.)

213 - Stephen, having watched Clonfert closely, thinks he understands the man's problem, and hopes that "...some resounding action will soon give Clonfert a real basis..." for feeling worthwhile and equal to Jack.

216 - Clonfert gets a "glory" leadership assignment in the landings on La Reunion - perhaps this will fix his ego problems?

Book 4 Chapter 7 - p234-270: (overview) With Gov. Farquhar's eager help, Jack and Keating plan an assault on Mauritius, even though they could readily use another 5000 troops - which could not arrive before next year. The English have military superiority, especially in ships, and Stephen believes his efforts at subverting (propagandizing) the populace are working well ("My broadsides [= printed propaganda handouts] are as effective as your roundshot!") Most importantly, they have a free hand - no orders from an uninformed distant command can possibly be sent to screw up locally-developed, knowledgeable plans. They will first take Ile de la Passe, a very small but strategic isle from which to stage the Mauritius invasion. Discussion of the Irish as highly civilized --- or maybe (alternatively viewed) as utter savages? Squadron vessel HMS Sirius -Capt Pym- arrives shortly after a small action in which Pym lost a cousin and several other men killed. In taking de la Passe, Jack captured the French code and signal book, and the French Commandant. Clonfert is in charge of the shore party and directs its activities - which seem largely random. Clonfert unintentionally interferes with Stephen's negotiations for a pillow stuffed with dodo feathers. Three French warships arrive (with two prizes). Clonfert's Nereide is deep in the harbor: he decides to lure the French to him, runs up the French ensign on Nereide and the fort. Sends up false signals also. Clonfert's leadership yields mostly confusion. Ruse works, but aboard Nereide a huge explosion on deck (due to a clumsy crewman) renders the ship functionally useless. Troops ashore are utterly confused, cannot fight effectively. The situation is close to irremediably bad, but Clonfert thinks he is winning. French warships anchor: two-day impasse. English ships arrive, enter harbor but one goes hard ground. A complex, multi-day action ensues, eventually going strongly in favor of the French. Several ships go aground, are mercilessly battered. Upper-level command wrangles prevent implementation of a plan that would -most believe- have given victory to the English. Stephen gets a sailing launch and adequate crew to take him to La Reunion, sneaks out of the harbor at night. Reaching Boadicea easily, Stephen must report the incredible debacle to Jack, who takes it phlegmatically.

240 - Stephen, going ashore with bales of handbills (propaganda) falls between ship and the boat, cracking two ribs: he is rescued by one of the black port-workers. A resulting inflammation of the lungs keeps him abed for some days. He is aboard Clonfert's ship and Clonfert proves a capable, caring nurse.

241 - Discussion of physicians' bedside manners and assumption of authority over the patient - difficulties so engendered. McAdam is officially Stephen's doctor (they are aboard McAdam's ship) - he advises a cingulum (heavy bandaging of the ribs), a black draught (we never do find out what this contains), and a bit of bloodletting. Stephen won't have anything to do with anything suggested by McAdam. Stephen takes only self-administered bark and recovers nicely.

243 - McAdam, drunk as usual, accuses Stephen of beclouding his mind with laudanum: Stephen instantly counters with alcoholism. Both men are right, Stephen somewhat more than McAdam. (Ste-

phen's use of laudanum is at least intellectualized and usually held in check - McAdam's drinking is neither.) Stephen goes introspective as to his personal use of laudanum.

244 - Mermaid on the starboard bow - a 'siren' (manatee or dugong). A nonsense argument has arisen between crewmen about the beast, and is growing potentially violent. Stephen quells the argument completely with an even more nonsensical statement - which because of his reputation is taken perfectly seriously.

259 - Clonfert is in charge of Nereide which is anchored in harbor. French arrive, Clonfert is frenetic in leading (badly: no coherent plan) the English forces. Makes a huge cock of things but runs madly about thinking he is doing brilliantly. Stephen and McAdam confer about Clonfert, wondering whether the man's conduct can be considered intelligent or even sane (the unstated question is, should Clonfert be removed from command?)

260 - Clonfert's behavior and speech make it completely clear that he is obsessed with outdoing Jack - he has no other goal.

263 - During the intense and confused battle in the harbor, Nereide goes partially aground, her first lieutenant and three army officers are dead (and presumably a great many more as well - "...blood ran over her quarterdeck not in streams but in a sheet...").

264 - Nereid's surgeon McAdam is now in an alcoholic coma. Stephen, technically a guest on Nereide, goes to work in the cockpit, case after case. Clonfert is very badly wounded in the head and neck - one eye out and dangling, shattered maxilla (upper jaw - hit by grapeshot), and a splinter has laid bare and shaved thin the carotid artery in his neck, which can be seen throbbing with his pulse, ready to burst if improperly touched. He is conscious and in shock - feeling no pain, trying to continue to lead. (Grapeshot were essentially large shotgun-charges: the individual balls were about 1" diameter, usually lead.)

265 - Clonfert gets up to go back to the battle, is warned by Stephen that if he touches the neck bandage, he may rupture the artery and die in under a minute. Returns to console the wounded: Stephen thinks Clonfert is in a state of "walking unconsciousness".

266 - Stephen now has over 150 patients, of whom he expects probably about 100 to survive. Twenty-seven have already died in the cockpit/sickbay, and he thinks that perhaps an additional 70 dead have been thrown overboard... a huge toll. At sunrise the battle resumes although Nereide is exhausted and battered. Gunner gets "...a gushing splinter wound in the forearm..." The bosun is also dead. Stephen checks on Clonfert one last time -he is ambulatory, apparently coherent- and then leaves Nereide in the last rowboat, to avoid capture and imprisonment by the French. Nereide has settled (sunk, actually) on the seabed.

Book 4 Chapter 8 - p271-292: (overview)   Aboard Boadicea, leaving La Reunion for de la Passe, which they find in French hands: the French fire unsuccessfully at Boadicea. French frigates Venus, Manche come out to meet Boadicea. Jack tries unsuccessfully to separate them for 1-on-1 engagements: the two return to de la Passe. Jack begins planning to mass his resources, then renew the attack. Miscellaneous pursuits off de la Passe, but no engagements. Pullings has Indiaman Wyndham, is arming her with cannon from beached English warships. Capt Corbett unexpectedly brings frigate HMS Africaine to La Reunion, a great augmentation to Jack's forces (Corbett is a good fighting captain but deeply despised by his crew). He is being pursued by the French (two frigates and a brig), and is flying Jack's broad pendant to confuse them. Jack takes entire squadron to La Reunion, where they eventually encounter Africaine 4 miles off, beset by two French frigates. Africaine strikes, but the French continue to fire point-blank for 15 minutes. This is unconscionable, strictly against the rules of war, and enrages Jack and his crew. New breeze reaches Boadicea first: they close, slowly. Boadicea engages the French, whose captain is not interested in pressing the engagement. English reinforcements heave into view but are coming slowly. Jack outlines for the captains his plan of attack and rationale. Events confound the plan, Jack retakes the Africaine: her surviving crew are so rabid for revenge that they swim over to Boadicea, beg Jack to chase NOW! He counsels patience. Capt Corbett, an infamous flogger, is gone missing, none of Africaine's crew know where he went. Clearly he was scragged (murdered by his own men) during the battle. Jack, having served before the mast himself, drops the question.

288 - After the short engagement Boadicea has only three wounded, plus "...poor Mr. Buchan." Buchan (the Master) was killed standing beside Jack - Jack is covered in the man's blood. Stephen reports: Colley has a depressed cranial fracture, is comatose, requires trepanning. The other two have splinter wounds, will survive.

Book 4 Chapter 9 - p293-322: (overview) Boadicea now towing the dismasted, badly battered Africaine. By evening the tow has three jury-rigged staysails and is manageable. Trepanning of Mr Colley's depressed skull fracture goes well. Jack regards Colley's survival (or not) as an omen for the entire Mauritius campaign. Farquhar and Stephen discuss politics (especially the Pope's secret excommunication of Napoleon) and Mauritius. Stephen uses his "extensive nautical knowledge" to educate Farquhar as to the odds (French vs English) and how those might be calculated. Jack and Keating are making plans for an invasion of Mauritius itself. Farquhar wonders aloud if perhaps Jack's enthusiasm is mediated by having some knowledge as yet unknown to Farquhar - is Stephen keeping secrets? Stephen says no. Stephen goes ashore on Mauritius to make contact with resistance/ opposition forces. On La Reunion (thoroughly held by the English now), French warship arrives, pursuing the small aviso HMS Pearl. Probably Venus, the ship that battered Africaine - Jack slips anchor and heads to sea, with the Squadron - has room for fifty volunteer Africaines, whom Jack must both calm and placate re revenge - gives them specific assignments to guns and for boarding. Stephen is aboard the Aviso, returning from the island. Stephen goes overboard tangled in a line when he tries to move to the Boadicea: rescued, he tells Jack of the ongoing sea-battle: two French frigates vs one English, and going badly. Bonden's report is more coherent. Venus and her escort Victor have taken a heavily-armed Indiaman, who has in turn inflicted heavy damage on Venus. Consideration of the disposition of forces, and plans. Victor is towing the prize 'Bombay', Venus is running as best she can. Plenty of time to prepare - inspection and dinner during the chase. Venus, although damaged, is extremely dangerous, but poorly maneuverable so she can get only one shot. She misses. Africaines from Boadicea board first, get one minute of time for personal vengeance, then the Boadiceans board. Venus strikes, the fighting aboard ceases. The French Commodore, Hamelin, is dead. The victory tilts all in favor of the English. Stephen reports that the island is ready to fall.

293 - Stephen is helping Africaine's surgeon Mr Cotton (who has just recovered from dysentery in time for today's carnage - he also has a withered leg): they still have 60-70 wounded patients in sickbay, and a shocking number of patients have died of wounds. French killed 49 Africaines outright and took away 50 prisoners.

294 - John Bates' foot is amputated - the surgeons feel he will survive, Bates asks if he mightn't keep his foot as a lucky charm. Corbett was badly wounded in the left foot, treated, returned to the fight, and then disappeared - so says Mr Cotton.

295 - Mr Cotton reports that after Corbett was gone, "Tullidge fought the ship and was wounded four times: Forder, the second, had a bullet through the lungs; Parker's head was shot off. Good officers." Captain Corbett's problem, per Mr Cotter, was being "...mad with authority...." when at sea, although sane enough ashore

296 - Cotton volunteers to help Stephen with the trepanning of Mr Colley, which will be done on deck (for the sunlight), with most of the ship's crew watching. Many enthusiastic watchers are in fact sickened by seeing Mr Colley's scalp flensed aside and his skull laid bare for the cutter. Cotton and Stephen discuss the failure of Colley's metopic suture to unite. (The metopic suture is the join-line of two bones of the cranium, which usually fuse solid in one's late teens.) The actual hole-making sickens still more observers. The shattered depressed bits of skull come off cleanly, and Mr Cotton goes fishing in the brain for splinters of bone - the procedure causes the patient to talk. A silver cover for the hole, scalp re-installed, and all cleaned up. The surgeons have done all they can, things went well, but "....no call for congratulation... it could not be said that any operation was wholly successful unless the patient at least outlived the crisis."

322: During the boarding of Venus by combined Africaines and Boadiceans, the French commodore Hamelin is killed by a grapeshot to the heart.

Book 4 Chapter 10-p323-348(end): (overview)   Jack's squadron is back at sea, with troops in transports, headed to invade Mauritius itself. Repairs being completed aboard Boadicea. Jack continues his installment-letter to Sophie. Prize crews from Boadicea had broken into captured Venus's spirit room, everyone was drunk and stayed that way ashore due to fetes honoring the Squadron's successes. Col Keating's hidden life-philosophy revealed whilst being returned to the ship in a barrow, bellowing "LET COPULATION THRIVE!" Best indicator of likely success of the invasion is the value of Mauritian paper money - now worthless. Rumors of a large force being assembled to take over from the Squadron. Col. Keating is apoplectic that he might lose his finest career opportunity. Shortly before the Squadron arrives at Mauritius, they encounter a fleet ("...a bleeding armada...") of English warships and troop transports, led by Admiral Bertie - the rumors were correct, Keating is done out of his glory and Jack is no longer in charge. The armada brings the mail: Pullings brings Boadicea's to Jack, asks cryptically if Jack has had any news from home, answer "NO". Pullings tells Jack that Sophie has produced a son, announced in the Naval Chronicle. Jack calculates mentally-the child was conceived the night before he left on this expedition. Jack gets orders, is superseded. Jack briefs the army/navy command staff, the invasion is done according to Jack and Keating's plan, succeeds with little blood and no problems... and of course no credit to Jack or Keating. Bertie (knowing full well what he has done) interviews Jack, expects to find resentment, probes deeper, finds none and is therefore deeply suspicious of Jack... even to feeling Jack may be silently making fun of him. Bertie suddenly discovers how well connected Jack is; that Jack's father is in Parliament; that said father might shortly be appointed to the Honors Board (which doles out knighthoods and such) - and Bertie does so heartily wish to be made a Lord Something. He gets cautious, and finally sends Jack, in Boadicea, to carry the news of the Mauritian campaign back to England, where Jack will reap the rewards attendant upon bringing such news. Meanwhile, Clonfert has heard of the Squadron's exploits and commits suicide by opening the wounded artery in his neck - this as praise and thanks for his defense of the Nereide, and a letter from his wife, are enroute to him.

323 - Boadicean officer Trollope down with heatstroke from overwork on repairs; a blacksmith likewise "...carried off in a dead swoon...".

340 - Stephen is ashore, talks with McAdam about Clonfert - the eye shows some improvement but the neck heals and sloughs repeatedly, the damaged artery is still exposed. Dr Martin suggests sewing flaps of skin over it for protection; Stephen pooh-poohs the idea. Clonfert seems reasonably calm and in his senses most of the time.

341 - Several of the wounded Nereides are still convalescing, Master's Mate Hobson has died, was "emasculated late in the battle." Stephen and McAdam discuss whether there is anything to the idea that a patient must die if he has "lost the will to live". McAdam makes another dig at Stephen's overuse of opium (as laudanum).

342 - Walking from hospital into town, Stephen passes two injured Nereide midshipman, one minus an arm, the other a leg.

345 - Clonfert commits suicide. He hears the town's enthusiastic cheering for Jack, then is told by McAdam that he will get Nereide back, from Jack Aubrey. Clonfert says "Never, not from Aubrey!", sends McAdam out of the room, rips open his own wounded neck artery and bleeds to death instantly.

Book 5 - Desolation Island

Book 5 Chapter 1- p5-39: (overview)   At Jack's home, Ash-grove Cottage. Jack has been ashore for some time as Command-ing Officer of the Sea-Fencibles, a semi-military "home guard"-ish organization of mostly fishermen and coastal shipping own-ers. Jack is being set up by mining con-artists who convince him to invest heavily in refining silver from the waste of old lead mines on his property. Stephen refuses to join in the project. Jack is frustrated by house remodeling etc. Killick buys a wife at the fair. Stephen's inamorata Diana Villiers (Sophie's cousin) is in America as Mr Johnson's mistress: Stephen is seriously de-pressed. Philosophizing about sex to Sophie, Jack almost shoots his own foot. Mrs Williams' home, Mapes, lost to foreclosure re-cently, has been regained. Jack turned down the new-building HMS Ajax (74) because it would mean serving in the Med under Adm Harte, who dislikes Jack because of his years-past affair with the Admiral's much younger wife, Molly. Jack's new ship is HMS Leopard (50), smallish two-decker (fourth rate), a notori-ously badly-built ship, also seriously outdated even before con-structed. But she has been renovated thoroughly: Jack is happy, has time to adequately prepare, gathers a good crew of men whom he knows. Destination - Spice Islands (East Indies), and Botany Bay (Australia), where Governor Bligh's officers have mutinied (again) and imprisoned him - Jack must investigate and resolve the problems. Stephen agrees to go. Flush with prize money, Jack gambles at cards, loses steadily. Stephen sees cheat-ing, warns Jack - who is Pollyanna at first but eventually calls Judge Wray on it publicly.

7 - Sophie's mother, Mrs Williams, is a hypochondriac, looking forward to today's long visit with her doctors. Mentioned in passing - Bonden, Jack's coxswain, was literally born amongst HMS Indefatigable's lower-deck guns.

8 - Mrs Williams: "I never complain...but I have here a list [of symptoms] that will make the doctors stare." Jack's son is cutting his

first tooth: Jack speaks to him too loudly for the women's taste - they claim little boys [as to hearing] are far more delicate than little girls.

14 - Mrs Williams' hairdresser arrives (late), to prepare her to meet with her doctors. She had a benign tumor removed some time before, and "...since then her spirit has been much oppressed by vapors..." according to Stephen. Her very expensive pair of physicians will likely just recommend taking the waters at Bath. The physicians cynically note the expensive remodeling and "...gauge their fees".

15 - Whilst awaiting Mrs Williams, the two doctors discuss medical topics: use of steel (i.e., iron as a supplement/treatment); side effects of colchicum (a poisonous flowering plant growing from a subterranean bulb - used to treat gout); valerian (a flowering plant used to treat insomnia and as a sedative - still sold for use today but not presently believed to be effective for either); leeches behind the ears; lenitives (= laxatives) and their effects on the spleen; use of pillows full of hops to promote good sleep (still sold today); "cold-sponging with a pint of water on an empty stomach"; therapeutic uses of opiates (with dangers of overuse acknowledged).

16 - Mid-discussion, Stephen walks in, the topic switches to the shocking price of corpses, which Stephen routinely buys for dissection - in this case because of a spectacular "calcification of the palmar aponeuroses" (PA). The PA is a web of ligaments and connective tissues in the palm, which sometimes becomes calcified (hardened) to various degrees, which then seriously deforms the hand and renders it inflexible - functionally useless. This condition is a special medical interest of Stephen's - as is also the human spleen, compared between nationalities (not races!) and between species. Stephen offers to "go snacks" (share the cost) with the two doctors, one of whom buys the liver to take to his medical students, saying "I am always happy to have a good fresh liver ... We will stuff it into the boot" (i.e., the luggage compartment of their carriage).

17 - Recommendation from the eminent physicians - Mrs Williams to take the waters at Scarborough not elsewhere, "...else we cannot answer for the consequences...".

23 - Recalling having poured boiling jam sauce onto their guest Mr Heywood aboard HMS Lively. Stephen treated him for the burns. (Heywood has served with Bligh, and is a source of information about the man.)

27 - Stephen has lost a patient in London, perhaps through Stephen's own fault. (ID on p39 as John Deering) - "...died under my knife".)

Book 5 Chapter 2 - p40-69: (overview)   A complex chapter seldom touching on medical or health issues. Stephen, traveling by coach, tosses his bottle of laudanum out the carriage window, despite his craving. He then immediately resupplies himself. At The Grapes Inn he has a permanent room: the landlady is used to weird specimens living or dead. He goes to Diana's apartment, she is gone, leaving many unpaid bills, which he settles. Stephen discovers that Diana was arrested on suspicion of aiding America's best female spy, her close friend Mrs Wogan. Diana, exonerated, has left precipitously for America, as Mr Johnson's mistress. Johnson arranges US citizen-ship for her, which she accepts. Wogan, convicted, will be sent via Leopard to Botany Bay. Diana leaves an explanatory letter for Stephen. Adm Sievewright of the Admiralty summons Stephen, whose name was found in Wogan's papers. Admiral is clumsily accusatory, Stephen explodes, overwhelms the Admiral, who threatens to arrest him but is stopped by the arrival in the office of Stephen's close friend Sir Joseph Blaine, Chief of Naval Intelligence. Blaine is in a position to, and does, threaten Adm Sievewright with career-destroying sanctions from above, in reprisal for the Admiral's unconscionable handling of Stephen. Maturin ponders what may happen to himself, once he is no longer useful to the Navy. Admiralty decides to ship a whole bevy of convicts to Botany Bay aboard Leopard, which infuriates Jack. Stephen calms him with hints that peace may break out - Jack better stick with what he has, namely Leopard. Jack finally catches Wray cheating at cards, accuses him publicly, expects a challenge to a duel: that challenge never happens. Wray is a politically powerful man with considerable sway over Jack's future career - Maturin says Wray will take revenge in other ways than a duel. Sophie laments the mess made of the world by men, and gets Stephen to encourage Jack to take to sea in Leopard: she

84

then goes to Jack and begs him to go to sea for Stephen's sake - "...Oh, Jack, he is so very low."

40 - Stephen, having thrown his laudanum away early in the day, buys a new supply during a stop for fresh horses

42 - Descriptions of the food available in the very poor part of town - rotten meat that the dogs will not eat but local children will.

44 - Among Diana's unpaid bills is one for large quantities of asses milk, in which she bathed 'for her complexion'.

51 - Stephen, at Grapes, gets in the mail a copy of The Syphilitic Preceptor, from the author. This is a genuine publication, not O'Brian's invention: *The Syphilitic Preceptor; or a Practical Treatise on the Nature and Cure of the Venereal Disease*. By G. Skelton, Surgeon. 2s6d. The publication is listed in Sir Walter Scott, Editor, "The Edinburgh Annual Register" Volume 2; Volume 3 [sic!!], Part 2 (1812). NOTE: Interesting that the title puts VD in the singular, as if there were only one.

Stephen sneers at a paper in Philosophical Transactions by Mellowes, who is pushing his theory that consumption (tuberculosis) is caused by an excess of oxygen (it is in fact bacterial).

52 - Mr Warren, a Naval Intelligence colleague of Stephen and Sir Joseph, has had a massive stroke, is not expected to live.

55 - Blaine tells Stephen he looks awful, begs him to "seek advice" - meaning, see another doctor. Stephen explains that he is on a course of 'physick' (self-prescribed). Stephen calls his laudanum a "Judas-draught" which he can stop (he believes) whenever he pleases, but he does suspect that a laudanum haze may have been responsible for Deering's death under his knife.

58 - Like any classical addict, when confronted with an uncomfortable situation, Stephen goes to his room, takes "his draught" (read "fix" in modern addiction terms) of laudanum (some hundreds of times the normal dose for an adult), then returns to the conversation fortified.

85

59 - Having clearly lost Diana to Johnson, and worried about his laudanum habit, Stephen is depressed by "...an indifference [to life] greater than he had ever known." and agrees to go on the Leopard's very long cruise, hoping new scientific horizons will re-enthuse him.

67 - Stephen, after heated discussions with Sophie primarily about men and their idiocies (including dueling), observes that Sophie needs to be let a few ounces of blood.

Book 5 Chapter 3 - p70-115: (overview)   At sea, aboard Leopard, Bay of Biscay enroute Botany Bay (9 months' sail) in a serious storm. Leopard is very unstable - makes even Jack seasick. Killick's bought wife has left him. The "passengers" (all prisoners) include several women. Prisoners scragg their "supervisor". Discovery of stowaway Mr Herapath, Prisoner Wogan's lover, trying to go with her to Australia.   Stephen plots to use Herapath/Wogan to impart disinformation to French Intelligence. Jack and Stephen order the prisoners' cage cleaned up, drained and ventilated. Wogan in her solo quarters in the aft cockpit is clean, neat, intelligent and handling the entire scene well, and has been killing rats with her shoe - Jack is impressed. Stephen has brought his friend and fellow-naturalist Rev Paul Martin, along as medical assistant. Stowaway entered in ship's rolls as "supernumerary landsman" - as low a rating as possible. Convict Wogan is, in an alarming number of characteristics, a good approximation of Diana - enough so to bother Jack and Stephen. English social-caste system critiqued.

74 - Convicts aboard Leopard have scragged their superintendent - beaten him to death with their shackles. All the prisoners are deathly seasick, one woman in a screeching fit. Convicts' surgeon fell into the hold, died of a broken neck. Prisoners' cage (= "quarters") is filthy beyond redemption. Stephen is very low spirited, in withdrawal from his beloved laudanum.

81 - Stephen and Jack inspect and condemn the iron cage that is the male prisoners' quarters. They order a thorough cleanup and healthy modifications, especially fresh air via wind-sail.

83 - Stephen examines a rat killed by Wogan: it is pregnant and also (more worrisome) has skin lesions that were not inflicted by Wogan's shoe.

85 - Discussing initial conditions for prisoners aboard Leopard, Jack and Stephen agree they have seen much worse ashore. Stephen is "...much caressed in the physical world..." (i.e., the world of medicine), in part due to his publications, including (1) Suggestions for the amelioration of Sick-Bays; (2) Thoughts on the Prevention of the Diseases most usual among Seamen; (3) New Operations for Suprapubic Cystotomy; (4) his *Tractus de Novae Febris Ingressa* (Latin - 'Management of the newly-arrived [i.e., recently encountered] fever' -- here, O'Brian takes obvious inspiration from a book of very similar name published in 1686 by Thomas Sydenham). All these publications are, we find, more or less required reading for naval surgeons. They are, in essence, the Aubrey-era's "Idiot's Guide to Medicine, including amputations and brain surgery inter alia", for literate but untrained ship's surgeons.

87 - Stephen requires that prisoners get access to open air on deck at least one hour twice daily.

89 - The prisoners are beginning to recover: Martin is helping with them.

90 - The prisoner most likely to have scragged the supervisor is still prostrate with seasickness: Stephen undertakes heroic measures, including 60 drops of 'sulphurous ether' administered through a funnel inserted in the man's pharynx. (NOTE 1): It is unclear what chemical compound this is, or what it is meant to do. It could be what we today call "ether", more technically diethylether or DEE - the original general anesthetic. But that was introduced in about 1846, far too late for this novel's action. Terminology is a problem - today's 'sulfurIC' and 'sulfurOUS' are quite different from one another, but in the novel's day (i.e., at the dawn of modern chemistry) 'sulfurous' was often if not usually used to cover both. Stephen prescribes for the other prisoners a water-extract of orange peel, and Peruvian bark (quinine). Other drugs here mentioned as being available on-board (i.e., Navy standard issue) include rhubarb (a common laxative); "grey powder" (un-

known); hartshorn (known today as Baker's ammonium and used in cooking - can also be literal shavings from a deer's horn); Lucatellus's balsam, polypody of the oak (a species of ground-dwelling low-light fern, *Polypodium vulgare*, the rhizomes (underground stems) of which taste like licorice and are incredibly sweet. Used to make cough soothers and to get rid of tapeworms); and three "Winchester quarts" of laudanum. (NOTE 2): "Winchester" refers to a set of standardized measures set up by Henry VII: this quart is about 2.25 liters. Because of his personal problems with laudanum, Stephen reflexively pours overboard the contents of one of the bottles, then reflects on possible legitimate medical needs for it, and retains the other two.)

91 - Stephen examines Mrs Wogan, concludes from looking at her tongue that she is healthy, praises the therapeutic effects of vomiting due to seasickness - "...as an evacuation of the gross humours and crudities, it has no equal." They discuss the state of her bowels.

93 - Stephen known by the troops as the fleet's "boldest hand with a saw". Bonden and his messmates have taken over the feeding of Herapath, who is severely malnourished and mustn't be fed too much too fast. They pound ship's biscuit with a marlinspike, add rum to make "pap" (babyfood), and then feed it to him with a tiny silver spoon, having confused the rate of supply with the sum total delivered.

95 - Detailed instructions for care of prisoners - airing on the forecastle for an hour morning and afternoon; new wind-sails to be rigged to ventilate their quarters; and exercise as possible - e.g., helping pump ship.

97 - Stephen still deeply morose: argues with Jack unnecessarily. Good food at the Captain's table improves his mood.

99 - At dinner, Stephen contemplates Babbington, whom Stephen has cured of "various discreditable diseases" over the years: also "...his enduring passion for the opposite sex had stunted his growth". Babbington is small (5'6"), apparently cute, and indefatigable in pur-

suit of women of any size, shape, race, age, etc. The Rev Mr Fisher has deeply-bitten nails, and eczema on both hand and wrist.

100 - Stephen analyzes his own condition - need for laudanum declining, appetite for food is returning.

101 - Four burials at sea: surgeon, superintendent of convicts, two convicts. The convicts died purely of seasickness, the only such deaths known to Stephen.

102 - The ship carries ten 'ships boys' of ages about 5-10: they get the daily grog ration regardless of age, and Jack has to stop that ration for one boy who apparently really cannot handle it.

103 - A junior officer Mr Byron relates a relative's experience of shipwreck, in which survivors ate the liver of a drowned comrade.

104 - Stephen comes to grips with his own bad behavior, apologizes to Jack; Stephen explains that he is "abandoning a course of physick, an injudicious course..." which leads to fits of petulance during the early stages of cessation. Two prisoners are idiots in a strict medical sense.

105 - Stephen analyzes and comments upon the several female prisoners - genuine hard cases. One procuress/abortionist, who "will not trouble us long..." She has a bad liver, plus ascites (accumulation of fluid in the abdomen) and other conditions. Stephen will, however, try to treat her using quicksilver (i.e., mercury), digitalis (heart stimulant from the nightshade plant), and a stout trochar (a sharply-pointed hollow tube, probably to be used here to drain the woman's abdomen.

106 - The Gipsy female prisoner is intentionally pregnant by her husband's brother: pregnancy is protection against the death sentence. She plans to reunite with her husband at Botany Bay. She is due to deliver about halfway to the Bay. Afternoon rounds - a few broken ribs and collarbones, contusions and crushed fingers - normal work-a-day seamen's injuries. Plus "the usual array of poxes", most of which are treated with 'mercurials' (i.e., compounds containing mercury, at least marginally successful against early-stage syphilis). Those treated must pay for their treatment - theory is they did it to themselves, not in line of duty.

89

107 - Working with Martin, Stephen reflects that the man "...treats his patients as though they were anatomical specimens, ... an inhumane, mechanical medicine".

108 - Stephen takes Mrs Wogan onto the quarterdeck for her airing: totally distracts and disrupts the watch, irritating Jack.

110 - Stephen notes that Wogan flushes and seems internally excited by the sight of an officer beating a sailor with a split-rattan cane. Her entire demeanor and behavior changes: implication is that she is a sexual sadist.

Book 5 Chapter 4 - p116-145: (overview) HMS Leopard just passing the Dry Salvages, enroute the Cape, then Botany Bay. Ship's routine has taken hold. Great-gun practice daily, using Jack's private powder. Crew assume Stephen and Wogan are probably lovers. Thievery rewarded with flogging. Herapath goes far aloft, falls, lands overboard. Saved by Jack, who is swimming. Jack is seen in the nude by Wogan: the crew respond with ribaldry that gets them stripped of their grog. Stephen mystified by his patients - cannot identify their malady. Herapath and Wogan are lovers, but she admits only to long friendship. She is, however, warming to Stephen - probably (he feels) to take advantage of him in some "intelligence" way. Turn-about: the Wogan/Herapath relationship is seized upon by Stephen, for use in his attempts to undermine the French Intelligence Service. Wogan's presence aboard is disturbing and disruptive of the ship's peace - some crew have drilled holes in bulkheads in order to peep at her... some of the officers spend time and effort on similar efforts. Jack cracks down hard on the perpetrators, is angry about having her aboard, but Stephen points out that she is blameless, the crew are the problem. As Leopard enters the doldrums, a rapidly-spreading illness is diagnosed as virulent gaol-fever (today's typhus), which can often have a 90% mortality. Twenty-three days in the doldrums whilst crew die steadily. Herapath worked heroically in the sickbay, Jack needs junior officers, offers a position to Herapath who cannot take it because he is American.

123 - Some of Stephen's 'miracle cures' as known to the crew: Cured Prince Billy (literally a Prince of the Realm) of the marthambles (imaginary disease - O'Brian invention), and of "the larynx" (No idea what this might be), and the strong fives (another O'Brian invention - implication of some monstrously uncomfortable perhaps deadly intestinal problem); wormed Admiral Keith in addition to curing his gout. Stephen the miracle worker.

125 - In port, St Jago, Cape Verde Islands. Several prisoners are still sick and Stephen still cannot identify the cause.

127 - Stephen, ashore, shops for "physick-nuts". (Note - this is a real item, a fruit vaguely described by explorer William Dampier in his 1688 report on a voyage of discovery around the world. It has a crunchy outer shell, juicy pulp beneath that, and a large seed - one chews up the whole item, spits out the seed and pulp. Likely a good source of vitamin C.)

130 - Voyage resumed, Stephen is worried about his sick prisoners - their symptoms do not correspond to anything he knows, and there is apparently a prolonged period of latency or incubation. This is a problem, because many illnesses are contagious through the latent period. He expects the next few days will show what the problem is.

135 - The entire sick-bay has been washed with vinegar and then whitewashed: wind-sails are working, bringing fresh air to the sick-bay. Three patients, all with similar symptoms - low fevers, fetid breath, severe headache, contracted pupils - and still he has no identification for the disease - the disease's progression is unique and therefore disturbing. Stephen ponders Wogan as a spy - her personality and connections and role - speculates (nonjudgmentally) that she has a very cavalier attitude about things sexual. He orders the patients' "slime draughts" to continue. In the after sickbay lies Jackruski in a deep alcoholic coma. Stephen wonders how seamen's bodies stand the conditions - continual damp, heavy work, never more than four hours of sleep uninterrupted, the tight packing of hammocks below-decks, the lack of sanitation.

136 - Herapath is doing well on the ship's food, but his soft, uncallused hands are nearly flayed from working with rough ropes. - he is ordered to wear mittens while working.

140 - Stephen chats with Wogan about love and its consequences - whether one can literally die from love or want thereof.

144 - All three patients suddenly break out in a mulberry-tinted rash (the "crisis" of the disease). The disease is now recognized - "gaol [USA – jail] fever", one of the most deadly known illnesses, highly contagious and quickly spread, often up to 90% fatalities in any outbreak: no cure or preventative. Often spread by direct human-human contact, also by fleas living on rodents, as is plague. (NOTE - "Gaol (jail) fever" is typhus (not typhoid), and is due to the bacterium *Rickettsia spp.*) Stephen confirms his diagnosis - all the symptoms of the worst, most virulent kind of gaol fever are present in all three men.

145 - Stephen doses fever patients with cantharides. (= "Spanish fly", a concoction of ground-up blister-beetles, *Lytta vesicatoria*, which can irritate the sexual organs including the urethra, yielding passive sexual stimulation - an aphrodisiac. Still available and so used today.) Also he prescribes "turpentine enemas", and shaving the head. All three patients go into delirium within hours of the crisis, and are dead shortly after midnight.

Book 5 Chapter 5 - p146-172: (overview) Fever spreads and kills whilst Leopard is caught in the doldrums. Quarantine measures fail. After the fever, there are ~200 remaining crew (+ 65 non-working convalescents), barely enough to sail the Leopard, not to fight her. Detour to Recife, to get convalescents into hospital, get greenstuff, and restock Stephen's medical chest. Stephen inspects Wogan's outgoing mail, looking for information as to her contacts or activities, finds code (apparently simple, but difficult for Wogan to use). Decoded, the text tells Stephen a great deal about America's newborn intelligence operations. He continues to set up the Wogan/Herapath relationship for his own 'counter-intelligence' use. Stephen re-loads his medicine chest, returns. Dutch man of war Waakzaamheid (74) is reported to be somewhere nearby, and faster than Leopard. Jack plans to give the Dutchman a wide berth. Leopard sails from Recife, once again for the Cape, thence to Botany Bay.

146 - Leopard caught in the doldrums, rolling violently, most hands are seasick plus terrified of gaol fever.

147 - Stephen tries to quarantine the patients so as to slow or stop the fever's spread. Nobody goes into or out of the greatly-enlarged sick-bay, except to bury the dead fever-victims.

148 - Stephen has had the entire ship fumigated with burning sulfur, and the sickbay bulkheads caulked and tarred in hopes of quarantining and slowing the spread of the disease (this makes people feel good but does nothing useful). Week #1 toll = seventeen dead, all of them prisoners or people working closely with them. Others now begin to die. Crew totally despondent, waiting to die - the disease strikes faster and kills more than the plague itself. Not every fever victim dies - there are eleven convalescing patients. Stephen confides in Martin that he thinks much of the mortality is due to men simply giving up once they show symptoms - that a rousing battle or major emergency requiring great activity, would save many. Stephen doses the men with more bark.

149 - Martin has the fever, makes notes for the record of his internal state, feelings, and symptoms as the disease progresses. Stephen out of medicines, resorts to placebos of colored chalk. Martin dies at some unspecified future date, but not of the fever - rather of a subsequent pneumonia.

151 - As Leopard regains the wind, fever mortality is diminishing, and no fresh cases are reporting in. Depression lifts.

152 - Evidence of the importance of mental state to physical health. In agreement with Stephen's theory, as soon as the weather becomes nice and activity returns to normal, patients who had been on the point of dying miraculously revive and return to duty.

154 - Final death toll from gaol-fever, 116.

155 - Stephen and Jack discuss the fever - Stephen knows that for gaol-fever, as for smallpox, a mild case confers lifelong immunity. Likely that most survivors had developed immunity elsewhere. Sixty-five convalescents, but most will not be able to work for months - the disease's effects are long-lasting, full recovery is very slow.

156 - Stephen demands that Leopard make for the nearest land hospital, else the convalescing cases will mostly die also - including Pullings, one of Jack's favorite officers. They head for Recife, Brazil.

Book 5 Chapter 6 - p173-205: (overview) Dutch warship Waakzaamheid, larger and faster than Leopard, has been spotted in the general area, could be almost anywhere. Jack is cautious - the Dutch navy is very good: gunnery practice increases. To further his plans, Stephen often gives Herapath the key to Wogan's quarters, and puts him "in charge" of her daily airings - Stephen expects the two will hatch a plot, into which Stephen can insert some destructive elements. Herapath unburdens himself to Stephen about his long-standing liaison with Mrs Wogan, which is the only reason he is aboard ship. Herapath is on the outs with his father - the young man is a student of ancient Chinese poetry: his father (a shipping magnate in America) is infuriated at the career choice. Leopard encounters Waakzaamheid. Jack turns and runs ("Ignominious flight is the order of the day!" he tells Stephen), hoping he hasn't been seen. Later they encounter Waakzaamheid again, sneak in to closer range to get positive identification; the result is a chase and minor cannon-fire, but no injuries or damages. Leopard escapes the not-very-determined Dutchman.

177 - Calm steady sailing towards the Cape: fever survivors are beginning to re-grow their hair (shaving the head then being a 'treatment' for many diseases). Stephen takes care of routine minor troubles - bad teeth, bad digestion, ague. He also "...wormed the entire midshipman's berth."

178 - Herapath reports to Stephen that he has treated seven hands for '*lues venera*' - almost certainly first-stage syphilis. Stage one does not last very long (external sore, visible but painless, lasts 2-4 weeks

94

only). These are fresh infections and there was no shore-leave at Recife. Conclusion: these cases of VD are due to contact with the few female prisoners - Stephen zeroes in on Mrs Wogan's servant girl Peggy Barnes. What to do? Jack suggests "...heading her up (enclosing her) in a barrel with no bunghole." Stephen ponders the lack of navy-issue chastity belts in fourth-rate men of war such as Leopard. Jack's medical superstitions are on view - he believes that basilisks (an imaginary reptile held to be "King of the Serpents") spread pest (disease) by glaring at people.

179 - One female prisoner is a Gipsy fortune teller who convinces the crew that there is an evil ghost aboard, living on the spritsail yard. Thereafter, the men will not go close to the place.

181 - Stephen undertakes to 'exorcise' the Gipsy's spook in the evening dark, and can get nobody -not Jack, not Bonden - to go with him.

189 - Herapath, in his rambling confessions to Stephen, admits to being an opium smoker: intrigued, Stephen pursues the question/problem of STOPPING - how best done, consequences, etc.

191 - About opium use, the crux is this interchange: Stephen - "...having broke the habit, were you able to return to a moderate, and pleasurable, use of the drug?" Herapath "Yes, sir" "And in the intervals, did you not crave? The craving did not return?" "No, sir, after the clean break it did not." (NOTE - Stephen can obviously use this to justify his own return to using laudanum ... "See? I really can quit whenever I want to, and a little bit now and then won't trigger true addiction.")

192 - Stephen admits to himself that he has sexual stirrings towards Wogan which she seems willing to entertain. He uses that to rationalize continued use of laudanum - as a professional agent, he MUST NOT fall prey to involvement with Mrs Wogan, and the laudanum will prevent that by dulling his sexual desires. As he puts it, mentally, "Duty directs me to my laudanum and thus to chastity."

95

193 - Stephen uses fake holy water, Latin incantations, and blue pyrotechnics to successfully exorcise the bowsprit ghost. The men are happy again.

Book 5 Chapter 7 - p206-236: (overview)   Waakzaamheid is within sight of Leopard at dawn, regardless of Jack's all-night attempts to put distance between them. There begins a slow chase with intermittent gunfire at extreme range - the Dutchman is good. Jack doesn't understand why Waakzaamheid merely parallels Leopard's course, does not attempt to close. Fluky winds foil Jack's attempts to depart unattended. Becalmed, at midnight the Dutchmen try to board Leopard via rowed boats, are spotted and driven off with grapeshot. Wind returns, Leopard sets off to escape, gains and is hull down by next evening. Jack's Chaplain, who has been helping with Wogan, declines to continue because he fears sexual entrapment by her. Leopard meets a whaler (Three Brothers: London) - she has not seen Waakzaamheid. Later that same day, coming out of a squall, there lies Waakzaamheid, hull up, three miles off. Now, in a rapidly growing storm, the Dutchman chases in earnest: Leopard is holding her own. Jack wonders why the Dutch captain is so intent on pursuit now... did Leopard's grapeshot into the Dutch boats (during the boarding attempt) kill the captain's son or do some equivalent injury? In any case, Jack now senses murderous intent on the Dutchman's part. Hawsers to the mastheads enable Jack to carry extra sail: Leopard gains. Storm intensifies, seas build to monstrous size - both ships are on the ragged edge of controllability where the least failure of equipment or technique will broach the ship to, inevitably then to capsize and sink. Mid chase, Mrs Bothwell goes into labor. Swell now so big that Leopard is partially becalmed when in the troughs - this allows the taller Waakzaamheid to gain steadily. Firing commences with bow and stern chasers. Waakzaamheid begins to overlap Leopard. Jack's overheated brass chaser explodes as he fires it, knocking him out briefly. He recovers in time to watch Marine officer Moore make a final desperation point-blank shot from the remaining chaser. That round takes out the Waakzaamheid's foremast: she broaches, capsizes, and disappears in seconds, taking all 600+ men with her. The ancient 50-gun Leopard has destroyed the Dutch 74, an unheard of result.

215 - Mr Larkin murders Marine Lt Howard. When Stephen arrives on scene, Larkin is in convulsions of *delerium tremens* (essentially alcohol poisoning). Larkin took a half-pike from the extensive weaponry on display on the wardroom bulkhead, stabbed Howard in the neck, which severed the aorta and Howard died instantly. Cause of the altercation was Howard beginning to assemble his German flute - an instrument which Larkin utterly detested.

216 - After Howard's death, the crew begin to think there is a Jonah aboard - a person who brings continual bad luck to the ship. They will scragg (= kill) anyone suspected of being a Jonah, making this a dangerous situation.

217 - Larkin, the murderer, is locked up below decks but howls so loudly as to upset the entire ship.

226 - In the middle of a severe southern high-latitude storm while being closely pursued by Waakzaamheid, Mrs Bothwell (convict) goes into labor - a difficult breech presentation (butt-first or back-first, instead of head-first - at the time often fatal to mother and/or child). Stephen has little experience with midwifery, and no proper forceps (= implements for manipulating a fetus during birth, and critical to rotating a breech-presentation into some other, less problematical orientation).

229 - Crewmen adding yet another sail have their hands bloodied by the flailing canvas and are sent to Stephen for treatment, including a shot of rum and a hot drink.

235 - Jack, firing one of his brass stern chasers, is knocked out when the gun explodes. He recovers to find Stephen busily sewing up his scalp. He watches as Marine Moore takes a final desperation shot with the other chaser: fired point-blank, the round destroys the Dutchman's foremast, causing Waakzaamheid to broach: it capsizes and immediately sink without a trace.

Book 5 Chapter 8 - p237-261: (overview) Still enroute the Cape. Jack ponders, gloomily, his sinking of the Waakzaamheid - he cannot feel good about it. Baby girl born to Mrs Boswell via

Caesarean section - mother and child survived. Snow, decreasing seas. Crewman Cobb, former whaler, says he can smell ice, it is nearby. Soon surrounded by large icebergs, in poor visibility. Leopard hits an iceberg while inadvertently moving backwards in a near-calm, destroying the rudder and starting a ferocious leak. They begin lightening ship immediately --- guns, anchors, stores, water all overboard. Fothering sail prepared (fothering = sliding a sail under the ship like a diaper, then pulling it taut to cover and slow large leaks, or those difficult to reach). The leak is most likely in the stern, but heroic efforts to find it fail. The Master, Mr Grant, has been a profound irritant to Jack the whole voyage, but rises to the occasion and reverses Jack's opinion. The men are becoming exhausted with pumping. Crew wants to take to the boats, Jack feels they can save Leopard, but allows the boats to be prepared. Given Jack's permission to choose, some crewmen decide to leave in two boats. Jack stays, as do most of the officers and some of the crew. Departure of the boats is a disaster: they are now 1300 miles from the Cape, and are seriously oversubscribed: with not enough room in the two boats to hold all who leave the ship, many wind up in the icy water, fighting to get into the boats. Life expectancy for a human immersed in Antarctic-temperature waters(i.e., -2 to +3 °C) is less than four minutes.

238 - Stephen warns Jack that the recent head-wound will spoil his beauty, and also tells him "As it is, I have great hope for your leg. Is there any feeling in it now?" Jack unaware of the leg wound, discovers the leg is numb. He also has a significant concussion.

239 - Stephen gives Jack a 25-drop dose of laudanum - Stephen's own "I can control it..." daily dose has at times been upwards of fourteen thousand drops. Mrs Boswell's giving birth resulted in a Caesarean section - she is in unstable condition - the baby (a girl) may live if they can find a lactating woman (the obvious candidate, Wogan's maid Peggy, is being transported to Botany Bay for repeated infanticide). Wogan volunteers to take care of the baby herself.

242 - Jack suffering headaches and nausea from the concussion, unable to eat breakfast. Stephen is happy with the leg's progress. The

newborn (in the orlop - lowest deck) can be heard from the main deck.

243 - New mother Mrs Boswell is recovering, can nurse the baby, which is both son and nephew to her. Wogan overtly flirts with Stephen as he gives her advice about underclothes. She volunteers that she may be pregnant herself. Stephen examines her: too early to tell. She does like babies and has longed for one of her own, so the pregnancy -if real- is not a burden.

245 - Jack's leg is 'coming to' - apparently mending well. We are never told exactly what happened to it.

246 - Jack's condition has been worrying the crew, generating outlandish rumors. He comes on deck for the noon observation, a bit uncertain and with his head bandaged, then manages to trip and fall in front of several crewmen, deepening the crew's unease.

249 - Jack's concussion is aggravated by loud noises: ship's bell has been muffled. Stephen tells Babbington to speak more softly in Jack's presence because "...the loss of blood renders the ears preternaturally acute."

Book 5 Chapter 9 - p262-284: (overview)   Chapter opens on Christmas Eve, Leopard is still afloat but with 8 feet of water in the hold. Christmas Day, the fothering-sail works, the pumps gain five feet. Renewed spirits. Still no rudder, hence ship not yet steerable:, despite multiple efforts to jury-rig a steering device. First steering oar cannot bring ship's head around sufficiently, the oar shatters from the effort, they skim past the first available island (the Crozets), those islands being clearly visible near at hand, yet "...as inaccessible as the moon", given the ship's lack of steering gear. Their last hope is Desolation Island, position uncertain but probably on their latitude. They make a very good landfall at Desolation, prepare the only remaining (small) anchor, augmented by a couple of cannons from the ballast. Jack is juggling a very large number of unknowns, mostly uncontrollable. A storm is rising as they approach the Island. In a mad race against the arriving storm, Leopard plows through a monstrous tidal rip and into smooth water under the lee of a huge cliff. They come to a fine anchorage. As they anchor, Jack is shat upon by a seabird – traditionally a sailor's good omen. (Author's Note: This exact thing happened to me as I was obeying my first order received in US Marine Corps bootcamp, 1964. As ordered, I stood on the yellow-painted footprints, and was copiously shat upon by a San Diego seagull.)

265 - Mrs Boswell's newborn daughter doing well, named Leopardina.

267 - Stephen and Herapath discuss the amazingly good state of the crew's health despite everything. Remaining crew believe their Jonah went off in the boats... Jonah generally believed to have been Mr Larkin.

271 - First signs of scurvy - Stephen suspects the lime juice is bad, is told some of the men don't drink their rum but trade it away - and the lime is administered in the daily grog. Stephen begins personally administering straight juice to all hands, one at a time, at muster or dinner.

276 - On deck again for air, Wogan comments on the heavy calluses on Stephen's hands from pumping ship.

Book 5 Chapter 10 - p285-325: (overview) A very complex multi-stranded chapter full of action on several non-medical fronts. At Desolation Island, moored to shore and anchored, emptying ship to get at the leak (an enormous task - hundreds of tons of materiel to be moved). One or two days' rest - fresh food plentiful on the Island - four meals daily of fresh meat. Sailors cannot be broken of indiscriminate slaughter of birds and sea-mammals. Stephen becomes slightly reclusive, has his own goodly island (a mile long), with his own tiny canvas boat - but due to his inherent clumsiness, he is continually accompanied by Herapath. Leak located - a long, nearly-fatal gash now fixed - the problem is building and then attaching a rudder. They have no forge, coal, or iron with which to make the needed hardware - in particular the massive iron gudgeons and pintles which both attach a rudder to a ship and allow it to swing port-starboard. Stephen ruminates extensively on the island fauna, on wit, and other topics. Stephen loses his canvas boat through inattention to the tide - it drifts out to where a strange small-craft, full of unknown men, retrieves it for him. American whalers, Brig La Fayette, anchored just around the point, crew ashore seeking cabbages. Their captain Putnam is in dental agony. La Fayette lost her surgeon due to "...the griping of the guts." (Dysentery?) Uneasy truce between Americans and English -the countries may be at war, the whalers recognize Leopard as the ship which savagely fired into an American ship during a search for Englishmen amongst its crew - an incident not to be forgiven regardless of who captains Leopard. Upon finding Stephen is a physician, Putnam entreats him to deal with his rotten teeth. Everyone knows the whaler will have iron, coal and forge. Tensions rise. Stephen goes to La Fayette to treat Putnam, finds more urgent cases needing first attention and handles them: this infuriates Putnam who has to wait for morning. Herapath aids Stephen, having promised not to desert into the whaler (he is American). Ultimately Stephen takes care of Putnam and the repair materials needed by Leopard are provided. Stephen indirectly encourages Herapath to think about being surgeon himself for the whaler - he has been formally offered the job. Herapath will not leave Wogan to her fate as a Botany Bay prisoner - if he goes, she must escape Leopard and go with him. It is obvious to Stephen that this must happen (for his own intelligence needs, at least). The problem is Herapath's overdeveloped sense of personal honor - he owes a trivial cash debt which he has not been able to repay, his ridiculously high-flown scruples about not absconding from a debt almost render him incapable of action. Wogan forces the issue and they plan to leave secretly aboard the La Fayette whilst the entire Leopard crew is helping with installing the new rudder. In their last interchange, Wogan tries to enlist Stephen into her own (American) intelligence service, and mentions the name of her main contact - perhaps her superior- in London – she insists that Stephen really truly should look up Mr Pole next opportunity. Stephen and Bonden sit in Stephen's boat and see the couple row out to La Fayette - Bonden recognizes them, offers to stop them but when told NO, he understands that this is just another of the Doctor's ongoing strange capers- capers that Bonden has been involved in repeatedly.

289 - Herapath complains that the local "cabbages" (eaten for their vitamin C) have turned his insides to water (= diarrhea). It is fine cabbage, says Stephen, even if it smells a little sharp and is yellowish under certain light. So what that it makes one's guts rumble and leads to farting? It cures purpurae (subdermal bruise-like purple blotches due to vitamin C deficiency). Earlier, the crew killed a sea-elephant, ate its liver, and broke out in clearly-defined dull blue blotches, which were, apparently, cured by the cabbage. The blotches may have been a result of scurvy, in which case the cabbage treatment could well have cured them.

307 - Whaler La Fayette arrives at Desolation, full of medical problems including scurvy, frostbitten toes badly amputated, a harpoon wound "gone bad" and the like.

308 - Stephen and Herapath go aboard La Fayette, just arrived at Desolation, find that two legs need operated on immediately if they are to be saved. Many teeth to be drawn (extracted) due to scurvy. Putnam's tooth has to wait for morning: he is furious. Stephen refuses any fee whatsoever. One patient refuses to remove his shirt for examination: he is English and has tattoos to prove it, so he justifiably fears being retaken and immediately hanged as a deserter. Stephen calms and treats him. There are many more like him aboard – men who, having run from the Royal Navy, are now forever subject to instant hanging if apprehended by British authority anywhere in the world. Herapath, as Stephen's aide, becomes highly regarded by the whalers, and is offered a job as their surgeon for a share in the voyage's profits - La Fayette will sail directly to America from Desolation. This raises the possibility of escape.

310 - Stephen praises Herapath, insists that he could be a good ship's surgeon even now, as-is and without more training he is better than many, perhaps most.

315 - Stephen notes (again) the widespread and peculiar dislike of dentists, and most crewmen's squeamish resistance to dental treatment. He notes that "…men who would submit to grave surgery, even amputation with a noble fortitude … grow unaccountably shy (cow-

ardly) when sat in a chair and told to open wide." Some things never do change!

317 - Sending Herapath off to (Stephen hopes) rescue Wogan and escape via the La Fayette, Stephen reminds him that asafoetida (a wrenchingly foul-smelling herb) is a great comfort to any seaman with the megrims (another O'Brian-invented malady).

Book 6 - The Fortune of War

Book 6 Chapter 1 - p7-38: (overview) HMS Leopard, badly damaged and thinly manned, is arriving Pulo Batang, having made it to Botany Bay, where the Bligh problem (Book 5) had already been solved and they delivered their surviving prisoners. Stephen's wombat is eating the gold braid on Jack's hat. Leopard given up for lost: Admiral Drury's greeting is enthusiastic, especially on learning that HMS Leopard (50; Captain Aubrey) sank the Dutch Waakzaamheid (72). One of Leopard's launches made it to the Cape with the news. Jack has been given HMS Acasta (40), a good sailer. To get to Acasta he and his followers must return home ASAP aboard La Fleche (20), under his friend Capt Yorke, due at Pulo Prabang momentarily. Man-hungry, the Adm argues vehemently with Jack, who wins and may take all his important followers. Cricket game: flagship vs Acasta. Stephen as Irish sports-hero for the cause- makes and uses his own hurly (hurling-stick) instead of a cricket bat. His being very good confounds all players. Jack's new mission will be to establish England-friendly governments, by whatever means but especially by the proper deployment of chests of "little silver ingots". Stephen and the Admiral's political advisor Wallis will work together. Sir Joseph Blaine, Stephen's friend and colleague, is back as Chief of Naval Intelligence. Stephen's plan to use Wogan and Herapath to sow destruction in the French and American Intelligence services has worked to perfection - a copy of his report went with Grant in the launch which made the Cape. Wogan was arrested, originally, with Admiralty papers in her possession. War of 1812 is imminent. La Fleche is carrying mostly passengers - plus Stephen's extensive natural history collections. Stephen once again is shortchanged on his scientific opportunities. Sophie's letter: she has heard of Jack's survival by way of the Diana-Wogan connection.

9 - Stephen is informed that his wombat is eating the gold lace from Jack's best hat: responds that it will not harm the creature's digestive tract.

16 - While away on Leopard, Jack has been assigned to HMS Acasta, which was to have been temporarily captained (in Jack's ab-

sence) by Burrel, who arrived and then died of the "bloody flux" (severe dysentery) as did half his crew.

20 - Stephen greets Wallis (political advisor) with "How is your penis?" - Stephen earlier circumcised Wallis, who needed to pass for a Jew. It proved a non-trifling operation. Wallis is downcast - the item will never be what it was pre-operation.

22 - Stephen's addiction to laudanum seems to be over, or at least under control.

31 - Mail. Jack's children have had the mumps. Stephen wishes that all children could be intentionally exposed to it at a very early age, since consequences of the disease in adults (especially males) are so severe ... "an orchitis that takes an ugly turn is a melancholy spectacle." (NOTE - Mumps in adult males often settles in the testicles, causing them to swell quite painfully - the condition can persist for some time and often causes sterility. Orchitis is specifically swelling and inflammation of the testicles.).

33 - Jack is depressed because of the ongoing mining/refining fiasco at home: Stephen recommends intense activity as a mood-lifter. "Be not idle; be not alone."

Book 6 Chapter 2 - p39-83: (overview) Jack's friend, Capt York of La Fleche (20) arrives on Leopard, bringing a letter from Sophie, who has been told of Jack's survival by Diana, who knows Wogan and Herapath ...Diana, Wogan and Herapath are all in America now. La Fleche is acting as a transport, will take Jack et al (including Stephen's extensive collections) aboard for England - and immediately, so as to catch the tide. Getting Stephen's collections properly shifted and secured in one hour creates problems aboard La Fleche, where it is now dinnertime. Music after dinner. Yorke's library and its special containers. Discussions of current English drama and novels. Love's analogies to war. Books unable to capture the multiple simultaneous timelines of real events, especially war. Jack's men have secured the collections perfectly. Stephen has no companion, confides to his secret encrypted diary: an idyllic sail, so far: Stephen meets ship's surgeon McLean -paralyzingly shy- who eventually praises Stephen's books. For McLean and Stephen, finding a place to smoke is difficult - every possibility comes afoul of one caste system or another. McLean, like Stephen, is a natural historian -they become close friends. The cruise is so long (15,000 miles) that there is no past or future, only 'here and now'. Warner is a closeted pederast, in torment from being close to the ship's boys. How Jack deals with the need to educate his young men. They make a perfect landfall at Simon's Bay. La Fleche is carrying despatches, cannot tarry. War of 1812 (England vs America) has been declared. Widely varied opinions of the war, within the quarterdeck. Now American merchants are subject to capture! American forces compared to English; the contrast is ludicrous - the Americans have only eight frigates and no ships of the line -- vs England's more than 600. Various famous battles refought, for the edification of Stephen, off of whom the effort bounces like sleet off a turtle. Implications of the war for Diana's situation considered. To go north they must go westward across the Atlantic almost to Brazil, following wind and current patterns. In the middle of a delightful calm night, the ship catches fire and blows up, giving them barely time to get away in un-provisioned boats.

63 - Stephen wonders how it can be that salt beef, salt pork, dried peas, hard work, too much rum, stifling quarters , and little sleep seem to make the crew healthy. Almost no sickness amongst crew at the moment - sickbay empty.

67 - Stephen recognizes that Warner is a pederast, muses on the agonies of being one whilst closeted in the utterly repressive atmosphere of the ship, and in such enforced proximity to attractive (and unavailable) males.

72 - Midshipman Fanshaw erred - cracked wise at Jack: he has been flogged with a knotted rope's end. Stephen will give him a painkiller and cover the lash marks with a linseed-mash poultice (poultice = any "medicinal" goop held in place with a bandage).

80 - A few sunstrokes plus a few cases of the usual diseases seamen get in town (aka VD)

83 - In mid-ocean under idyllic conditions, La Fleche burns, explodes, sinks. Crew has time to man the boats, not to provision them.

Book 6 Chapter 3 - p84-124: (overview) La Fleche has exploded and sunk. Two boats were launched: they were separated by a storm that night. Now Jack and 12 men are afloat in an 18' rowboat (the 'cutter'). Bosun long ago stole and sold the cutter's sails. Men's shirts patched together as a sail: heading for Brazil. Biscuit and water dwindling - sky clear blue, sun blazing: 1/3 mug water, 1/3 biscuit per man per day. Drinking urine mixed with seawater and freshwater. Men have saved random miscellaneous personal items. Jack has his chronometer, one midshipman his own sextant - Jack can navigate if they get wind. Bonden stands up and spots a sail. An Indiaman. They row towards it, close to under 1/2 mile, but are not seen The fact she carries a top-light means she is in shipping channel: they still may find another ship. Deluge of rain refills their storage, fills all bellies. Squids fly into the boat, are devoured alive. At dawn, a pair of ships lies only two miles off. They are stopped to chat. Nationality and functionality unknown, no matter. They row madly: closing, Jack announces "OURS!" - Frigate HMS Java (38). Rescue, a couple of days before Christmas. Food and drink. Captain Lambert, with a passenger, Lord Hislop, the new Governor of Bombay enroute to that city. Java seriously overcrowded -over 400 souls- and acting as transport. (On punishment days there was scarcely room to swing a cat effectively.) Entire ship's complement downcast, no visible reason. Eventual explanation - War of 1812 has opened horribly badly for the English Navy - HMS Guerriere taken by USS Constitution; USS Wasp took HMS Frolic. HMS Macedonia struck to USS United States. This is NOT the natural order of things naval - England ALWAYS wins... doesn't she? Stephen's thoughts on the situation. Java has a prize, American merchantman William (a slowpoke). On the difficulties of turning rabble into skilled seamen. Sail spotted: Bonden says it is USS Constitution... a vessel to be feared, especially because Java's crew has had inadequate live-fire training on the ship's long guns. Sail positively identified as USS Constitution. Jack volunteers himself and his men to remain aboard Java (no transfer to William, as earlier planned), to fight some of the Java's guns. Constitution seeks to draw Java away, alone. Lambert's strategy is to charge in and board the enemy (the passengers will participate) - Jack worries, would prefer a long-distance cannon exchange but it is not his ship. Sharp, fierce battle - Java makes several serious blunders, compounded with errors by inexperienced gun-crews and loss of all masts: she strikes to Constitution.

84 - Most immediate problem is sunburn on never-exposed backs now red, purple: fear, hunger, and thirst will come soon.

85 - Starvation rations: drinking fresh water diluted with urine and seawater. The men have "chewed all the goodness out of their belts and shoes".

89 - Jack continually at the helm, has lost "...about as much weight as a man can lose and live."

90 - Raikes (La Fleche's quarter-gunner) dies: they decide not to throw him overboard - they might have to eat him.

92 - Raikes' corpse swelling, part of his thigh has been eaten. His mates won't ditch him - agree he must have a parson.

95 - Saved by HMS Java: Java's entire ship's company seems mildly depressed: Stephen cannot figure it out. His prescription for the problem would be add women to the crew... to "...inject a little civilization... even at the risk of moral deviation."

96 - Stephen roundly perceived as weird: gets health advice from the crew - "...eat little and chew ever bite forty times."

97 - Midshipman Forshaw, a small child, is especially depressed: Stephen wonders if he has gotten some horribly bad news? Decides to give him half a blue pill (placebo). Shortly thereafter, Stephen is told the reason for the gloom - three consecutive defeats of RN by the Americans' inexperienced, minuscule Navy.

116 - In battle with Constitution, an officer beside Jack is shot, then killed by a 24# ball. Jack's head grazed by a musket-ball.

117 - Bonden down - scalp wound - Jack sends him below to Stephen, for stitching, with words of comfort "...your pigtail's all right." Amidships on Java there are "dead and wounded by the score".

120 - Java's captain is down. Jack takes a musket-shot to the right arm

121 - Stephen binds Jack's arm so that he can return to the fray - the wound is serious, may result in loss of the arm. One victim in the cockpit is "lying on his own liver".

122 - Midshipman Forshaw has been blasted over the side - dead. Age about eight.

Book 6 Chapter 4 - p125-157: (overview) Constitution, victorious, burns Java, which explodes. Aboard Constitution as prisoners, Stephen is mildly suspected of intelligence work but adequately explains his diaries as scientific workbooks. Jack's having captained the unfortunate HMS Leopard makes him unfairly badly received. American and French intelligence working cooperatively in Boston - worrisome for Stephen. Frenchman/agent unknowingly reveals a detailed knowledge of Stephen's diaries and notebooks. Philosophizing about the best form of government - must man be ruled illogically? American politics and political theories discussed - also the American accent and propensity for joking and chewing tobacco. Jack has pneumonia, must go ashore to hospital. Jack and Stephens' POW exchanges are predicted to be mysteriously delayed. In Boston, the American officers personally advance cash loans and clothing to meet prisoners' needs. Herapath reappears - his father is a rich and powerful ship-owner, deeply affected and upset by the war. Jack is befriended in the asylum by three madmen, and shortly mistakes the official American interrogators for more of the same - and treats them accordingly. HMS Peacock sunk by USS Hornet... more gloom. Jack has a telescope, studies the warships in Boston Harbor - this terrifies Stephen - Jack can readily be hanged for espionage for doing so. Jack is innocently astounded by the idea. Jack and Stephen variously interrogated, no discussion of their exchange date. Mrs Wogan (aka Mrs Herapath) finds them.

125 - Huge number of wounded: Stephen helps Constitution's surgeon, Mr Evans, a deft operator: a rare doctor who tries to treat the whole patient, not just the problem itself.

126 - The doctors have lost Capt Lambert (more of misery than of his wounds), nearly lost Jack, who shows signs of gangrene in his

wounded arm and is "…too near death to be moved…" Jack is seriously depressed, although he can now "…defecate with ease…"

135 - Jack is in "truly shocking pain" from his arm, now described as "shattered".

136 - Stephen and Surgeon Evans consult, actively considering amputation of Jack's arm, decide NO.

137 - The doctors add "inspissated (thickened) juice of lettuce" to Jack's treatment, to treat his "light, quick, irregular" pulse, and also his irascibility.

141 - Jack down with pneumonia, ordered out of the chill winter winds.

142 - Jack basically comatose with pneumonia. Evans' brother-in-law Dr Choate runs a private hospital in Boston, to which they send Jack despite the attendants being Papist Irishwomen and the building full of certified lunatics.

148 - Choate's treatment for mental patients (half-wits, lunatics) is humane, far removed from the usual whipping, chains and barred-cell milieu of most English mental hospitals. Jack's quarters are away from almost all the mental patients.

149 - Jack has recovered from pneumonia, his arm is mending and saved from amputation, and his appetite is voracious.

Book 6 Chapter 5 - p158-184: (overview)   When last seen, Wogan was pregnant: she and Herapath had escaped from Leopard, and were headed for America on a whaler. She renews their friendship: she is a top American spy, but nonetheless an amateur and has never realized how Stephen used her to convey disruptive misinformation to her own and the French intelligence services. Wogan is Diana's close friend - Diana is now the mistress of the very wealthy and powerful American, Mr Johnson - a bird enthusiast who know of Stephen's studies. The elder Herapath acknowledges that he owes a debt to Stephen and Jack for aiding his son. Stephen trained Herapath (son) as a surgeon, recommends to the father that he send him to medical school (son is currently enamored only of medieval Chinese poetry, for which

110

father despises him). Father also dislikes Wogan, would ditch the couple entirely except that he loves the child (his granddaughter). Herapath (father) meets and gets along famously with Jack. Wogan meets privately with Stephen and tries to recruit him. Stephen considers letting her seduce him, decides against it. Diana's Mr Johnson hates Leopard and by association Jack. Johnson is in fact Wogan's superior in American intelligence circles. Stephen's extensive thoughts on the business of intelligence (= not espionage!).

158 - Wogan gave birth to a girl, in an appalling tempest off Cape Horn. Stephen is happy - he had feared for both mother and child.

174 - Michael Herapath's sister has been in Choate's care for years - "...she is a werewolf." Stephen mulls this over.

175 - Jack is asleep, Stephen studies him - mentally prescribes yet more bark and steel, but what Jack really needs is news of any sort of English naval victory.

Book 6 Chapter 6 - p185-216: (overview) Stephen is extraordinarily nervous as he prepares to meet with Mr Johnson, who is Diana's paramour, protector, and handler. Johnson knows there is some sort of relationship between Stephen and Diana, but it is unclear how much he knows. Diana has been very discreet - Johnson knows little. The men discuss boobies. Stephen sees Diana in private - she is ecstatic. Diana desperately wants OUT of the Johnson affair. Wogan, Johnson, Stephen, and Diana are together, a delicate affair. American intelligence has found mysterious papers among Jack's effects, demands an explanation. They are victualling notes - a million pounds of salt beef, etc. The agents are too ignorant to understand how much even a small ship requires in the way of supply for a 9-month voyage and crew of 400+. The agents have read private mail written (apparently to wife or lover) by Jack's Admiral Drury. Jack is incensed, refuses further cooperation. A huge Native American doorman helps Jack and Stephen against the officials: Stephen has been addressing him only with grunts, now discovers the man is highly educated and literate, both of his grandfathers attended Harvard Indian College (established 1665, this school still exists: Harvard's first brick building). He hates all governmental officials equally, hence his help. HMS Shannon, frigate, is on the Boston blockade, comes close inshore every morning to check the American fleet. Capt Lawrence of USS Chesapeake brings Jack news of Mowatt (one of Jack's protégés) who was injured aboard the sunk Peacock, then taken prisoner and with whom Lawrence got along famously. Diana panicked over the possibility of being taken up for spying when Wogan was caught, was taken to America by Johnson, who got her to accept American citizenship... she is now an American insofar as the English are concerned. Johnson overtly tries to recruit Stephen into American intelligence.

192 - Jack still in the hospital, has recovered to the point he is actively rehabilitating his damaged right arm, using a side-table as an exercise weight.

197 - Choate asks Stephen for help with an urgent suprapubic cystotomy, Stephen's famous operation.

198 - Stephen, worried about lonely, difficult nights, gets a pint of laudanum from Choate: apparently he intends to dose himself again. He is depressed, does not know if he does, or even can, still love Diana - much less what to do about it. The operation itself is a success, and there is "...a real likelihood that the man might live."

200 - Having realized that he is likely human and subject to the emotional sturm and drang he sees in others around him but to which he has always felt himself immune, Stephen knocks himself out with laudanum.

209 - Stephen musing on Diana as a woman of courage, wonders --- if constipation can affect a man's courage (and he clearly believes that it can!), then "...how much more might an adverse phase of the moon affect a woman's?" Even the highly educated, scientific-minded and rational Stephen is still imbued with pre-medieval claptrap and superstition.

Book 6 Chapter 7 - p217-252: (overview) Stephen is deeply worried that Johnson, together with French agent Dubreuil, will figure out his role as agent provocateur. Jack's blundering conversations with Johnson do not help at all. Jack has known Capt Broke of Shannon since childhood, gives Stephen a multipage synopsis of the man's life and career. Stephen's room and papers are rifled, but discreetly. Stephen is now in fear for his own life, takes defensive measures - asks Jack to get a brace of pistols, and arms himself with a heavy surgical knife. The French clumsily attempt to capture Stephen in a crowd: he foils them by screaming 'stop thief!!!' and falling to the ground. The gathering crowd believes Stephen, and the French depart in haste. Stephen makes arrangements to marry Diana - this will get her English citizenship back. The French make another, more concerted effort to abduct Stephen - they chase him on foot through the nighttime fog. He goes to ground at Diana's apartments, literally under her bed-covers while a search is made of the premises - it misses him. Two French agents enter Johnson's quarters where Stephen is hiding. In the dark, Stephen uses a heavy obsidian phallus paper-weight from Johnson's desk to literally cold-cock the first agent, whose throat he immediately cuts in perfect cold blood. Shortly thereafter the second agent comes in search of #1: This is Dubreuil, whom Stephen shoots through the heart point-blank. Diana returns, is unfazed by the gore and bodies; Stephen collects all of Johnson's private espionage and intelligence papers, Diana retrieves her huge diamond. They send an explanatory note to Jack. Now they have no choice, must escape before Johnson returns. The situation thoroughly re-unites Stephen and Diana: she agrees to marry him. Jack calls in favors and asks the senior Herapath to hide Jack, Stephen and Diana in one of his merchantmen. Next morning in the fog the three take a skiff and sail it out to meet Shannon (Capt Broke) as she comes in for a morning survey of the American fleet.

245 - Stephen has been injured while being chased on foot by the French agents: in Johnson and Diana's quarters, he self-diagnoses cracked 8th and 9th ribs and a mild concussion.

248 - Stephen cuts the throat of a French agent whom he has beaten into unconsciousness.

249 - Stephen shoots point blank another French agent (Dubreuil), killing him as well.

Book 6 Chapter 8 - p253-293: (overview)   Herapath Senior helps arrange a carriage to one of his ships wherein there is an excellent hidey-hole for seamen, to keep them from being pressed. Horses bolt, they walk to the ship. Herapath (son) provides guidance and food. Early morning, they take the ship's skiff and sail off to meet the incoming Shannon. Enroute they are passed and ignored by Capt Lawrence's boats from Chesapeake, practicing high-speed rowing for cutting-out expeditions. They are welcomed aboard Shannon with amazement. Aboard Shannon, food and water are running short: Jack helps Captain Broke compose a gentleman's challenge to Capt Lawrence, proposing that Chesapeake and Shannon meet in single unsupported combat. Accepted. (NOTE - Historically it seems unlikely that this written challenge was ever received, although it most certainly was written and sent.) Discussions of steamboats - trepidation for the future of the sailing navy. Broke has burnt all 24 of his prizes so as not to reduce Shannon's crew by sending in prize-crews. Broke like Jack believes in the great guns - in practice his ship beats Jack's personal best for time between broadsides.

272 - In the skiff in the harbor enroute from Herapath's ship to meet Shannon, Diana gets seasick immediately.

280 - In the open Atlantic's midwinter swell and chop, Diana is monstrously, debilitatingly seasick. There is an open question as to whether she is pregnant or not.

 288 - Discussions between Stephen and the Shannon's surgeon as to the mind/body connections, with examples from naval combat.

Book 6 Chapter 9 - p294-329: (overview)   (NOTE: Aboard Shannon is a very young Lt Provo Wallis, a real participant of this non-fictional battle, who progressed to become Admiral of the Fleet and died at the age of 100 still on active duty.) Broke is prepared to meet Chesapeake if it can be arranged. Stephen asks Broke to marry him to Diana - Broke does not know the regulations and is busy - the wedding is postponed because Chesapeake is coming out for battle. Diana stowed well below-decks out of harm's way... unless they should be recaptured by Chesapeake, in which case they can all be assured of being hanged. Stephen binds Jacks bad arm tightly, with a steel dish over it as armor. The ships close. Battle, furious indeed, one of the deadliest frigate battles ever fought in Royal Navy history. Broke lays Shannon alongside Chesapeake, leads the boarding party. Lawrence is gut-shot with grape, stays conscious, understands his injuries are fatal, dies four days later. Broke takes a savage saber-cut to the head, loses a large chunk of skull so that the brain is exposed: it is more than a year before he recovers, but he does so. Fifteen minutes from first gun until Chesapeake strikes: an error by the boarders' Lt Watt in striking the Chesapeake's colors results in one final cannon shot which literally in the moment of victory kills Watt and several others. Broke is conscious despite his head wound, indicates to Jack that he understands he has won.

295 - Jack ruminates on what his increasing age will bring him in terms of reduced health and activity

324 - Heat of battle aboard Shannon - the man next to Jack falls, astonished, eviscerated by a bar-shot. Jack sees Chesapeak's helmsman killed at the wheel. In the boarding, the bosun has his arm cut off by a saber.

Book 7 - The Surgeon's Mate

Book 7 Chapter 1 - p9-42: (overview)   Halifax, Nova Scotia. HMS Shannon brings in USS Chesapeake. The quite junior Mr Wallis now captains Shannon; Mr Falkiner is prize-captain of Chesapeake. Jack, Stephen and Diana escaped from Boston to Shannon just before the battle. Admiral greets Jack, knows of Stephen, meets Diana and invites her to stay with his family. Jack expects to get the frigate HMS Acasta (40). Jack's financial affairs ashore are in a horrible muddle due to Jack's gullibility - he invested with a charlatan, to refine silver from old waste from ancient lead mines on his property. Stephen and Diana are engaged to be married - sometime, somewhere: until that, she is an American citizen in a difficult position. Her keeper in Boston, Mr Johnson, is enormously rich and vindictive, and head of American Intelligence. Stephen meets with Marine Major Beck, head of Intelligence in the N. American station. Beck knows some of Stephen's exploits, is disappointed by Stephen's nondescript appearance, regains respect in spades when Stephen says he personally killed the two senior French agents in Boston, and stole all of Johnson's private "intelligence" materials, which he discusses with Beck. Stephen clears Diana, with English Intelligence, of any espionage or disloyal activities: he also (as always) refuses all payment for services, which surprises Beck. He ruminates on marriage. Wray, the top-level security leak in the Navy administration (a fact unknown to Stephen) is now acting second secretary. Jack long ago accused Wray, in public, of cheating at cards. Having Wray be so directly above Jack is unfortunate for Jack's career. In addition, Adm Harte is to be Jack's commanding officer - Jack cuckolded the Admiral years ago (his wife Molly had quite a coterie): this is known to the Admiral. Change - Jack is not to have Acasta but to return to England. Funeral for Capt Lawrence - Brits and Americans all attend. Later, a grand ball: Diana's gown a hit. Scientists and their work held to be above the squabbles of war - travel, meetings, publications - all freely engaged in, without problems, despite hostilities.

116

10 - Captain Broke of HMS Shannon has a severe head-wound, barely alive. Shannon's losses include Lt. Watt and 22 crew: sickbay has 59 wounded.

11 - Chesapeake's casualties: Capt Lawrence, plus "...above 60 killed and 90 wounded."

13 - Jack's musket-ball wound to his right arm is still debilitating. Stephen says Broke cannot be disturbed even for the Admiral to congratulate him - not until "...the draught has had its effect." (As usual we get no specifics about the 'draught'.) Stephen has been on duty continuously for some days, treating wounded.

14   Stephen has "...an amputation on my hands" at the moment. Admiral, congratulating Jack, recognizes Stephen, who is known for having been called in to treat the Duke himself.

15 - Diana is helping Stephen, encounters the Admiral whilst she is carrying body parts in a basin, for disposal. Someone - presumably Stephen's amputee - is shrieking in the sick-bay belowdecks.

16 - Wounded taken ashore to hospital: Broke to the Commissioner's house for convalescence.

18 - Brief discussion between Jack and Diana as to Jack's wife Sophie having had a "bad time" in her most recent labor. Jack is oblivious, simply does not know.

30 - News of Capt Broke - he is very slowly recovering from his near-fatal head wound. Physician of the fleet Dr Harrington shows Stephen a case of 'military' fever (typhoid – aka one form of 'miliary' fever) in twins – they have perfectly symmetrical symptoms.

39 - At the Admiral's, a footman (Bullock) recognizes Stephen as the surgeon who saved his leg from amputation aboard Surprise years earlier. His leg is missing now -- lost to a bar-shot in another ship.

40 - Stephen upbraids Jack about his weight, appetite and diet - for the umpteenth time.

41 - Stephen meets a doctor specialist in birthing, and pumps him for details to seek in determining pregnant vs not so. Suspicion is that Diana may be pregnant, by Johnson.

Book 7 Chapter 2 - p43-71: (overview)   At the Admiral's ball, Stephen ruminates on the huge social and educational diversity found in the Navy officer corps - with an even wider diversity of wives, a diversity startling in both physique and couture. Jack is targeted by a reasonably attractive harpy -Miss Smith- against whom nobody will warn him openly. Diana knows the woman and has seen her in action in India. Smith is wily and resourceful - - Jack is seduced, then publicly embarrassed, and ultimately blackmailed with a false tale of pregnancy. Jack is so thoroughly an innocent that he would never believe any woman could follow such an evil, underhanded course.

61 - Jack returns in early morning to his quarters at the inn (shared with Stephen): Stephen notes that Jack's injured arm is clearly irritated from overuse (Jack spent a very active night with his Harpy), orders the arm back into a sling.

63 - Stephen finally allows Diana's pregnancy to break through his unconscious resistance to its existence, berates himself for being a common man and seeing what he wishes to see rather than what actually is there.

69 - Confrontation between Stephen and Diana - the source of both her increasing distance from Stephen, and especially of her on-going postponement of their marriage, is revealed - she acknowledges her pregnancy by Johnson and declares she will not marry any man whilst carrying another man's child. Stephen calms her, points out that marriage to him will solve her citizenship problem and eliminate the problems of bastardy for the child, at a stroke. She absolutely refuses, and begs Stephen (a strict Spanish Catholic) for an abortion. He refuses, continues to offer marriage.

Book 7 Chapter 3 - p72-95: (overview)   Jack et al. are aboard private British ship Diligence owner/captain Dalgleish, headed to England: incidentally and unofficially they are carrying first-news of Shannon's victory. Private ship Liberty discovered nearby, a notorious privateer. Liberty and a partner schooner chase Diligence, ignoring all other concerns and distractions (e.g. prizes). Dalgleish knows the other captain too well to want to fight - flight is best. Pursuit goes through the Grand Banks cod-fishing fleet, into heavy fog and ice. Jack and Dalgleish work the ship together to avoid capture, it being clear that for some reason Diligence is the pursuers' sole concern - Diana, almost in a stupor, leads speculation that Johnson, vindictive and angry, has hired the pair of vessels, seeking to retake Diana, the diamonds he gave her, and his intelligence papers. Discussions of the banks, fog, currents, codfish, birds. Liberty chases Diligence through dangerously dense fog laced with small icebergs- very single-minded indeed. Wind becomes fluky, slightly favoring the pursuers who gain. Liberty opens fire: Stephen goes below to fill powder (one of his very rare non-medical active participations in battle). If necessary, he will also aid Jack in fighting the Diligence's carronade. Pursuers set up a pincers-movement to take Diligence from both sides at once: Diligence prepares to give its best, when Liberty at full speed runs squarely into ice, dismasts herself, shears away her stem and forefoot and sinks within minutes, ending the chase. Diligence continues towards England, likely to make a record crossing due to the speed displayed in avoiding capture.

77 - Diana utterly prostrated by seasickness.

80 - Stephen doses Diana with laudanum to stop the dry heaves.

94 - After the chase ends, Stephen checks on Diana who is suddenly fully recovered and sitting in her cabin with two loaded pistols in hand, fearing capture by Johnson, a fear now needless.

Book 7 Chapter 4 - p96-131: (overview) [NOTE - no significant medical activity – chapter is devoted to politics and domestic problems.] Dalgleish cracks on mightily to get to England, but arrives behind the news of Shannon's win - all England is in an exultant uproar. Jack rides to Ashgrove Cottage, his family home ashore. Re-acquaints himself with his twin daughters and younger son, not to mention wife Sophie. Jack's evaporated command of Acasta is softened by her captain volunteering to send Jack whatever members of the crew he might want for his next command - but Jack is in no hurry for a new command. Jack's uncontrollable

father, the General, is running for parliament, where he will undoubtedly be forever on the wrong side, continually embarrassing
Jack and doing irreparable damage to Jack's career. The General's
parliamentary antics have already prevented Jack's getting a
knighthood for sinking the Dutch warship Waakzaamheid. Jack
dashes off to give the news about Shannon, and a health report,
to Capt Broke's wife. Jack becomes deeply involved in straighten-
ing out the Kimber-silver mess... but Sophie is beginning to understand business and has mostly taken charge. Stephen undertakes (through his boss, Sir Joseph) to find a competent lawyer
for Jack, to disentangle his affairs over the silver. Stephen gives
all of Johnson's papers to Sir Joseph, who is ecstatic - he now has
complete inside knowledge of the entire American intelligence
operation. Stephen is his star, and this his best coup yet. Description of the political and military scene in Europe. Worries that
Napoleon may yet succeed in taking all of Europe. Militarily,
things are delicate - five minutes of conversation in the right
place might be worth a whole squadron of the line, or an army,
especially in Spain - Stephen undertakes to provide that conversation, clandestinely - but first he will go to Paris to address the
Academy. Sir Joseph will provide documents to clarify and confirm Diana's status as a loyal English subject.

107 - Some of Jack's household "servants" - former sailors all -
return from town 'paralytic' meaning in an alcoholic coma or close to
it: they have been celebrating Shannon's victory.

Book 7 Chapter 5 - p132-160: (overview) Another chapter with
essentially no medical activity. Diana's pregnancy by Johnson is
progressing. Discussions and thoughts on pregnancy and especially on actually having small children about. Paris still open and
cultured, the hub of Europe despite the war: Stephen opines "We
are at war with Napoleon, not with Paris." Stephen and Diana go
to Paris together, where she is established as houseguest of male
socialite Mssr. LeMothe who is thoroughly gay but believes himself undetected. Knowing he may have to travel soon, Stephen
engages for Diana Paris's best accoucheur (male midwife), Mssr.
Baudelocque. Extensive ruminations on architecture, girlfriends,
fox-hunting, corruption of various sorts, etc. Jack's American

embarrassment, Miss Smith, writes to declare her enduring love, that she is pregnant by him, and she needs a few hundred pounds which will enable her to come to his side in England. Jack is aghast, cannot conceive of a woman being part of a scam, and sends money, with reasons for her not to come. In Paris strictly as a scientist, Stephen is repeatedly asked to carry messages back to England - refuses all such requests as probable traps. Discussions between Stephen and Diana on clothing and other minor social issues. Stephen mumbles his way through his talk - a monstrously bad presenter: his "...beginning was bad, the continuation worse." So bad that French intelligence agents in the audience, studying him, conclude he cannot be smart enough to be a threat. M. Ponsich, a Catalan like Stephen, and also a very senior English intelligence agent (well loved by Stephen) has been sent on a critical mission to Scandinavia, where his ship "met with a disaster" and was lost with all hands. Stephen is offered that mission, and accepts.

132 - Diana's pregnancy renders her in blooming good health, but Stephen senses an underlying distress.

134 - Diana is following Stephen's advice - little wine and no tobacco during her pregnancy.

138 - Touring Paris with Diana, Stephen points out where as students he and a now-famous anatomist "...used to share our corpses."

Book 7 Chapter 6 - p161-192: (overview)   Jack is worried about Miss Smith's letters falling into Sophie's hands, hence daily intercepts the post when it arrives. His worries interfere with his relations with Sophie. Stephen vaguely describes his own new mission in 'northern waters', asks whether Jack might be interested in a short interim command connected to that mission. Jack accepts eagerly, poorly-charted shoal waters, rocky shores, active enemy ashore and likely bad weather notwithstanding - it will get him away from all his domestic problems, including Miss Smith. (It is never made clear just how any further letters from Ms Smith are to be kept from other eyes (e.g. Sophie's) during Jack's northern command.) The mission is dangerous - Agent Ponsich's ship was set afire and blown up by coastal gunfire, and Stephen will have to be put ashore essentially under those guns. The mission's goal is to gain control of the territory by subversion, not direct force of arms - subversion being a Stephen specialty. Success would remove a major northern support (the Scandinavian countries) for Napoleon's "all-Europe" ambitions. Ruminations on marriage, celibacy, monogamy. Catalan troops occupy and control the major island: Stephen of course is Catalan. That force is commanded by Stephen's own Godfather, to whom he is exceedingly close. All this makes Stephen the ideal agent to attempt subversion, particularly since those troops are largely disgruntled (mostly due to no wine and no tobacco). Reminiscences of Stephen's growing-up with Godfather. Jack meets Jagiello, a ridiculously handsome -even beautiful- blond Swedish officer - minor royalty- in his pink uniform. He will be part of the expedition. Women of all ages and social standings continually throw themselves at him (almost literally), but he appears immune - disinterested, deeply naive and thus puzzled, but certainly not gay. The mission is urgent: Jack takes command of HMS sloop of war Ariel (18), evicting her captain in the midst of a formal dinner, sets sail instantly, and has the guns practicing live firing before he clears the harbor. Ariel is a fine, responsive little French-built ship - Jack chased her twice -unsuccessfully- when she was still in the French Navy.

162 - Sophie asks Stephen to check Jack - he seems not to be himself lately. Jack is allover nerves about Miss Smith.

166 - Jack tells Stephen about Miss Smith, her condition and demands. Stephen points out the possibility of fraud (Jack instantly and vehemently declares this to be impossible), and the likelihood of miscarriage if true: the possibility of false pregnancy: from a medical point of view, he advises wait-and-see.

168 - At their inn, The Grapes: the inn's people like Stephen and Jack - Stephen has cured the proprietress Mrs Broad of the marthambles, and two servants of "a less creditable disease" (undoubtedly some form of VD). Grapes' personnel are used to Stephen's odd ways, up to and including the occasional dead orphan child he purchases for dissection and stows in the closet.

176 - Visiting Sir Joseph at his home, Stephen notes that the erotic vases and art have disappeared. Blaine asks Stephen's professional medical opinion on a man his age marrying - clearly worrying about sexual capacity and capabilities. Stephen reassures him that all things are possible.

188 - In the first few minutes aboard Ariel, Jagiello (a tall man unaccustomed to the confines of small ships) drives his head into a beam, receiving a not-serious but bloody gash.

Book 7 Chapter 7 - p193-220: (overview) Sailing north towards Denmark, Ariel's crew is much better than Jack had expected. Jack is an adrenalin junkie: thoughts about war-fighting at sea being a "proper life for a real man", etc. Jagiello, landlubber, is accident prone and incredibly lucky - many falls and other mishaps including going overboard, yet he has only an injured hand to show. He is invaluable for his humor, conversation, skill at chess, and his innumerable contacts ashore. Pontifications about the (im?)possibility of true friendship between men and women. Jagiello thinks he could love and befriend a genuine Amazon, but certainly nothing less. Ariel encounters a 28-ship Baltic convoy (friendly). Port of call Gothenburg, a town whose citizens are melancholy and "...much given to self-murder..." The port liberally supplies Ariel with munitions. They head north again, in difficult waters (narrow, shallow, strongly tidal) with enemy batteries on shores too close for comfort. They pass Elsinore: Jagiello has been there many times, points out Hamlet's grave. Danes lob 200-pound explosive mortar shells which fall just short. Ariel collects fish killed by the shells' subsurface explosions. Jack reminisces about playing Ophelia aboard ship as a youngster, got three curtain calls. All watch the mortar shells in flight. A storm produces extremely choppy seas and almost all aboard are seasick. Ariel reports in to the Admiral of the Baltic Fleet - Sir James Saumarez: the Admiral's brother and Stephen are acquainted. Jack's thoughts on the art of command. The Admiral's political officer briefs Stephen and Jack. Objective is to put Stephen ashore to convince the Catalan troops to retire from the field without a battle they do not want, and with full military honors. Perhaps they may even be convinced to join the English side on the continent against Napoleon... who clearly intends no good towards Catalonia. Stephen must go ashore in a civilian non-British vessel, with alcohol and tobacco to enthuse the Catalan troops. Ariel must try to find such a vessel (a merchantman catboat), one of which they bypassed enroute.

195 - Jagiello, a complete lubber aboard ship, almost loses a finger to a slipping lock on a nine-pounder. Treated by Stephen.

197 - Mr Hyde tends to confuse right and left, and is left-handed - Stephen ponders whether there is a cause/effect relationship, and if the confusion results from "an inversion of sounds" (whatever that may be).

211 - Stephen is seasick, unimpressed by the ship's surgeon ("a mere sot"), seeking ten drops of sulfurous ether (= today's diethyl ether) or "acid of sulfur, dulcified". (NOTE: Today's diethylether is the original surgical anesthetic, first so used ~1840s but available much earlier and then taken either by inhalation or swallowing - some effects resemble those of alcohol. 'Dulcified' is mysterious - it means 'sweetened' but adding sugar to sulfuric acid is a common junior-high-chemistry demonstration, and merely chars the sugar.) The surgeon has drunk up all the sulfurous ether and spilt the liquid sulfuric acid, which is eating into the deck.

Book 7 Chapter 8 - p221-260: (overview)   Ariel is re-provisioned with breathtaking speed, sets off to find the catboat which has about 48 hours of head-start and is on an uncertain course. Encouraging the lookouts: 10-guinea reward plus 'remission of sins short of mutiny, sodomy or damaging the paintwork' for the first man to sight the catboat. Thoughts on aging and relative ages. They encounter an unexpected ship, the Danish Minnie, pursue her instead of the cat. They overhaul Minnie but daren't shoot at her - they need her intact. They encounter a brig, HMS "Humbug" and enlist her aid in pursuing Minnie, who is headed for shoal water. Jagiello is still wearing his spurs, which catch in a rope and trip him: he removes them. Minnie goes aground; some crew/passengers are desperate not to be taken, and abandon ship in a rowboat headed for shore. A warning shot does not work, Ariel sinks the escape boat, killing all but one occupant. Together Ariel and Humbug refloat Minnie. A recalcitrant Minnie officer refuses to answer questions until Jagiello takes him below decks privately - the information flows thereafter, including the private signals declaring nationality. Stephen invents a ruse, which he sells to Jack - Minnie (with a crew of Ariels disguised as Danes) to sail into harbor being pursued by Ariel, to confuse the garrison and render an improper private signal acceptable. Ariel's men hate the idea which requires them to exchange clothing with the Minnie prisoners - who are lousy. Jack announces a bonus "hard-duty pay" for the effort. Stephen lectures on the different species of human louse, reassures the crew. A Catalan flag flown on the breakwater will signal Stephen's success. The ruse works - Minnie sails in un-opposed, the shore batteries drive Ariel back to sea. Going ashore to do subversion, Stephen falls into the water between the boat and dock whilst trying to disembark, roars for help in Catalan, stuns the reception committee. His Godfather is present, they greet one another energetically. Next day an agreement is reached to embark the Catalan infantry and all gear, with full military honors: a bloodless coup. Ariel is badly overloaded with warm bodies. Extensive overblown honors (21 guns, etc.) to the Catalans and especially Godfather himself - a first-class egomaniac in the best Spanish tradition.

240 - The only survivor from the rowboat, a 17-year old French officer badly wounded and unconscious is brought aboard Ariel, treated by Stephen for head and leg injuries.

244 - Stephen's patient seems to be doing well, is still in a coma - but Stephen intuits oncoming death for him.

252 - The young wounded prisoner dies, never recovering consciousness.

Book 7 Chapter 9- p261-311: (overview) A triumphant return to meet the Admiral. Jack exhausted both from work and from handling the Godfather with kid gloves, and without a mutual language. Great conviviality at the Admiral's table for dinner. Ariel to go to Hano Bay, thence with a convoy to the Broad Fourteens: Stephen will be sole determiner of what to do with the

"Spanish" troops. The convoy and escort constitute 783 vessels. (ASIDE: this is not a ridiculous number – convoys of over 2000 sail are recorded.) Jagiello has found a woman in his bed - a well-known actress nicknamed "The Gentlemen's Relish"; the Governor's personal harlot; a singing harlot of great price, who came aboard with the Catalonians. He is embarrassed and distinctly not interested: Jack will send her ashore immediately via rowboat. Other women are pursuing Jagiello - including two Admirals' daughters. Convoy sets off, dead slow. Storm coming. Chronometer broken. Discussion of navigation. Stephen's pocket watch must do, and it is good only to a minute a day. Stephen gives infantryman Jagiello a miraculously accurate explanation of winds and relative motions, including leeway, using coins on the tabletop to diagram things. Jack misses out on it, would never believe such a thing possible! They encounter a chase - HMS Jason two miles behind Meduse, a French 72 - new and clean and very fast indeed. Jack is ordered to leave the convoy and help. Pursuit through increasingly nasty weather: Meduse turns, fires, loses her foretopmast. Ariel's fire destroys a sail on Meduse and slows her: she disengages and heads for port again. Jason continue pursuit: the major ships vanish into the storm. That night, with a week of thick weather and no observations behind her, the lookout reports "Breakers under the lee!", then "Breakers ahead!". Jack manages an emergency anchoring essentially in the surf, between two deadly reefs. Daylight, they figure out where they are: a fort nearby shells them, accurately. Jack has to club-haul Ariel. The leadsman casts badly, the lead cold-cocks Jack, and at the critical moment left-handed Hyde, suddenly in command, mistakes left for right and sends the ship ashore through the surf, breaking her back as she bounces across the reef.

279 - The Colonel (Godfather) is in bed seasick.

282 - Stephen has his first erotic dream since getting back together with Diana.

288 - In the transports accompanying Ariel: "Hundreds of seasick soldiers belowdecks."

Book 7 Chapter 10 - p312-344: (overview)   Ariel's crew go ashore after the wreck, near Brest, and are interned. Semi-facetious complaints about food, especially bread being too full of holes to be nutritious. Fully facetious information given to French authorities by the Brits - all but one of Ariel's officers claim descent from Queen Anne; father's name = Creeping Jenny. Etcetera. Jack is threatened with incarceration in Bitche, a notoriously rigorous and unhealthy French prison. Jagiello is instantly pursued by a prison serving girl who brings far more food than requested and asks Jagiello to step out into the hall with her to make payment. French Intelligence agent Duhamel escorts Ariel's officers (by carriage) to a Paris prison: Duhamel is a gourmand and puts himself in charge of food, which is excellent... except that a bad batch of crayfish gives all a serious case of diarrhea and there is almost no privacy in the entire passing landscape - being prudish sailors, privacy is a MUST. They arrive at the prison at a dead run for the facilities. Stephen ruminates on the continental intelligence service, then on Diana (now living in Paris in M LeMothe's home). In "Temple" prison: the three share a cell far above ground, with windows and a private privy - a stone shelf overhanging the moat, which might yield an escape route. Jagiello flirts with a nearby girl, she does laundry and food for prisoners, he gets her to send them supplies and -led by Jack- they begin trying to open an escape route. Meanwhile, helping cover their rock-mining exercises, Temple is literally being disassembled around them. Stephen calls for a local physician, Dr Larry, introduces himself, makes certain that the fellow will tell all of Paris about Stephen's presence in the Temple - thus precluding their being clandestinely disposed of by the French Intelligence services. Hearing that Diana will likely miscarry, Stephen philosophizes about bringing children into the world. Dr Larry provides Stephen with "ampullae" which are probably glass capsules of cyanide. Weeks pass whilst the Temple's razing continues and they keep excavating the privy seat. Eventually the girl sends a cold chisel, tiny pulley and some line - all in the food/laundry basket.

321 - The prison-bound party dines on tainted crawfish - massive diarrhea follows. Stephen gets permission to buy medicine (and a "horse-sized enema") from a nearby apothecary, and knocks Jack out

with laudanum - then the same for Jagiello and Duhamel. He could have killed Duhamel out of hand with poison included in the purchase... but that would be against Stephen's sense of medical honor and also useless due to their escort. The drugs temporarily control the problem.

324 - Nearing prison "Temple" in Paris, all have urgent renewed need for facilities as diarrhea returns with a vengeance.

332- In prison, Parisian physician Dr Larry, overawed by Stephen's reputation, brings Stephen a message from Dr Baudelocque that Diana's foetus is not likely to be viable... possibly due to prolonged seasickness.

Book 7 Chapter 11 - p345-382; (overview)   Stephen is interviewed by French Intelligence: they are not particularly adept. Stephen confuses them about his identity, and basically refuses to cooperate at all, citing rules of war. To persuade him, the French, in Stephen's sight, execute a man by firing squad. Stephen has seen much worse, is unmoved, remains convinced that the French have no solid information about him. Someone has offered a huge sum for Stephen's release: he is puzzled. Stephen and Duhamel execute a finely structured verbal and logical minuet concerning whether Stephen is in fact an agent capable of carrying vital information to the proper recipients in England - information about potential anti-Buonaparte activities or tendencies at high level in France: neither man is willing to actually concede or reveal anything substantive. Duhamel appears, possibly, to be himself anti-Napoleon: to show good faith, he surrenders his pistols to Stephen when asked. He, or his office, has accepted the mysterious offer of a huge diamond for Stephen's release. Stephen knows the offer can only come from Diana... the huge diamond "Blue Peter" is her personal treasure. Stephen realizes that much of his impression of Diana is profoundly wrong. Duhamel brings a Navy Gazette, which bears the news of Miss Smith's marriage to a Captain of Marines named Lushington, thereby relieving Jack of her further pursuit. Stephen is at last confronted and identified by Johnson: now escape is both more critical and more difficult. Returned at night to the communal cell, Stephen demands that they move on making their escape - they shove the privy-seat (a huge slab of rock) loose and it falls, the sound of a falling rock being nothing special due to all the disassembly. Duhamel arrives with several other apparently high-ranking officials who are part of the plan to return the three prisoners - presumably mostly for Stephen's ability to carry to the right places in England the news of disquiet at high French levels. The missing slab makes Duhamel et al.'s job (spiriting the prisoners away, to a ship bound for England) easier because the opening could have been their escape route... no illicit aid from anti-Buonapartistas need be invoked. Duhamel provides transportation, offers money (which Stephen as usual refuses). He gives Stephen an amethyst Episcopal ring as a sign of good faith and of intent to return the Blue Peter to Diana. Even better, they can tonight produce the diamond's owner, who is eager to travel with them. They collect Diana at laMothe's home: she and Stephen have an emotional reunion in the carriage, she says "Fie" about the large diamond and the necklace, she has miscarried and is at pains to tell Stephen she did nothing to encourage it. Duhamel gives Stephen documents to carry to England: together they do a final edit whilst belting along in the carriage to Calais.   Safely aboard the ship HMS Oedipus (sic!), with Babbington as captain. Babbington, one of Jack's protégés, has for years, since he was a young teen-ager, pursued Diana like a puppy with its tongue out, utterly infatuated and completely hopeless. Now married to Admiral Harte's daughter, he gets to marry Diana to Stephen aboard Oedipus in mid-Channel, with Jack to give away the bride and using Duhamel's Episcopal ring.

356 - Being taken for another round of interrogation, Stephen slips one of the glass ampullae (ampulla = capsule, designed for suicide - probably containing cyanide) into his mouth as a precaution. It is not needed.

357 - Duhamel asks Stephen's medical advice for his bowel problem, which was caused by the crayfish episode, and has never fully resolved. Stephen prescribes for him.

364 - Stephen is interrogated, held in a cell with a false prisoner (a planted agent) who is provided with "little bladders of gore" - presumably to make the man appear to have been badly beaten and thus to frighten Stephen.

375 - Diana reports to Stephen on her miscarriage, which was spontaneous and unavoidable according to her doctor - a doctor whom Stephen chose and in whom Stephen clearly believes. Stephen understands.

382 - Stephen and Diana are married aboard ship by Babbington.

Book 8 - The Ionian Mission

Book 8 Chapter 1 - p9-38: (overview) (Very little 'medical') - Thoughts on marriage: what are the best living arrangements for "un-housebroken" Stephen (slovenly; socially reclusive) and new wife Diana (intensely social and fashionable)? Separate apartments blocks apart. Stephen's penchant for unorthodox biology does not bother his landlady. Jack has temporary orders to HMS Worcester (74), a miserably-built ship, so badly constructed as to be dangerous to sail. Jack takes the temporary command to avoid the law ashore: he apparently responded physically - inappropriately- to some form of legal service. Worcester is headed for blockade duty against the French fleet in Toulon, in the Med. Stephen will go ashore in France near Toulon to meet clandestinely with a secret anti-Napoleon coalition. Stephen arrives dockside late, as usual, and almost causes Jack to miss his tide.

11 - Discussion of the use of "whole orphans" for Stephen's anatomical dissections - in good supply near winter's end.

22 - Stephen advises Diana not to stretch too intensely in playing billiards - there is a strong possibility that she is pregnant again (this time by her husband, Stephen).

31 - Jagiello's arm severely wrenched in lost-wheel carriage incident enroute to ship.

34 - Ship's crew includes many who have been treated (e.g., amputations, VD) by Stephen aboard other vessels. The crew likes him extremely.

38 - The officers' "port" seems to be mostly impure raw alcohol, perhaps lead acetate, and cochineal (ground red beetles used as dye). A not unusual situation.

Book 8 Chapter 2 - p39-69: (overview)   Bringing ship up to full complement, mostly via pressed men - largely inexperienced - and drafts of criminals. Stephen inspects new seamen: Jack rejects -diplomatically- candidate midshipmen and ship's boys. Jack may have to transport seven clergy - bad luck in the extreme! Philosophical discussion of social rank and the concept of subordination. Moral vs natural philosophy (aka religion vs science). Jack bought the gunpowder stock of a fireworks factory: various ages, grinds, and colorants, but CHEAP. The gunner sorts them out by taste while randomly filling cartridges for long-gun exercises. The guns fire huge clouds of brilliantly colored smoke and flame, to the endless amusement of the entire ship's crew. Next exercise - to cruise the French shoreline, shooting up shore installations. Jack encounters and pursues French Jemmapes (74): the intensely-colored fireworks powder is accidentally used in the great guns, and the shock of the sight (what new secret weapon is this?) sends the Frenchman racing for cover, ending the chase.

41 - Stephen, vehemently opposed to impressment, invents medical reasons for rejecting men who are established in trades or have families.

46 - Lt Pullings, one of Jack's long-term protégés - is angry with Stephen for rejecting impressed men - Stephen considers giving him "a comfortable dose" of laudanum, which will by morning restore the Lieutenant's original amiable personality.

58 - One colorant additive in Jack's powder is antimony: Stephen is worried that the master gunner may have tasted too much of it - it is somewhat poisonous. Used as an expectorant and emetic.

68 - Butcher's bill for brief encounter with French Jemmapes (74) is no fatalities, three splinter wounds, and one

crushed foot. Plus the ominous report "...the Doctor has copped it."

<u>Book 8 Chapter 3 - p70-97: (overview)</u> Stephen is wounded in the feet and scalp, suffers endless medical advice and prescriptions from visitors. At Gibraltar he discusses with Rev Graham deception as a military tactic - what can and cannot be done. Graham tries clumsily to enlist Stephen as a spy - offer rejected. "The nautical mind has its own logic." Stephen does a play on words - "being jocose" - on Graham, who cannot stomach and will not stand for any humor or jokes involving himself. When he discovers the joke, at dinner, he rejects any further contact with Stephen, eventually leaving the ship in a considerable huff. Five of the clergy debark. Mr Martin, a one-eyed clergyman and also natural historian like Stephen (his eye was destroyed by an owl), will remain as Stephen's assistant; he is not booked as clergy - the crew are relieved. Mr Somers, a new officer, is a braggart and drunk - and no seaman. Martin is a jewel, fits in perfectly.

70 - Stephen has been unlucky in this short battle - hit by a falling block, then a lump of wood ripped off half his scalp, and finally a large splinter pierced both of his feet. All non-critical but exceedingly bloody and painful. Stephen self-prescribes laudanum for the pain. He is pestered by an incessant parade of visitors, each of whom prescribes some personal-favorite nostrum for his injuries.

89 - Somers is seriously drunk at supper: Stephen gives him Lucatellus' balsam next morning, for the after-effects.

97 - Adm Thornton and the Physician of the Fleet both want to see Stephen.

<u>Book 8 Chapter 4 - p98-127: (overview)</u> Meeting up with the blockading fleet under Adm Thornton - Jack is appalled at how the Adm has aged. Discussion of the Med Admiral's overload of important/critical duties. Discussions of courts-martial - their misuse for settling trivial wardroom differences. Admiral is aware of Stephen's mission, agrees with it, badly needs better intelligence. His support for Stephen includes Jack and HMS Worcester. Discussion of the problems of running an intelligence operation consisting of many uncoordinated, even opposing, parts. Jack has plenty of time, and good sailing weather, to work up his crew aboard Worcester. Jack visits Adm Mitchell, a very old acquaintance: they race to the jack-crosstrees - the crew study Jack for signs of possible apoplexy: Jack's face is purple, the crew are happy.

106 - Stephen confers with Harrington, Physician of the Fleet. Fleet, overall, is remarkably healthy: no scurvy (Mediterranean fruit readily at hand). No VD (ships rarely enter port, hence no exposure).

107 - More discussion of the effects of mind (happiness, resolve, etc) on the state and functioning of the body. Adm Thornton as a difficult patient, worn down physically by his duties, and being treated only with bark and steel.

108 - Aboard the flagship, Doctor Harrington shows Stephen an odd cadaver: the corpse lies supine, arched off the deck, suspended on heels and head. Apparently a classic case of tetanus, but it cannot be so, because it occurred so quickly. They speculate about poison ("...a wild overdose of St. Ignatius's beans...") but cannot see how such a dose could have been gotten into the man's hands. Must be either suicide or murder, however, and with an accomplice because the corpse is still manacled hand and foot. The dead man was employed by the Admiral's Secretary, and was due to be court-martialed for selling secrets: unspoken high probability is that he was poisoned

by the Secretary himself, to avoid a public trial and its attendant loss of secrecy and cover. (Ignatius's beans are seeds of the plant *Ignatia amara*, and are poisonous, their effects resembling those of strychnine.)

112 - Stephen takes charge of the Admiral's health, orders him to submit to an examination and to stop self-dosing with Mungo's Cordial. The examination finds no specific problems, just age compounded with heavy work and worry. A battle with the French fleet would fix everything for the Admiral.

116 - Secretary Allen informs the Admiral of the apparent suicide: the Admiral probably intuits the reality, gives Allen a hard look, and carries on.

120 - Stephen comments on Jack's apparent loss of two stone (28 pounds), declares "I must look into you. We may all of us entertain an unknown guest." Stephen suspects intestinal parasites (either tape- or round-worms) - the "look into you" is meant literally.

125 - Jack's hands are raw from sliding down a backstay at the end of his race against Admiral Mitchell. Stephen anoints them with an ointment (probably hog's lard with herbs).

<u>Book 8 Chapter 5 - p128-151: (overview)</u> Worcester loses the good weather. Jack's immediate superior is Adm Harte, who is civil but not pleased to have to deal this closely with a man to whom he owes at least one of the many sets of horns he bears. Musical talent aboard-ship is good and plentiful - both singing and instrumental... including five seamen word-perfect in singing the Messiah. The ship becomes a final refuge for thousands of migrating quails exhausted by endlessly beating into a strong headwind: quails land everywhere, including on Jack's epaulettes during inspection. Worcester nearly collides with HMS Pompee, another blockade ship: the error is part of Somers' ongoing incompetence. Somers mouths off to Jack, moves to grab a belaying-pin but is physically restrained by Mowett. This threat is a court-martial offense with the only possible outcomes being death or ejection from the Navy. Jack chooses to ignore it but requires Somers to leave the ship: Somers arranges a swap, himself for Mr Rowan of Colossus. The incident instantly becomes the stuff of legend, ever-growing with each retelling. The entire crew is recruited into preparing a complete Oratorio (from the Messiah): whilst working up to that, they will do Hamlet. They meet Jack's old ship Surprise (28), delivering mail to the Toulon fleet. Babbington reappears: a first-class womanizer, he was apparently caught (by Adm Harte himself) in flagrante delicto with Adm Harte's daughter Fanny - Babbington is being attached to Harte's squadron. Stephen's high-level intelligence leak, Mr Wray, is likely to become Secretary of the Admiralty, a near-certain disaster for both Jack and Stephen.

137 - Jack's thorough inspection ends in the sickbay: two gleets (pus-weeping genital sores usually due to gonorrhea); two ruptures; one fractured clavicle. To protect the quail from the crew, Stephen announces that the quail "...may be poisonous..." hence must not be touched. His advice on any such matter is absolute law to the crew.

147 - Jack's letters from home: his children have had chicken pox, and daughter Caroline's teeth have been "filed" - this is another occurrence of the term - it does not seem to be a typo for "filled" (modern sense), but exactly what "filing a tooth" might mean in English society of the day, is a mystery.

148 - Stephen's wife Diana mentions in a letter that she was mistaken about her pregnancy. Stephen is unaware of the possibility: perhaps a letter to him went missing?

Book 8 Chapter 6 - p151-188: (overview) Rambles covering shipboard personal space and privileges available to various ranks. A captain's need for some companionship outside the rank structure, as is Stephen for Jack. Crew still working on the Messiah and Hamlet. Adm Harte assigns Jack to deliver a new envoy (Mr Consul Hamilton) to the Barbary State of Barka. The goal, long-term, seems to be to have good English-Barbary State relationships and to exclude the French from the region. Orders - Jack (in Worcester) to be accompanied by Babbington in HMS Dryad. Dryad will leave Jack when a day's sail from land, and sail in alone to deliver dispatches to Medina. An odd order. Jack insists on formal written orders: Harte objects but cannot refuse, given the whole room is full of admirals. A live rhinoceros aboard supply-ship Polyphemus as a gift to the Pasha of Barka amuses the crew endlessly as they figure out how to exercise the 3-ton critter. Dryad returns to Worcester at panic speed, having discovered unexpected French warships ships in the harbor: Dryad had been sent on a suicide mission (of which neither Jack nor Babbington were informed), to provoke the French into firing first, thus enabling the English to retaliate in good accord with the letter of international rules of warfare. Neither side fired during this incident. Following the precise wording of his orders, Jack takes Worcester into the harbor and physically alongside the French ships, a 74 and a frigate. Twice they pass alongside with every man on both sides prepared for action, but both sides have identical orders not to fire first. Nobody fires, Jack is able to retire peacefully.

157 - Back on blockade. Jack has a serious cold

158 - Jack self-treats his cold with a glass of hot lemon shrub, which is basically hot lemonade with a good dose of rum.

160 - Summoned to the Admiral aboard the flagship, the Flag-Captain notices Jack's cold, orders for Jack his own nos-

trum, a physically hot liquid concoction called a "fearnought draught" whose main ingredients are boiling rum, black pepper, and Spanish Fly (a urinary-tract irritant and supposed aphrodisiac). The Captain of the Fleet pooh-poohs the draught - his own nostrum is a raw onion. All blame Jack's cold on his habit of swimming in the sea.

162 - Harte advises Jack to be bled, to fix the cold.

170 - Jack's cold worsens, turns him into a reclusive grouch. Wardroom discusses each man's personal theories about colds... their causes and cures.

Book 8 Chapter 7 - p189-222: (overview) Jack returns to the fleet and meets with Adm Harte who angrily explains (now – well after the fact) that the plan was for Dryad to be fired upon and probably captured or sunk. Jack is furious at what he feels is utter betrayal of his ships and men by the upper command including Harte himself, and flaunts his written orders in Harte's face, with various admirals looking on. Harte, embarrassed, finally backs down - he is clearly in the wrong is a great many ways. Jack's crew do not understand why no fight occurred during the Medina confrontation, and are cool to him, and this occasions introspection about valor, honor, bravery, cowardice etc. Worcester is off to Port Mahon for resupply, and to pick up Stephen. Jack will deliver Stephen to the French coast, presumably to help those ashore foment troubles for Buonaparte. At his inn ashore Jack re-encounters an old lover, Mercedes: flame rekindles but is frustrated by the very untimely arrival of Stephen, in a tearing hurry to get going to a rendezvous in France. He is rowed ashore in the dark, is involved in a complex utterly bungled -and betrayed- rendezvous. At the rendezvous he finds Prof. Graham, who has just shot off his own little toe.

198 - Jack goes ashore, Midshipman Willits goes along on liberty but Jack assigns bow-ore Eldon to accompany Mr Willits, to keep the lad from "buying a pox" with his cash.

212 - After long discursions about sails, prizes and proprieties, Jack asks Stephen if there exist "pills and draughts against the blue devils (depression) and ill-temper"? Jack is depressed because he has been forced into bypassing combat and prizes and the crew are deeply upset thereby.

214 - In passing, Stephen admits to himself that cigars, and smoking generally, yield him pleasures equal to those of sex. He is utterly convinced that smoking is not merely harmless, but very much beneficial.

Book 8 Chapter 8 - p223-255: (overview)   Stephen feels his meeting ashore was bungled due mostly to too many uncoordinated intelligence services (mostly rank amateurs) floundering about. Stephen saved Graham, now feels he owns him. More wardroom poetry. Mumps aboard Worcester truncates the Oratorio for want of the proper male voices, but togas made from unused sailcloth save Hamlet. French fleet (17 ships of the line) comes out during a storm. Rigging the Worcester for heavy sailing in severe weather. Stephen as usual is in the way, is ordered below-decks. Discussion of fleet tactics. A long, difficult chase so strains the ancient Worcester that to keep her afloat Jack has to wrap the hull with hawsers (frapping) and fother her (use a sail to wrap the bottom, so as to stop or at least slow serious leaks). In the end, the entire chase is futile: there is no engagement except chasers at maximum range, to no effect.

228 - Mumps has invaded the Worcester: thoughts about the problems of mumps in an adult male (e.g., orchitis [swelling of the testicles] leading to sterility, perhaps impotence). Graham is

worried - he has not had mumps yet: he declines the wardroom's dinner invitation, fearing contagion.

245 - Prof Graham apparently has been injured by losing his footing: no specifics.

246 - Stephen gets some rest - via laudanum once again.

251 - The wild motions of the ship during the chase have caused casualties - many sprains, contusions and simple broken bones. Plus one spectacular complex compound fracture - Stephen is happy the man is unconscious, for that lets the surgeon work unimpeded by a patient's panic, fears and worry.

Book 8 Chapter 9 - p256-288: (overview)   Another chapter with little of medical import. The chase (and more importantly the weather) did enormous damage to the fleet generally, not just Worcester. One of the few French shots during the chase came aboard Surprise and killed Captain Latham and his first officer. The Admiral gives Surprise to Jack, to go to the Seven Islands (probably Islamic small states like the Barbary Coast kingdoms - a real impediment to English trade). The hope is to expel the French entirely from the region: for this, friendly relationships need to be negotiated with various local rulers (Beys, Deys, Pashas, Emirs and the like, most of whom report to or are part of the Turkish Empire) - diplomatic quicksand. Stephen and Graham will deal with things diplomatic. In the midst of intense unpredictable internecine warfare, Jack and Stephen must choose the best ruler to back, for English purposes. Adm Thornton is leaving, Harte will be in command of the Med fleet (and of English foreign relationships with the entire region): he is utterly out of his depth - and knows it. Humbled, Harte has Jack's orders written to Jack's specifications, leaving him immense freedom of action.... including manning Surprise (~125 men) with the pick of Worcester's crew (~500 men). The new crewmembers agree - Jack's luck has returned. At sea enroute, more poetry reading and contests in the wardroom. Stephen jumps overboard to swim just as Surprise starts packing on sail, but is rescued. Surprise takes a famous blockade runner, the Bonhomme Richard - a fine prize....with a large amount of silver coin in the hold. Jack does a partial distribution of shares - the crew is ecstatic. Dryad arrives loaded with women - Babbington (notorious as a womanizer) has saved a large gaggle of "Lesbians" from their captors. Jack hears Babbington's amusing explanation, then sends him off in Dryad to repatriate the women. Jack's choice for an English ally is among three 'chieftains' or beys; at least one, named Mustapha, has a pair of small men of war, the Torgud (30) and Kitabi (20).

276 - Stephen after a week back afloat is still covered head to toe with Maltese bedbug bites - plus flea and mosquito bites.

Book 8 Chapter 10 - p289-326; (overview)   Anchored off Mesenteron (Turkish-held). Salute due Surprise is slow in coming (worrying Jack) and weak.   Candidate Beys are Mustapha, Ismail and Sciahan who are all at one another's throats. Jack has cannon to give to the winner; they all know it and are fiercely competitive for English support. More discussions on the oppression both possible and likely given a navy-like rank structure.   Extensive feasting and simple-minded negotiations. Discussion of the idiocy of the new informal naval custom of having candidates for officer pass both a proficiency test and an informal test "...for being a gentleman". Surprise encounters Torgud and Kitabi - they are well handled, and Mustapha Bey is captain of Torgud - which mounts two enormous long-36#ers athwartships. They have no cannonballs, only nine handmade spherical marble shot (this last learnt by Bonden when one of the Torgud's crew recognizes him). Mustapha argues that he is the best choice to help the English get rid of the French on shore here. Jack doesn't quite believe the man. Surprise sails to meet with Sciahan Bey in Kutali. Sciahan initiates contact by sending a Greek Orthodox priest out to Surprise as envoy - all are impressed by the man. Sciahan's battle experience is extensive, his arguments strong. Jack chooses to support him.

315 - Stephen is again taking laudanum, needs four successive doses to drive himself into sleep.

Book 8 Chapter 11 - p327-367; (overview)   At dinner with Sciahan, with Prof Graham along as negotiator, Jack feels good about Sciahan and without detailed negotiations simply agrees to support him. Graham is furious at being left out, and at Jack for not pressing for a complex negotiated treaty. Jack and Graham have a shouting-match: Stephen declines to participate. Per Sciahan's and Jack's plans, the Surprise's crew sets a line of heavy cables from wharf to the heights behind Kutali, planning to haul several cannon up to the ridge, whence they can completely dominate both town and harbor. Graham eventually cools, goes ashore in his role as Turkish-speaking intelligence agent, and collects extensive information about the overall situation. Whilst awaiting a wind change that will being the ship carrying the "gift" cannon, Jack has severe second thoughts, worries about having perhaps backed the wrong man. Extensive rumors upset the entire town: they are calmed largely by Stephen's analysis, reinforced by information from Graham. Ismail prefers alliance with the French, set up rumors which Mustapha believed and acted upon (specifically, he rebelled against his superiors), thereby giving all parties clear notice of his perfidy. Jack has backed the right man. Torgud and Kitabi come up with the wind and attack Surprise. A serious battle, in which superior seamanship by Surprise is the critical factor. Prof Graham, feeling exposed and vulnerable beside Jack on the quarterdeck, volunteers to fire at the enemy with a musket. Kitabi runs into Torgud, confusing things horribly (Torgud fires many rounds into Kitabi) just as Surprise begins to board. Near the end of the hand-to-hand, Jack sees Pullings go down, fears he may have been killed, finds out shortly that Pullings survived uninjured save for having his waistcoat ruined. Kitabi sinks as Jack steps off, having "Come it the Nelson bridge" – to wit, attacking and taking a second enemy vessel, using the captured first enemy as a bridge.

359 - Men wounded in the battle with Torgud and Kitabi are carried below, screaming, for Stephen to handle.

361 - One Surprise shows his mates how he has just lost a finger and never felt it go. Six badly-wounded men and three dead - a very low butcher's bill for such an action.

362 - As Jack is giving ship's boy Williamson orders to carry forward, Torgud's 36# ball takes the boy's arm off at the elbow. Jack improvises a tourniquet and sends him to sickbay.

364 - Stephen tells Jack that Williamson will likely survive.

366 - In the final melee of boarding, Jack is wounded: a pistol-ball across the ribs, a partly-blocked sword-thrust also to the chest.

Book 9 - Treason's Harbour

Book 9 Chapter 1 - p9-28: (overview)   Malta. Many officers ashore, without ships or with vessels under repair including two for Jack - Worcester (74) (badly built and recently damaged by weather), and Surprise (28), damaged in battle with Turkish vessels Torgud (sunk) and Kitabi (captured). Pullings promoted to Commander. Philosophical discussion between Stephen and Prof. Graham (Turkish language expert) comparing Greek and Irish scholars. Intense dislike of Rousseau: likewise of colonial powers generally. Stephen is being watched by French intelligence agents, who know he is their English counterpart. Red-haired beauty Laura Fielding's husband (RN Lieutenant) is in French prison: under threats to him, she is recruited to extract information from Jack and Stephen (she is teaching Jack Italian), by any means up to and including seduction. Stephen understands her position and goals, gallantly deflects her advances, explains things to her, and uses her to his own advantage in intelligence matters. Jack and Stephen's nemesis Adm Harte is temporary Commander in Chief - a position wildly beyond his capabilities. Alternative nemesis Wray, the thoroughly corrupt and dishonest acting Second Secretary of the Admiralty, is on-scene presumably to do counter-intelligence work, for which he is quite unsuited and of which he is incapable. Wray is married to Fanny, Harte's daughter, who is in love with Jack's protégé Mr Babbington. Embarrassment of crew to be seen carrying Stephen's fiddle through the streets - must hire a boy. Laura's huge mastiff falls down the cistern, is rescued by Jack, who falls into the cistern in the process.

9 - Pullings was wounded in the Turkish actions that yielded his promotion – impressive major saber-damage to his forehead and nose, largely but not perfectly repaired by Stephen. We find out in future books that Pullings' injuries received here include damage to the hinge of his jaw, such that it is easily dislocated.

10 - Stephen is irritable - he is giving up tobacco - a strange thing to do inasmuch as he has often praised it as a panacea for human ills.

15 - Stephen discourses on tobacco, is convinced that "mere lack of tobacco" cannot be what is making him testy: he admits to himself that his sexual desires have resurfaced with a vengeance, caused by his contact with Laura Fielding on Malta.

27 - Mention of Stephen's "best works", one scientific the other a medical treatise: (1) Remarks on *Pezohaps Solitarius* (this is a species of dove, from Rodriguez Island, gone extinct at human hands about 1780), and (2) Modest Proposals for the Preservation of Health in the Navy (no title quite like this has been uncovered).

33 - Pullings, celebrating his elevation, is comatose drunk - "paralytic" - transported unconscious to the ship by crewmen, who lash him to a stretcher for the trip.

34 - Jack's steward Killick has never seen a fresh green pea, only the Navy's dried version.

Book 9 Chapter 2 - p39-62: (overview)   Jack is strongly rumored (and generally believed) to be having an affair with Laura. Problems of dealing with the Navy's corrupt dockyard system. Pullings realizes that his promotion has set him ashore shipless for the indefinite future, and volunteers to help Jack with repairing and readying Surprise for her "CONFIDENTIAL" mission to the Red Sea, the essence of which is known to everyone on the island save Jack, to whom the accurate rumors have not been conveyed - much less official orders. Difficulties of sailing the Red Sea generally and near Mubara (the objective) particularly. (NOTE - today's village of Mubara is in the desert half-way between Basra and Baghdad, Iraq – and far from any navigable bit of seawater.) Jack visits with Adm Hartley, a central character in Jack's early career - is appalled at how aged the Adm is. Mating tortoises observed. Stephen encounters Wray (now a high Admiralty official, and high-level spy for the French cause) whilst listening to plainsong: a mutual appreciation of the music leads to discussions of tyranny, including Buonaparte, and a gentle attempt by Wray to get information from Stephen, who is as yet genuinely clueless about Wray's intelligence (espionage) doings. French agent Lesueur tells Wray that Stephen is a first-class English agent. Lesueur complains about Wray's gambling addiction, which the French do not wish to support.

40 - Aphrodisiacs? Jack has a pound of sardines for breakfast - supposedly an aphrodisiac for men of his makeup. With usual male egotism, he begins to believe Laura may be signaling him to advance on her.

41 - Jack's crewmen ashore work hard to make their quarters (black-painted wooden sheds) as ventilation-free and otherwise nasty as their shipboard accommodations.

56 - Jack muses on the ageing process and its inevitable consequences, including impotence.

Book 9 Chapter 3 - p63-93: (overview) Jack's prize is sold: he sends home to Sophie some ten years' pay. Bribes in the shipyard finally get repairs started on Surprise. Jack is puzzled by Laura's behavior towards him during his Italian lessons. Stephen's two-ton brass and glass diving bell (designed by astronomer Halley) arrives and is discussed. Only because it can be disassembled, it may go aboard in pieces and act as ballast when not in use. On the complexities of properly seating a menagerie of dinner guests all of whom are caste- and rank-sensitive, but who operate in multiple social systems, often with no cross-connectivity. Prof Graham (also of English Naval Intelligence) apprises Stephen of Lesueur. Stephen, having walked on the subsea ooze by means of the bell and fouled his hose, now stinks and borrows hose and shoes from Prof Graham so as to attend Laura's party, at which she tries to seduce Stephen: he deflects the move, then extracts from her information about her captured (threatened) husband. She admits to having been forced to try to seduce Stephen in pursuit of information. Together they conspire to make fools of the French.

77 - Graham's shoes chafe Stephen's feet raw within two hundred yards' walking.

85 - Aphrodisiacs again. Laura's after-party pass at Stephen includes feeding him doses of Spanish Fly (ground-up cantharides bee-

tles - a potent urinary-tract irritant but not [as is widely believed even today] an aphrodisiac).

86 - Stephen detects in himself the effects of the Spanish Fly, and worries about the male guests (who also were dosed) turning into raging sexual bulls, now turned loose upon the innocent local women. (Never considering that many of the ladies might heartily enjoy such an occasion – a different Running of the Bulls?)

Book 9 Chapter 4 - p94-133: (overview) Stephen's and Laura's ruse includes the couple's giving every appearance of having an affair. This eventually bites Stephen when his wife Diana hears of it. It also upsets Jack, who is now lecherously pursuing Laura - once again, it seems to him that he and Stephen are after the same woman, as they were years earlier over Diana. Stephen's meetings with various intelligence officials - "...a great many words were uttered and very little was said." Adm Ives has a problem, offers Jack a quick important cruise up the Red Sea in Surprise, to deal with the French-supported efforts of one Mehmet Ali to conquer the entire region in cahoots with the French. A French treasure ship is also in the area, to support the effort. Jack and crew will take HMS Dromedary (transport) to the Nile Delta, then march across the desert to man the small but well-armed East-India Company ship Niobe (about 18 guns?). Political advice will come from Mr Hairabedian, highly recommended by Mr Wray (making Hairabedian a French agent). One-eyed parson Martin re-appears, accidentally accompanies Stephen et al on this 'confidential' expedition, about which he has detailed information picked up on the street. Stephen gets anonymous letters stating that Diana is being unfaithful - he ignores them. More wardroom singing and poetry: problems rhyming the word 'dromedary'. Crew's odd delicacy as to things gynecological.

94 - At their rooms ashore, Stephen doses himself heavily with "sleeping-pills". He has intense erotic dreams of himself and Laura.

100 - Awkward Davies (mis-spelt here and on p148 as DAVIS) has been "laid up" by the Scots Guards - presumably beaten senseless

and locked in the guard-room. Three other Surprises are in similar straits.

101 - Eleven men recently taken to hospital - four with Malta fever (probably malaria), four with the "great pox" (likely smallpox), two with broken legs, another mildly knifed in a fight. One man is in prison awaiting trial for rape.

118 - Dromedary pitches a sleeping Stephan from his chair: cuts his forehead "a hands-breadth across" on a table-edge. Martin is expert at sewing up bird skins for scientific uses, and immediately sews it up with twelve neat stitches.

120 - Stephen mulls over [presumed] sexual appetites of various classes of women. Jack tries to prescribe diet for Stephen (as a result of his new head-wound) and the unsolicited advice is roundly rejected.

125 - Stephen wanders about ship with a bloody bandage over his wound: the crew are sure he was dead drunk at the time. Stephen confirms two new cases of syphilis.

126 - Treatment for syphilis (early stage) - no grog, number two low diet, a course of salivation, cost of treatment to be deducted from the patients' pay because the problem is personal, not service-related. (Unclear what 'salivation' is, as a medical treatment – probably it means inducing excess salivation in an attempt to clear the body of some sort of humor or vapor, per medical theories of the day.) Pulled one tooth for a seaman.

128 - Discussion of the use of loud noises and startle as a form of anesthesia, especially for tooth-extractions. Discussion of how in the heat of battle men fail to notice even severe wounds - or their treatment, up to and including amputation.

Book 9 Chapter 5 - p134-165: (overview) Aboard Dromedary enroute to Suez from Malta. Church: Martin sermonizes ineptly - discussion ensues. Treasure - rumors of 5,000 purses, each of 5,000 piasters - an enormous sum, all in one small vessel. Worries about proper salutes: Hairabedian a wonderfully strong swimmer,

good diplomat. Problems with camels and too-beautiful boy servants. Crew utterly terrified by night-time sounds and rumors of
evil spirits. Jack is lent the finest horse of his life, for the trek.
Jack mulls over his recent combat record, is dissatisfied with
himself, worried about 'competition' with other post-captains.
Jack meets the Bey (=local ruler); instant rapport. The Bey's
odabashi (military rank, probably non-commissioned officer) is in
charge of the party's escort, speaks perfect English (his mother
was a Londoner).

141 - Stephen prepares "physick and powders" for those crew
who will be left behind at Tina whilst the rest march across the desert
to Niobe.

148 - Crewman Awkward Davies (here mis-spelt Davis) was casually described as negro in an earlier book, here has a "hairy hand" -
unlikely for a dark negro.

159 - In the desert, Martin is bitten by a camel - not seriously but
worrisome because a camel's bite is locally thought to convey syphilis
(= nonsense). An equally local wound-dressing "...derived from the
skink" is applied to prevent the infection. (Skink = almost any
smooth-scaled lizard, world-wide.)

Book 9 Chapter 6 - p166-210: (overview)   Aboard Niobe, in
Suez. Camels knock down tents, Jack's fancy "chelengk" (a non-
fictional device) cannot be found afterwards - it is a very high
military award, a spray of diamonds with a watch-work spring to
make it vibrate. Jack had intended to take it home for Sophie. Difficulties with internal local politics. entertainment and food during negotiations. Lethargy of local troops until treasure is mentioned. Discussion of the problems of sailing in the Red Sea - incredible and unpredictable winds, plus reefs and pirates. Intense
heat: sea-surface temperature is "...84 degrees by Fahrenheit's
thermometer". (NOTE - this is a truly high temperature for the
sea-surface - nearly a world record in fact.) Jack worries about
the weather, which he does not understand but which causes him
intense unease. Shortly his unease is fully justified by an incredible days-long high velocity sandstorm called an "Egyptian". Jack
uses the storm to investigate Niobe's sailing characteristics whilst

running south (the desired direction). Turkish/Muslim fatalism leading mostly to inaction. Post storm, Niobe is becalmed for days. Hairabedian, the ship's strongest and most enthusiastic swimmer, dives into the sea and is immediately torn apart and eaten by sharks, in full view of many of the crew. Turks aboard Niobe do not understand sailing, try to bribe Jack to set more sail, assuming that more sail equates to more speed. Distant drums are heard - it is the treasure-galley setting its rowing pace. Jack pursues, but things are odd - the galley is toying with Niobe, leading her on. Jack figures this out, believes this is NOT the treasure ship but rather a decoy, and sinks the galley with one shot. The galley rests on the bottom with mast-head above water. Maturin and Stephen go down in the diving bell to recover the treasure - which turns out to be lead, not precious metals. Jack was correct. Local fishermen pass the rumor, however, of another similar galley nearby, loaded with silver.

168 - Jack's steward Killick passes out from overwork (sifting sand to find the chelengk) and terror of night-spirits and bats... must be transported draped over a camel. Hairabedian is stung in the foot by a scorpion that had hidden in his boot - the leg is hugely swollen, "like a bolster".

177 - Stephen expounds on scorpions - common, sting only when provoked, rarely lethal although they can cause "a certain amount of discomfort, even coma..."

179 - Air temperature over 125°F in the shade.

185 - As storm abates, Stephen has the usual collections of bruises and strains to deal with, including broken bones. No specifics. Hairabedian's leg nearly recovered from the scorpion sting.

189 - Stephen muses about bleeding the entire crew (unclear why he thinks this a good idea) - and Jack in particular, to reduce the danger of "siriasis or apoplexy" (to which danger Jack's 'always-too-heavy' tendency towards corpulence is a major factor) "Siriasis" (sic) does not appear to be a proper English word, even in medical circles. By 'siriasis' Stephen may be referring to today's "psoriasis" – a sometimes debilitating skin condition. Corpulence could make a per-

son sweat more freely and that might in turn exacerbate psoriasis. Hairabedian eaten by sharks. Stephen finds Jack's chelengk hidden amongst Hairabedian's effects.

206 - Temperature 128 F in the shade on deck, as Stephen and Martin struggle - in the diving bell - with small very heavy chests aboard the sunken galley. Lead - not silver.

Book 9 Chapter 7 - p211-226: (overview)   Niobe returns to Suez low on water and provisions, utterly disappointed. Ashore, they learn details of the silver and more about local politics. Local rumors are that Niobe and her diving bell succeeded, but are keeping the fact secret. Leaving Niobe and marching back to Surprise, the crew are bashful over anything related to body functions - especially wastes… hence the utter flatness and treelessness of the desert are monumentally disconcerting. Attacked mid-desert by mounted horsemen, the party loses much valuable property in the melee, but suffer no injuries. Exhausted and dehydrated, they straggle into Tina to find Dromedary waiting for them. The expedition has been an utter failure in all particulars.

212 - Many crewmen badly sunburnt working unprotected in Suez. Stephen anoints their burns with "sweet oil" - the panacea for his watch whenever it gets a ducking. There are several candidates for "sweet oil", the most likely being orange, lemon, or perhaps almond oil.

216 - Doctor Simiaka, a Coptic physician, visits Stephen. They chew khat and discuss, inter alia, "Egyptian adultery, fornication and pederasty". Khat is a plant common in the mid-east, often and widely chewed as a stimulant (apparently the plant contains at least one form of amphetamine).

217 - Awkward Davies has been bargaining for a Syrian bear-cub, which apparently attacked him - greatly to the bear's detriment, for Stephen must go "repair the bear"… and this is not not Stephen's first foray into veterinary medicine.

Book 9 Chapter 8 - p227-260: (overview) Jack reports the mission's complete failure to his commander-in-chief. The Admiral properly lays blame on faulty intelligence rather than on Jack. Surprise is to go home and be broken up. Jack was promised the new heavy frigate HMS Blackwater - in whose fitting out he had been deeply involved. Jack is now over half-way up the Navy List, climbing towards rear-admiral. He is farther up than expected, because several captains have recently died of disease or been killed. Stephen visits with Laura: her husband may be dead - recent letters are suspiciously off-key, probably ghost-written in his name. Laura is in great danger. Stephen spends the night at her home - innocently. The French - and also the Surprises - notice and assume that the couple's (faked) affair continues. Anonymous letters inform Stephen that Diana is having an affair with their mutual friend, the 'absurdly beautiful' Swedish officer Jagiello - none of which Stephen believes. Stephen goes aboard the flag for an intelligence evaluation and consultation as to the recent mission. Wray (acting undersecretary) lays all mission problems on Hairabedian, now deceased. The French really want a base at Mubara. Stephen realizes that Wray is a pederast. Wray invites Stephen to gamble at cards: Stephen is both lucky and very skilful (and has also learned from a professional gambler how to read faces): in two separate high-stakes encounters, he strips Wray, who has to give Stephen an IOU. Stephen and Laura plant a half-encoded message (in Stephen's handwriting, which is known to Wray), to confuse Lesueur and Wray. Wray has given away the new frigate Blackwater (long promised to Jack) to someone with more influence in Parliament. Stephen demands that Wray make good on a seagoing command for Jack - plus one for Pullings. More "secret" orders are brewing - tasks for Jack whilst enroute home in Surprise... orders so secret that Stephen learns their details from Laura who got the information in the street. Surprise will shepherd the Adriatic commercial convoy. Stephen leaves behind one superbly crafted packet of disinformation for the French.

233 - Stephen takes three new patients to the hospital ashore: also checks on patients left behind for the desert journey.

238 - Sophie's letter mentions "coming to the town [London] twice for the children's teeth" - no further explanation.

Book 9 Chapter 9 - p261-289: (overview) (NOTE - this chapter has little of 'medical' note.) Aboard Surprise, bound for Kutali. More discursions by Stephen on poetry. Jack discovers he has lost the Blackwater, takes the news well. Passing Marga, scene of one of Jack's triumphs ashore, they arrive at Kutali and meet with his former allies in that affair - the Turkish Father Andros and the ruler, Sciahan Bey, whom Surprise helped install. Jack and Sciahan hunt a bear for diversion, the hunters' discretion results in no bearskin, but a good story. Enroute they encounter a small commercial vessel (an hourario). Some days ago Nymphe had rescued a man now identified as Laura Fielding's husband – who is now the patient (at p278) carrying a wandering subcutaneous musket-ball now ripe for removal. Stephen worries how he will debunk to Mr Fielding the carefully-nurtured and widely-believed rumor of a Stephen/Laura affair. Some pages of details about Fielding's escape. Stephen has believed all along that Jack and Laura were the real, clandestine affair: Jack is hugely amused when Stephen warns him about Fielding's presence aboard Nymphe.

277 - Stephen performs his signature surgical operation, a suprapubic cystotomy, aboard HMS Nymphe, and is applauded by her surgeon.

278 - Nymphe's surgeon's next case is merely a wandering ball (=bullet) lodged beneath a patient's skin - usually a trivial operation.

281 - Mr Fielding (Laura's husband) is the "next" case - asks why he has not been cut yet - he has been prepped with mandragora and his own rum. Stephen is unimpressed by the use of mandragora. The ball removal goes well. Now Stephen is worried about the revelation to come.

Book 9 Chapter 10 - p290-334: (overview) [NOTE - this chapter, although full of action, has little of 'medical' import.] Surprise and Dryad, heading south. Stephen discourses on dolphins. Plans on how best to use Laura to pin (i.e., expose, render null, even kill) all French agents in Malta. Stephen still has not discovered Wray's role as top-level French collaborator and spy, prepares to tell all to Wray as necessary. English Mediterranean fleet badly mauled by storms. Surprise meets HMS Edinburgh (74), Capt Heneage Dundas, Jack's longest-term friend. Encounter and chase a French privateer which runs for the Barbary Coast, eventually is taken. Stephen hurries to Malta aboard the cutter, but when he reaches shore, he finds the news of Fielding's return is public. Fearing for his and Laura's lives, Stephen arms himself. Stephen goes to Laura's house - empty - lets himself in and waits in the dark for assassins to arrive seeking Laura. They arrive, discuss in Stephen's hearing the "best practices" for murdering a woman. Meanwhile, Jack gets orders to Zambra - to consult with English Consul Eliot and warn the Dey of Mascara not to cross English interests under pain of naval retribution including all-out war which the Dey cannot hope to win. If the Dey is in any way recalcitrant, Jack has a free hand to take, burn, etc. Further, he will sail to Zambra in HMS Pollux (74) as a show of force - with Adm Harte aboard. Jack demands reassurances that Harte will not meddle in Jack's negotiations with the Dey. The assassins leave Laura's home: she arrives home minutes later, tells Stephen that her beloved watchdog died earlier in the day. He realizes that the dog –always in robust good health- was certainly killed by the assassins to clear the path for their attack. Stephen tells her that Mr Fielding is escaped, and his health is fine. Stephen hides her aboard Surprise - the perfect refuge. The crew nod knowingly - Stephen/Laura illicit connection affirmed! Worry now about explaining the Stephen/Laura connection to her husband and also to Stephen's wife Diana. Six days' sail to Zambra are a delight. Jack dines aboard Pollux, is quizzed as to his mission by a drunk Adm Harte, who astounds Jack by giving him money with which to buy freedom for several Christian slaves of Jack's choosing. Alone, Surprise stands in to Zambra Bay – there to be ambushed by an 80-gun ship flying Turkish colors (the Turks have no such ships - obviously a French + Dey plot), plus two frigates (38, 28) - a force vastly beyond Surprise's combat capabilities. Pollux comes to Surprise's aid, fights fiercely against the much-superior 80. Pollux explodes with loss of all 500+ hands including Admiral Harte - doing extensive damage to the French 80. Pursued by the two frigates, Jack's superb seamanship causes one to go hard

154

aground at the mouth of the bay, totally dismasting her and breaking her back, which forces the second frigate to come to the grounded ship's aid. Surprise escapes. Enroute home, Stephen hatches a plan to finally expose the high-level undercover French agent - very few people knew where Jack was going and why - the ambush had to have been arranged with that person's help.

312 - Stephen, seeking relief from sleeplessness, once again gives in and doses himself with laudanum.

315 - Stephen, observing the crew's mental state and much more genteel behavior with Laura aboard, invents a prescription for naval mental health - as part of ship's equipment, "...a really handsome, thoroughly good-natured but totally inaccessible young woman, changed at stated intervals before familiarity could set in..."

Book 10 – The Far Side of the World

Book 10 Chapter 1 - p9-40: (overview) Surprise, lying-to off Gibraltar. Jack is summoned aboard the flagship to explain to the Commander-in-Chief, Mediterranean (CC Admiral Ives – a very stern man actively seeking a knighthood or baronetcy) why Jack's most recent mission had failed. The failure was no fault of Jack's - British interests had been actively betrayed. Jack nonetheless dreads having to report the debacle, in which Admiral Harte (Jack's long-time nemesis) was killed when the British Pollux (60) had exploded under fire from a French 80, which vessel was also destroyed by Pollux's demise. Admiral Ives' concerns about women aboard warships using an inordinate amount of fresh water to wash their underwear; also the manner in which salutes are rendered; and the punishable stylistic atrocity of Navy personnel wearing colorful civilian clothing when ashore. Aubrey's report indefinitely delayed. Surprise and crew are to be disassembled shortly – ruminations on the idiocy of dissolving a wonderfully efficient crew. Jack's long-promised new frigate Blackwater has been given to a more influential captain. Jack can have no certainty of another ship of any rate. Ashore, Jack encounters Hollom, a passed-over midshipmen now unable to find a ship: Jack is prevailed upon to accept him into Surprise. Maturin finds that the main French spy, Lesueur, has escaped unhurt. Discussion of parricide (killing one's own father) and its use in intelligence operations, that act held to be "...a usual factor in Eastern politics." Aboard flag, the C-in-C allays Jack's worry over the evaluation of his recent performance: he tells Jack in friendly fashion "...you are no goddam good at blowing your own trumpet; nor, by consequence, at blowing mine." C-in-C regards Jack's & Pollux's destruction of the French 80 as a thundering great victory, will edit Jack's report to show it so. Sharing a bottle of sillery, the Adm does Jack the signal honor of being the first to her of the Admiral's being made a Peer (Lord of the Realm), an enormous national honor for which he partially –and openly- credits Jack. Jack, deeply worried about his future in a Navy rapidly shrinking, is delighted to be given the task, in Surprise, of dealing with an American light frigate, Norfolk (32), that has been sent to harass British whalers in far southern Pacific waters. Surprise thus avoids the ship-breakers' attentions. In celebration of his elevation to the

Peerage, the C-in-C offers to make a few promotions upon Jack's recommendations, another honor to Jack. Stephen is briefed on Norfolk's likely whereabouts, route, mission, etc. Difficulties of dealings in S. America discussed. The Admiral sends Jack and Stephen off to the Navy Yard with a personally-signed 'caret-blanche' chit for all necessary supplies and repairs, under the usual "Not a moment to be lost!" invocation.

11 – It is not Ives but rather the Captain of the Fleet (ranks just below C-in-C) who called Jack in - to discuss their being new neighbors, on land. Influenza has confined CF to his cabin, where they meet.

19 – Belief in "Jonahs" – superstition that there exist individuals bound to bring bad luck to their ship. Jack denies being superstitious but feels Hollom likely to be one.

31 – Aboard flagship, Maturin is shown two cases of "military fever" (sic) – complete with a spattering of "dots" (rash? pustules?). The patients are identical twins, and the patterns of infection on their two bodies are identical. Probable error by book's editor – text reads "military fever", but (from the symptoms) must properly be "MILIARY fever" – a catchall term of the time for unidentified illnesses that cause high fevers, sweating, severe body rashes, and the like. The skin of victims was said to resemble a variety of cereal grain named 'proso millet', hence "miliary" (not military). W. Amadeus Mozart's death certificate invokes "miliary fever".

Book 10 Chapter 2 – p41-75 (overview): [NOTE - a chapter largely devoid of medical affairs.] Jack's cruise preparations are impeded by formal 'thank-yous' from men he got promoted. A gathering of major characters ensues – Pullings, Stephen, Rev. Martin (Stephen's co-worker in intelligence and natural history), Jack's steward Killick. Pullings is recently promoted and out of a command: he volunteers to help with preparations. Jack has inadvertently shipped six squeakers (preadolescent ship's boys) and needs teachers for them – namely Rev Martin and the wife (now residing aboard) of Gunner Mister Horner, for whose presence aboard Jack inadvertently gave permission. When approached,

Martin is delighted, Jack less so due to superstitions about "parson aboard = bad luck"… not even to mention the horror of having WOMEN aboard! Concept introduced of "committing an innovation" (in any matter maritime)… nothing should ever change. Jack is short-handed, gets a draft of lunatics from the local asylum, courtesy the C-in-C, apparently. Jack's total ignorance of whales and whaling. Fortuitous enrolling of experienced whaler Mr Allen, in Surprise's crew. Martin and Stephen atop Gibraltar, studying migrating birds, drive away Jack's messenger with an urgent invitation (NOT to be refused!) to dine with the Admiral: they are retrieved just in time, by a force of men from Surprise. Stephen (and not Jack) is told there is a huge sum of money aboard the British Brig Danae, now in N. or S. American waters – she must not be taken by Norfolk. The funds are adequate to, and intended for, bankrolling an unspecified South-American revolution favorable to British interests. Even Danae's captain does not know how much wealth she carries. Pullings agrees to go on the Surprise's cruise as "volunteer" – at least he may gain some glory to help his career – far better than staying ashore and moping. Bribes at the shipyard and ropeyard have their hoped-for effects as cannons and cables magically appear. Ultimately, after all the pressurized preparations, Jack is told that Norfolk was delayed a full month, there is no need to hurry!

43 – Seaman's official Navy daily rations and diet presented without discussion.

52 – Stephens musing on the psychological (mood) effects of alcohol.

53 – Stephen and another doctor, at dinner, agree that a mere 10% of the Navy's casualties are due to combat, 90% to disease and accident. Stephen, anticipating scurvy on a long voyage, requests an assistant, preferably one highly skilled at extracting teeth, a procedure at which Stephen himself is no good and which is inevitably needed.

54 – Discussion of Stephen's famous skill with a saw (i.e., at amputations), curiously contrasting with an inability to pull teeth. A good extraction-man is found – Mr Higgins.

65 – Admiral is "taking physic" – this is a difficult concept to clarify. Apparently, the highly-ranked or wealthy would occasionally take a day off-duty to engage in various semi-medical health-related practices, generically called "taking physic"… perhaps including sulfur water baths, poultices of various sorts, day-long diets, purges, enemas and the like. The broad concept also seems to include specific treatments (e.g. pills, enemas) for specific needs.

58 – Noise and distraction as anesthesia: Higgins' demonstration of his extraction technique – using a drummer beside the patient's ear (plus slapping and pinching the patient's face) to distract him. All are impressed with Higgins' skill.

71- Admiral recalls his family going to watch the mentally ill in Bedlam, for amusement. Admiral: "Most lunatics are only shamming…"

73 – Stephen must examine candidate seamen who are being sent to Surprise from the local lunatic asylum. Rejects most of them as unfit for even the lightest duties at sea.

75 – For security reasons, Stephen accepts as his personal medical aide an illiterate man who cannot speak English, and who has a severe harelip. There can be no finding-out of secrets by this man, much less transmitting of them.

Book 10 Chapter 3 – p76-119 (overview): Jack studied USS Norfolk whilst a prisoner in America: a formidable opponent with a magnificent crew. Surprise can use the extra month in port for full overhaul and provisioning, plus extensive crew training. Killick spreads suspicions that Hollom is a Jonah. Surprise weighed without a real cook, the nominal one being capable only of boiling salt beef. For a formal officers' dinner, several volunteers from the crew try to make various dishes, and all fail to varyingly serious degrees. Discussion of the god-awful food with Rev Martin, new to such a diet: he heroically asked for more. Massive infusions of cheap wine save the occasion. Jack describes the mission. Mr Allen then discourses on whales and whaling, Southern-Ocean weather, whale oil, ambergris, and spermaceti. Also the vagaries of the market for whale-stuffs.

Mowett revealed as resident poet of Surprise. Hollom is recovering from near starvation, has a marvelous singing voice. Aspasia the goat (kept for milk, used in Jack's tea) begs her daily cigar-stub from Stephen. Landfall at Teneriffe… and of course they cannot pause to go ashore, to the disgust of Stephen and Martin as natural historians. Compton tries to be a ventriloquist but his complaints, delivered audibly with witnesses, are instantly known to be his product. Stephen declares the Bosun's cat (feline) must be named "Scourge" – "…the only possible name for a bosun's cat!" says he. (A complex pun - the bosun keeps and wields the ship's Cat-o-Nine-Tails used for flogging: 'scourge' is both a whip (noun), and the process of using it (verb). All present recognize the superb pun.) Seaman Nagel openly fails to salute a passing officer as required, and does it in Jack's presence. Nagel is flogged, takes it philosophically. Excess blood from the preventive-medicine bleeding is used to attract sharks. The surgeons catch two sharks on hooks, have no idea what to do with them when they come aboard snapping and flailing. Crew proves a deep pool of musical talent and ability. Nagel begins an affair with Mrs Horner – an extremely dangerous man, her husband – and Surprise is hardly an environment conducive to maintaining secrecy about such an arrangement.

85 – Tobacco (Stephen is addicted) to be smoked only in the open, on the quarterdeck, for fear of fire.

92 – Mr Allen's most recent whaler carried a "most capital surgeon" who treated the crew's scurvy with "James's powder". This nostrum is not a fiction: it was sold for nearly a century. Composed largely (say, 50% by weight) of antimony, which has various forms quite like arsenic (to which it is closely related) -a powerful and dangerous poison with no preventive or therapeutic uses in medicine.

103 – Grog described – the universal seaman's dream and panacea. Three water to one rum (rum of the day probably 95.5 proof, or just under 50% alcohol by weight), plus sugar, lemon juice and often cinnamon. One pint of grog per man per meal. This works out to well over two fluid ounces of pure grain alcohol per serving, either twice or thrice per day. Such a dose hase profoundly different effects on a forty year old two-hundred pound seaman vs on a 75-pound ten year

old squeaker… and both got the same ration, regardless of the relative biomasses etc. Pree-teen alcoholism was common both ashore and afloat.

107 – Surprise crosses the tropic line: the weather is of course hot and getting hotter as they run south, and Stephen worries about the crew having "calentures" (fevers and seizures believed to be induced by the tropical sun). Stephen plans a preventative blood-letting for most of the ship's company, to avoid those effects. Not a popular treatment with the crew.

108 – Higgins has pulled teeth already for at least two crewmembers, is otherwise seen to be a medical charlatan preying on the crew. Occasional crewmen are going to him instead of Stephen, from whom they formerly got their weekly placebo "cure-all" pills made of chalk and dye.

111 – Crewman Horner, whose wife is aboard, comes to Stephen worried whether the planned bleeding will render him truly impotent – he has been unable to have sex with the Mrs for quite some time and is getting distraught. Horner is a violent man of barely-controlled-anger, and seen as such by the whole crew, who give him a wide berth. Horner is impotent only with his wife, and she "…is not particularly understanding". Horner thinks he may have been hexed, has paid charlatans a good deal to remove the spell, to no avail. Crew uniformly unable to understand that the total quantity of alcohol is the important parameter in drink – they believe that a pint of grog further diluted with a pint of water is only half as effective as the unwatered original.

113 – Stephen watches Nagel be flogged (24 strokes – a severe punishment indeed), will try "Mullin's Patent Balm" (an O'Brian invention) on the man's lash-wounds.

115 – Bloodletting for all hands, a "mere 8 ounces" per crewman, but totaling to "…nine good buckets with foam of an extraordinary beauty…" At least the two surgeons (Stephen, Rev Martin) bleed one another, as seemed only fair.

161

Book 10 Chapter 4 – p120-157 (overview): [NOTE – a chapter presenting very little medical activity.]   Fleet of Indiamen encountered where Jack expected them. Stephen's inability to swim. Indiamen captains invited aboard Surprise for dinner: champagne hung overside to cool. (NOTE: even in the tropics, at a depth of about 200m the water is quite cold.) Reports of fitful, inconstant winds for unusual distances, making for difficult, slow sailing. Puzzle – balancing uncertainties, where best to look for Norfolk? Crewman Mowett, at the wheel late at night, quotes Homer to Stephen, who is impressed – the topic is ship's speed through the water. Discussion of the Iliad as a screed against adultery. Into the doldrums: ship drifting aimlessly for want of wind. Rev Martin's musical abilities not up to Surprise's standards. Ship's boats put to towing Surprise – backbreaking work. Major danger is Surprise rolling so hard as to snap her masts. Ship's water-supply is dwindling, another major problem. Jack's experiences before the mast let him feel an undercurrent of unrest in the crew. Jack is an innocent, completely unaware of the widely-known Hollom+Mrs Horner liaison, the cause of the unrest. Crew fully expect Hollom to be found out by Mr Horner, then killed. Surprise successfully chases a rain-squall and collects eight days' worth of fresh water. Jack is supremely able to extract performance from Surprise. Eventually they find the trade-winds again. Music and humor finally return to the great cabin. Approaching St Paul's Rocks, ship is priddied to the nines just in case. Blue-footed boobies (variety of albatross) immensely please the naturalists. As usual, there is no time to spare for naturalizing. Martin wishes to propose marriage, gets Stephen to edit his written proposal. Surprise considered as a completely untypical Navy ship - nearly ideal, with a fine well-trained crew in a sterling vessel (despite being small and old). Equator crossed with traditional ceremonies. Jack positions Surprise to patrol across Norfolk's most likely path. Great-gun exercises daily, with Jack's private powder. Water dwindles to nil, Surprise head for shore and a watering place. Mister Allen knows personally some of the locals, from his whaling cruises. Lightning hits Surprise, destroys the bowsprit, melts the shank of the best bower anchor and sets off seven cannon, but causes no injuries. Finally ashore on un-explored turf, Stephen and Martin are enthralled by the flora and fauna.

162

129 – Stephen still longs for his laudanum (= alcoholic solution of opium), although he has renounced it successfully.

131 – Even the hardiest of sailors may, and here do, become sea-sick from the ship's wild rolling when trapped in the doldrums – the rolling due to a large underlying swell from distant storms.

144 – Stephen mulls over the plus/minus of marriage and its attendant complications, joys, sorrows.

151 – With Surprise on very short water rations, Stephen is asked his opinion of a cup of green fluid purporting to be water – Jack asks, "…is it drinkable without fatal effect?" Stephen delights in using his magnifying glass to study the larger creatures therein. Stephen and Martin exclaim over the variety of macroscopic life in the 'water'. Conclusion – eminently and utterly non-potable. Perfectly ordinary condition for a sailing-vessel's water supply on such a voyage.

153 – Stephen drugs himself with laudanum, sleeps through a magnificent thunderstorm. His rationale is that he must sleep so as to be at top form if required in his medical capacity.

<u>Book 10 Chapter 5 – p158-206 (overview)</u>: Upriver a bit, Surprise gets a new bowsprit. Martin and Stephen can botanize freely. Norfolk is reported to have sailed past the river-mouth almost immediately after Surprise moved upstream. Work accelerated to 24/7. Surprise manages to sail at precisely the highest tide of the month. An idiot pilot runs her solidly aground in deep mud: ship must be unloaded, cannot be refloated until NEXT highest tide, 28 days hence. She is successfully refloated then, sets off in pursuit of Norfolk, known to be about sixteen days ahead. Crew believe Hollom is a Jonah even more strongly now. Running south, occasional news of Norfolk far ahead. Cooling waters, whales. Encounter with HMS Danae, which ship seems shy about approaching Surprise. Jack believes she has been taken, is being sailed by the enemy, and goes in chase. If they capture her, Jack will have Pullings sail her home – essentially guaranteeing Pullings the next available captaincy, perhaps even of Danae herself. Surprise catches Danae, manned by an American prize crew, retakes her without a shot. Stephen drafts Jack's report. Norfolk is already raising havoc with British whalers. Stephen knows of the enormous treasure aboard Danae, Jack does not. Stephen decides they must transfer it to Surprise, and only Jack can help him. Together they find the real 'treasure' – not the already-transferred chests of specie, but a hidden box full of bank notes and promissory notes and negotiable paper 'payable to the bearer', altogether worth a staggering sum. Jack is impressed. Stephen trephines another skull, with audience. Severe storms, much prolonged. Allen helps Jack think about the likely whereabouts of Norfolk. Danae's captured American captain had earlier captured Surprise's Mowatt, treated him exceedingly well: Jack intends to do the same in return. Nightmare seas in trying to round the tip of S America, weeks of work beating upwind.

160 – A Peruvian re-introduces Stephen to use of chewed coca leaves as a mental and physical stimulant. He provides "…of course, the best flat-leaved mountain coca…"

162 – Martin bitten to the bone by an owl-faced night-ape: he poked his finger at the beastie whilst it was at home in its hollow tree.

172 – Stephen offers coca leaves to Jack to aid him in his attempt to re-float Surprise, and is turned down flatly.

176 - Dental assistant Higgins is interfering badly with the crew's medical affairs – nostrums, quackery, apparently extortion, magic… most ships had at least one such charlatan aboard. Stephen is annoyed.

177 – Stephen's daily sick-calls – foremast hands in fore-noon, then afternoon sick-bed checkups with Jack in attendance. Mrs Horner calls for an examination – she is pregnant by Hollom, and if her husband finds out he will surely kill her. She begs stout Catholic Stephen for an abortion. He cannot and will not consider it.

178 - Stephen's only advice to Mrs Horner is, essentially, "Grin and bear it".

182 – Mrs Horner attempts an abortion aided by Higgins – it is very badly bungled. Massive tissue damage hinted at, blood everywhere. Stephen and Mrs Lamb care for the patient, lie to Mr Horner

164

about the problem – NOT his fault, merely a serious but common female disorder. Prognosis quite poor, death likely, only hope is 'resilience of youth'.

192 – Re Mrs Horner, Stephen tells Jack "…I do not know if she will live!" Jack is dumbfounded (still the perfect innocent).

193 – Joe Plaice fractured his skull in a tumble down a ladder; and Mrs Horner is responding not at all to any of Stephen's ministrations.

194 – Stephen has a new surgical toy, an advanced French trephine for cutting circular pieces from the skull and thereby relieving pressure on the brain (usually due to swelling from severe impact injury – e.g. depressed fractures). He has done exactly this operation before, in public, early in his naval career - and is famous across the British Fleet for it. Now he does the operation in full view of the crew, patching over the trephined hole with a silver disc made from a three-shilling piece forged into the proper shape by the armorer.

196 – Stephen says he has shaved Mrs Horner's head – presumably (by implication) to reduce her fever – a nonsense treatment nonetheless used in many circumstances.

197 – John Nesbitt, youngster, has a broken collar-bone. Plaice is recovering nicely from his skull-surgery.

202 – Ship's wild cavorting throws Stephen violently down a ladder – nothing breaks but he receives lots of bruising, battering, and strains. Seaman Warely, aloft replacing a split sail, loses his footing and disappears into the sea.

203 – Antics needed to fix sails and other gear mid-storm have sent many to sick-bay: Jenkins' chest is largely stove in, most likely he will die. Rogers will probably lose his shattered arm. Jack himself has had a batch of fingernails torn out. Signs of scurvy appearing. Rogers' arm amputated.

204 – Stephen depressed, turns again to coca leaves by day, laudanum by night. Stephen personally caring for Mrs Horner, who is on the mend, albeit slowly. Stephen is beginning to have feelings for her.

Book 10 Chapter 6 – p207-237 (overview):   Surprise moored in Cumberland Bay for refitting. Crew camping and hunting ashore. Men atop the local mountain with the naturalists spot a ship far off: Surprise immediately unmoors and gives chase – it might be Norfolk. Gunner Mr Horner went ashore with Hollom and Mrs Horner, returns to ship alone, silent, blood-splattered, announces that the pair has deserted. All hands except Jack understand that he has murdered the couple. Stephen finally informs Jack about the Hollom-Horner affair, without breaking any patient/doctor confidentiality rules. Surprise catches up to the ship Estrella, a Spanish merchantman – she has information of Norfolk, who is far ahead, and continues to take and burn British whalers. Gunner, thoroughly drunk, accuses Stephen of performing an abortion on Mrs Horner ('using an instrument on her'). Stephen angrily and truthfully denies it, refuses to discuss with Horner the man's opinion that his wife was pregnant ("in kindle"). Dental assistant Higgins is terrified of Horner, begs Stephen's protection. Too late – Higgins seems to have disappeared, probably given a "Jonah's Lift" – i.e., been thrown overboard by crewmen who believed him to be a jinx. At any rate, he is no longer aboard. Gunner finally hangs himself without doing violence to anyone else. In the attempt, he has strangled himself rather than broken his neck: Martin thinks he might be revived through heroic efforts – thinks he can detect a faint pulse. Stephen refuses to try to resuscitate him, which if successful would only mean the man would have to try again. Gunner dies and is 'accidentally' buried at sea without any ceremony. Encounter another vessel at night: a British-built whaler. Surprise pursues it. Jack analyzes the prey's performance, concludes she is being operated by an American prize crew. Prey is Acapulco (whaler), surrenders to Surprise. She is full of oil ($100,000 worth), plus spars and other supplies – a magnificent haul. Captain of Acapulco is a disappointed naturalist, soulmate to Stephen and Martin. Discussion of the island Huahiva (O'Brian's imaginary Tahiti-like island in the Marquesas). Huahiva's people are "…scarcely an orthodox Presbyterian Paradise…" Seems the people are amiable, "…their only faults being cannibalism and unlimited fornication." Norfolk's captain may be of a missionary frame of mind. Prize dispatched (captain is Mr Allen) to Valparaiso, there to be ransomed by her owners, the results to be paid to Surprise's crew as prize-money, the military sailor's eternal hope and delight.

208 – Stephen has a large 'hospital tent' to handle "…severe cases of scurvy", and the usual assortment of other invalids.

209 – Mention in passing the recent death and burial at sea of two crewmen (a very minor toll). Surprise now well re-provisioned with island produce and meats. Entire crew again healthy or mending fast. Gunner Horner drinking heavily, "…probably going mad." Passing mention: Boyle had three ribs stove in. Williamson lost toes and tips of his ears to frostbite coming round the Horn. Scurvy rendered Calamy totally bald.

211 – The last three invalids are hurried aboard ship – one broken leg that will not knit (a common effect of scurvy), one amputated forearm removed after going gangrenous (ultimately due to frostbite) and one tertiary (final) stage case of syphilis.

222 – Stephen accosted by Horner: Stephen gives him a powerful draught of laudanum, with little effect.

227 – Gunner Horner hangs himself. Not a well-done effort… may have a pulse when cut down.

228 – Stephen prevents any attempt to resuscitate Horner, and the man finally dies. An interesting contrast in Stephen's moral makeup, abortion vs suicide.

Book 10 Chapter 7 – p238-277 (overview): Surprise is sailing through the Galapagos – difficult due to powerful, weird tidal currents. Norfolk is likely anchored in one of several bays. Naturalists cannot go ashore but shore is almost within touching distance and the view keeps them ecstatic – new flora and fauna everywhere. Encounter with a whaleboat (six men pulling) from whaler Intrepid Fox (London). The boat had been away from Fox, pursuing a whale when Fox was taken and eventually burnt by Norfolk. Information given as to Norfolk's course after the burning: Surprise off instantly in pursuit, the six men taken aboard, status not specified but apparently not (yet?) recruited into Sur-

167

prise's crew – in any case, despite war most whalers are immune to impressments into anyone's navy. Stephen furious at being denied 'promised' time ashore on Galapagos. A Marine sergeant was in another life a poacher of birds: he resuscitates those skills to provide Surprise with delectable seabirds (teal) in plenty. Discussion in wardroom of poetry, rhyme, meter, humor. One of the rescued whalers was once a pastry cook, produces magnificent puddings for the wardroom. Very light winds, 100 miles is now a good day's sail. Whalers' informality discussed. At night, during an all-hands dance and sing, Stephen falls overboard, noticed only by Jack, who dives after him without alerting anyone. In the misty dark, Jack finds Stephen, who really cannot swim. Surprise does not hear them hailing, and disappears into the fog. Jack swims continually, supporting Stephen. All night and into the day they swim, hoping for a log or other floating object. Rescued by a large 2-masted outrigger canoe crewed entirely by women – who apparently want nothing to do with men, judging from the human scrotums nailed to the mast. All the carved male figures in the bow have been castrated. The women's bosoms are uncovered, to the interest of both men. The women sail so well that it thoroughly startles Jack: they are also very well-armed and clearly adept with weaponry. When a 12-foot shark investigates the boat, one small girl slips casually into the water and guts the animal, then just as casually re-boards the vessel. The women, mostly attractive youngish Polynesians, find the Caucasian men both ugly and upsetting – worse than useless. Skulls rolling about in the catamaran do not calm Jack and Stephen. After arguments within the crew, a decision seems to be reached - the catamaran makes for a small island and deposits the men ashore, then leaves.

241 – Galapagos "cactus" pointed out as source of emergency water, but it will cause "the wet gripes" – i.e., diarrhea.

249 – To soothe his anger at not being allowed ashore, Stephen downs two ounces of laudanum – a heroic dose that would kill the unaddicted average man.

250 – Stephen, in laudanum stupor, awakened - Mister Blakeney is thought to have swallowed a 4# shot (a physical impossibility, thinks Stephen). Actually the lad swallowed one plum-sized lead ball

from the nine making up a four-pounder's grape-shot charge – still a considerable feat of swallowing. Purging the swallower with salt water recovers the ball intact.

Book 10 Chapter 8 – p278-294 (overview):   Jack and Stephen are marooned on a small island – green and lots of palms. Jack calculates as to likely search-and-rescue efforts by Surprise. Jack climbs for coconuts: from treetop, he first notices the catamaran some 12 miles away, then sees Surprise, some 8 leagues off (24 nautical miles, about 28 statute). Jack builds a signal of his shirt, sets it atop a palm. Surprise sees and sets course to intercept the catamaran. Jack is downcast, has to place all his faith in Mowatt's abilities and persistence. Jack and Stephen are chattering idly away about island geology when Stephen interjects "There is the boat." Their signal was successful - Surprise's launch arrives to retrieve them, after an 8-hour pull into the weather. Surprise has recently found a floating pristine USN beef keg – Norfolk must be nearby. Considerable number of wounds to crew, given them by the catamaran's women.

291 – Surprises Martin, Hogg et al. spoke the catamaran, were repulsed violently – five men in sickbay with serious wounds from war-clubs, a half-dozen more with lesser damage. Stephen treats them all: Martin has a shark's-tooth embedded in his buttocks (from a war-club), which Stephen removes using a tool designed to remove musket-balls. Martin demands the tooth so that he may identify the shark to species. Martin also has 36 stitches distributed about his head. His shoulders are also lacerated. Most of the Surprises had been "…ingloriously wounded from behind…" as they retreated from the women. Martin also has a barbed spear-point embedded in his calf, which Stephen cannot push through since it is obstructed by the tibia – it must be cut out. Martin is in a happy drug-fog of rum and laudanum for the operation.

Book 10 Chapter 9 – p295-335 (overview):   Surprise at sea, Sunday. Jack's musings about his mostly-absent father, General Aubrey, now an MP and seemingly bent on inadvertently destroying Jack's career. Inspections of ship and personnel. Stephen's ruminations on the sexual trap in which women find themselves caught – damned if you do, ditto if you don't. Deplores "male tyranny", has full empathy with the catamaran's women for whatever turned them against men. Another Norfolk beef-barrel sighted. Reading the Articles of War to the crew. Stephen's interest in prize-fighting (boxing) revealed: he has known or watched several well-known champions, which astounds the crew. A monstrous storm with severe lightning pitches Stephen headfirst down a gangway: he smashes his skull on a cannon, is now unconscious, probably with a depressed skull fracture. Severe storm produces more injuries for Martin to treat. Stephen looks dead, but is still breathing. Discussions about Martin's diagnosis, the obvious treatment being trephination to relieve pressure on the brain – as they had seen Stephen do at least twice. Martin is very much in doubt of his abilities, eventually decides to try, no other choice, Stephen is fading. Hogg spots an island by the color green reflecting off the underside of the island's cloud-cap: they head for it, to go ashore so as to provide Martin a stable operating platform. While running in towards shore, they find Norfolk, sunk, her back broken. All preparations made for the operation, the surgical team accidentally drizzles a mist of finely-ground snuff into Stephen's face, which makes him sneeze and instantly revives him. Martin, who has not yet begun the operation, is seriously disappointed. Meeting with the Norfolk's officers (Jack met Palmer, Norfolk's captain, whilst a prisoner in Boston) – the war, they say, is over, they heard so from a whaler. Jack is suspicious, this may be a ruse. Norfolk's crew, ashore now, is edgy because many of the crew are deserters from the Royal Navy, subject to instant hanging if recaptured. Jack understands this, tries to plan accordingly. Norfolk's own surgeon greets Jack, whose arm he saved some years earlier after it was shattered by a musket-ball.

296 – Mr Adams treated with a clyster (large enema) for "...a fit of the strong fives..." An imaginary ailment invented (along with the "marthambles") by a London quack named Tufts (of ~1700), with which to promote sales of Tuft's nostrums.

297 – Jack is now fat, cannot button his pants.

309 – Stephen cold-cocked by a head-first fall onto a cannon, is unconscious, barely breathing, under the care of his assistant Rev Martin. Stephen is unconscious, but probably not in full coma – his breathing is too regular for that. Martin declines offers of brandy for his patient, and will do no bloodletting on him.

310 – Martin's diagnosis is probable bruising or bleeding in the brain. Ongoing discussions about possible trephination, while Stephen remains unconscious for days.

312 – Severe storm: Hogg's arm is broken, Martin sets it. Martin himself is injured in some way – sports a bloody bandage.

324 – Norfolk's surgeon volunteers to help with trephining Stephen – has vast experience.

329 – Ashore, about to be trephined, Steven is accidentally dosed with snuff, sneezes himself to consciousness, declines to be cut upon.

Book 10 Chapter 10 – p336-366 (overview): Jack spends the night ashore with a few Surprises, expecting Stephen to be trephined momentarily. Stephen wakes up, seems okay. That night a huge storm tears Surprise from her moorings, which forces Mowatt (in command when Jack is ashore) to weigh anchor and head out to sea for safety. Storm lasts about three days, drives Surprise an unknown distance. Meanwhile the Surprises ashore are seriously outnumbered by the Norfolk's crew, who claim the USA vs England war is over – which Jack fears is an outright lie by Palmer. Discussion of other well-known similar ruses. Now waiting for Surprise to return (Jack feels a week is about right, given luck, but a month is a real possibility), Jack reminisces to Stephen about bad-weather cruises. The two sides are on very uneasy terms: who is whose prisoner? Is one captain subservient to the other, and if so why? Jack makes plans to enlarge the barge in which the Surprises came ashore, so as to escape the island with all Surprises. Preparations for island warfare are begun. Battles over ship's wood-working tools. One American crewman is a British deserter, has tried to ensure his own safety in exchange for his naming to Jack all others like himself. Norfolk's other crewmen hear of this, chase him down and disembowel him. Outnumbered, the Surprises try to launch their enlarged barge, and lose

171

that fight in a pitched battle with Norfolk crew. Just as the barge-fight ends, a whaler under full sail comes into view from behind the point – as they watch, she loses her main and fore topgallants, comes up into the wind, strikes her colors as Surprise, in full pursuit, comes into view, folds her wings, and lowers boats.

343 – Perils to crewmen of being ashore include stepping on poisonous spines of sea-urchins; being bitten by moray eels whilst seeking clams; eating a harmless-looking fish that gave diners a skin rash, black vomit, and temporary blindness. Stephen presumably treated all these conditions.

Book 11 – The Reverse of the Medal

Book 11 Chapter 1 - p9-39: (overview) Bridgeport, West Indies: Surprise (28), Captain Jack Aubrey, coming into port towing a prize – a fully-laden British whaler, recaptured by Surprise and therefore a lawful prize, worth $US 97000. Admiral Pellew gets a twelfth share, is pleased by the prize and a chance for a musical evening with Jack and Stephen. Jack's reputation as seducer and rake discussed. Surprise is decades out of date, long overdue to be scrapped. "Black Parson" introduced. Jack and Stephen intentionally do not inform Pellew about the huge sum they recovered from Danae – not the Admiral's business, rather Stephen's, in his role as "intelligence-agent/provocateur". Pellew declares Jack's just-finished cruise a resounding success – Norfolk is sunk, prize money in hand. [ASIDE - On p25 O'Brian makes an odd error – he was an avid birder all his life, yet he has the Admiral say, to Aubrey, "Doves don't suck." In fact, pigeons, doves and other related birds DO SUCK – they drink by suction, unlike almost all other birds.] Dinner aboard flag: no mail for Surprise. Securities market discussed: Jack only vaguely interested. Strange ebony-black man, huge, handsome. well-educated, a parson, is seeking Jack. Crew seem almost giggly over some hidden thing apparently associated with Jack – he is puzzled. The black man is Samuel Panda, son of Sally Mputa – Jack's until-now unknown son from an early tryst. Panda was most likely conceived in the depths of then-Midshipman Aubrey's Surprise – this very ship. He has now come to find his father and get Daddy's blessings. He brings gifts from his mother to Jack. Jack is flabbergasted. Worries arise about Jack's wife, Sophie's likely reaction, but evaporate when Panda gives Jack a letter he is carrying from Sophie – in seeking Jack, Panda went to their home. Obviously Sophie knows… the two men have identical faces and carriage. The crew is uniformly, secretly, hilarious over the event. Panda is in Catholic holy orders, enroute to the priesthood: despite being an adamant anti-papist, Jack does not let religion interfere with his relationship with Panda – after all, there is precedent - Jack's best friend Stephen is also a devout Catholic.

15 – Major health problem is whores coming out to meet Navy ships – certainly because of venereal diseases, but also –perhaps mostly- because they bring large quantities of alcohol. Jack waves the whore-fleet away from Surprise: the crew will have to go ashore for their refreshments.

22 – Admiral Pellew needs to consult with Stephen about too-frequent urination.

26 – Flag's surgeon Mr Waters has an abdominal tumor he wants seen by Stephen, a renowned expert diagnostician.

31 – Mrs Goole has met Mrs Aubrey, tells Jack his children have had and recovered from the chicken pox. Waters' tumor is benign but awkwardly situated – must be removed, which is not a favorite option, pre-anesthesia.

32 – Martin will aid Stephen with the abdominal surgery – he has "…never seen the opening of a living human abdomen."

Book 11 Chapter 2 – p40-69: (overview) Panda and priestly companions – lubbers all- have their own ship and are headed off together, apparently to S. America, likely to proselytize. Jack mildly bemoans the fact of Panda's blackness – Stephen reproves Jack, pointing out that the Queen of Sheba (inter alia) was shining black, and also that Caucasian skin color is rather bland if not disgusting, compared to most others. Jack concedes the point. Jack to Flag to attend the court-martial of the deserters he re-captured on the whaler, an odious duty. They will be allowed to defend themselves, then they will be hanged immediately. Stephen's ability to fall between any ship or boat and an adjacent dock is now legendary in the Fleet. Stephen's intelligence connections explained. There are two highly-placed but not yet known moles in Navy intelligence, named Wray and Ledward, both "… besotted admirers of Buonaparte." Perils of self-publishing one's slender volume of poetry discussed – Mowatt is about to do so. Privateers and letters-of-marque vessels discussed, compared to men-o-war. Deserters convicted and hung: long discussions at dinner of various topics mostly non-military. Surprise sails instantly for England, once the court is dissolved.

46 – Discussion of hospitals as instruments of death – successful amputations, for example, if kept in a hospital almost inevitably die of infection, those kept outside a hospital generally survive. This is well known to, but not yet understood by, the medical community. [Germ theory of disease is still many decades in the future.]

47 – Post operation, the patient seems fine, alert and chatty, just a little "laudable pus" from the incision. "Laudable" in sense of "desirable, or good" – pus that runs freely from a wound rather than being trapped inside – believed to aid in draining unhealthy 'humors' from the body. Pus indicates mild sepsis, often but not always indicative of general infection of the abdominal cavity, inevitably a fatal outcome. Prognosis neither good nor bad.

51 – Capt Palmer (Norfolk) has "quartan ague" – a fever that recurs ever four days, likely malaria. Stephen has been treating it successfully with Jesuit's bark and sassafras. Sassafras has no medicinal value. Jesuit's bark is from the plant *Chinchona spp*, contains quinine, a reasonably effective anti-malarial still in use today. Palmer is also suffering from a steadily-worsening melancholia – should be on suicide watch.

69- Stephen leaves Mr Waters with a prescription, presumably for extract of Jesuit's bark.

Book 11 Chapter 3 – p70-113: (overview) [NOTE - no medical events of consequence occur in this chapter.] Surprise is a vaguely unhappy ship, very likely enroute to the breakers. All aboard are hoping for some action during this final cruise. Luck as a tide – cyclic, and Jack currently low in the cycle The passage itself is almost idyllic, ship totally reprovisioned to everyone's satisfaction, performing perfectly, clad in mild disguise to mislead any outside observers as to her true nature. Gunnery practice – the crew is superb. They spot the heavy privateer Spartan three times, then find him close aboard in morning fog. Disappointment, the nearby ship is actually British, the privateer Prudence (12), her captain an acquaintance of Jack's now in humbler circumstances, no Navy command being available. Extended descriptions of training aboard Surprise: also discipline on Surprise vs other ships. Spartan is seen, and pursued - a very extended and difficult pursuit, in horrible weather, lasting for days. Ships dead-evenly matched except for a small advantage to Surprise in really dirty weather. As Surprise closes to bow-chaser range, Jack is rudely awakened by a shot across his bow from a British 3-decker... Surprise and her prey have sailed blindly and at breakneck speed straight into the British Channel Fleet. Spartan escapes.

72 – Stephen has "...almost certainly lost his last patient," the Flag's surgeon.

Book 11 Chapter 4 – p114-138: (overview) [NOTE – No medical events occur in this chapter.] Jack is haled before the Fleet Admiral and given a serious dressing-down. Surprise now at anchor awaiting orders, her crew disbanded, almost all dead drunk ashore. Jack speculating to Sophie as to his own likely Navy future – e.g. perhaps running fireboats. Stephen has "inherited" from his Godfather – Jack knows nothing more about any inheritance than that bald statement. Jack still hopes Surprise will be mothballed rather than broken. Ashore and headed home to family, Jack helps a stranger fight off an attacker in the drive, shares a carriage with that man and his companion – both strangers to Jack, who apparently have inside knowledge of soon-to-happen stock-market fluctuations. Eventually they impart to Jack this information in thanks for his aid during the scuffle... with suggestions to invest in specific funds, monies, or stocks at specific prices. Jack, financial cretin, shortly does so, having been convinced that his initial doubts as to the legality of doing so are utterly incorrect – that such is the normal course of business ashore. Jack tries to interest Stephen in the scheme, fails. Jack encounters his idiot father, retired Army General, tells Daddy of the scheme, with specifics – successfully urges the General to invest in the scheme.

Book 11 Chapter 5 – p139-174: (overview) [NOTE – little of medical import occurs in this chapter.] Stephen is ashore, preparing to reconnect with his wife Diana. He is told Diana has moved, does not live at her old address. His and Jack's favorite inn, The Grapes, has burnt to the ground. She has left behind with his

176

clean underwear a note, essentially saying that they should separate because clearly his passion for her had died... this due to his having not yet explained to her that his rumored running-about with another woman was in fact part of his intelligence operations, not an affair. Her notes make it clear – she believes he is having an affair, the morality of it is NOT her concern, rather it is his appalling lack of gentlemanly good behavior that offends her. Stephen's intelligence boss, Sir Joseph Blaine, now considered moderately elderly, seeks Stephen's advice on male sexual vigor – he is thinking seriously of marriage. Blaine seems to be losing an internecine war for control of Naval Intelligence, which he at present heads. But he has plans to set all right again...once the primary opponents can be identified. Stephen give to Sir Joseph the box of funds recovered from Danae. Blaine disavows any knowledge whatever of it. Blain warns Stephen to decline any engagement offered that requires crossing the Channel. Aubrey is without a ship: meets with Admiral Melville at the Admiralty. Surprise will be sold out of the service, not broken. Jack would like to buy her. Stephen's nemesis in intelligence (this is not yet known to him) is Mr Wray, whom Stephen has beaten thoroughly at cards and who owes him a huge debt. Wray is actively ducking away from Stephen. Stephen is well acquainted with the Crown Prince, William Duke of Clarence (an Admiral in his own right) whom he has treated: this flabbergasts some of Stephen's enemies. The huge sum retrieved from Danae is put into the hands of Wray and his superior. A trans-Channel mission is proposed to Stephen: forewarned of the danger of such a mission, he neither accepts nor declines.

157 – Stephen is at Naval Intelligence HQ whilst Jack is seeing Adm Melville. Stephen dosed himself heavily with laudanum the previous evening, so as to sleep.

163 – Stephen mentioned to have cured the Crown Prince of a serious illness (unspecified).

164 – Other physicians recommend Stephen to one another for his expertise in treating 'marthambles'.

166 – Stephen meets Wray socially, notes severe eczema on Wray's hands, attributes it to extreme nervousness.

170 – Stephen declines an invitation to attend public hangings at Newgate, London.

Book 11 Chapter 6 – p174-199: (overview) [NOTE – another chapter with no medical events.] Stephen in a coach enroute to Jack's home near Portsmouth, advises a fellow-passenger not to invest based on mere hopeful rumors of peace. She takes the advice. Other passengers discuss investments, believe that the one Stephen heard about from Jack is a fraud. Jack is fully committed to it… all available funds. At Jack's home, a cricket match is under way. Maturin the eternal stumblebum arrives afoot, collides with a fielder. Jack describes to Stephen his hope of buying Surprise – done with open bidding, cash on the barrelhead. Cricket defined and explained for the unwashed (sort of: ineffectively for this Yankee, however). Adm Harte's daughter Fanny has been married off to Mr Wray, with a very large dowry (probably in cash – Harte is rich). Much to Wray's consternation the lady's monies (upon which Wray based his attraction to her and for which -quite openly- he married her), are perfectly bound up – he cannot get at a penny. Babbington is presently having an affair with Fanny, feels immune to possible bad effects because he and his family have several seats in Parliament – plans to run off with her. Martin arrives, dismayed at the complexity of setting up de novo a married household. Sophie arrives unexpectedly, the house is a shambles of cleaning and overhaul, she and Jack have dinner in the stable, his worries about her reaction to his bastard son Sam Panda (a jet-black Catholic priest) are allayed – she liked Rev Panda, wants him back to get to know the children – but clearly she understands the genetics. Jack is arrested at home on a warrant, not for debt but for conspiracy to defraud the stock exchange.

182 – Jack says two of his more excitable cricketeers would benefit from one of Stephen's "…comfortable slime draughts…" NOTE – nobody writing about the Aubrey novels seems to have uncovered a reasonable description for this O'Brian invention – but it must be something evilly slimy and nasty to fit the implications one gets during its recurrent use through the entire series. Such a disgusting item

178

would help convince the average sailor that the dose was truly strong and effective.

Book 11 Chapter 7 – p200-228: (overview) [NOTE – another chapter with no medical occurrences.] No doubt about stock-exchange fraud having been committed by SOMEONE, but not Jack. Jack's naïve belief in the purity and accuracy of English law and justice is very hard to shake. Trial is a bad joke, very much put-up, transparently a total miscarriage of justice, entirely driven by politics which the system cannot be persuaded to abandon. Jack's father, deeply implicated in the actual fraud, has disap-peared, perhaps to Scotland. Everyone believes the General did the dirty deed and is actively fobbing off guilt onto his son. Jack's lawyer nearly incompetent, ill with a severe cold, fails to keep track of the case, a court-manipulated midnight decision goes against Jack, who stays in prison with Stephen, Sophie and oth-ers, awaiting sentence. Stephen owns up to his huge inheritance – more money than he could believe existed in the world. Stephen will not change his spending or living habits despite infinite rich-es: he will however endow an academic position, a chair of com-parative osteology (study of bones). Jack is warned that his naive-té is going to destroy him: Jack refuses to believe how the system actually works. Jack's supporters cannot make a case for his in-nocence – all the important intermediaries and witnesses have been brutally murdered. Stephen sees that Jack will be convicted and then almost certainly stricken from the Navy List – ending his career. Stephen feels that eventually the truth will out and Jack will be restored to the list, but it will take a long time... meanwhile, to keep Jack sane, Stephen will buy Surprise, get let-ters of marque, and set Jack up as a privateer. Jack still believes in the English Jury's inherent ability to discern truth... cannot be persuaded otherwise.

Book 11 Chapter 8 – p229-255: (overview) [NOTE - Few medical events of consequence occur in this chapter.] Stephen beats himself up in his diary for mishandling Jack's case. Meets with Blaine, who suggests that Aubrey will be convicted, that much is wrong with the scenario, that it is entirely fabricated and will eventually be fixable but not soon or easily. Stephen and

Blaine hatch a plot, supported by shadowy figures in the British government, to have Stephen, Jack and Surprise unofficially foment a revolution leading to a British-favorable government in a major South American country... or countries. England would greatly prefer a batch of disconnected small states to a continent-wide coherent empire. Stephen and Pullings buy Surprise at auction, aided by Jack's lifelong friend Heneage Dundas, who provides the crew needed to move the ship from the auction area to safer moorings. Jack is found guilty, the only remaining question being the punishment – everyone is hoping for a simple money fine: all fear the possibility of something more extreme, e.g. being pilloried.

230 – Stephen is angry with himself over Jack's case, returns to his laudanum-drinking.

236 – Jack's lawyer Williams has Spanish influenza, debasing his skills and ability to think.

239 – Jack's attorney taking "physic" – doses by spoon from a bottle – not prescribed by Stephen... Attorney is miserably ill and simultaneously preoccupied with saving a very young boy from being hung for stealing a small watch. Lawyer also has his own nostrum of choice, to wit 'Quinn's Draught' (another O'Brian invention).

Book 11 Chapter 9 – p256-267: (overview) [NOTE - no medical events of consequence occur in this chapter.] Jack is sentenced to a fine of 2500 pounds, and to the pillory for an hour, a total disgrace and also physically dangerous because the public may throw at him whatever they might choose as missiles. Those responsible for the trumped up charges and rigged trial realize they've utterly misjudged the public reaction which they hoped would be aimed at Jack, but which is instead purely directed at the government, Jack is recognized as a hero by the Navy, and by the populace, who have always enjoyed hearing about his exploits. Nonetheless, Jack will be stricken from the List, the worst possible outcome for him, psychologically. Already, Stephen and others are plotting how to get Jack restored to the list – an eventuality which is now the ONLY real question. The hope is to eventually begin the process by using Stephen's friendship with the Crown Prince, Duke of Clarence, but the Duke is presently somewhat out of his father's good graces and such a venture must wait indefinitely. Seamen and officers from all over the British Isles attend the pillory, thousands of angry, heavily armed men intent on defending one of their own: they drive away the hired professional louts, and keep the muck-throwing rabble entirely away from the pillory whilst Jack is in it, cheering him nonstop through the entire hour.

265 – In prison, Jack preparing for the pillory, Stephen offers him a draught (likely laudanum), which he says "…will make the time in the pillory pass like little more than a dream…" Jack thanks him, refuses to take it.

Book 11 Chapter 10 – p268-287: (overview) [NOTE – another chapter with no medical events.] Stephen is remarkably astute in bargaining re letters of marque, and also in his definition of Surprise's "South American agenda". He gets a letter of exemption for the crew – nobody can be pressed for any reason. Also a letter giving Surprise access to any British Navy yard, including any needed supplies and repairs. Blaine tells Stephen that the trail to the overall "intelligence" problem and to the perpetrators of Jack's misery, are becoming clearer – urges patience. Stephen receives a mysterious message written on the skin of an armadillo, which is made clear by a passing Admiral who understands the nautical import of some of the words. The reference is to the Blue Peter, a very large diamond once owned by his wife Diana, and years ago used by her to rescue Stephen from certain death in an enemy prison: its eventual return was guaranteed (after the fact) by high enemy officials. This is the first Stephen has heard of the stone for many years. A clandestine meeting results between Stephen and Duhamel, the highest level of operative in the French Intelligence – the meeting is friendly, Stephen leaves with the diamond in his pocket. In a final act, Duhamel makes known to Stephen just who the mole is in British Intelligence – Mr Wray.

Book 12: The Letter of Marque

Book 12 Chapter 1 - p7-32: (overview) [NOTE – Little of medical import occurs in this chapter.] Jack is now a civilian, has been stricken from the Navy List: life now fundamentally meaningless. Aboard Surprise at anchor in Shelmerston, choosing his new crew – Jack has his pick of the very best volunteers. They expect to get rich with Lucky Jack, privateering. Maturin, secretly owner of Surprise, is late. Now bleeding rich, Maturin's carefree attitude towards money has changed – a bit miserly. Stephen meets a self-proclaimed author in an open field, composing novels orally. Perils of publishing discussed: he cannot quite finish any manuscript. Martin has been turned out of any role within the Navy due to his vitriolic pamphlet on sex practices in the Navy, will join Surprise not as chaplain but as Stephen's medical second. To dinner ashore with an Admiral, an early commanding officer of Jack's. Balloons discussed – nasty, dangerous things. Admirals at dinner reassure Jack of their ongoing efforts on his behalf. Adm Russell gives Jack a letter written and signed by Adm Lord Nelson, Jack's particular hero – a magnificent gift indeed.

26 – Stephen given a book, "_An account of the means by which Adm Henry has cured the rheumatism, a tendency to gout, the tic douloureux, the cramp and other disorders; and by which a cataract in the eye was removed._" This book by Adm. Henry is real, published in 1816.

Book 12 Chapter 2 – p33-65: (overview) [NOTE – little of medical import in this chapter.] At sea, Jack does not know Stephen has obtained exemption from pressing for the entire crew. Jack is taken aback at having to do, on his own, the ship's complex accounts. Oddities of being non-Navy – no man-o-war pennant, no Marines, open chatter and humor by the crew. Rumors rife aboard small ships – Rev Martin supposedly banished to sea for rogering (= fucking) his bishop's wife. Problems of making an integrated crew from mixed Surprises and Shelmerstonians (civilian sailors, mostly pirates and/or smugglers). Surprise encounters

Navy cutter "Viper", commanded by a snooty brat, who is flummoxed when he proposes to press a few Surprises and is shown the exemption letter. As Viper leaves Surprise's crew man the ratlines, send the cutter a full salute of naked "protected buttocks." Stephen explains, to Jack, both Jack's own situation, and their mission to the Americas. Stephen and Martin go aloft, to the terror of the crew. Surprise encounters Tartarus, commanded by Babbington (with Mrs Wray aboard as his companion): Mowatt and Pullings are also aboard.

54 – Mention made of crew's injuries in practicing with the great guns – bruises, burns, crushed toes and fingers, a broken leg. No specifics given.

55 – During great-gun exercises, Stephen's monoglot Irish loblolly boy Padeen saves the day by holding onto, bare-handed, a loose and extremely hot cannon that has broken its breechings. He prevents injuries to men and ship, but is horribly burnt – "... his blood hissed as it ran down the metal." Padeen gets heavy doses of laudanum for the pain. Laudanum praised as a panacea for insomnia, toothache, wounds, headache, morbid anxiety (i.e., depression) and hemicrania (severe, persistent or recurring headache confined to one side of the head). Martin worries about possible addiction. Chapter ends with a massive storm brewing.

56 – Stephen pooh-poohs the idea of addiction to opium..."...no more injurious than smoking tobacco."

62 – The "digesting machine" bursts in the galley – a large early pressure-cooker readily subject to misuse – particularly cook's helpers tying down the safety valve to make things go faster. "Nobody dead" is the report: the scalds are "...of no consequence and will heal in a month or so."

Book 12 Chapter 3 – p66-107: (overview)   A truly violent storm at sea: Surprise almost founders. Surprise finds the damaged merchantman schooner Merlin, which tries to get away, fails. She is also a privateer, and consort to the formidable privateer Spartan, nowhere to be seen just now. Jack's cabin and stores

are destroyed, he wants to play host (there are ladies aboard Merlin), asks the Merlin's Captain Dupont to hold Jack's dinner
aboard Merlin. Dupont is astounded not to be summarily stripped
by a fellow privateer, a fine party ensues. News about a huge
shipment (150 tons) of quicksilver (mercury – valuable in its own
right, very useful in gold-mining) – in a chartered ship, the powerful privateer Azul, a vessel closely resembling Surprise. An
elaborate ruse is hatched: disguise Surprise as Azul. Slow sailing
for days, hunting for the quicksilver-carrier. Joe Plaice falls overboard, is rescued. No Spartan or Azul. Surprise encounters a running two-ship battle, identities unknown. Probably Spartan chasing Azul, thinks Jack. During the chase, Azul grounds on a barely
submerged reef. Azul's crew abandon ship, Spartan is preoccupied with Azul. Surprise closes in to take Azul, then they work
across her (using her as a bridge per Lord Nelson much earlier)
and take Spartan as well. The attack comes off well, Azul (preoccupied) is taken, followed by Spartan, whose crew have abandoned her in boats. No Surprise casualties, although much overall
carnage. Azul sinks, but the mercury has been transferred to Spartan, now Surprise's prize. They make sail as quickly as possible,
for Fayal, where Spartan's five prizes await Spartan's return – a
new plot hatched to take those prizes: the bosun is encouraged to
whip up several spare French ensigns.

67- Ship's motion pitched Jack against the overhead in his cabin:
he is dripping blood: shortly he has a bloody bandage around his
head, covering one eye.

78 – Stephen awakes feeling stupid, due to his last-night's
draught of laudanum. Sick call today: action is imminent, nobody
comes to complain of anything except Padeen, who has a tooth very
badly infected, likely abscessed, perhaps merely an impacted wis-
dom-tooth but agonizing in any event.

79 – Padeen dosed heavily with laudanum – palliative only, nothing in the way of treatment that either Martin or Stephen can do.

88 – Padeen, in continual agony and with freedom of the medicine chest, doses himself with laudanum and tops off the laudanum
bottle with brandy from Martin's store.

95 – Jack asks after Padeen, Stephen is unaware of the man's growing consumption of laudanum, says only that he is stoically bearing up well.

99 – Stephen tells Jack he has seldom seen so healthy a crew.

104 – In attacking Azul, Jack's sword is taken out of his hand by a musket-shot, and a pike cuts him badly on the neck.

105 – Surprise's Webster has a belly wound, Gunner's arm is in a sling, presumably broken, but the only those two serious casualties for Surprise.

106   Jack's neck wound confirmed as "a trifle".

Book 12 Chapter 4 – p108-138: (overview)   Stephen and Martin buy medical supplies – laudanum available in 11-gallon carboys. Grapes Inn has been rebuilt. Stephen engages a room for Padeen's recovery from dental surgery. Stephen visits his Intelligence superior Blaine at the man's home – Blaine seems to have won the battle for control of the organization, both men are happy. Concept of pardoning Jack – for something he never did. This will not sit well with Jack. Privateering even if successful does not count towards reinstatement on the Navy List. Surprise did in fact convince all five of Spartan's prizes to sail themselves directly into the Surprise's guns – her being disguised as Azul worked perfectly, Jack is again monetarily rich (quicksilver + 6 prizes). Diana (Mrs Stephen) has become a balloon show-woman and rider. Stephen decides to go meet with her in Sweden, where she has gone to live for the nonce – he will return the Blue Peter diamond to her there. Deadly perils of ballooning discussed. Stephen discovers the very existence of insurance – e.g. for ships and diamonds, inter alia. Jack at home, express mail arrives: Jack has a chance at a real naval action vs the French, which could get him reinstatement. French ship Diane (30), being set up for a mission to S America paralleling their own. In Jack's name and without his permission, Stephen has accepted the assignment to deal with Diane. Surprise (a private ship) is now leased to the Government (thus becoming temporarily a Royal Navy vessel once more), commanded under contract by John Aubrey, Esquire, hereby sent on a special service, with orders requiring absolute noninterference by any of His Majesty's forces. A wonderful document!

185

Jack nearly cries. Mission and Plan – take Diane –cut her out from where she lies quayside at St Martin's, a difficult well-defended harbor. A master stroke if successful.

109 – Stephen speculates on the apparent decrease in effective-ness of laudanum after prolonged use. He is still unaware that tooth-ache-driven Padeen is steadily diluting the bottle from which both he and Stephen are dosing themselves. Martin asks what might be con-sidered a 'moderate dose' and is shocked by the answer "Not above a thousand drops or so." – Martin knows the standard hospital dose is 25 drops, sixty for 'severe pain'.

112 – Padeen finally scheduled for a tooth-drawing "tomorrow".

123 – Power of money to influence patients... the more expensive the doctor, the less difficulty getting willing –even enthusiastic- ac-quiescence from the patient. Padeen as an example.

125 – Padeen's operation difficult but successful – more lauda-num for pain.

131 – At Jack's home, the postman fell off his horse in the drive, is 'covered in blood'.

Book 12 Chapter 5 – p139-165: (overview) Complex problem of religion (Sethian sect - protestant of course) in the crew – Jack smoothes things over nicely, all content. Discussion of religion as a phenomenon. Martin's wife coming aboard to be introduced. Lack of experienced gunners and Marines is a problem. Sail to St Martin's - extensive detailed rehearsals out of sight of the enemy (Diane et al) moored in port. Detailed roles, information, educa-tion for every participant. Crew extremely happy, excited, deep into their individual roles. Jack freed of his melancholy due to in-tense activity. More discussion of various forms of religion. Padeen, "confirmed opium eater" goes ashore to try to find his own supply, at the pharmacy he does not know the drug's name (except to call it 'tincture', of which there are literally hundreds), cannot speak English, is a terrible stammerer and illiterate to boot... and cannot identify what he needs. Stephen has been un-knowingly weaned off the drug by Padeen's serial dilutions. This unknown cleansing bites Stephen later. Surprise sets sail as soon as possible: only possible clinker would be Babbington, a King's Officer, getting all the credit for a successful action, and both Jack and Stephen wonder if the man is sufficiently astute to see how he must act so as not to wind up with credit – all of which MUST accrue to Jack alone. In the event, Babbington is magnificent.

157 – Mention in passing of injuries during training exercises – strains, cracked ribs, a few badly broken bones, e.g. Thomas's compound fracture of the femur. He fell from a yard, fetched the leg up against the mizzen-stay - snapped the leg but stopped his fall, saved from certain death.

158 – Thomas's leg gives medicos pause – any trace of gangrene and off it will come. Diagnostic tool used to check for onset of gangrene is the human nose. Thomas is doing well, no stench from the wound.

159 – Still undetected by Stephen, Padeen is now a "confirmed opium-eater"… and Stephen has been weaned down to almost no laudanum – the contents of the laudanum bottle are now nearly pure brandy due to Padeen's self-dosing.

Book 12 Chapter 6 – p166-197: (overview)   Final council of war aboard Tartarus – still an official Navy vessel commanded by Babbington, who knows nothing whatever of the plan or his possible role as spoiler if he fails to correctly understand the situation. Babbington has just been made Post, is ecstatic, in no need of further glory for the moment – and his orders are to aid the Surprise as needed… which is exactly what he proposes to do: he will totally subordinate his own interests to those of Jack. Babbington has matured, takes masterful command of the meeting, defers entirely to Jack's plans. During practice, Stephen demonstrates consummate skill (unsuspected by all) as a first-class swordsman. All is in readiness. Surprise launches the complex plan. The cutting-out party is completely successful: with some difficulties the Diane is overcome and unmoored in an intense close-fought battle. Cavalry horses are being ridden onto the ship from the quay. Jack wounded. Operation successful in all respects, including Babbington's noninterference. As an extra, they take two French gunboats.

196 – Taking Diane, Jack is wounded – saber cut on his forearm and a musket-ball in his back (he thought he'd been kicked by a horse).

Book 12 Chapter 7 – p198-219: (overview)   Back aboard Surprise, Jack's wounds are excruciating. A superb victory for Jack – capturing a frigate of greater strength than his own, capturing two laden merchantmen and two French gunboats into the bargain – without fatalities. Stephen boarded the Diane with the rest of the Surprises, was seen energetically and effectively pistoling the French captain and otherwise attacking the Diane's men. In England, news of the action causes a big public uproar of applause. Stephen chagrined –on Diane, he had captured a top French agent, but the man escaped, disguised as an injured woman. Huge amounts of French cash are expected to be found in Diane, now being closely searched. If Jack had been on the List he'd have received a knighthood or baronetcy: as things stand, no such award is possible. The public is angry over perceived mistreatment of Jack et al. At lunch, Jack is accosted by HM Duke of Clarence, Crown Prince whom Stephen has treated: the Duke sits down at the table and demands an account of the action, being himself an Admiral and a good sailor. Sir Joseph (head of Naval Intelligence) sets a dinner to honor Jack, attended by a dozen men whom Jack respects and who wield considerable political power. All praise Jack. Later, Jack is approached with the offer of a pardon, which he vehemently rejects, inasmuch as accepting it would be (to Jack) to admit guilt, which he does not carry and to which he will never admit.

198 – Stephen and Martin working to treat Surprise's wounded, including Jack. Jack has a musket-ball in the back, causing him great pain in the leg (the ball is pressing on the sciatic nerve). The ball must be extracted, a very painful procedure for which Jack is strapped down with leather-padded chains, given a leather pad to bite on. Re-

moval is successful. Jack also has deep gashes in both forearm and thigh, which have cost him a lot of blood.

200 – Butcher's bill (casualty list) – No fatalities yet, but many wounded, including three very dangerous abdominal wounds. Mr Bentley somewhat injured (tripped over a bucket, headfirst down a hatchway). Many Surprises kicked or bitten by the cavalry horses ridden aboard... says Stephen of the equine injuries, "...an unreasonable number for a naval engagement."

Book 12 Chapter 8 – p220-255: (overview)   Jack's refusal of a pardon has vexed all his powerful friends, who are more pragmatic and less honor-bound than is Jack. The idea was badly presented to Jack, they agree. Jack's father found dead in a ditch, presumably murdered by fellow conspirators in the stock market fraud. At the funeral, an old family friend and relative -"Cousin Edward"- offers Jack the seat in Parliament that goes with some of Edwards' land-holdings – the 'borough of Milport.' Jack is ecstatic, even though he must do some campaigning to ensure the seat. Jack meets his much younger half-brother, now aged about ten, the result of the General in his dotage having married his illiterate teenage milkmaid. All is happiness in the Aubrey household. A trip to Sweden looms: Stephen will use the chance to met with Diana to test the degree of their estrangement over his imaginary affair. Ruminations on the sequence of events needed to reinstate Jack to the Navy List. Stephen's thoughts on the strangeness of wife Diana's mind... wondering what he really represents to her, other than perhaps comfort within her need for independence. Surprise reprovisioning in Shelmerston, Jack's wife Sophie is beloved by the town's women (mostly prostitutes) both as Jack's wife and on her own account – she is completely nonjudgmental. It is now an open secret that Jack is shortly to be restored to the List. Enroute to Sweden aboard Leopard (almost a hulk now), Stephen is identified by the crew as a former Leopard and participant in the ship's famous battle – wherein Leopard (50) most improbably sank the Dutch Waakzaamheid (74). Stephen is much caressed by Leopard's present crew. Stephen gets deeper into melancholia (depression) as Leopard nears Sweden. Jack is now happy, Stephen is miserable, Jack understands Stephen's situation but cannot bring himself to say anything comforting.

230 – Stephen is still taking laudanum nightly – but it is so diluted by Padeen's depredations that the actual dose he receives is trivial. His body is now utterly unaccustomed to the opiate – his long-time near-immunity to laudanum's effects is gone, but he does not know it.

249 – Stephen mentioned to Leopard's crew as author of famous "The Diseases of Seamen" – standard Royal Navy medical text, put aboard every Navy vessel. (The actual book is by Sir Gilbert Blane, "Observations on the diseases of seamen", published 1799.)

254 – Stephen in his misery, preparing to confront Diana, fumbles and breaks the laudanum bottle. He will buy more in Stockholm.

Book 12 Chapter 9 – p256-284: (overview)   Arriving in Stockholm, Stephen takes an apartment, sees his banker, sets out to buy laudanum – and of course gets full-strength tincture. Stephen is walking cross-country towards where Diana is living: she passes by driving a buggy, recognizes him, picks him up – seems ecstatic to see him, kisses and embraces him. She is exquisitely beautiful, being both happy and set off well by the climate and surroundings. She has been reported to Stephen (erroneously and with scurrilous intent) to be having an affair with Jagiello, an absurdly beautiful rich noble officer in the Swedish army – she tells Stephen there is nothing to the stories – this to keep the men from one anothers' throats when they meet, which is inevitable and will happen soon. Diana never got Stephen's letter explaining his phony affair – it was given to Wray for delivery, which he failed to do. Stephen is exhausted, asks to retire to his room where he will take a dose of laudanum to encourage sleep. He measures the dose, is startled at the strength, attributes that strength to use of a different liquor as the tincture's basis, and takes a dose such as he was wont to take at the height of his addiction and immunity. The dose works, quickly and effectively. Both parties forgive one another, although both feel there is nothing needing forgiving on the part of the other. In an opium haze, Stephen returns the Blue Peter diamond to Diana. They go up in an observation tower. Stephen, senses dulled, falls through the trapdoor and is badly injured, in addition to being nearly dead of an overdose. Diana undertakes to nurse him back to health... his coma and delirium last for some

190

days. During his recovery, they discuss the missing letter of explanation, and are fully reconciled. Padeen caught by Martin in the act of stealing laudanum. Stephen suddenly understands his own laudanum experience. As Surprise prepares to sail from Sweden to its duty in South America, Diana boards the ship, introduces herself as Stephen's wife to the utter astonishment of the entire crew (what is that scarecrow doing with such a gorgeous woman?) and takes possession of Stephen's cabin.

265 – Stephen doses himself with full-strength laudanum, in the quantity he was used to taking back when his addiction and immunity were both at full strength, too.

269 – Under the emotional strain of the reunion, Stephen takes another (second) dose of the newly-bought full-strength laudanum.

271 – Upstairs in the observation tower with Diana, Stephen is clearly ill, opens a door and pitches headlong down the access. He is still alive, hallucinating, almost comatose from the overdose.

273 – Swedish physicians called in, diagnose the problem, treat the badly-broken leg via "Anderson's Basra method". This is a generic term for immobilizing a simple fracture, using external splints of various materials, then further protecting it with a coat of plaster – a good approximation to today's modern plaster or fiberglass cast. In his fall, the laudanum bottle broke, cut him severely but not quite into the abdominal cavity, which would likely have been fatal.

277 – Even in recovery from his near-fatal laudanum escapade, Stephen rationalizes his own use thus: "...this frequent and indeed habitual use was not true addiction, but just the right side of it."

Book 13 – The Thirteen Gun Salute

Book 13 Chapter 1 – p7-36: (overview)   Surprise just leaving harbor enroute to S. America, as a private ship (owned by Stephen, carrying letters of marque) leased to the Government, captained by Jack Aubrey as a civilian hoping to be reinstated to the Navy List shortly. Task – study the continental situation, then foment an England-favorable resolution to the "emerging nationalities" problem – England does NOT want a coherent South American Empire (i.e., potential competitor) to emerge. Diana is pregnant by Stephen. Jack's black bastard son, a Catholic clergyman, is doing well. Discourse on banks and banking. Differences in atmosphere and interpersonal relationships on civilian vs military ships. Padeen, away in Scotland, broke into a pharmacy seeking laudanum for himself, was captured and tried – a capital offense: only Jack's influence as a Member of Parliament had enabled a commutation to life, in exile at Botany Bay. Jack once more dives overboard to rescue Stephen, again fallen into the sea in a calm.

18 – Stephen has given up his laudanum habit: post-addiction return of his sex drive yielded Diana's pregnancy.

29 – Stephen unpacks, inventories and locks up the ship's medical supplies and equipment.

33 – Mister Standish, the purser, is cut about the ears by a boathook energetically wielded in the uproar of saving Stephen from drowning.

Book 13 Chapter 2 – p37-56: (overview)   [NOTE – No medical events in this chapter.] Surprise sails in seldom-used sea-lanes to avoid problems. Stephen, off of laudanum, is extremely horny… with no relief available. Encounter with a 10-gun snow – a vessel clearly outfitted for speed and almost certainly a privateer. Wind dies, Surprise mans the sweeps (long oars, each powered by several men) to close the snow – which does the same and with much greater effect. Calm ends, strong winds enable a chase. Snow, overhauled, is seen to carry Mr Gough, an acquaintance of Stephen's from Irish Revolution days, no longer an ally. Stephen wants no confrontation, considers trying to use his new "medical magnet" to deflect the ship's compass, cannot figure out how. Snow escapes when Surprise loses a topgallantmast in the blow.

39 – Fellow Physician Pratt has gifted Stephen with a powerful magnet for use in removing splinters of shattered cannon-balls – especially from the eye.

45 – Standish is violently seasick for days on end.

Book 13 Chapter 3 – p57-82: (overview) [NOTE – nothing of medical import occurs in this chapter.] Sailing across the Atlantic, seeking the westerlies. Great-gun exercises. Surprises are becoming a Jack-Aubrey-style crew. Discussions of techniques for weighing anchor. Ashore in Lisbon, the French make a clumsy attempt to kidnap Stephen. Relationships between Jack and crew astoundingly informal and close. Purser Standish resigns due to ongoing seasickness. Mail call. Diana has bought a horse-breeding farm, but is living with Jack's wife Sophie at present. More problems dealing with banks. Sam Panda (Jack's illegitimate black son) will be ordained a Catholic priest. Stephen meets with his intelligence-service superior, Blaine. Ruminations on entomology, a passion to both men. Surprise's mission suspected by the Spanish. French trying to recruit the Sultan of Pulo Prabang, a piratical Malay state – Surprise may have to deal with that. The French effort is led by top intelligence operative and Stephen's nemesis M. Ledward, plus a new player, M. Duplessis. The English are sending a trained diplomat, Mr Fox, to engineer a counter-move – Surprise will carry him and his party to the fray in Indonesia – the South American venture is on brief hold for this errand. There will be considerable diplomatic and other maneuvering as French and English interests and inducements are presented, in competition, to the Sultan seeking his alliance.

63 – Standish, after many days of seasickness, can keep an egg down, but there is no real cure for the malady.

193

Book 13 Chapter 4 – p83-119: (overview) To support the plan, Jack must take command of Diane, reluctantly leaves Surprise in Pullings' hands… a rendezvous is planned. Jack must go to Diane part-way overland, a difficult journey. Enroute, a land-lubber's position is found for Standish, as aide to a British Army officer – Standish's outstanding musical abilities cinch the deal. Stephen's reminiscences of the Irish Revolution. The Surprise's party arrives in London to get detailed orders. Stephen and Jack head for the Aubrey house to see their wives. Diana is near full term now. The men send word of their imminent arrival, the women take a coach, meet them at an inn without warning. Jack meets with Lord Melville (First Lord of the Admiralty) at the Admiral's private home – gets first news of his reinstatement to the Navy List with his original seniority. Jack's and Stephen's mission restated and clarified. Yet more difficulties with his bankers – Stephen in a snit. Banks of the day were private affairs, known to frequently go belly-up, so choosing the right bank is of major concern. Diane has a full crew, but not of Jack's choosing or training. The son of Jack's nemesis Adm Harte is serving aboard Diane: Jack packs the man off – Jack cuckolded Harte long ago, the son takes his father's view of the affair. Fox meets the group, and appears (incorrectly) to be a true gentleman. Discussions of forms of Buddhism, and human vs other spleens. Fox hates Ledward. Sir Joseph Blaine noted for 'masterly flashes of silence'. Stephen re-reads his diary, relives some of his revolutionary experiences. Hiring a servant for Stephen – a black man with blackened teeth – much racial and other prejudice to be overcome. Jack's much younger half-brother Phillip (aged about ten or twelve) is determined to run away to sea. Jack cools the boy's ardor. Confidential ship's joiners (cabinetry-men) come aboard to build secret hideyholes for serious treasure. Jack goes aboard Diane as her skipper leaves, reads himself in to the crew. Back in the Navy for real, now!

99 – Killick in an alcoholic stupor from celebrating Jack's reinstatement.

110 – Stephen busy observing an interesting delicate operation performed by a friend – the condition not specified. Patient screams nonstop.

Book 13 Chapter 5 – p120-169: (overview)   Surprise carrying Envoy Fox to Pulo Prabang. Dead calm: a prodigious swell is setting the ship into a vertical cliff 1000 feet tall, a desperate situation... no bottom hence anchors unusable: manning boats to tow ship is too little too late. Stephen and Fox sit below decks, playing chess, as doom approaches. A roll throws the chessboard to the deck – game ends. A tiny puff of wind at the last instant enables Surprise to clear the cliff, within touching distance. Now reinstated, Jack ponders the relative freedom of action that was his as a privateer... he rather misses it. Various drawn-out ruminations by Jack, including his self-imposed duty to properly educate the youngest crew-members, who are caught copying one another's work. Sailing mostly south now, getting very cold, very fast. Icebergs appear. Bergy bits (aka drift ice) rapping on the hull. Confusion – there are several islands named "Desolation". Rations getting meager. Eventual uneventful arrival at Java Head, Indonesia.

139 – Killick has passed the word to Surprise and the Ambassador's party that Stephen is so esteemed by the Navy as to have been offered the position of Physician to the Fleet – which he had declined! Stephen's belief that forcing men to pay for their own treatment for venereal diseases was in fact a disastrous policy – it meant treatment was often delayed (simply to avoid payment) until there was no hope whatever. The men particularly respect him for his tact and for being completely non-judgmental. Stephen announces an amputation to take place momentarily (no explanation or identification of the patient given here: identified at p141). Return to lower latitude, weather improves. Boston Tea-Party motto garbled into "No reproduction without copulation!"

140 – Sick list includes two with advanced syphilis (both dying now), plus "some serious pulmonary cases" (likely flu or pneumonia). The amputation succeeded, patient doing well.

141 – Amputee identified as Mr Raikes, the injury identified – a compound break, broken tibia and fibula, caused by a recoiling great gun – one side of the gun's breeching failed, throwing the gun side-

ways. Initial good indications gave way to rapidly-progressing gangrene, hence the amputation.

142 – Stephen busy rigging an enlarged sick-bay to handle the usual flood of high-latitude health problems (e.g. scurvy, pneumonia) and work-injuries.

147 – Fox visits Stephen – has a pain in his lower belly, difficult defecation. Stephen gives him a laxative and sets a strict diet.

148 – Pills given to Fox are placebos only. Mr Fox's true ailment is psychological, the effects on him of self-imposed (due to snootiness) loneliness, alienation.

149 – More injuries due to ship's antics in violent weather… rope burns, twisted joints, torn muscles, cracked ribs, another broken leg, scalds and burns amongst the galley crew. Most of the crew is in some minor way continuously injured.

155 – Not mentioned earlier, Arthur Grimble has been operated on (probably trephined) to relieve pressure on his brain – he is a terminal-stage syphilitic. "He may recover, but don't be too hopeful. If not, an easy death."

158 – Grimble buried at sea.

163 – All of Fox's livestock die of a 'murrain' (an unspecified highly-infectious disease (often anthrax), usually of cattle or sheep). Fox feeling poorly, sees Stephen – diagnosis still loneliness.

165 – Fox's complaint more real, less mental – something (unknown) amiss in his belly. Fox bled 15 ounces, and purged. Fox in pain – prescribed rhubarb, calomel [a strong laxative, also quite a strong poison, to wit mercurous chloride - Hg_2Cl_2], hiera picra ("sacred antidote" in medieval Latin - a cathartic [i.e., strong laxative] powder made of aloes and canella bark). The laxatives "work powerfully". (They certainly should; this is an extreme use!)

166 – Fox returned to apparent health.

Book 13 Chapter 6 – p169-202: (overview) [NOTE – Little of medical import in this chapter.] At java Head - Diane filling water, re-provisioning. Comments on complexity of manners, social structure in Indonesia. Word of bank failures at home – ongoing worries about Stephen's bank. French delegation has already left Java Head, headed for an eventual meeting with the Sultan. Ten Diane crewmen run, cannot be found before sailing. Eventual arrival at Pulo Prabang, delivering Fox to his mission-territory. Stephen seeks information on the French delegation. Stephen's interest in spleens of humans and other primates: host van Buren shares that interest. Execution by peppering. Problems (e.g., decay) of scientific dissection of animals in a tropical climate. Planning to upstage the French at a communal diplomatic meeting with the Sultan. Stephen's foes from French intelligence - Wray, Ledward, Lesueur, and Duplessis - finally realize they are in the same room with Stephen, almost panic. Homosexual intrigues in the Sultan's properties include the Sultan's favorite gazelle-boy, plus some of the French delegation – disastrous to them all – especially the boy.

169 – Mr Fox (a friend to Mr Raffles, British Governor of the island) returned to good health, probably due to "acceptable" companionship.

Book 13 Chapter 7 – p203-230: (overview) [NOTE – No medical incidents in this chapter.] Diplomatic negotiations. Stephen arranges colorful fireworks for the Princess's birthday celebration (muzzle-flashes of the ship's great guns, firing decorative gunpowder). Money properly spent produces the intelligence Stephen needed. He plans the demise of the French intelligence-gentlemen, especially Wray and Ledward. Sultan comes aboard Diane for a short cruise and firepower demonstration – enjoys himself. The French came on an unarmed merchantman – Diane is incomparably more impressive. Ledyard (and also, not here mentioned, Mr Wray) have become the secret gay lover of the Sultan's gazelle-boy-inamorata – a truly stupid move. Negotiations delayed a week for religious celebrations requiring celibacy. Stephen goes to the volcano-crater, befriends an ancient orangutan who is suffering rejection by her much younger lover/mate, makes extensive cultural and historical observations. Chapter ends with Stephen in the volcano, watching a territorial combat between rival rhinos.

Book 13 Chapter 8 – p231-264: (overview) [NOTE – little of medical note occurs in this chapter.] Stephen returns from the crater, for once satisfied with his biologizing. Jack is off surveying the coast, for centuries a required activity for Royal Navy officers when in unfamiliar territory. Other people's attitudes show that Stephen – much to his distaste – is regarded as elderly now. He blames it on his ancient threadbare wig. Returns to town through the swamps in a downpour, gets infested with leeches. Gazelle-boy seized in bed with Wray and Ledward. Lesueur murdered, apparently over gambling debts. Gazelle-boy executed by being peppered, meaning beaten to death with a bag full of peppercorns over his head. Sultan's earlier safe-conduct is keeping Ledward and Wray alive, but nobody will aid them in any way. They eventually end up on van Buren's dissection table, both of them having been shot by a party never named but obviously Stephen himself. Stephen and van Buren together dissect both corpses. By Stephen's specific arrangements with the Sultan's Vizier, the Englishmen are reduced to bits and the skeletal elements boiled clean of flesh. The "English spleens" are saved for van Buren's collection: he is officially unaware of the who-what-where-when-why and how of the two specimens. Jack goes sailing in the skiff, lands for lunch, finds the French warship Cornelie, careened (= intentionally heaved down on her side on a bank) and having her bottom copper repaired. A Cornelie officer spots Jack – he is an acquaintance from an important long-past battle, reminiscences and friendship bloom. Agreement not to attack one another. Fox is happy, finally. The treaty is concluded very rapidly, with much advantage to the British. The short text is written out in duplicate, to be sent to England via two separate routes, for insurance. Diane sails, with the entire British contingent aboard again.

243 – Mister Elliott, a poor excuse for a seaman, has a wounded shoulder upon which falls a bucket of tar, from aloft.

259 – The Sultan gives magnificent gifts to the major British players – Stephen's is a "chest of the Honourable East India Company's best Bengal opium".

Book 13 Chapter 9 – p265-297: (overview) Plans to meet with Pullings and resume the South American mission. Meanwhile, Fox has been a complete insensitive overbearing ass aboard ship – *inter alia*, he makes no gestures of thanks to the crew that brought him to his successful mission. The entire crew despises the man. Fox's men are trying to interfere with the sailing of Diane, so the officers also hate him. Stephen hopes for word of "Diana and our daughter": Jack (parent of three) tries and fails to disabuse him of the notion that being a day-to-day parent is 100% joyous fun. Fox's social boorishness accidentally causes a magnificent dinner party for the ship's officers only. Arriving at the first set rendezvous they find no Pullings, and no Surprise. Fox mistakes the ship's Coronation Day salute as being for himself, is furious when told it is not. The two worlds – Navy and diplomacy – have no lines of communication and nothing in common save sovereign and (marginally) language. Stephen manages in one awkward fall, to destroy most of Jack's expensive oceanographic instruments. Diane runs hard aground at full speed on an uncharted subsurface rock…at the highest possible tide, making the chance of re-floating her fall in-between improbable and impossible.

271 – Stephen wonders about Mr Fox's mental stability and condition.

280 – The "usual port diseases" (meaning various venereal infections) are mentioned in passing as being present among the crew.

283 - Loderer (of Fox's retinue) consults Stephen privately. He has an unnamed condition, clearly a venereal disease caught in Prabang – "…the Prabang infection is particularly virulent". Prescribed are dietary restrictions, plus ointment and pills (probably of mercury). The disease should be controllable, as it is in the very early stages.

<u>Book 13 Chapter 10 – p298-319: (overview)</u>   Lightening ship, assessing and then repairing damage. Pumps going nonstop. All hands moved to stay ashore. At high-tide, with the ship somewhat repaired, the guns go overboard to reduce the ship's draft when next they try to float her. Hopeless. Must wait the next spring tide in four weeks. Fox angry, insists he must go off in a ship's boat (actually, a boat that is Jack's personal property) to deliver the treaty (it is his entire career) to Batavia (some 200 miles off- a mere two days' sail), for shipment home. Warned not to do so because of possible typhoons, he goes anyhow, taking one of the two copies. The Marines and sailors set up an organized camp ashore. A savage storm arises, the wind and breakers destroy the ship's small-boats: finally the Diane herself is beaten apart on the rocks. The storm leaves them a large chunk of Diane, and in addition much miscellaneous timber has washed ashore. The book ends with the crew surveying the available wreckage, and deciding that they can construct a reasonable small schooner from it – presumably a small crew will then go to Batavia to obtain and return with serious rescue capabilities.

299 – Many falls, sprains, a hernia – all resulting from work on salvage and repair. Mister Blyth hit in the head by a flung hen-coop, deep scalp wound, sewn up, bleeding stopped.

Book 14 – The Nutmeg of Consolation

Book 14 Chapter 1 – p9-31: (overview): Jack, Stephen, and the crew of Diane (a temporary alternative to Surprise, with whom they were to rendezvous) are castaways, busy building a usable schooner from the wreckage of Diane, destroyed by a violent typhoon. Stephen is the group's chief hunter (mostly of pigs) and is escaping the crew's Sunday cricket match. Stephen is so physically inept that he has been thankfully shunted aside from other work on the schooner or camp. Hunting a pig, he finds a cliff full of edible swallows-nests. Supplies of rum, tobacco, sugar running out. Stephen, himself taken ill, expounds on the misfortune of being a doctor and therefore knowing in detail what the body can and cannot stand. Native Malay girl (a member of the fierce 'Dyak' tribe) and crew arrive in a small proa, study everything about the camp (riches galore!). Girl uses her knife to shave Stephen's arm – the blade is literally razor-sharp. Gunner, excited by Girl, spills the entire stock of drying gunpowder. The Dianes hire Girl et al. to take a message to Batavia, 200 miles (two days' sail) away. Girl's uncle is mentioned by her – he is nearby in a much larger proa. Most Dyaks being piratical, this makes the Dianes nervous, particularly Stephen, who knows that she has seen and studied the layout of the entire camp.

12 – Stephen, the ultimate "all-thumbs" worker, has driven a pick through William George's foot.

21 – Stephen is suddenly taken violently ill, no cause specified.

22 - Macmillan (assistant doctor) suggests twenty drops of tincture of opium (= laudanum) for Stephen. Stephen, recently recovered from severe laudanum addiction, vehemently rejects the idea.

23 – Stephen self-prescribes – bark, steel, saline enemas, rest and quiet. Realizes he has a severe fever, cause unspecified. Chews coca-leaves to relieve symptoms (probably queasiness).

24 – Stephen kept cool and hydrated in the shade, fever breaks by morning, with "a profuse laudable sudation" (= heavy sweating).

Book 14 Chapter 2 – p32-54: (overview)   At dawn, the larger proa (a large ship) launches an attack on the shipbuilding site, stealing tools and killing at least two Dianes. Insufficient powder to defend or counterattack with firearms. Yesterday's Girl is among the Malay dead: she had killed Mister White in the battle. The sides separate, most of Diane's supplies and tools in Dyak hands. Diane's Marines are capable and experienced, study the ground, come up with a defensive plan since it is obvious the Dyaks intend to attack again. Maximum use of terrain and available firepower. Marines' orders: one shot per Marine, no reloading, fix bayonets. Available small cannon from Diane loaded with grapeshot, wreak havoc, massive killing, amongst Dyaks during second assault. Dyaks retreat. Jack has the 9#-er (his personal brass cannon) carefully reloaded with solid shot. Jack is an expert with this gun. Suggestion to shoot the anchored proa rejected – that would leave 230 desperate, waterless Dyaks stranded ashore in the Dianes' faces. Dyaks regroup, assault in a charge, going uphill at the Dianes' defensive positions – into a barrage of rocks and line of bayonets, plus grapeshot. Dianes mount a countercharge, Dyaks retreat, losing many. Dyaks set fire to the half-built schooner, the hundred remaining clamber aboard the big proa. As the proa leaves, Jack sinks it with a shot from his 9#-er, dumping all the Dyaks into the water – and they are in a millrace current carrying them out to sea: all will inevitably drown. The schooner project is unsalvageable... they must start over. More planning for both survival and successful escape. They will build a cutter, not a schooner. Hunting, Stephen kills a large wild pig. Enroute back to camp, he encounters four small children – three girls and a slightly injured boy. They are collecting swallow's-nests, and come from a junk visible offshore. Stephen befriends them, treats the boy's injury. One girl delegated to go tell Father (on the junk) what is going on... the rest will go with Stephen to the Diane camp. Boy's injury greatly exaggerated, as is his treatment, to impress Father and put him into Diane's debt. Negotiations for passage to Batavia for all Diane personnel on the junk, which is roomy.

34 – Bosun sewn up – has had his hamstring slashed by a Dyak – "He will never dance again".

37 – Both medicos busy treating "several wounded" Dianes. Two more Dianes injured by shots from a small Dyak swivel-gun.

38 – Purser killed instantly by a swivel-gun shot through the heart, whilst standing beside Stephen.

43 – Stephen is getting older – now requires glasses for fine surgical work. Several crewmen received nasty burns trying to salvage the schooner.

44 – In post-battle talk, Bonden tells Jack that Jack's scalp needs sewing up – Jack had not noticed the wound.

45 – The young ship's boy Reade has his arm amputated... he is about 12 years old, perhaps less. Luckily he had been knocked unconscious and remained so through the operation. Long will be the butcher's bill... many dead and wounded, not even counted yet. No final accounting ever provided. Wounded are beginning to develop gangrene, many are dying (2 or 3 burials per day). Stephen treated the wounded Dyaks also – they die just like other men.

46 – Reade has no gangrene, is recovering.

50 – Stephen treats a local boy-child for minor leg injuries, exaggerates their severity and need for ongoing care.

Book 14 Chapter 3 – p55-80: (overview)   Aboard the junk, having left the island. Career possibilities for Edwards (Fox's assistant) are contingent upon delivery to London of the remaining copy of the treaty between England and the Sultan of Pulo Prabang. The duplicate carries a letter venting Mr Fox's spleen on his entire party – career-ruining bad marks and totally undeserved. Equally likely to forever deeply tarnish Mr Fox's (deceased)own reputation. Stephen, as intelligence agent, knows of the letter and its contents, is torn about telling anyone. An even larger pirate ship approaches the junk: captain of the 'pirate' is a business colleague of Stephen's from Pulo Prabang. All is suddenly sweetness and light: the junk merely pays a 'customary toll' for safe passage. Cornelie is operational and now in Pulo Prabang: its route is known, passed to Stephen. Cornelie suspected of being desperately short of gunpowder. Safe arrival of the junk - ashore in Batavia, seat of government: Stephen consults with Raffles (Governor of British Indonesia) about Fox's nasty letter – what to do? Stephen's bank may be bankrupt, his fortune gone up in smoke –penniless once again. Stephen has plenty of government funds immediately to hand, proposes to buy a recently-raised delightful small Dutch-built 20-gun warship (nice vessel, but too small - not capable of directly setting upon Cornelie). The ship was intentionally sunk in the harbor for six months "because of infection". Stephen buys dolls for the three girls – they are utterly flummoxed by the toys. Stephen's peroration on Irish history. Jack is delighted with the little ship, which will be outfitted immediately in the local yards, carte blanche. Chapter ends with naming the vessel by Jack – "Nutmeg of Consolation" – the phrase taken from the Sultan's formal title.

58 – Stephen's sneaky staging of care for the boy is finally understood by Macmillan. They agree to cauterize (physically burn away) a "naevus" (= "nevus" modernly, = raised birthmark, usually red or black, an inconsequential item seldom going malignant). This unnecessary but spectacular "treatment" is to impress the boy's father and further indebt him to the Dianes.

59 – Macmillan admits to Stephen that he is married and impotent.

64 – Edwards down with severe dysentery.

Book 14 Chapter 4 – p81-110: (overview)   Nutmeg in the yard being fitted out gloriously well for a change. Problems of union work-rules solved by judicious bribery. Anticipating encounters with the superior Cornelie, Jack outfits Nutmeg with 32-pound carronades – "smashers". Replacements recruited for casualties of the Dyak battle. Stephen has a new species named for him – an exceedingly foul-smelling plant: he ponders possible hidden message. Nutmeg sails, fully manned, armed, provisioned and ready for anything. Nutmeg is a phenomenally fine sailer. Ship trials, training. Speculating as to Cornelie's most likely course, and the likely location of Pullings in Surprise.

85 – Passing mention of survivors of Dyak battle being on the mend.

89 – Raffles' butler is a cadaverous Brit, victim of "Javan ague" (vicious sub-species of malaria).

100 – Killick has a new mate, an old shipmate of himself and Jack, the only survivor of seven men from warship "Thunderer" - all had Batavian fever, were left ashore to convalesce or die.

106 – Medical rounds: one broken collarbone, five obstinate cases of Batavia pox (unclear: may refer to smallpox or syphilis).

Book 14 Chapter 5 – p111-139: (overview)   Nutmeg in steady winds, sailing the Celebes Sea enroute to South America, but actively seeking Cornelie. Nutmeg speaks the merchantman Alkamaar, stopped very recently by a French frigate (32: presumably Cornelie) which took all her powder – Cornelie is now effectively armed. Nutmeg plans to disguise herself as a merchantman, hoping to close Cornelie once the Frenchman is found. Stephen ruminating on his financial loss due to his bank's failure: his philanthropic and personal plans all dashed. Stephen cannot even perceive the supposed "filth" constituting Nutmeg's disguise. Finally they spot the Cornelie moored and taking water on (fictitious) island Nil Desperandum. Nutmeg makes to close her as inconspicuously as possible (an oxymoron? – she is approaching via zigzag through the reef at perhaps 2 knots maximum!?). Disguise fails, Cornelie fires immediately: she obviously has plenty of powder, fires rapidly and accurately. Nutmeg hit repeatedly whilst closing, gets the range (now ¾ mile) and fires at twice the rate of Cornelie, and with 32#-ers vs the enemy's 18#-ers. Cornelie's main problem is severe shortage of men: she cannot both fight and unmoor.

116 – Two dental cases: both molars are far gone in decay, difficult to extract. Stephen's assistant Macmillan knows nothing useful about dental work. Oil of cloves directly into the rot-holes (even today this is a useful primitive emergency palliative for the pain of a decaying tooth). Holes then packed with lead foil in hopes the tooth will come out entire, but neither does – they must then be dug out

piecemeal, a nasty job for everyone involved. Stephen hates dentistry, makes do without proper instruments, succeeds but ends up feeling perhaps worse than the patients.

117 – Youngster Reade in good health, recovered from loss of his arm, wearing a padded appliance to protect the healed stump. His increasing agility largely compensates for the loss.

132 – Daily hospital rounds, discussion between Stephen and Macmillan in Latin to confound the patients. One hernia, two "obstinate" remaining Batavian poxes… whatever the disease is, it seems to be curable by Stephen, which suggests syphilis – if it were smallpox (or a relative) the disease would not "hang on". Seaman Abse is dying of the marthambles (an ugly multifaceted intestinal disease conveniently invented by O'Brian). Stephen considers doing an autopsy, but must consider the crew's feelings – they hate the idea, find it distinctly sacreligious. But Abse had no friends, so an autopsy is quietly laid on.

133 – Stephen's preparations for treating the inevitable battle-injuries: laying out equipment including saws, chains, gags.

134 – Ship's Master cannot climb the foremast to con the ship through the reef towards Cornelie – his bowels are too upset.

136 – One 18# raking shot down Nutmeg's deck kills two men on the forecastle and three on the quarterdeck, including Miller, standing beside Jack, who is splattered with Miller's blood.

137 – Battle injuries begin to occur immediately – splinter wounds, broken forearm. Nothing yet unusual or excessive.

139 – Stephen visited by Jack: Stephen reports three men dead of splinter wounds (bled to death), six other wounded but are all in "a very good way", plus many minor injuries.

Chapter 6 – p140-166: (overview) Cornelie manages well, pursues Nutmeg but stays outside the smashers' range. Cornelie is a slug as a sailing machine, Subterfuge – Nutmeg deploys a submerged sea-anchor to slow herself down despite full sail… must not outrun the prey! At maximum range, slow careful continual exchanges of cannon-fire. Building a ship's-stern-like decoy for night use. Pursuit is extended. Unexpectedly strong tidal currents interferes badly with the chase. Cornelie gets wily, in the dark closes to killing range, does Nutmeg great damage. Tom appears, in Diane - as do Surprise and three American warships. Surprise joins Nutmeg in chasing Cornelie. Rainsquall hides the action briefly, Cornelie disappears – foundered, all her men off in small boats headed for rescue by Surprise. Jack greets Cornelie's captain Dumesnil as a long-lost friend, refuses to accept the Captain's sword. Dumesnil is the nephew of Capt Christy-Palliere who captured Jack (in Sophie), and treated Jack very well indeed. Favor being returned. The American colors were Pullings' misdirection, and all the ships with him are prizes.

144 – Simple ceremony for the Nutmeg's dead, buried at sea.

149 – Stephen complains – he had held back a corpse (Mr Abse), dead of the marthambles, for dissection, but the crew included the specimen in the burials early that day, unknown to Stephen.

157 – Discussion of splinter-wounds and their impostumes (= abscesses).

166 – Stephen and Macmillan cannot leave Nutmeg because "They are going at it with a saw, sir." An unspecified amputation.

Book 14 Chapter 7 – p167-197: (overview) Jack gets a letter from his son Sam Panda: more of Stephen's ruminations on Irish vs English (pointing out that the Irish taught the English to read, inter alia). Quasi-ceremonial dinner for all the various ships' officers. Traditional seating arrangements explained. Surprise's crew has worked hard to be ready for the party – requests a whole-ship tour of inspection by Jack-in his most formal uniform, please. With his medals and ceremonial sword. They get it. Sethians (a very odd minor Christian sect) are still aboard Surprise. Jack's share of the prize monies will enable him to buy Surprise from Stephen (at the same price), thereby satisfying Jack and helping a tiny bit to restore Stephen's apparently-lost fortune.

178 – One of the officers at Jack's dinner is violently seasick due to the glue-like 'portable soup' served at dinner.

183 – One of the Surprise's Sethians lost two toes to frostbite; another 'sinned with a woman in Tahiti and is in sickbay yet…" Next page, the disease is named: Tahiti pox. Aka syphilis (again).

184 – Inspection of sickbay by Jack. Surprise has lost "only five hands" since Jack departed: three Lascars dead of pneumonia, one washed off the head whilst easing himself, the final one killed in action with a prize. Wilkins' broken arm will not mend (sign of scurvy). Ship reeks belowdecks, due to men shitting and pissing in dark corners rather than go be exposed to the elements on the head. This turns the bilges and lower holds into cesspools.

185 – Stephen arranges for better ventilation in his sickbay, using "windsails". Sethian sinner Brampton is despondent, feels he will surely go to hell. He gets slime-draught and asafetida (a medicinal and culinary herb with a terrible smell – related to parsley).

186 – Stephen (psychological counselor?) sets the "Tahitian-poxed' Sethian aside in isolation until his treatment of salivation is done – this is a mental-health move by Stephen to keep the man from exposure to his fellow-Sethians' mirth and needling - he already feels bad enough.

188 – Martin and Stephen confab whilst sitting on spare sails in the crosstrees. Martin was ship's doctor by himself on Surprise while Jack and Stephen were gone: Stephen tells him he has done a fine job, lost a mere three hands across 100 degrees of latitude; successfully done surgery on West's nose (a mere snip with scissors, a few stitches) – frostbite, not syphilis. An altogether good record indeed.

192 – Martin relates his being bitten by a tapir – perhaps a worldwide first! Wilkins' arm is properly set, immobilized in Basra-method plaster, but will not knit – suspect scurvy. Ship's lime juice seems to be adulterated, not an effective antiscorbutic. Wilkin's broken arm resulted from a fall out of the top whilst drunk – a lucky man to have survived at all.

Book 14 Chapter 8 – p198-239: (overview)   Both doctors have
learned to safely climb via the shrouds, and unattended, to the
fighting tops and beyond – Surprise is the only ship known where
that is the case. Landfall at Sweeting's Island is important for getting green vegetation (vitamin C) for the crew. Discussion of
Botany Bay, Capt Cook, Banks, and their naturalist's findings.
Landfall and mooring in an eerie silence, boding ill. The island's
entire human population is very recently dead, probably of smallpox, and in advanced stages of decomposition. Stephen finds two
surviving children, starving, jet-black sisters perhaps 5 or 6 years
old. At first sight (from a distance) he declared them to be small
apes. Martin agreed, called them "glabrous" (i.e., smooth and
hairless). The children are trying futilely to open coconuts: Stephen does so for them, takes them to the water. The kids return to
Surprise with Martin and Stephen, become the ship's mascots instantly. Jemmy Ducks (caretaker of ship's poultry and other livestock) has seven children, hence is assigned to care for the two
girls, with a pay adjustment accordingly. Antiscorbutics (anti-
scurvy substances – plants containing vitamin C) galore on the island. Girls adopted by entire crew – phenomenally good at learning languages. Ruminations on language learning, forgetting.
Great Barrier Reef skirted. News that Buonaparte has escaped and
is raising hell again. Rats ate most of Jack's private food-stores,
plus Stephen's coca – resulting in fat and very aggressive (i.e.,
stoned) rats. Long discussion of Botany Bay, invitation to dinner
at the Governor's house. Boorish resident Englishmen at dinner
infuriates Stephen by ignorantly and incorrectly criticizing Ireland. Stephen runs him through the shoulder, threatens to kill him
if he does not apologize, which he does, exuding malevolence.

206 – Entire native human population of Sweeting's Island dead
of smallpox, and decomposing. Stephen orders the few Surprises who
have landed to strip, bathe immediately in seawater, isolate themselves from the others, and touch nobody.

208 – Mr Reade has not had smallpox but was the most likely to
have been exposed ashore – ordered to shave his head, wash with vinegar, and stay isolated from everyone for a week.

213 – Antiscorbutics working – Hayes' arm knit, signs of scurvy in the crew have vanished. In treating scurvy, vitamin C works very quickly.

219 – Stephen reveals that he regularly doses Awkward Davies with hellebore to calm him. Davis is a marginally psychotic, stupid, and extremely powerful man. Hellebore is a common herb often used as a purgative, or to calm people who are nervously (mentally) upset.

220 – Discussion of rats, well known by sailors to "fatten on the odor" of an unclean bilge – Surprise's bilges are flooded and pumped daily, now quite sweet-smelling.

224 – Rats have eaten all of Stephen's coca leaves.

225 – Girls Emily and Sarah bitten by their pet rats, which are now stoned on coca. Bites cauterized by Stephen.

230 – Apparent mild food poisoning among those who ate a turtle the day before. Stephen prescribes "physic" that will "confine them to the seat of ease" for many hours – the physic is a strong laxative. Stephen and Jack discuss various pills – Jack unimpressed by small pills.

232 – Sarah swallowed a pin: recovered, presumably using emetics, perhaps laxatives as well… the child is "emptied".

233 – Jack, still mistrusting Stephen's small pills, begs another dose from Martin and winds up in the head for hours ("…he has taken a 90-year lease on the quarter gallery…").

Book 14 Chapter 9 – p240-279: (overview)   [NOTE – Nothing of medical import occurs in this chapter.] Stephen's encounter with the boor is the stuff of instant fame and legend aboard Surprise. Sethians have relatives imprisoned at the Bay; Stephen's gentle Irish aide Padeen is here somewhere – jailed for breaking into an apothecary seeking laudanum for his addiction. Stephen locates Padeen, aids Sethians. Stephen receives a letter from his old bank – he had mis-signed the documents that were intended to transfer his fortune from old bank to new bank, the transfer could not be made and had NOT been made, hence when new bank failed (of which Stephen had heard correctly), that failure did not affect Stephen at all. Pure dumb luck. More ruminations on money, wealth. Attempt to leave the girls behind at an orphanage or with the Governor's wife fails – they escape, return to the ship, climb to the highest rigging and stay put – unreachable. Eventual decision to take them home to England: they are officially entered on Surprise's books as paid crew. Lessons about boomerangs. Padeen located in the penal hospital, severely injured by a ferocious punishment (200 lashes apparently – the intent of such a sentence is to kill). Stephen calms Padeen, determines to help the man escape.

240 – Captain asleep after hours on the head.

250 – Martin deeply bitten by a cockatoo.

277 – Every ship leaving Sydney/Botany Bay is "smoked" – fumigated with sulfur... not against disease but to expose any stowaway convicts trying to escape.

Book 14 Chapter 10 – p280-315: (overview)   Martin and Stephen explore the outback with a native guide payable in whiskey. Behavior towards Surprise and its crew by authorities ashore is inexcusably bad and infuriating. Jack anchors mid-harbor to be safe from local authorities. Stephen's necessary arrangements to spirit Padeen away aboard ship transgress many aspects of Jack's morality and code of ethics. Although the plan works and may – with legal technicalities- have been just-barely acceptable, the breach between Stephen and Jack is serious and will be difficult to paper over. Stephen gets indirect word of the birth of his daughter, reported in the Naval Chronicle. Stephen is stung by a male platypus, almost dies of the venom. Surprise sails away with all safely aboard.

288 – Stephen's thoughts about sailors' horniness and what they will undertake ashore to relieve it.

313 – Stephen severely stung by a male duckbilled platypus, comatose, hallucinating and nearly dies. In recovery at end of chapter, which is also the end of Book 14.

Book 15 – The TRUELOVE

Book 15 Chapter 1 – p7-34: (overview)   Aboard Surprise, finally headed to S. America, hopefully to strongly promote British interests – especially seeing that no competitive empire arises. Encourage smaller states. Competition = France. Highly placed traitor, still unknown, in Whitehall (Navy HQ, London). Jack's musings on Surprise, the Navy, his eventual rise to flag rank. Jack offers Rev Martin (Stephen's assistant) several 'livings' – the income from some of Jack's property, which income is to support the local church. Full formal inspection of ship and crew – all is fine. Rumors that the French bury their dead in the ship's ballast. Stowaway found in the cable tier – female (Clarissa Harwell)… a gentlewoman convict smuggled aboard by Mr Oakes. Her presence onboard is common knowledge in the ship, but unknown to Jack in his splendid 'commander's isolation'. Warned by Stephen against throwing first stones, Jack allows Clarissa to be openly aboard, but very grudgingly… his own shipboard antics with women being the stuff of legend amongst his crews, he can hardly do otherwise.

15 – Jack wants to consult Stephen – who suspects venereal disease, since they'd been ashore quite some time. Wrong – Jack wants a pill giving "good-nature". Stephen examines Jack for liver problems. Unknown to Stephen, Jack has been consulting a Sydney quack – weird diagnoses, treatments of oil rubbed into the spine.

16 – Stephen bleeds Jack – the all-purpose panacea. Jack asks, hopefully, for some drug to eliminate his horniness – no such thing available, says Stephen. Recommendation is for greatly increased exercise.

26 – Several men are in sickbay due to "burning" venereal diseases – undoubtedly gonorrhea. Several other patients present, identities and problems not related.

27 – Jack has had no chance to contract any venereal malady – much to his disgust.

Book 15 Chapter 2 – p35-64: (overview) [NOTE – little of medical import occurs in this chapter.] Stephen muses on the strange morality imposed on doctors – giving placebos = lying, etc. yet seems both necessary and ethical. Jack's faithful cox-swain Bonden understands perfectly when Jack sends him to scout an island for possible landing places – Jack requires (but the need is unspoken) a "not possible Sir", which will absolve him of having to abandon his stowaways, about whose escapes he feels profoundly bad – his personal code of honor has been broken. Bonden intuits this, surveys the island, reports "No landing at all, Sir." Surprise sails off, stowaways still aboard. Ship Éclair (cutter) appears, gives chase to Surprise, Jack wants no contact, oddly enough he cannot see the cutter through his telescope. Neither can he see the cutter's repeated signals. (He worries that Éclair has been sent to reclaim the escapees.) Oakes and Melissa married aboard Surprise: she cannot legally be taken by Éclair now. Crew has a great good time with the wedding and preparations. For a wedding dress, Jack gives her part of a bolt of unusual, bright-scarlet silk he'd bought for his wife. A fine all-hands celebration. Cutter overhauls Surprise, its captain comes aboard, Padeen deeply hidden belowdecks. Éclair sends across men and packages, including mail: its primary mission is not recapture, but delivery of orders to Jack. Trouble in Moahu (an O'Brian-created fictional Hawaiian island). Jack to investigate, take the side most likely to benefit England. He has a free hand as to force, negotiations, etc. The new Mrs Oakes is a delight to all. Clarissa diagnosed as sterile, quite happy about it, loathes children and wants none of her own.

38 – Two patients for surgery – one is a simple cystotomy (= opening the bladder, usually because the urethra from bladder to the outer world is blocked by a kidney stone that has moved down from its formation site in the lumen of a kidney). Probability of infection is much lower at sea than in a hospital ashore.

Book 15 Chapter 3 – p65-90: (overview) Diana not happy in role as mother, worries about the child's mind. Jack being over-whelmed with legal papers re his new properties and Parliamentary duties. Steady sailing. Stephen discovers that Clarissa Oakes

213

is having multiple affairs aboard ship. 500 pound swordfish impales itself in the ship's flank, Awkward Davies harpoons it, fine eating for some time (sailfish = swordfish for culinary purposes, even today).

72 – Clarissa thinks she is pregnant, consults with Stephen. Examination carried on in French: she is not pregnant and likely never will be (cause of sterility not given).

76 – Martin and Stephen discuss the difficulties of accurate diagnosis of venereal diseases – even the eminent printed authorities disagree strongly.

87 – Dyspeptic (= stomach upset, usually prolonged and occasionally leading to depression) seaman told 'no grog, chew every bite 40 times..."

Book 15 Chapter 4 – p91-118: (overview) The two black girls are awesome assistants in surgery – agile, coordinated, utterly non-squeamish. Equally helpful with Stephen's hurried dissection of the swordfish. Clarissa's attitude towards men is becoming clearer... likewise her dislike of questions in conversation. Her bestowing of sexual favors is causing considerable disruption, beginning to affect the smooth running of the ship. Despite tensions, a very long and friendly dinner party is held for all officers plus Clarissa. Reade, dead drunk after the party, mumbles about how Clarissa is lying with so many men. Jack is utterly clueless about the "Clarissa" problem.

93 – In a letter to Diana, Stephen says Clarissa has a poor complexion, to be improved with steel and bark.

95 – Clarissa's complexion not improving, Stephen increases her dosage, adds noontime glass of wine to the treatment regime.

100 – Stephen consults his books, convinced he is missing something in Clarissa's condition, but the authorities are all over the place, no agreement. Davidge has been hit hard on the temple – Stephen suspects a fistfight but the story is "...fell down a companionway..."

111 – After the party, youngster Reade is dead drunk – he is "emptied…with a powerful emetic", then tucked away to sleep it off.

Book 15 Chapter 5 – p119-144: (overview)   Stormy weather, Jack driving the ship hard, crew expects action soon. Reade is injured, and in laudanum stupor talks about Clarissa receiving men - "…they go in and out of that door, like a bawdy-house…" Reade is in early adolescence, deeply in love (at least a hearty crush) with Clarissa and unable to come to grips with her sexual behavior. Crew is on Clarissa's side, beginning to despise husband Oakes for beating her. Meeting with huge double canoc full of south-sea islanders plus Caucasian Mr Wainright, master of whaler Daisy. Gifts exchanged, miscellaneous native thievery aboard Surprise. Cannibalism common here.

121 – Storm-caused injuries: sprains, cracked ribs, broken bones, one hernia. The usual bad-weather galley-burns. Time and patients allow experiments with the Basra Method (plaster casts for broken bones).

122 – Reade hit on the head by a falling block, fell on his marlinspike, drove it deep into his chest, between the ribs – extremely painful because a bone-splinter is pressing on a thoracic nerve. Laudanum for anesthesia, removal of splinter is successful.

127 – Clarissa shows signs of physical abuse, most likely from husband Oakes – official story is a stumble and fall.

130 – Clarissa again shows bruises from a probable beating by her husband.

143 – About rabies and its treatments: Ship Daisy's surgeon Dr Falconer visits Surprise: he and Stephen are compatible. Falconer's forte is hydrophobia (rabies). He discusses treatments and patients. Treatments include being dipped into icy seawater, followed by a sticking-plaster to the wound. One victim was given all of the following - a "bolus of musk" with opium and turpeth (a vine resembling morning glory, its roots are a purgative); five grains of opium (a considerable dose) per hour; strong mercurial ointment rubbed into the

cervical vertebrae (surely a poison, but unlikely to get through the skin); an embrocation (liniment aka rubbing-salve) of two ounces of laudanum mixed with an ounce of acetum (= vinegar) saturninum (a plant species invented by O'Brian); the embrocation was 'applied directly to the throat', and sent the patient into convulsions which persisted whether or not the patient's eyes were covered (light was thought to make rabies worse). Changed the embrocation for a plaster of powdered camphor, opium, and "confection Damocritis" – this latter being obscure, probably invented by O'Brian. [Confection implies sugar; Damoctitis, being capitalized in the text, implies a person or place-name - perhaps some medicinal substance (mis?)-named after the Greek philosopher Democritus?] Later, when symptoms fade briefly then return, the patient gets an enema of 6 ounces of mutton broth plus an ounce of laudanum. Patient (oddly enough) died that night. (**NOTE** – as of 2016 there has been exactly ONE known instance of a human recovering from rabies – these Doctors' efforts whilst heroic were by any standards utterly useless.)

Stephen relates, from his own practice, an apparent cure following the patient's drinking two bottle of whiskey over one day.

Martin sticks his oar in – has seen used an embrocation of sal-ammoniac (= ammonium chloride, an expectorant) plus olive oil plus "oil of amber" (having nothing to do with fossilized pine-tree resin – rather from overheated succinic acid; used historically to encourage menstruation, perhaps to cause abortion), plus laudanum. Goal was to induce "ptyalism" (= excessive salivation), that being further encouraged by filling the patient's mouth with "smoke of cinnabar." (This is problematic – cinnabar is a rocky ore of mercury and cannot burn.... Perhaps "cinnamon"? Or perhaps "smoke" merely means vapors from hot rocks? In any case, breathing vaporized mercury is not a healthy thing to do, but if one has rabies, it cannot hurt. Note that the only medicines that actually do much of anything are (a) purgatives and laxatives, and (b) alcohol + opium as a pain-killer and [marginally] as an anesthetic.

Book 15 Chapter 6 – p145-168: (overview) [NOTE – no medical events occur in this chapter, but two extensive discussions center on rabies, and sexual abuse of children.] Ashore in the "Friendly Isles" (O'Brian's imaginary extension of the Hawaiian chain –e.g. islands such as the present landfall called "Annamooka", and the larger distant central island "Moahu"). There, Jack reveals to Stephen his new orders, received via the mail cutter. Two evenly-balanced factions are at war on Moahu, Jack is to study the situation and strike an alliance with the side most likely to be of use to England. French privateer is on-scene, upsetting the balance. Aboard her is Frenchman Dutourd (an interesting O'Brian play on words and sounds) who is known to Stephen as a utopian seeking an untouched place to despoil. Introductions twixt Surprise and natives go well. Red feathers are the valued currency here… one feather can get a man whatever he might want or need. Stephen's collections of bird-skins have been plucked bare by the crew enroute to shore. Ashore with Clarissa in the jungle, Stephen gives her his rifle, asks if she knows how to use it: she almost laughs: yes, indeed, she does. She and Stephen go swimming in the nude but without erotic intent or content. She explains herself to him as her physician – she is dispassionate and analytical - a victim of severe sexual abuse as a child (partly incestuous). She finally rebelled and blew the head off one of her serial-rapists – for which she was tried, convicted and sentenced to life in Botany Bay. She is today utterly indifferent to sex for pleasure - it is just another physical activity. She dispenses her physical favors willingly to those needy Surprises who work up courage to ask – e.g. to Pullings himself, and other officers… and apparently also to the very young Mr Reade. This makes her a terribly disruptive influence in a 150-foot-long ship full of horny men. Clarissa seeks to protect Sarah and Emily from a like fate. As a slave/prostitute, she had serviced Mssrs Ledward and Wray many times, but the pair was mostly interested in boys – Clarissa came in mostly for specials involving chains and leather. A casual, unremarkable bit of information from Clarissa's personal, detailed knowledge of highly-placed men is of huge value to Stephen in his ongoing search for the very-highly-placed (but unidentified) mole known to be embedded in the British Naval Intelligence Office.

Book 15 Chapter 7 – p169-195: (overview) Stephen finally identifies Clarissa, writes to his superior Blaine "...she is the lady who blew Mr Caley's head off with a double-barreled shotgun some years ago; ...and ... (MP) Essex had her sentence commuted to transportation." (Transportation = incarceration at Botany Bay.) In a wrestling match, Awkward Davies, by far Surprise's strongest man, is quite casually reduced to blubbering helplessness by one burly islander. Surprise sets sail. Discussions of volcanism and of volcanoes as objects of worship. Jack is now worried about the discontent he senses among the crew and officers – unknown to him, it is caused by Clarissa. Pullings finally tells Jack straight out about the problem – Jack (the eternal innocent) is flabbergasted, then furious, reads the men the riot act – they will, By God, immediately return to behaving as adults and members of His Majesty's Navy. Jack writes home to Sophie about the whole business. Jack goes swimming, is seen naked by Clarissa, who later discusses with Stephen the multitudinous wounds and injuries which Jack carries. Even Rev Martin confesses to Stephen his lustful thoughts about Clarissa... Martin broke his own viola intentionally, so as not to have to continue giving her lessons – too much close contact therein! Later, Mr and Mrs Oakes are seen together at dinner, seem to have reconciled.

170 – Emily reports to Stephen for inspection, is chewing tobacco – Stephen forbids it.

174 – Natives have unintentionally injured Bonden (broken nose from boxing) and Davies (unspecified, from wrestling). Emily is ill, having both eaten too much sugarcane, and been told how the kava she was drinking had been made (fermented well-chewed taro root – the chewing being a communal activity).

Book 15 Chapter 8 – p196-222: (overview) At sea, enroute to Moahu. Crew returning to proper discipline after Jack's dressing-down. Jack is working the crew extremely hard, mad at himself more than anything else... changing topmasts, endless great-gun exercises. Live-firing of the great guns discussed in detail for

Clarissa's benefit. Disguised Surprise as a whaler, dirty and scruffy. Landfall at Moahu.

198 – Punishment – Flogging for seven men including Weightman, who got 12 lashes for insolence and inattention to duty.

199 – Sick-call brings in only the butcher and the bosun's mate, both for dressing of their floggings – ointment, padding and a wrapping-bandage.

Book 15 Chapter 9 – p223-256: (overview)   At Moahu – no land batteries, no privateer. Surprise approached by native canoe, occupants refuse to come aboard. No men in the villages – all gone to war. Encounter with Truelove, which has taken a British ship and very badly mistreated the Truelove's English crew, who recognized Surprise despite her disguise, and are now being freed. They are drowning their French jailer, aka coxswain, who killed their skipper. Surprise sends an armed party ashore to thwart French ambitions by force. Land battle, Surprise prevails, with two Surprises killed. Truelove and her captured merchantmen are both legitimate prizes, because they were in enemy hands for over 24 hours. Even Emily and Sarah will share, getting about 9£ each, everyone else aboard proportionately more. The girls want to buy Stephen a blue coat lined with white. Stephen gives Clarissa advice about how to be inconspicuous if she chooses to return to England "before her time is up". Her being married is a great help – plus Stephen will use his considerable connections towards her safety. He even offers to have her stay with his wife Diana. Surprise's armament moved ashore for land use. Jack as diplomat, engages the Queen, forms the required English-Moahu alliance. Jack gives Mr Oakes command of the Truelove, to carry word of the alliance to England: tradition is that the bearer of such news is promoted – Oates will be rewarded there with his first real command. Surprises ashore join battle on the Queen's side, deploying the ship's carronades. In native warfare no quarter or retreat are allowed. Slaughter ensues. Feasting (beware of meat dishes – it is common to eat one's enemy who was killed in battle) and celebration follow. Jack spends the night in bed with Queen Puolani. Truelove sails next morning for England, carrying the Oakses and the news.

229 – Davidge and Weaver killed in skirmish ashore with French forces. Four Surprises too badly hurt to be moved, plus other sundry walking-wounded. No Frenchmen survived the encounter.

230 – Stephen considered amputating Stewart's leg (injured in the skirmish), but desisted, now thinks the man will survive and keep the leg. Stephen's comment says worlds about the state of medical knowledge and practice: Looking at his blood-covered hands, "…though I nearly always clean my instruments I sometimes forget my person."

232 – Sickbay air is foul despite all attempts at ventilation. Two rescued Truelove crewman have been neglected and now have "mortifying" wounds – here mortifying means death of large chunks of tissue, usually putrefying, due to loss of blood supply.

238 – Clarissa has been taking mercuric compounds as a precaution against possible exposure to syphilis, but has no symptoms whatsoever. More steel and bark, to improve her complexion.

250 – Battle ashore has lifted Jack from his long-standing depression.

Book 16 – The Wine-Dark Sea

Book 16 Chapter 1 – p1-23: (overview)   Surprise (formally a privateer, now His Majesty's Hired Vessel) is pursuing privateer Franklin (22 @ 9#). Surprise's mission is to help Peru and Chile become independent of Spain. Sea is a strange dark color. Air heavy, oppressive. Sea twitches – never seen before. Chase discards cannon and fresh water supply to gain speed. Lightning (mistaken for gunfire), heavy clouds – all due to a very active nearby volcano.

2 – Rats have eaten Stephen's store of coca leaves.

7 – Stephen and Martin make sick-bay rounds. The usual seamen's diseases plus various injuries, mostly due to over-exertion.

10 – Interesting injury – seaman ashore had fallen on a sharpened bamboo which pierced and let air into the pleural space (between lung and chest-wall). One lung strangely affected – no details given.

20 Mr West flattened, bleeding due to being hit by something, probably a lava-bomb from the as-yet-unrecognized new volcano nearby.

21 – Several hands go to sick-bay injured like Mr West. West has a severe depressed skull fracture, is in coma. Another man has a compound fracture of the arm, plus numerous gashes in his side.

22 – All available sick-bay help is busy- Stephen, Martin, Sarah, Emily. Unspecified man has unspecified limb amputated: "...This will hurt for the moment, but it will not last." Another lacerating wound.

23 - Wilcox has some wounded fingers amputated.

25 – Post-storm, Stephen has worked in surgery nonstop all night, is still busy. West remains comatose from the skull fracture, Stephen cannot operate on the violently-moving ship.

Book 16 Chapter 2 – p24-43: (overview) Surprise and chase (whaler Franklin) both dismasted by the storm, but Surprise is in much the better condition. Franklin surrenders to Surprise, asks for medical help, Stephen and Martin go across. Stephen fears recognition by Dutourd, which would imperil the "subversion in S America" mission. Dutourd comes aboard Surprise, does not have the proper documentation to be a privateer, hence must be considered a pirate (death penalty = only punishment available for piracy). Reade takes command of the Franklin. Dutourd is an idiot idealist, taking prizes without authorization from any country. Pullings will take the whaler Franklin home as a prize – this will gain him standing at the Admiralty, thus improving his chances of getting a ship.

30 – In Franklin's cabin are over a dozen seriously wounded French crewmen, commingled willy-nilly with the dead-drunk and the merely dead. Dead go over the side, and Stephen begins work. Dutourd has a head/scalp wound. Severe burns due to the volcano. One hip-level amputation specifically mentioned.

38 – Stephen and Martin discuss an earlier failed trephination of West's skull to reduce the brain-swelling, but the brain damage was too severe - West is now dead.

Book 16 Chapter 3 – p44-64: (overview) Various promotions into vacancies. Stephen muses on the nature and uses of authority, then on marriage and happiness. Steady repair-work yields acceptable sailing characteristics: much musing about non-maritime topics as the two ships sail side by side through very light winds.

51 – One of the ship's boys, Arthur Wedell, falls through Jack's cabin's skylight – no injury.

52 – Stephen again misses his coca leaves.

53 – Mr Bentley had a top-maul (a very large, heavy wooden hammer used aloft) fall on his foot – not a dangerous injury, but confining. Stephen resumes his habit of naked sunbathing and occasional salt-water paddlings alongside the ship.

54 – Final burial service for Franklin crew members.

Book 16 Chapter 4 – p65-93: (overview) Dutourd, captive aboard Surprise, is a nuisance because of his egalitarian sentiments mixed with absolute ignorance of naval custom or behavior. Martin discovered to be self-dosing for syphilis – his lecherous thoughts have terrified him into producing false but convincing symptoms. Although actually far too young, Reade plans to try for Lieutenant when Surprise returns home, using a thinly disguised false age (a common practice). Dutourd finally recognizes Stephen as someone he has met, but cannot place him. Stephen's views on slavery – extremely against it in any form. Determination of prize value and shares angers Dutourd. Rousseau seen as a blatant, immoral fraud. Preliminary distribution of prize money delights all hands.

65 – In a calm, Jack weighs himself – he has gained half a stone (stone = 14 pounds), doesn't like it.

69 – Martin, having been given livings by Jack, is now acting a bit hoity-toity, criticizing Stephen for past excesses with laudanum.

70 – During live-firing exercises, Pullings (now captaining Franklin) dislocates his jaw – something that happens regularly, the result of an old facial wound from a Turkish scimitar during a land engagement.

72 – Vidal sees Stephen for more ointment "for the parts" – presumably mercuric ointment to treat syphilis. He complains about how the salt accumulating in clothing will rub a man's skin raw.

75 – Stephen has some persistent cases of syphilis, decides to treat them "…in the Viennese manner…" (no details specified). One standard treatment for venereal diseases, used by Stephen, is a daily dose of calomel (more mercury – here mercuric chloride, Hg_2Cl_2) and guaiacum (resin from one of several species of plants in genus *Guaiacum* – most commonly used to treat gout, not VD).

77 – Stephen finally realizes what Martin is doing – inventing phantasmagorical illnesses in himself. Reade's stump needs dressings changed.

Book 16 Chapter 5 – p94-119: (overview) Yankee-made whaler's-barrel found floating by: two Surprises recognize the maker's-mark. Encounter with whaler and its runaway whaleboat (towed far from mother ship by a harpooned whale). Franklin (Capt Pullings) takes the whaler. Whaler had obviously intended to abandon the men in the runaway whaleboat… those men being retrieved by Surprise et al and brought aboard, the harpooner impales his captain on the mast with an accurately thrown harpoon to the chest – instant death. No comment or argument results. Whaler's crew report a heavy privateer (32 9#-ers) in the area. In a storm, distant gunfire is heard. Eventually they encounter two ships, four-masted privateer Alastor –literally wearing the black flag of piracy- has grappled Franklin, hand-to-hand battle rages. Jack in Surprise comes up fast, grapples tie the ships together as Surprise joins battle: Alastor is taken, Jack wounded – his men are infuriated, go on a revenge rampage, slaughtering the enemy sailors.

97 – Stephen busy "…rubbing blue ointment into Douglas Murd…" – no further details.

100 – Whaler's captain harpooned by his own crewman for abandoning the whaleboat – heart and spinal cord severed. Martin ill, unknown causes.

104 – Seaman Smyth was given liniment, has apparently drunk it instead of rubbing it on himself – no further details of the event or its consequences.

105 – Stephen notes [accurately] that metallic mercury is metabolically inert, a person can drink a quart with no ill effect – as compared to its various compounds (e.g., "blue pills" for VD and/or constipation due to obesity – an all-purpose medicine indeed).

106 – Martin haggard, is ordered to bed by Stephen.

108 – Martin sleeps, Stephen examines him seeking signs of VD, finds none. He does find numerous recent, oozing sores – but they are caused by Martin's unspoken self-diagnosis (that he has VD) and self-treatment (more penitential suffering than medical treatment)…due to extreme anxiety, guilt and self-loathing for having lusted (mentally only) after Clarissa. A purely psychosomatic illness.

115 – Stephen explains to Martin what the problem is with his health –the sores are salt-sores from rubbing skin against salty cloth.

117 – First shots in a new action terrify and derange Martin: Stephen ties him in the bunk, gives a powerful dose of laudanum.

118 – Jack's skull is creased by a bullet, and he is brought down by a pikeman.

Book 16 Chapter 6 – p120-142: (overview) French pirates who choose not to enroll on Surprise will be dropped off ashore. Dutourd escapes with that group. Ashore, Stephen meets a colleague, a fellow medical student with whom he had shared a corpse. Surprise is now in Callao, Peru. Alastor takes considerable cleaning-up after the carnage of battle. Jack's illegitimate jet-black son Sam Panda has been sent to S America as a sort of Papal legate, comes to see Jack. Discussion of slavery between Stephen and Panda – the institution hated by both.

120 - Jack's wounds include injury to one eye (we later find out it was a nearby pistol discharge that blew burnt powder and wadding into the eye), a spectacular scalp-wound of no great consequence, and the leg through which the enemy pike-man stabbed.

121 – Stephen leaves Jack to Killick's tender mercies – specifically dressing the eye and the pike-wound - whilst Stephen is away from the ship.

122 – Jack is actually seriously wounded: "weakness, loss of sense of balance…"

123 – Many wounded from Alastor are in sickbay aboard Surprise – several have died so far. We first hear of Bonden (Jack's coxswain)

225

having been wounded – a "...great cutlass-slash that had required such anxious sewing." Other patients will likely lose limbs soon.

124 – First patient of the day is the bosun, who pursued enemies into the rigging whilst roaring drunk, fell onto a mass of weapons, got much cut about. Mister Grainger received a musket-ball which took a very strange route through his body and required considerable finding.

127 – Martin admits to having self-administered the "Vienna treatment" (for VD) to himself. He admits to taking four grains of mercury – a mere 16 times the normal dose. His survival at all is a wonder.

128 – Stephen prescribes copious ongoing drinks of rainwater to try to purge the mercury from Martin's body.

130 – We find that the marthambles is "...as deadly as measles or the smallpox to islanders..."

132 – Symptoms of profound mental problems such as Martin's discussed – as are the results of some treatments (e.g., loss of all body hair).

139 – Stephen, enroute afoot to Lima, meets Panda, describes Jack's current injuries – this is where we finally learn that the pike-thrust went through Jack's upper thigh.

Book 16 Chapter 7 – p143-165: (overview)   [NOTE – there is little of medical import in this chapter.] High mass in Lima: Sarah and Emily attend, get thoroughly drunk at post-service party. Discussions of things political – local vs national vs international interests. Who's Who in S. American politics of the day. Spain may be aware of the English mission – not sure. What to do with the English funds, whom to back, what conditions? Dutourd finally known to be missing. Jack and a picked crew of the best sailors leave on a mission, in the launch. A day's sail out, a serious storm hits the launch which is dismasted and loses all sails. Epic saga of survival at sea ensues – no sails, no food, very little water. Seven attempts to return are foiled by winds: no chance of rescue – the winds will have driven the larger ships far out to sea, and damaged them as well.

153 – Killick endlessly exercising his Stephen-mandated 'medical' authority over the Captain (in matters of treatment for eye and leg wounds). Jack acquiesces, reluctantly: Killick adds to the eye ointment some "Gregory's Patent Liquid" because "...it rectifies the humours..." - another of O'Brian's invented patent medicines. Miscellaneous "treatments" known to Jack include Gregory's Patent Liquid, Harris's Guaranteed Unguent; Carey's Warranted Arrowroot, brimstone (sulfur) and treacle (molasses) ... and many others not here named.

155   We are told of the severity of Bonden's cutlass-slash received in the Alastor battle – apparently it laid bare, open to view, both his breastbone and a few ribs. But it is healing nicely now.

Book 16 Chapter 8 – p166-187: (overview)   [NOTE – nothing medical occurs in this chapter.] Whilst Jack et al. are trying to save themselves in the launch, Stephen engages in intelligence activities and politics ashore, in pursuit of the overall mission's highest goals. A long letter to his superior Blaine, explaining things to date. Reflections on his wife, Diana. Foibles of "great [male] leaders" discussed. Stephen makes an epic, long, slow foot-and-mule slog over the very high Andes mountains to get to various meetings with rebels and patriots. He gets a native guide: together they survive a ferocious off-season snowstorm. The guide is politically savvy, asks what should be done with Dutourd, now in jail ashore, but still noisy and obnoxious. Stephen suggests quite seriously to denounce him to the Inquisition. Sam Panda eventually gets the task of shepherding the dealings with Dutourd who is, in fact, denounced as a heretic to the local "Holy Office" a.k.a. the Inquisition. Stephen must go on to Chile to meet that country's upper level of revolutionaries, check them out. Meanwhile, the huge store of British gold will not (as had been planned) be portioned out to the locals for support of their revolution – which Stephen finds to have been very badly managed. Dutourd is shortly arrested by the Holy Office and taken beyond reach of civil or military authorities.

Book 16 Chapter 9 – p188-218: (overview)   Jack and his crew finally arrive at the harbor, paddling 3-oared and nearly dead from thirst. Their calls for help are first thought to be sea-lions' calls. Pullings, out for a row, recognizes Jack and the Alastor's launch. He guides them to the ship, all saved, probably would have been all dead in one more day at sea. Jack's first concern after food and drink is to recapture Dutourd – Jack feels that he has let Stephen down terribly by allowing the escape. Discussion of idiot impracticability of utopian schemes, including Dutourd's. More of Stephen's mountain adventures with rebels and revolutionaries: natural history *in extenso*. Stephen and guide caught (again) by a mountaintop snowstorm: they huddle in a rock fissure, save themselves by sacrificing their llama, and chewing coca.

217 – Stephen reports to his guide, after their overnight amidst the rocks in a blizzard, that his leg is "deeply frostbitten" – if lucky he will lose only "a handful of toes". Guide cheers him up with the opinion that toes are perhaps overrated, that many of his people lose toes to frostbite, nothing unusual about it. Stephen rubs snow on the frostbitten leg – precisely the wrong thing to do, but prevalent treatment in many folklores.

Book 16 Chapter 10 – p219-261: (overview)   Jack aboard Surprise, heading to rendezvous with Stephen in Valparaiso. Shooting the sun: scientific observations made. Speculations on amounts and value of gold rumored to be available in the local mountains. Calculations about values of various prizes yields large numbers, to the satisfaction of the entire crew. Surprise et al waiting far offshore for political decisions – a huge storm causes major damage to Surprise. Two sail sighted. Potential prizes. Fog descends, battle in a slow-motion quiet. Many icebergs confuse things mightily. Jack in Surprise has unfortunately taken on an American heavy frigate carrying 38 18-#ers, a bad choice of opponent. Chase ends up taking both ships into an ice-field from which Jack can escape but the American cannot. Surprise runs safely through the ice-field as the ships exchange Christmas greetings via signal-flags. Surprise struck by lightning. Eventually Surprise meets up with a British 64, captained by Jack's lifelong best friend, Dundas. Word from home, dinner aboard the 64. Jack's slightly morose analysis of the overall mission – primarily a failure – ends the book.

222 – Stephen examines Jack's recent wounds – the thigh is fine, but about the eye he is noncommittal.

224 – Stephen confesses to the loss, due to frostbite, of several unimportant toes – a good bargain inasmuch as he had initially expected to lose the entire leg below the knee.

225   Reade asks how Stephen removed his own frozen toes: "Why, with a chisel, as soon as we came down to the village." By that time the toes were already gangrenous, had to go regardless.

228 – Crewman John Proby had died two days out of Callao, despite bark and steel and linctus (linctus = sweet sticky cough syrup, usually laced with an astonishing mount of opium, later codeine). Proby had a deformed hand, which was privately kept back for Stephen to dissect.

247 – The encounter with the American 38 yielded two splinter wounds, one man hit in the head with a falling block, all are likely to survive. One man with a foot badly crushed by a recoiling gun: the foot is amputated. No dead, no masses of wounded.

252 – Lightning casualties: one man unconscious with a charred spot over his heart (suffering from fatal arrhythmia); two foremast hands with oddly-patterned electrical burns over their bodies…not life-threatening, just odd.

254 – The lightning victim with the charred spot dies.

Book 17 – The Commodore

Book 17 Chapter 1 – p1-29: (overview) Surprise is back in English waters, in the Channel, homeward bound, traveling with Berenice (64), Captain Heneage Dundas, Jack's lifelong friend. Exchange Stephen's medical services (needed on Berenice) for repair supplies to fix Surprise. Surprise has done magnificently in terms of prizes (single-share = £364-6s-8d [units of pound-shillings-pence] – and many of the ship's company rate more than a single share). Jack lends 1000 guineas in gold (from his share of Surprise's prizes) to Dundas, who otherwise faces instant debtor's prison when he touches English soil. Stephen ruminates on age and desire – worried about both wife and as-yet-unseen daughter. Jack is unexpectedly offered command of a squadron, to cruise off the W. African coast. A temporary rank of Commodore, just short of Admiral, is included... Jack's first formal multi-vessel command. Jack arrives home to a drunken party of servant-sailors but no wife- she is staying elsewhere. Jack rides to join Sophie, is thrown, lands headfirst on a stone marking the boundary of his lands.

2 – Stephen goes aboard Berenice (whose doctors drowned to-gether), finds crew decimated or worse by Sydney Pox (probably this is ordinary smallpox – perhaps 'merely' chicken-pox) and Cape Horn Scurvy. (Scurvy is just scurvy the world around – there are no identi-fied varieties.)

4 – Jack, reminiscing, shows off a large scar on his forearm, sou-venir of battle aboard Bellerophon (74 - aka "Billy Ruffian").

12 – Sick-bay contains two men who while drunk sparred with one another using "loggerheads" – a long iron rod ending in a cast-iron ball some inches in diameter. The balls are heated, then carried to where one is working with tar. The tar is safely (no flames) melted for use by plunging the ball into the tar-bucket. The men have severely injured one another, damage not specified.

26 – Hanging as a public amusement – seven men and one child on a single gibbet. Unexpected births amongst the crew's female stay-at-homes, not the least bit unusual in mariners' families.

Book 17 Chapter 2 – p30-55: (overview) Stephen meets with his superior in Naval Intelligence, Sir Joseph Blaine. Jack will hoist his broad pennant (mark of a squadron commander), go to Africa to protect merchantmen and discourage slaving. Stephen will be sent along to help. Mrs Broad's London inn "The Grapes" has been rebuilt after a fire, she welcomes Stephen, having gotten used to his odd habits and pursuits – he maintains a permanent room there. Stephen's banked fortune is intact. Clarissa's inno-cent remarks about her erotic customers has enabled identification of the top-level mole in Naval Intelligence, to wit, the Duke of Habachtsthal. Family attends the injured Jack. Sophie's shrew of a mother feels Diana/Stephen's child is an idiot, mentally defec-tive, insists on trying to take command of the child's life and treatment. Jack has to threaten the shrew with banishment to get her to stand down. Shrew has set up an amateur unlicensed bet-ting/gambling operation – when she tries to direct the child's treatment, Stephen says he will put her in jail for illegal gambling if she doesn't quit. She finally does so. Pullings has been made post captain and been selected by Jack as one of his squadron's captains. Consumed with worry, and accompanied by Sarah, Emi-ly and Padeen, Stephen visits Clarissa who is caring for his daughter Brigid. He meets Brigid – a beauty but apparently unin-terested in speaking, as if autistic. She seems utterly indifferent to her surroundings, except for the family dog. No eye contact with fellow humans. She understands everything, speaks almost not at all. Diana has essentially run away from the situation, unable to handle it emotionally.

43- Jack is abed with a concussion, no mental stimulation al-lowed; soup and cheese only for diet.

47 – Stephen recommends hellebore to calm Jack's spirits. (Roots of the two medicinal plant species of genus *Helleborus* have strong purgative and narcotic properties.)

231

48 – All Jack's children have measles: precautions necessary to keep the two black girls away from the patients – the girls have zero immunity and the disease would almost certainly kill them... as deadly to innocents as is smallpox itself.

Book 17 Chapter 3 – p56-88: (overview) Jack's commodore's uniform (more or less an Admiral's rig) fascinates all. The evil shrew tries hard to exert personal control over Stephen's daughter. Shrew is ordered by Stephen to cease and desist, else he will immediately send her to jail personally for her illegal gambling, and ban her for life from his estates. The child Brigid has been heard to speak only rarely, and is seldom interested at all in things around her. Padeen, monoglot Irishman, a severe stutterer with a saint's ability to calm any kind of animal, takes her under his wing and teaches her Irish – overheard by Stephen who declares a miracle. The girl emerges from her shell under Padeen's companionship and teaching, turns out to be not only normal but quite bright. And during his interactions with the child, Padeen stutters not at all. Jack's skills as a mathematician and astronomer and telescope-grinder revealed. Jack is ordered to fly his commodore's pennant at once – an honor. First view of "his fleet". His flagship Bellona (74) is well over 50 years of age... but well built and maintained. Aboard Bellona Stephen finds several very long-term friends amongst the crew – a happy reunion, but the sickbay is a disaster, infuriates Stephen – with Jack's help he fixes the problems.

63 – In the wake of Padeen's 'miraculous' success with Brigid, Stephen must discuss her case with the world authority on mental development, in Barcelona.

65 – Brigid has been diagnosed as an idiot (a proper medical term for one grade of mental mis-development). That diagnosis is clearly quite wrong.

66 – The shrew's gambling-man Mr Briggs is beaten by thugs for cheating or informing – looked at by Stephen. Battered and bruised, nothing broken. Shrew worries that he might have been castrated, a not uncommon revenge, but not so here.

68 – Stephen threatens the Shrew (Sophie's mother, Mrs Williams) with prison and estrangement from the family if she does not stop meddling with Brigid. Further, Stephen will use his influence to see that her man Briggs is pressed into a particularly bad crew – from which impressments he is unlikely to return. Suspect an affair between Shrew and Briggs. Shrew backs down entirely.

84 – Sickbay of Bellona is quite literally a pigsty, with no ventilation, light, or hygiene – Stephen is infuriated by it, threatens to quit instantly, but with Jack's help all problems are quickly fixed. Previous surgeon died of an alcoholic coma, all ship's patients have been put ashore into the naval hospital.

Book 17 Chapter 4 – p89-106: (overview)   Formal dinner at Jack's home – Killick in a fury over allocation of roles and tasks. Stephen's rumination on sex and sexuality, the varieties thereof, various societies' differing approaches to the topic. The crews of many ships in Jack's squadron are barely capable, cannot be replaced (says the Admiral), and Jack will have to train them up to Jack's own standards. Stephen gets secret orders during a personal meeting with his superior Sir Joseph Blaine of Naval Intelligence, Stephen's superior. Habachtsthal knows that his agents Ledward and Ray were disposed of by Stephen personally – and knows Clarissa is the source of information about himself. There may be a movement afoot - led by Habachtsthal - to try Stephen for treason. Stephen, with family and all of his considerable fortune, must leave England immediately. Blaine will try to protect him.

92 – Ruminations on human sexuality. Phrenology (study of the bumps on an individual's skull) still considered (even by Stephen) as part of medical science.

97 – Partial inventory of medical supplies – anitmonials (compounds of antimony), jalap (a vine resembling morning glory, yielding a strong purgative), camphire (sic, not 'camphor' - the henna plant, use unspecified), linen bandage, tourniquets, mercury, various alexipharmics, portable soup, asafetida. Note the incredible variety of

purgatives mentioned… if nothing else, Stephen's medicines could induce vomiting and bowel movements!

98 – Stephen has a good supply of coca, explains yet again how useful and safe it is … "…in no way dangerous", "…an enhancer of daily life, particularly by the labouring classes of men."

99 – Mention of coca as useful in fighting fevers, and especially in fighting melancholia (modern = depression) but there are no good test subjects available.

Book 17 Chapter 5 – p107-146: (overview) Stephen's difficulties controlling his mount Lalla, a mare in deepest heat, seeking stallion. News of a French squadron being assembled of about the same strength as Jack's: enemy squadron's course, sailing date, and intent. Jack furious with one of his captains for massive overuse of flogging. Long discussion of bastardy (Stephen himself is one; Jack has one of his own, namely Sam Panda). Discussion of Jack's crewmembers from Shelmerston – England's very best smugglers, hence best sailers-of-small-craft – valuable men indeed on occasion. Stephen going up Thames in Jack's personal schooner Ringle at emergency speed, to take care of his fortune before leaving the country. Ringle is sailing through the fleet anchored in the Thames, literally thousands of ships. The schooner sets an apparent record for the particular run, logged and witnessed by Stephen, with all titles flying. Stephen retrieves his many small chests of gold from the bank, takes them aboard Ringle for return to Bellona. Interminable wait for a proper wind. Setting sail finally, between Hammer and Anvil (dangerous rocks). Bellona will sail to Spain, there to deposit with Stephen's relatives the refugees and Stephen's gold. Stephen and child developing a good rapport – she has emerged from her shell completely. Unfortunate dinner – Clarissa and Sophie arrive in dresses made from the same bolt of scarlet. Jack gave Clarissa part of the cloth for her wedding dress months ago, at sea – the rest of the bolt went to Sophie. Disaster… was Sophie appearing clad in the remnants, the leavings, of some Jack/Clarissa arrangement? Brigid ecstatic about sailing and the sea. Stephen promises Padeen a small estate in Ireland, with sheep and cottage – but NO OWLS! Ringle chased by a French privateer – almost everything

Stephen values is aboard the boat, endangered. Reade captaining Ringle quickly outsails the Frenchman completely. All safe in Spain, time to head for rendezvous with Jack at the Berling Islands, off the coast of Portugal.

118 – Stephen leaves Jack with the admonition that if his bowels do not move by evening, take rhubarb next morning.

128 – Reade gets Stephen to autograph the log's report of their record sail… "Please would you sign, small and neat in the margin, with all the degrees you can think of, and FRS as well? Otherwise they will never believe me, sir!"

140 – General discussion of children's needs for milk and cheese, yielding "good bones".

Book 17 Chapter 6 – p147-164: (overview) Near the Berling Islands, Ringle hears a ferocious, perhaps fleet-sized, naval battle in the distance, clears for action. It is Jack's entire command, practicing. Jack's intensive training – the ships are firing both sides – a very difficult maneuver for any crew – and a disaster this time… sloppy and slow. Jack has heard from Sophie about the scarlet dresses… Jack is in deep trouble and upset by it – for once, he is guilty of nothing whatever except an excess of charity. Jack's own crews on Bellona (over 500 men total) will show the rest of the Squadron how to fight both sides... those hands delight in the chance to show off. They do well. Bonden and Killick climb to privacy, discuss morale – which is very low because of the Jack/Sophie contretemps… it affects EVERYthing aboard ship. Jack is particularly worried about Sophie's recurrent visitor, Hinksey, Sophie's long-ago pre-Jack suitor – relieved when Stephen tells him Hinksey is betrothed elsewhere. Stephen and Jack discuss morality in marriage and elsewhere – consider what is or is not 'truth'.

149 – Stephen, coming aboard Bellona, inspects a sailor's ear which he sewed back in place, years before – all is well. On Thames, Jack replaces Thomas, who leaves angry, in high dudgeon.

155 – Mr Gray seems to have a severe attack of "stone" (kidney or bladder stones – perhaps the most painful condition to which a man may be subjected – arguably equaling the pains of childbirth).

156 – Laudanum in large doses for Mr Gray. Chips is preparing a chair in which the patient can be chained in the proper position for the operation… an incision into the bladder or (usually) kidneys to enable removing the stones. This is a deep-abdominal operation ("being cut for stone") that carries a very high risk of death from post-operative infection. Patients are chained down as if for amputation.

Book 17 Chapter 7 – p165-193: (overview) Bellona sails well for her age and size. Capt. Thomas of Thames is a very poor seaman and commander, and is disliked for that by Jack. Jack leery of the stated purpose of the Squadron (namely, stop the slave trade). There is far too much loose talk and obvious deep knowledge amongst the public back home– what is going on? Sealed orders opened. The French fleet is probably part of yet another attempt to invade Ireland. Jack should stop it - consulting and advising with Stephen. Separate orders for Stephen, also. "All captains to flag" – meeting re mission. More training –small-boats and great guns. Mister Whewell called to Flag to aid Jack's understanding of slavery and the trade – he is a 'slavery expert'; from Jamaica – and a highly qualified but passed-over officer-candidate. Detailed discussion of the trade, especially the ships and shipping involved. Common to lose 1/3 of the 'cargo' to disease and malnourishment. Ship as an approximation to a small town. Jack's written orders are classically vague. Bellona intercepts slaver Nancy, fake Spanish papers for the English ship, now Belonna's prize. Jack appalled to the core at conditions aboard the slaver, makes the white crew and officers do massive cleanup mostly of human excrement. Custom in taking slavers as prizes: prize to be sawn in half and her value distributed as prize money.

165 – Mr Gray died of a deep infection not long post-operation.

167 – Stephen's opinion on Napoleon's health recently requested: Stephen went to see the patient in person, an interesting interview.

168 – Stephen prescribed for Napoleon some unspecified dose that would calm him – "would purge his more malignant humours".

179 – Stephen told in confidence by Giffard that the problem with Capt. Thomas (Thames) is that he is a pederast, calls the younger attractive men to his quarters in the dark. Discipline gone all to hell on Thames.

187 – Stephen's virtues as a medical man: listener, treated all equally, no concern about money, extensive experience.

188 – Some of Stephen's vices: using a lot of nitrous oxide himself (laughing-gas) and ditto hemp smoke (aka marijuana). Ditto bhang (marijuana resin, today's 'hashish'). Ditto tobacco. Ditto opium as laudanum. Ditto coca leaves. Also failure to recognize that in dosing himself, he fails to take account of his actual age (middle, not young), leading to consistent overdosage.

192 – Conditions on slave ship appalling, Stephen treats some slaves for manacle-abrasions.

Book 17 Chapter 8 – p194-222: (overview) Nancy sunk by broadsides, rather than sawn apart – done immediately offshore, to properly impress the slavers still on the beach. Crew thoroughly enjoys having such a delightful target for practice. Squadron takes initial prizes: five schooners, two brigs and a ship – plus the bounty-money (a per-head payment for slaves freed), a magnificent haul already. Setting up multiple cutting-out operations using small boats. Most of the slavers' papers seem to have been misplaced or (mostly) to have disappeared overboard as soon as Jack's men boarded, making the slavers into perfectly legitimate prizes regardless of their verbal claims. Discussion of naturalist Adanson and his accomplishments. Jack tells Stephen of the plan of action for the Squadron. Dinnertime discussion of sodomy and sodomites – "…they can never be real men…" etc. almost causes blows between Stately's officers and some from other vessels.

198 – Stephen orders NO SHORE LEAVE in Sierra Leone – crew grumbling, no fresh fruit, and more importantly no women. Sewing up a slash in Whewell's arm, gotten taking one of the prizes.

205 – Stephen orders a supply of the best available coca leaves, for his own use.

206 – Quite a few slavers are now in Belonna's sickbay, they having been somewhat mangled by yesterday's cannonade. Wounds and burns.

207 – Weather is excruciatingly hot and dry – the blacks rub their skin with palm-oil or tallow to prevent the skin cracking in the heat. Stephen worried about miasmas ("bad air" causing disease) ashore, refuses shore leave for the crew.

211 – Seaman Black cracked his fibula tripping over a bucket: in sickbay he is found to have a hyper-swollen bladder due to blockage by stone… Like many a seaman he was too shy to come forward and seek help.

222 – Stephen states correctly that running waters are healthier than stagnant – particularly so as regards "miasmas". Miasmas are known today mostly as mosquito-borne diseases, and stagnant water is ideal habitat for mosquito larvae.

Book 17 Chapter 9 – p223-259: (overview) Leaving Philip's Island, where Stephen spent some days ashore, naturalizing. He catches yellow fever, diagnoses himself, lays out treatment needs and no-nos, makes his will – death rate for the disease is often over 80%. Studies himself from within as the sickness progresses through its three well-known stages. He is intensively nursed by all. Recovers. Whilst he was ill (mostly unconscious) the Squadron has taken 18 slavers. Over six thousand slaves freed – at per-head-money of 60£. Plus the vessels' own value. There have been fights and personnel losses, not specified. Jack's problems with his sodomitic captain of the Thames are driving him to distraction. News of the Squadron has spread widely among the slavers – all the near-shore slave camps are now empty. Stories about the Dahomi tribe's battalions of amazon warriors – "terribly bold and fierce". Stephen is given a live potto, brings it aboard, a fine pet, it helps soothe the crew. Sail eventually to Freetown: the Governor's young wife is a superb naturalist - she and Stephen hit it off nicely. Stephen's letters from "home" (now Spain): Brigid progressing well. Stephen offers his potto to the the Governor's daughter – to take the animal north would kill it with cold. She accepts. Squadron loads powder and provisions, has a party ashore, and sails.

224 - Stephen feels poorly, his tongue is flame-red, to match his eyes. Takes own temperature, about 100° F. Suspects yellow fever, a deadly killer disease.

225 – Stephen understands the disease well. He lays out the course of the disease, and the treatments he will need. Self-prescribes "radix serpentariae Virginianae" – an oil extracted from the roots of the "snakeroot" plant, of some value in treating symptoms of intermittent fevers (e.g., yellow fever, malaria). Bemoans a lack of calumba root (*Jateorhiza calumba* – another herbal with properties like snakeroot, used for a wild mix of conditions and symptoms, probably ineffectively). He also specifies no bleeding, no purging, lots of bark (quinine), plenty of fluids. Sponging (for cooling to reduce fever).

227 – Stephen struck down by the disease as he sit and talks with Jack – all know that the disease (yellow fever) is not infectious.

230 – Stephen survives – recovery very slow. On p 243 we find that he has lost at least a stone (14 pounds) of weight, perhaps a good deal more, from his rather small frame.

242 – Bellona now houses most of the very large number of fever-stricken men from around the entire Squadron. Stephen's difficulties explaining to the crew that yellow fever is not infectious.

244 – Duel fought ashore between two men who participated in the earlier argument/discussion of sodomy and its consequences for Naval discipline. Each man shot the other in the belly, thereby resolving nothing of the argument.

245 – Both duelists die of their wounds, reconciling with one another as they did so – had either survived, he would have likely been tried for murder.

247 – Stephen and Jack discuss sodomy yet again, compare it with the problem of bestiality with the ship's goat (on a much earlier cruise).

254 – Several patients have a severe rash of unknown cause.

257 – Once again, ship's fauna (this time not rats, but cockroaches) have eaten Stephen's cache of coca leaves.

Book 17 Chapter 10 – p260: (overview)   [NOTE – nothing of medical import occurs in this chapter.] Heading to intercept the French Squadron, which is supposed to have sailed recently on a known course. Comparison of Jack's crews' readiness earlier in his career with the changed present situation - present quite iffy and unknown. Dirty weather, but the Squadron finds the enemy. Jack discusses possible tactics for the action to come (hopefully) soon. Enemy strength – 2 @ 74, two frigates, other ships including transports. French frigates likely to be larger and better armed than Jack's. Frenchmen take a difficult-to-defend position amongst small islands. Close, furious engagement. Bellona takes the French flagship: second French 74 leaves the scene. Two more British 74s appear and join up under Jack as senior officer present. Remainder of French squadron, less one escaping frigate, are captured. Sail to Ireland, the region where the French had planned to land. Stephen explains to the landsmen what is going on – speaking in Irish, which helps calm fervor ashore. Stephen heads off to find Diana, who is overjoyed to see him again.

278 – Stephen volunteers his medical services to the captured French vessels, who have extensive wounded and a dead surgeon.

Book 18 – The Yellow Admiral

Book 18 Chapter 1 – p1-23: (overview) [NOTE – no medical events in this chapter.] Extensive preliminary background - Sir Joseph Blaine (head, Naval Intelligence) et al. discuss the suicide of the high-ranking mole (Duke of Habachtsthal), and Stephen's role in various foreign affairs: ditto for Jack's career. Formal pardons finally signed for Stephen and Clarissa. From his seat in Parliament, Jack speaks bluntly about Naval affairs – far too bluntly for the good of his own career - Jack has now risen on the Navy list to just short of admiral, must worry about being promoted to "Yellow Admiral" – i.e., holding Admiral rank but without an actual command. "Right to a flag" is not the same as "Right to hoist that flag". Legal problems and financial misadventures mean Sophie must sell the homestead, Ashgrove – it is Sophie's personal property. Jack's legal problems stem from his arguably improper seizure of a slave vessel during his latest command.

7 – Stephen explaining the virtues of his coca leaves yet again – apparently he is an avid user even after his experiences with laudanum addiction. (Coca is not opium-based.)

Book 18 Chapter 2 – p24-51: (overview) [NOTE – no medical events in this chapter.] At Ashgrove, ruminating on various topics, including the enclosure movement which is kicking smallholders and freemen off the land entirely – mostly to assemble large plots of land amenable to then-modern machine-driven agricultural processes. Jack hates the enclosure movement, moves to thwart attempts to enclose more of the local commons (Parliament must give its consent to enclosure, under special bills.) For this he is deeply loved by his tenants.

24 – List of various soporifics or sleep-inducers Stephen has used – poppy, (i.e., opioids), mandragora (mandrake root), inspissated (= thickened) juice of aconite (monkshood, extremely toxic and unpredictable) or henbane (*Hyoscyamus niger*); datura stramonium (= Jimson weed in N America – aka Loco Weed for its effect on livestock); creeping skerit and leopard's bane (both seem to be O'Brian inventions).

48 – Stephen's choice-du-jour of mammal to study is the shrew – well known in folklore to age you a year per touch, to cause rheumatism, and to cause cattle to abort.

Book 18 Chapter 3 – p52-81: (overview) Jack's best friend Dundas Heneage visits at Ashgrove, gets orders. Jack's coxswain Bonden is fleet champion boxer, readying for a match. Boxing discussed. Extended discussion of whys and results of enclosure – as being pushed on Jack by his landowner neighbors. Orders arrive for Jack – report immediately – but he is attending Parliament, so says Diana, covering for Jack to Sophie's befuddlement. Jack is actually at the fair, attending to the business of enclosure or not, and Bonden's boxing match.

53 – To toughen his hands for bare-knuckle boxing, Bonden soaks them in a solution of vinegar, very strong tea, spirits of wine, tar-bark and dragon's-blood (bark and/or juices of the New-World plant *Croton lechleri*) plus barber's styptic (aluminum chloride, still in use today to stop bleeding from small superficial cuts as in shaving).

68 – Bonden knocked out and concussed in his match.

72 – Bonden's opponent seems to have "...copped it worse [more badly hurt than Bonden] and is despaired of..."   --- Bonden apparently recovering.

Book 18 Chapter 4 – p82-107: (overview) The 'familial group' misses the sailing due to an ox-cart traffic jam, and is left ashore. Jack finds two of his midshipmen in a tavern with their girls – clear dereliction of duty- but 'persuades' them to use the Ringle (the cutter) to carry the family to the Squadron. Stephen almost incapable of dressing properly – object of amusement to the crew. Jack called to flag for conference. Stephen asked for advice by Charlotte's surgeon. Aboard flag, Adm Lord Stranraer tries to use Stephen's supposed influence over Jack to encourage a Parliamentary vote (by Jack) in favor of Lord Stranraer's favorable position on inclosure. Stephen refuses, reports the incident to Jack. Patrolling, enforcing a trade embargo on the Bay of Biscay. "Yellowing" explained and discussed: also the likely future of revolutions and nation-building in S. America.

90 – Seaman gets a crushed foot when a block of stone is dropped on it (the stone being a deck-scrubbing item called a 'bear').

95 – Bonden has recovered, but his scalp is now hairless – loss of his pigtail an ego blow.

97 – On the use of maggots (fly larvae) to cleanse wounds. They are very picky eaters, consuming only dead flesh and avoiding the living – perfect little surgeons – still in use today, all squeamishness aside. Even badly gangrenous legs have been saved by their use.

98 – Still aboard Charlotte – a days-old coma due to a head blow (but without skull fracture). Stephen given as author of the treatise "Mental Health of Seamen". (There exist several early books on the topic, but apparently none published in the proper time frame for this story.)

99 – Admiral Stranraer wants to consult Stephen – sudden sharp "heart-pangs" in the chest.

102 – Top of page, one or more entire lines of type are missing.

<u>Book 18 Chapter 5 – p108-139: (overview)</u> Detailed discussion of long-gone sea battles. Stephen is his usual clumsy self aboard ship in only moderately heavy weather. Discussions of handedness – inborn? Changeable? Jack dislikes being strapped for funds – he cannot set a proper table for his officers. Great gun exercises come off tolerably well. New crewman Geoghegan is a superb flutist, welcome in the Captain's cabin as a musician. He is killed almost immediately in a fall from the main topmast. Bellona et al. busy putting agents ashore at night in a fog in dangerous waters.

123 – Casualty from the great-gun exercise – a three-ton 32-#er had recoiled into a seaman's foot. Tourniquet, some sewing, then a bandage. Stephen's aide, Macaulay, is a wizard with bandages.

131 – Flutist Geoghegan falls from the main topmast, lands on a carronade, instantly dead.

<u>Book 18 Chapter 6 – p140-167: (overview)</u> [NOTE – no medical events occur in this chapter.] Navigating Bellona in very shallow nearshore waters guided by a pilot and a wax-armed sounding lead. Encounter with English vessel Alexandria: no mail, no news. School for the ship's boys. Mail eventually arrives, letter to Jack from Sophie displays her open knowledge of Jack's affair months earlier with Amanda Smith in Canada – who is now claiming pregnancy and asking for financial support. Jack kept Amanda's letters, stored them where, in retrospect, they were almost certain to be found. And they were – by Sophie's mother, the Shrew. Some French ships slip past Jack's screening blockade in the dark and fog: Jack called to account for that by Adm Stranraer – who eventually accepts Jack's explanation, blaming very heavy weather and low visibility. Jack's request for private leave (to go visit Sophie and make amends) flatly denied. British fleet meets the French in heavy weather, Bellona pursues and takes privateer Les Deux Freres, an exceedingly valuable prize, herself being laden with the spoils of several large prizes. Problems – Bellona has been damaged and their position is uncertain. Bellona must go to the yard for repairs. Jack goes to Sophie, who is furious: he attempts to apologize and beg her pardon, she refuses to hear him, says she wishes never to see him again. He leaves angrily, his parting words "Then be damned to you for a hard ill-natured and pitiless unforgiving shrew!"

Book 18 Chapter 7 – p168-180: (overview) [NOTE – No medical events in this chapter.] Bellona repaired, back at sea with the blockade. Ringle gone to pick up Stephen. Jack in trouble for having failed to heed the Admiral's signal – went off-station to capture the privateer. Jack gets orders (more blockading, surveying), throws himself into activities to escape dealing with his marital problem. Stephen meets with Sir Joseph: discussions of amateurism vs professionalism in intelligence agents. Stephen reports on his activities in S. America. Stephen asks Sir Joseph about the chances of Jack's being yellowed upon reaching flag rank… the problem would be with Adm Stranraer and his disagreement with Jack over inclosure… nothing wrong with Jack's military record. Sir Joseph and Stephen set a trap for a top French agent, in Sir Joseph's quarters – it works to perfection.

Book 18 Chapter 8 – p181-207: (overview)   Stephen's Chilean work meets with approval in London. Authorized to proceed towards a Chile independent of both Spain and other S American countries or movements, always acting with plausible deniability. Stephen returns to Ashgrove, is greeted with new of the marital disaster. Sophie still monumentally upset, but regrets turning Jack away so abruptly. On the other hand, Diana has it "…on the best authority that

Jack is no artist in these matters..." Diana undertakes to explain to Sophie some of the pleasurable aspects of sex... and Sophie listens attentively. She also learns about birth control (by implication, condoms)... properly accoutered, she need not fear more pregnancies, hence might perhaps be enabled to concentrate on the couple's pleasures. Diana drives the four-in-hand from London to Torquay strand, a two day journey, to meet with Bellona. Jack gets a letter from Sophie, carried by Stephen, apologizing for having been a shrew. Jack is ecstatic. The war with France is likely to end soon, if so, the Navy will be reduced by perhaps 75% almost instantly. Jack would be well advised to continue in his present role of studying S. America with intent to foment an English-favorable revolution or two... that need is seen in London as being a very long-term investment in England's future, and will be maintained, peace or no. It would also keep him from the perils of being yellowed.

185 – Sophie has never taken any pleasure in sex, has had difficult pregnancies – the antithesis of Jack in sexual temperament and interest.

195 – The Admiral wants to consult with Stephen – the Admiral is aging rapidly, does not like what he sees and feels in himself.

196 – Stephen listens to the Admiral's breathing using a primitive stethoscope (then commonly used in Europe, but unknown in England!), decides the patient is not in such terrible shape, but does find fluid in the pericardium (the sac within which the heart lies), prescribes a course of treatments - particularly digitalis as a heart stimulent. Plus, of course, laudanum. Admiral is not medically trustworthy, believed to be discarding most of the medicines prescribed to date.

201 – We learn that the time in the yard has yielded its usual fruits – a large number of cases of pox (syphilis); three men were lost overboard in the pre-yard storm; partial dismasting of the ship had produced four broken limbs.

202 – Bonden's head examined, his boxing injury is nicely healed.

Book 18 Chapter 9 – p208-232: (overview)   Christmas with Bellona on endless patrolling – blockade duty. Accidental encounter with a mackerel fisherman provides a lovely Christmas dinner. Jack deeply worried about possible yellowing. Extensive discussion of ships of various ratings, plus accounts of various actions. Heard at great range   a likely naval battle. Bellona heads that way. Two French 74s, other vessels, doing great damage to the British. Stephen lent to British ship Aboukir, damaged by the French, who disengage and run for home. First rate Charlotte arrives, assembles all captains. Napoleon is being driven back, towards Waterloo. Peace is threatening to break out all over.

211 – Another suprapubic cystotomy (cutting for stone), on crewman Bowden. The usual 'operating' chair, with chains, and laudanum as anesthetic. Stephen pours 'spirits of wine' (distilled ethyl alcohol, a fine antiseptic even today) over the incision site, not as sterilizer but to cool the area (by evaporation). Implication is that this has been a regular routine of Stephens, and perhaps helps account for his remarkable percentage of success with this operation. His teacher in medical school did the same: both men have unusually good records of success – meaning few patients dying of post-operative deep infections.

226 – Admiral thanks Stephen, he seems fully recovered, vigorous and full of life. Stephen examines him, is satisfied.

Book 18 Chapter 10 – p233-262: (overview)   Peace – most of the Navy is being decommissioned, paid off. Bellona will, at best, be stripped and laid up in mothballs (aka "being laid up in ordinary" – deactivated and put into fleet reserve). Meetings with Chileans ashore set up. Jack must be officially removed from the Navy List if he is to undertake full employment working the S American 'independencies' projects that Stephen has helped nurture. Jack is unhappy, but knows he is amazingly fortunate – success in S America will bring him back to the List in his original seniority. Buonaparte is in exile on Elba. Meetings with Chileans go very well: using Surprise, Jack is to survey and chart the S American coastlines, informally he is also to provide military and political assistance as needed and possible. The promise of post-project reinstatement to the List is revisited, will be put in writing… for the project, Jack is a civilian lent to the Navy Hydrographic Office. Jack has issued an "all-family" invitation to board the Surprise for a picnic-like two-week excursion to Madeira (Sophie has not yet been to sea with Jack, nor has she been abroad.) All is in high readiness for the S American expedition – the Navy is being remarkably liberal with assistance and funding. Jack has been worried about a possible snubbing he received from Lord Keith (who is married to a much younger woman with whom Jack has a longstanding close friendship (nothing at all improper)… the anxiety relieved by an apologetic note stating that Buonaparte has just now escaped and is on the loose, and Jack is to hoist a broad pennant as Commodore (a second fleet command!), take command of various ships, and proceed to Gibraltar, where he will block all transit of any vessels whatsoever through the straits.

260 – Admiral Stranraer, acting on the seaman's belief that "if a little is good, a lot more will be much better!" has overdosed himself with digitalis. The flagship's captain has fallen down a companionway and has a broken tibia and fibula for Stephen to examine ashore.

Book 19 – The HUNDRED DAYS

Book 19 Chapter 1 – p1-35: (overview) Napoleon escaped from Elba, is loose on the continent trying to re-establish himself. Royal Navy scrambling to re-commission ships for yet another war. Lord Keith, Jack's friend, is Commander-in-Chief. Jack's Squadron has not yet been disbanded, stands guard over the Strait of Gibraltar. Ruminations on 'happy' marriages: do they exist? Keith changes Jack's assignment. Discussion of the military situation on land – awkward and dangerous. French are building lots of warships in small yards on the Adriatic. Napoleon seems to be supported by Muslim (Turkish) money. Now, Jack must protect Constantinople's trade, prevent enemy movements by sea, and most importantly seek out and destroy French shipbuilding in the Adriatic. Turkish mercenaries will support Napoleon but must be paid (else no work!) – all movement of cash or gold to pay them must be stopped. Hard fast work bringing Surprise up to proper condition for the expedition. Jack attends the court-martial of an officer for homosexuality, says to the court "No penetration, no sodomy" – thereby saving the man's life, punishment reduced to being cashiered out of the Navy for 'gross indecency'.

3 – Adm Stranraer now dead of a self-administered overdose of datura (heart stimulant). Stephen's wife Diana and several others have been killed in a carriage accident.

16 – Comments on the placebo effects of some of Stephen's prescriptions.

26 – Captain of Jack's vessel Pomone (30) has a badly broken tibia and fibula, not available for duty. Discussion of impotence, its connections to opium use.

32 – Maturin meets with Dr Jacob, who gives him a preserved human hand – developmentally malformed, a fascination to Stephen.

Book 19 Chapter 2 – p36-63: (overview) Training new crews on the great guns. Discussion of women as actual soldiers and sailors – throughout history there have been many, some quite

249

well-known and successful, some even on a few of Jack's own ships. Stephen gets a very experienced medical-woman "Poll" as his assistant – she has 20 years at sea on His Majesty's ships. Nearby pirates (from Laraish) are interfering with British trade: Keith sends Jack's Squadron to fix the problem. Reade sent to check out ships in Laraish harbor. Indiamen under pirate attack by xebecs and galleys. Enemies sunk or scared off.

43 – Grinding blue ointment (mercury-based salve for syphilitic ulcers) with Poll. They hit it off well, she explains the whys and wherefores of women like herself.

47 – Ashore on Gibraltar, Stephen does two suprapubic cystotomies with the Surgeon of the Fleet in attendance (a job for which Stephen has been approached several times).

55 – Stephen has (again) given up laudanum (for the Nth time), coca leaves, tobacco… every little pleasure save a bit of wine.

59 – Surprise's casualties from encounters with pirates at Laraish – two dead, a dozen variously injured, now in sick bay. Other ships from the Squadron suffered similarly.

62 – Some of the casualties are seriously wounded – nurse Poll worth her weight in gold. After a dinner Pomone's Captain Pomfret consults privately with Stephen – he has very guilty pangs of conscience since deliberately running down a galley full of slaves in the Laraish engagement – some of who were bound to be Christian prisoners. Stephen gives him a box of pills (active principle, if any, not specified) that will aid his sleep.

Book 19 Chapter 3 – p64-90: (overview) Back at Gibraltar – Keith commends Jack for Laraish, sends him immediately to deal with the Balkan Muslims who are apparently themselves willing not only to fight for Napoleon, but also to provide the needed gold to pay mercenaries. Capt Pomfret has committed suicide aboard Pomene, an exceedingly ill omen under which to set off on an expedition. Stephen's narwhal tooth considered by the crew to be a unicorn's horn and to make the ship proof against poisons. Squadron sails to Port Mahan, enroute to the Adriatic. Stephen gets the latest intelligence. Extensive timing and coordination problems amongst the land forces opposing Boney. Time to destroy the shipyards supplying the French. Noted scientist Wright agrees to examine Stephen's narwhal tooth – what are the spiral windings for? Cabin boy is drunk, Killick also drunk, playing with the narwhal tooth, drops and breaks the tooth – enormously bad omen, the crew are aghast. Wright can reassemble the pieces, he says, as good as new

64 – Three patients failing – one leg amputated for Thomas, one resection needed (resection meaning removal of part of an organ or limb), and one depressed skull fracture badly in need of trephining (a Stephen specialty). All three sent ashore to hospital.

65 – Aboard Pomene, Capt Pomfret has committed suicide ("His pistol discharged whilst he was cleaning it" = official story).

71 – Stephen chastises Jack for gaining weight.

Book 19 Chapter 4 – p91-121: (overview) Exiting Mahon harbor for the Adriatic. Pomene is a mess – poor and new officers, lousy training to date. Stephen's "Hand of Glory" (a malformed human hand regarded by the entire superstitious crew as magically protective of the ship) eaten by a crewman's dog named Nasby: emetics yield the bones, which Stephen can wire together. Jack plays diplomat over the event, and the treatment of Nasby. The reassembled skeletal hand satisfies the crew – luck is back aboard Surprise. Stephen is beginning to fantasize about Christina Wood, a superb young naturalist whom he has had dealing with repeatedly over the past few years – she is now a widow… perhaps available? Surprise encounters (again) Christie-Palliere, get thorough update on military situation. Stephen discovers that tunas are warm-blooded (a true statement). Reade reports significant –but not overwhelming- French forces at anchor.

94 – Pomene undertaking serious training and discipline – her injured men come to Surprise for treatment because her own surgeon is "far gone with the double-pox" (this is probably a combination of pustule-producing diseases, perhaps chickenpox plus syphilis, or even

251

chickenpox plus smallpox (unlikely – the smallpox would result in an epidemic aboard ship). In any case, Pomene's surgeon sensibly does not want to treat patients while he has such a disease.

96 – A plague of boils breaks out aboard Surprise – "remarkably like the Aleppo button" (that being a protozoan parasite that can infect humans via sand-fly bites, rather like the protozoa/ mosquito arrangement for malaria).

111 – Inspection of entire ship, with French captain Christie-Palliere along – two cases of bloody flux in sickbay, nothing more.

Book 19 Chapter 5 – p122-149: (overview)   Seeking out and taking on various piratical vessels. Also planning a land attack by Squadron's Marines – will try to destroy a fort. Fake battle arranged that will allow the graceful surrender of French ship Cerbere (captained by an anti-Boney officer) to Surprise. The point-blank "blanks-only" exchanges amuse and deafen all participants. Then to the business of burning French ships-abuilding and/or the many smaller shipyards doing the construction – also to convince the local ruler not to support Boney. Burning boats that are under construction, and shipyards also, is something that does not appeal to Jack (above all due to not yielding prize-monies), but he agrees it makes very good sense indeed. Surprise burns a good many such enemy items.

129 – Battle joined with pirates, Surprise prevails. Casualties include a broken arm, six splinter wounds, one man dead of a musket-ball, two men hurt by falling blocks – a modest butcher's bill.

132 – Jacob bleeding profusely from a self-inflicted wound (snagged himself on a shot-damaged wooden gunwale whilst coming aboard).

143 – Too much levity prevailed during the "blanks" exercise – damage includes rope-burns and impact injuries from not clearing the gun-carriage during recoil. John Daniel (gun crewman) has been hit in the chest by a wooden disc that was part of a blank charge (added to increase noise output)… a broken collarbone is all.

144 – Daniel given a dose of laudanum for his pain.

Book 19 Chapter 6 – p150-174: (overview) Back to sea after the burnings. Goal now – prevent the local Dey (governor) from shipping gold to support Napoleon's activities. Stephen in negotiations ashore, takes a boy from Ringle with him – the child is endlessly gob-smacked by the wonders of the orient – camels, silks, the entire bazaar.

151 – Mr Daniel takes a tumble, re-injures his broken collarbone. (See page 143.)

152 – More detailed examination of Daniel's injuries. Problems of using auscultation (listening for body-sounds using a primitive stethoscope) aboard a noisy, pitching, creaking ship. Daniel may have pneumonia. Ashore, new intelligence – there is a new Dey, an unknown quantity.

153 – No leeches remain in the medical supplies – the midshipmen stole them all for bait.

156 – Daniel's collarbone is slow in healing - he requires light duty until the bones fully knit.

159 – Capt Hobden has fallen down in a fit – alcoholic coma. Carried to his bunk.

160 – Jacob predicts "crapula" (nausea; hangover) will be Hobden's lot in the morning. Evening rounds – two obstinate gleets (gonorrhetic oozings) and one tenesmus (a persistent feeling, usually false, that one has not quite finished emptying one's bowels). Bone splinter extracted from Daniel's collarbone region has been the problem with his healing.

168 – Ashore, Stephen (with Jacob) visits the consul – whom he has met and who is semi-permanently confined to bed with hip-gout. Stephen treats the gout with a very hot poultice and Thebaic tincture (a ten-percent-by-weight solution of powered opium, here as anesthetic and/or sedative) – quite effective relief follows.

253

Book 19 Chapter 7 – p175-207: (overview) Jacob grew up amidst the local cultures (Turkish, etc) and is the perfect envoy/spy/negotiator for British concerns. Plan hatched – simple initial bribery of underlings, then see what might follow with the Dey himself. Jacob remains incognito. Meeting with the Dey during his lion-hunting: Stephen and the Dey go hunting, Stephen –a crack shot- saves the Dey's life by killing a lion during its charge at them. This Dey claims he is not interested in supporting Boney. But gold is already enroute to support Boney, aboard a very fast-sailing xebec.

190 – Discussions between Jacob and Stephen about an apparently permanent remission of (1) tetraplegia (= today's quadriplegia – all four limbs paralyzed), and (2) pthisis (pulmonary tuberculosis).

Book 19 Chapter 8 – p208-236: (overview) Stephen and Jacob go overland to Algiers, through a monstrous sandstorm: Jack is at sea, cannot be apprised of the treasure's existence and route. Ringle has been blown far offshore in the storm, limping home apparently jury-rigged. Yet another new Dey – Ali Bey, known to be favorable to English interests. In the marketplace Stephen finds two Irish children, brother/sister, enslaved and offered for sale. Stephen buys them with intent to return them to their home when possible – they were a fishing family blown out to sea by a storm and found there by the Moors, hence slavery. News of the treasure-ship; it is in port Arzila. Children, Jacob and Stephen hire a ride out to meet Ringle. Ringle and Surprise were for several days aiding ship Lion, totally dismasted in the storm. Jack explains the situation to the Admiral. Surprise in port, Wright returns the fully repaired narwhal tooth to Stephen. Now the ship's luck has truly returned… perhaps as a result they will catch the gold-courier?

209 – The gouty consul is almost miraculously recovered – he and wife adore Stephen's blue pills.

Book 19 Chapter 9 – p237-257: (overview) At sea, headed to intercept the treasure-xebec if possible. New area commander, Lord Adm Barmouth, and Jack had a few disagreements early in Jack's career – his opinion of Jack may be crucial and is presently unknown. At sea, they encounter Jack's best long-term friend Heneage Dundas in Hamadryad. Jack attempts –yet again- to explain to Stephen the moon's phases and effects on tides, so as to explain Surprise's tactics: this seems only to raise in Stephen's mind a sort of dense fog. Adm Barmouth orders Jack to lower his commodore's broad pennant and revert: he is depressed, they cannot go after the gold. Stephen has, however, fixed that with the highest authorities – Barmouth will be overruled. Lady Keith volunteers to handle the two Irish children.

237 – Sickbay full of the usual consequences (to sailors) of being allowed ashore.

254 – Abram White of Surprise is in an alcoholic coma from drinking illegal alcohol he brought aboard and drank at one draft when he thought he'd been discovered. Stephen examines him, pumps his stomach, and has him put to bed.

256 – Sick list is now trivial – some obstinate poxes and a hernia.

Book 19 Chapter 10 – p258-281: (overview) News of the gold xebec – time for Surprise to give chase. Lord Adm Barmouth finally realizes that Jack is a childhood friend of the Admiral's own very much younger second wife. Wife has followed Jack's career assiduously… this completely changes his interactions with Jack – much for the better. And said wife is arriving today aboard Acasta, which has not hurt his mood a bit. Corsair captaining the xebec is wily, has decoys out – Jack smokes them. A chance shot from the Xebec kills Bonden (and two other men) at gun #2 starboard – Jack's longest-term shipmate and his personal coxswain for decades. Xebec hauls into very shallow water where she moors quite safe from attack by Surprise. Jack's crew haul a cannon up the mountain behind the xebec's berth: one shot makes the pirates aware they are now functionally dead men. The pirates behead their captain in full view of Surprise, will not fight if given their lives and water. Many of the surviving slaves are British

255

citizens: they undertake to secure the pirates' persons and weaponry, they are offered a share of the prize if they will help sail
the xebec into Gibraltar with Surprise. Many small, very heavy
chests are transferred to Surprise. Later there will be moments of
doubt as to whether this is a valid prize, but eventually all is resolved in favor of its validity. Jack is once again wealthy. Arriving back at Gibraltar, the news is that Boney has been beaten. After a lovely reunion and dinner, Surprise finally sets sail for Chile,
on her original mission, which is still deemed by the government
to be critical to Britain's future.

268 – Pursuing (in slow motion) the xebec, three cases of sun-
stroke. Xebec is panicking, throwing overboard manacled slaves
(rowers) to lighten ship.

Book 20 – BLUE at the MIZZEN

Book 20 Chapter 1 – p1-29: (overview) Surprise anchored at Gibraltar. Crew gets huge payoff of prize money. Medium heavy weather. Surprise is run down in the dark –and very badly damaged forward- by a large unidentifiable ship. Jack is having an affair with Barmouth's wife… of which the Admiral is aware. Adm Barmouth –understandably- puts Surprise dead last in shipyard priority – She's not an official Navy ship, after all! Extensive discussion of the land campaign at Waterloo. Temporary repairs are needed, then a trip to a first-class shipyard – the resulting delay in dealing with the action-oriented Chileans (about nationhood) is worrisome to high officials in the English government.

6 – Stephen's aide Dr Jacob knocked down and bloodied by ship's antics.

7 – Jacob was handling a glass scientific instrument when he took his tumble – shards cut the brachial artery and other lesser vessels. Stephen stanches the flow, sutures the damaged vessels.

22 – Ashore, Stephen treats an old, dazed but basically uninjured civilian who had been caught in the riot of drunk seamen (many from Surprise).

25 – Jacob says he has recovered from his wound – "…a mere bloodletting…"

Book 20 Chapter 2 – p30-56: (overview) Adm Lord Barmouth considers politics, his own marital situation, decides to ignore Jack's affair with his wife, and to help Jack get Surprise repaired and back enroute to Chile as quickly as possible. Surprise moves to the head of the shipyard queue. Stephen is beset by memories of Christine Wood (his widow-scientist), is writing to her, confused as how to express his (partly carnal) interest in her from such a distance. The most critical repairs are done, Surprise sets sail for a better shipyard, which is burning to the ground as they arrive. A certain Mister Wantage reports to Jack: he had an affair with a shepherd's daughter, was kidnapped and castrated ("cut"), then freed. He wants a position on Surprise, gets it. Stephen gets encoded instructions, commandeers Ringle and Mr Reade, sails to London for intelligence meetings.

35 – Stephen returns to using laudanum to get to sleep.

40 – Stephen's passing thoughts about the "…shocking prevalence of pox in its dismal varieties…"

Book 20 Chapter 3 – p57-86: (overview)   Stephen meets privately with Sir Joseph to discuss Chile – so many leaders, so few followers! Another independent group with a vessel is pursuing a course of action similar to Jack's, but with different parties and intent – real competition! Stephen's black girls Sarah and Emily have become superb cooks. Christine Woods sends Stephen his potto's skeleton, cleaned and articulated. Affection reciprocated. Surprise into Sepping's shipyard (the very best) for repairs. Prince Regent the Duke of Clarence (long Stephen's patient), a qualified Admiral, meets "accidentally" with Jack. HRH's favorite son (named "Horatio" Hanson, oddly enough - a bastard so far not legitimized by royal decree) is cautiously offered to Jack as a trainee midshipman – Jack takes him but with great reservations openly discussed with His Highness, who is at first taken aback by the frankness, then is pleased by it and agrees completely. At home: a happy gathering, Jack's son George serving aboard Lion (74), Capt Dundas. Surprise is recruiting fine seamen from among Shelmerston's smugglers.

73 – Still ashore, Mister Wells' pony threw him into a ditch – taken home, stripped, anointed with hog's lard, balm and sticking-plaster (adhesive bandage). Trivial injuries. Stephen's hypocrisy about personal use of drugs – he routinely uses opium, hemp, bhang (today's 'hash', i.e., hemp resin), coca leaves, nitrous oxide, tobacco, alcohol in all varieties – yet vehemently condemns other people for just such usage.

86 – Long voyage ahead, massive inlay of supplies including seven casks of rhubarb – the commonly-prescribed "purgative" of choice.

Book 20 Chapter 4 – p87- 107: (overview)   At sea, enroute Chile. Mister Hanson is quick, able, and instantly in love with the sea and Surprise, to Jack's delight and relief. Stephen comments on his doing comparative-drug experiments on crewmen – "Of course I do so!" Jack takes Hanson aloft for the boy's first time at the masthead – he is enthralled. Rejoined by Ringle. Ashore, Dr Jacob startles Stephen by engaging –quite professionally– in precious-gem trading. Political situation in Chile very confused. Surprise will definitely be in competition with the "other party", which has a ship and is repairing another. At sea bound for Freetown, where Widow Wood lives - Stephen plans to ask Christine Wood to marry him.

88- Sickbay apparently full of seriously seasick crew, all on various purgatives. (**Author's aside** – I am a sea-going oceanographer and have been seasick a good many times. I have no idea why anyone would give a violently-vomiting person a good strong laxative – I cannot imagine running at both ends simultaneously! Purest idiocy.) Hanson has overcome seasickness amazingly quickly – Stephen attributes that to "Vera Cruz jalap" ('jalap' = any strong laxative [the usual meaning of 'purgative'] – here, specifically a drug made from the roots of *Ipomoea purga*, a relative of morning glory et al.).

Book 20 Chapter 5 – p108-133: (overview)   At Freetown: Governor's dinner for Surprise's officers the hostess seats Stephen and Christine side by side. The couple shortly explores the nearby jungle, going skinny-dipping to observe turtles. They accumulate mud and leeches, which must be removed – presumably each deals with the other person's collection. Stephen admits to himself that he cannot maintain strict objective neutrality in the situation. Much discussion of natural history. Stephen proposes: Christine declines, citing her disgust about things sexual, that disgust having been specifically engendered by her husband who was totally impotent. Eventually, she agrees to think on the idea whilst Stephen is handling the Chilean mission: meanwhile she will sail (commercially) to England to visit with Clarissa, Brigid and the whole Aubrey clan: Stephen fills her cabin with flowers. Another discussion of being yellowed.

259

127 – No bed-ridden patients; only patient is a victim of Hanson's blows in a local boxing match – a mild concussion.

130 – Hanson has been sparring again, now needs stitches in his own eyebrow.

Book 20 Chapter 6 – p134-160: (overview) Hanson promoted to Master's Mate when Wantage dies – a well-deserved promotion even if rapid. Long, slow voyage: around the Horn; doldrums again; amazingly heavy storms; meeting with ship Daniel whose chronometers gave out and she needs a position. Stephen both diagnoses and cures Daniel's chronometer malfunction – and without opening the clock's case, which is a capital crime.

134 – Wantage, master's mate, buried at sea: also, recently lost two crewmen to yellow fever.

156 – Aftermath of a post-doldrums storm – three recent fractures need to be reset, nothing else reported.

157 – Stephen has donated to the Daniel a cask of tincture of hogweed (a relative of the carrot, the seeds are boiled in oil and the liquor applied to skin rashes such as shingles and acne). No explanation is given for that donation.

Book 20 Chapter 7 – p161-196: (overview) Surprise, in sight of Sugar Loaf, near the American coast. Asp (the competition) is an entirely-rebuilt ship, heavily armed therefore worrisome. Trading encounters with Tierra del Fuegians. Hard work, short rations, and no vitamin C. Stephen appalled by the merciless slaughter of seals, needed as provisions for Surprise and Ringle.

165 – Stephen's letter to Christine recounts a great gun being forced from its position by pressure of ice, and injuring several crewmen.

168 – A whaler named Bjorn has three cracked ribs from a personal accident during a recent major storm.

172 – First signs of scurvy appear. Three men and a boy have died from plain pneumonia; Woodbine has self-medicated for many years and is dying (of what we are not told).

Book 20 Chapter 8 – p176-196: (overview) Cape Pillar (S end of the continent) in sight from Ringle, near Surprise. Finally into the Pacific – the weather fits the name. A whaler comes alongside, seeking a doctor's help for a man whose arm has been horribly mangled – caught in a running line attached to a harpoon struck into a whale. A gift of coffee motivates Stephen. Ringle grounded and damaged, heaved down on a beach, repairs conducted whilst the ground trembles from volcanoes. Jury-rigged Ringle: sailing with Surprise to a shipyard for repairs. Encounter with an old ship, the old Lisbon Packet (renamed Isaac Newton), carrying a crew of scientist-Members of the Royal Academy on a round-the-world research cruise – many of them friends of Jack and Stephen. Jack inspects Asp: her captain Lindsay is a boorish ass, exceedingly arrogant and overconfident… assumes incorrectly that Jack has been sent to aid Lindsay's efforts. The political situation is murky – there is a junta (or several?) which has (maybe?) ships and perhaps even an embryonic navy? … etc.

176 – Woodbine buried at sea.

177 – The sudden diet of rich seal-meat has led to large-scale constipation: Stephen and Poll have been administering enemas steadily. There have also been, apparently, a good many frostbite cases.

182 – Stephen is hung over (poppy, hellebore, Jamaican rum) and must amputate a whaler's mangled arm at the shoulder, which is "…still a clean joint…" says Poll to Stephen, having evaluated the patient whilst Stephen sobers up. She has prepped the whaler's crew on what to do to make ready for surgery.

183 – Amputation went smoothly; good flaps of healthy skin.

188 – Reade, commanding Ringle, drove her aground, is so upset with himself that Stephen provides hellebore and laudanum to help him sleep.

Book 20 Chapter 9 – p197-226: (overview) Stephen explains the political and military situations. Among other concerns, the nominal Chilean Navy has almost no trained officers and men, and its singleton major vessel the O'Higgins (50) is unserviceable even if the personnel were available. They do have several schooner-sized vessels, but no idea how to fight them. Discussions of electricity (no general theory yet); the delicate art of cut-

261

ting-out a vessel. Jack is emotionally rattled by a fine, long letter from Sophie. Stephen's daydreams of Christine, certainly physical but mostly an almost abstract longing and love. Dinner for Bernardo O'Higgins (ASIDE – he is actually the G. Washington of Chile) aboard Surprise – with a great-gun target practice to impress him. Peru threatens to invade Chile, Peru has a navy of one heavy cruiser the Esmeralda (50: unready for sea). Reconnaissance and preparation to assault the port of Valdivia from the sea, using O'Higgins's troops which are carried aboard Surprise. A bloody but very successful battle.

216 – Sickbay rounds – two stubborn hernias, some obstinate poxes.

Book 20 - INTERCHAPTER – p227- 233: (overview) Maturin's long letter to Christine summarizes the Valdivia affair and battle. Nobody from Jack's command was killed, the fortress was destroyed and the navy yard captured. Large amount of prize money to be distributed. Internecine jealousies and squabbles among the Chileans. Lindsay (Capt of Asp) was challenged to a duel by one of his own officers, and was killed. Jack takes the body without local permission, moves Surprise safely offshore, buries him at sea. Locals are enraged, Jack has usurped local authorities. Jack plans to cut out the only serious Peruvian warship, the Esmeralda.

228 – Hanson brings Stephen to Capt Lindsay, felled by pistol shot in a duel with his own officer. He is already dead – shot in the aorta.

Book 20 Chapter 10 – p234-262: (overview) Scientific party from Isaac Newton come aboard Surprise for Sunday services and dinner. Some of them will go home to London via crossing the Panama isthmus – they volunteer to carry urgent messages (to Government) and letters (friends and family) – saving many months of communications dead-time. There is a new "South African Squadron" known to be a-building. Surprise is again disguised as a merchantman, lays herself alongside Esmeralda. Boarding after several broadsides, the Surprises take Esmeralda.

Horatio conned Surprise into position – after boarding, Jack has him take Esmeralda out – yet another (his final) successful cutting-out for Jack. Stephen reminds Jack of Jack's true status: Jack is rueful, has Stephen write to the Chilean Government, reporting the action. Major problem – the crew is upset, because the prize money (from Esmeralda) has not been paid, nor has the treasure seized at Valparaiso been distributed. Jack pressures the Chileans, gets totally unsatisfactory excuses. A long, dragging formal dinner aboard Surprise, for the Chileans mostly. Jack angrily confronts the Chileans, demands payment, gives an ultimatum and absolute deadline for an answer. Jacob returns from Panama as an informal courier of a coded signal, and is met at Surprise by Stephen. Together they decode it. Stephen meets privately with Jack to give him the message in italics just below.

> *"Immediately upon receipt of the present order you will proceed to the River Plate, there joining the South African Squadron: you will go aboard HMS Implacable, hoisting your flag, blue at the mizzen and take command of the blue squadron."*

239 – While boarding Esmeralda, Jack has his thigh run through by a Peruvian swordsman. He is also pistol-shot in the left shoulder from very close range.

241 – Jack's shoulder is intact – the bullet struck the buckle of his sword-belt, ruining it.

243 – Passing comment that most of Esmeralda's officers were wounded and are now under Dr Jacob's care. Mister Linklatter lost an arm making Surprise fast to Esmeralda.

246 – Jack rests in bed, being fed chicken soup and an un-named liquid medicine.

248 – Ringle's crewman William is mentioned as having "…copped it good and hearty…" but also "….we hope to save the leg."

250 – Stephen worries about Jack's irascibility, examines him carefully for possible deep-seated infections from his wounds, finds nothing.

The Chilean Government welshes on its obligations to Jack, thereby freeing him from any obligation whatever to Chile.

The book, and the entire Aubrey series, ends with Surprise headed out to sea per Jack's first order under his lifelong ambition, the blue flag of a brand-new admiral -

"Mister Hanson, pray lay me a course for Cape Pilar and Magellan's Strait."